FROM
New York
With Love

With Love
COLLECTION

February 2017

February 2017

February 2017

March 2017

March 2017

March 2017

FROM *New York*
With Love

CAROLE NIKKI WENDY
MORTIMER **LOGAN** **ETHERINGTON**

First Published in Great Britain 2017
By Mills & Boon, an imprint of HarperCollins*Publishers*
1 London Bridge Street, London, SE1 9GF

FROM NEW YORK WITH LOVE © 2017 Harlequin Books S.A.

Rumours on the Red Carpet © 2013 Carole Mortimer
Rapunzel in New York © 2011 Nikki Logan
Sizzle in the City © 2012 by Etherington, Inc

ISBN: 978-0-263-92791-7

09-0317

RUMOURS ON THE RED CARPET

CAROLE MORTIMER

Peter, as always.

Carole Mortimer was born in England, the youngest of three children. She began writing in 1978, and has now written nearly two hundred books for Mills & Boon. Carole has six sons, Matthew, Joshua, Timothy, Michael, David and Peter. She says, 'I'm happily married to Peter senior; we're best friends as well as lovers, which is probably the best recipe for a successful relationship. We live in a lovely part of England.'

CHAPTER ONE

'ENJOYING THE VIEW…?'

Thia tensed, a shiver of awareness quivering down the length of her spine at the sound of that deep voice coming out of the darkness behind her, before turning quickly to search those shadows for the man who had just spoken to her.

She was able to make out a tall figure in the moonlight just feet away from where she stood, alone on the balcony that surrounded the whole of this luxurious penthouse apartment on the fortieth floor of one of the impressive buildings lighting up the New York skyline. Only dim light spilled from the open French doors of the apartment further down the balcony—along with the sound of tinkling laughter and the chatter of the fifty or so party guests still inside—making it impossible for Thia to see any more than that the man was very tall, dark and broadshouldered. Imposingly so.

Dangerously so…?

The wariness still humming through her body just at the sound of the deep and seductive timbre of his voice said a definite *yes!*

Thia's fingers tightened about the breast-high balustrade in front of her. 'I was, yes…' she answered pointedly.

'You're a Brit,' he observed deeply.

'From London,' Thia confirmed shortly, really hoping that he would take note of that terseness and leave her to her solitude.

The New York night skyline, amazing as it was, hadn't been Thia's main reason for coming outside into the balmy evening air fifteen minutes ago, when the other guests had all been preoccupied with their excitement at the late arrival of Lucien Steele, American zillionaire business-man, and the party's guest of honour. That so many high-profile actors, actresses and politicians had turned out for the event was indicative of the amount of power the man wielded.

After all Jonathan's hype about him Thia had to admit that she hadn't found him so prepossessing—a man of middle age and average height, slightly stocky and bald-ing. But maybe all that money and power made him more attractive? In any event, Thia had just been grateful that he had arrived at last—if only because it had allowed her to slip outside and *be* alone—instead of just *feeling* alone.

Thia certainly hadn't intended to find herself alone on the balcony with a man who exuded such an intensity of power and sexual attraction she could almost taste it…

'A Brit, from London, who's avoiding the party in-side…?' that deep voice guessed with dry amusement.

Having been to three other parties just like this one in the four days since her arrival in New York, Thia had to admit to having become slightly bored—jaded?—by them. The first one had been fun—exciting, even—meeting people she had only ever seen on the big or little screen before, world-famous actors and actresses and high-profile politicians. But the artificiality of it was all becom-ing a bit samey now. The conversations were repetitive and

too loud, the laughter even more so, with everyone seemingly out to impress or better everyone else, their exces-
sive wealth literally worn on their sleeves.

This constant round of parties also meant that she'd
had very little opportunity for any time or private conversation with Jonathan, the man she had come to New
York to visit...

Jonathan Miller, the English star of *Network,* a new
American thriller television series set in New York, directed by this evening's host, Felix Carew, and co-starring
his young and sexy wife Simone as the love-interest.

The show had been an instant hit, and Jonathan was
currently the darling of New York's beautiful people—
and, as Thia had discovered these past four days, there
were a *lot* of beautiful people in New York!

And not a single one of them had felt any qualms about
ignoring the woman who had been seen at Jonathan's side
on those evenings once they'd learnt that Thia was of no
social or political value to them whatsoever.

Not that Thia minded being ignored. She had very
quickly discovered she had no more in common with New
York's elite than they had with her.

She was pleased for Jonathan's success, of course. The
two of them had known each other for a couple of years
now, after meeting at the London restaurant where Thia
always worked the late shift, leaving her free to attend her
university course in the day.

She and Jonathan had met quite by chance, when he
had been appearing in a play at the theatre across the street
from the restaurant and had started calling in late in the
evening a couple of times a week for something to eat,
once the theatre had closed for the night.

They had chatted on those evenings, then dated casu-

ally for a few weeks. But there had been no spark between
them and the relationship had quickly fallen into the 'just
friends' category. Then, four months ago, Jonathan had
landed the lead role in the television series over here, and
Thia had accepted that even that friendship would be over
once Jonathan moved to New York.

He had telephoned a couple of times in the months
that followed, just light and friendly conversations, when
they had caught up on each other's lives, and then a month
ago Jonathan had flown back to England for the weekend, insisting he had missed her and wanted to spend all
his time back home with her. And it had been fun. Thia
had arranged to have the weekend off so that they could
have dinner together in the evening, visits to museums
and walks in the parks during the day, before Jonathan
had to fly back to New York to start filming again on the
Monday.

But no one had been more surprised than Thia when a
first-class plane ticket for a week-long stay in New York
had been delivered to her by messenger just two days later!

She had telephoned Jonathan immediately, of course,
to tell him she couldn't possibly accept such generosity
from him. But he had insisted, saying he could well afford it and, more to the point, he wanted to see her again.
He wanted to show her New York, and for New York to
see her.

Thia's pride had told her she should continue to refuse,
but Jonathan had been very persuasive, and as she hadn't
been able to afford a holiday for years the temptation had
just been too much. So she had accepted, with the pro-
viso that he cancelled the first class ticket and changed it
to a standard fare. Spending that amount of money on an

airfare seemed obscene to her, in view of her own financial difficulties.

Jonathan had assured her that she would have her own bedroom in his apartment, and that he just wanted her to come and enjoy New York with him. She had even gone out and spent some of her hard-earned savings on buying some new clothes for the trip!

Except Jonathan's idea of her enjoying New York with him was vastly different from Thia's own. They had attended parties like this one every night, and Jonathan would sleep off the effects the following morning. Meanwhile his late afternoons and early evenings were usually spent secluded somewhere with Simone Carew, going over the script together.

Seeing so little of Jonathan during the day, and attending parties in the evenings, Thia had started to wonder why he had bothered to invite her here at all.

And she now found herself irritated that, once again, Jonathan had disappeared with Simone shortly after they had arrived at this party he had claimed was so important to him on account of the presence of Lucien Steele, the American billionaire owner of the television station responsible for *Network*. That desertion had left Thia being considered fair game by men like the one standing in the shadows behind her...

Well...perhaps not *exactly* like this man. The way he seemed to possess even the air about him told her that she had never met a man quite like this one before...

'Beautiful...' the man murmured huskily as he stepped forward to stand at the railing beside her.

Thia's heart skipped a beat, her nerve-endings going on high alert as her senses were instantly filled with the light smell of lemons—his cologne?—accompanied by an insidious maleness that she guessed was all him.

She turned to look at him, tilting her head back as she realised how much taller he was than her, even in her four-inch-heeled take-me-to-bed shoes. Taller, and so broad across the shoulders, with dark hair that rested low on the collar of his white shirt and black evening jacket. His face appeared to be all hard angles in the moonlight: strong jaw, chiselled lips, long aquiline nose, high cheekbones. And those pale and glittering eyes—

Piercing eyes, that she now realised were looking at *her* in admiration rather than at the New York skyline!

Thia repressed another quiver of awareness at having this man look at her so intently, realising that she was completely alone out here with a man she didn't know from—well, from Adam.

'Have they all stopped licking Lucien Steele's highly polished handmade Italian leather shoes yet, do you think?' she prompted in her nervousness, only to give a pained grimace at her uncharacteristic sharpness. 'I'm sorry— that was incredibly rude of me.' She winced, knowing how important Lucien Steele's goodwill was to Jonathan's success in the US. He had certainly emphasised it often enough on the drive over here!

'But true?' the man drawled dryly.

'Perhaps.' She nodded. 'But I'm sure that Mr Steele has more than earned the adoration being showered upon him so effusively.'

Teeth gleamed whitely in the darkness as the man gave a hard and humourless smile. 'Or maybe he's just so rich and powerful no one has ever dared to tell him otherwise?'

'Maybe,' she conceded ruefully. 'Cynthia Hammond.'

She thrust out her hand in an effort to bring some normality to this conversation. 'But everyone calls me Thia.'

He took possession of her hand—there was no other way to describe the way the paleness of her hand just disappeared inside the long bronzed strength of his. And Thia could not ignore the jolt of electricity zinging along her fingers and arm at contact with the warmth of his skin...

'I've never been particularly fond of being a part of what everyone else does,' he murmured throatily. 'So I think I'll call you Cyn...'

Just the way he said that word, in that deliciously deep and sexy voice, was enough to send yet more shivers of awareness down Thia's spine. Her breasts tingled with that awareness, the nipples puckering to tight and sensitive berries as they pressed against the sheer material of the clinging blue ankle-length gown she wore.

And it was a totally inappropriate reaction to a complete stranger!

Jonathan might have done yet another disappearing act with Simone forty minutes ago, but that certainly didn't mean Thia was going to stand here and allow herself to be seduced by some dark-haired hunk, who looked sinfully delicious in his obviously expensive evening suit but so far hadn't even been polite enough to introduce himself!

'And you are...?'

Those teeth gleamed even whiter in the darkness as he gave a wolfish smile. 'Lucien Steele.'

Thia gave a snort. 'I don't think so!' she scoffed.

'No?' He sounded amused by her scepticism.

'No,' she repeated decisively.

He raised one dark brow. 'Why not?'

She breathed her impatience. 'Well, for one thing you aren't nearly old enough to be the self-made zillionaire

Lucien Steele.' She estimated this man was aged somewhere in his early to mid-thirties, ten or twelve years older
than her own twenty-three, and she knew from the things
Jonathan had told her about this evening's guest of honour that Lucien Steele had not only been the richest man
in New York for the last ten years, but was also the most
powerful.

He gave an unconcerned shrug of those impossibly
wide shoulders. 'What can I say? My parents were wealthy
to begin with, and I'd made my own first million by the
time I was twenty-one.'

'Also,' Thia continued, determined, 'I saw Mr Steele
when he arrived.'

It had been impossible to miss the awed reaction of the
other guests. Those incredibly rich and beautiful people
had all, without exception, fallen absolutely silent the moment Lucien Steele had appeared in the doorway. And
Felix Carew, a powerful man in his own right, had become
almost unctuous as he moved swiftly across the room to
greet his guest.

Thia gave a rueful shake of her head. 'Lucien Steele
is in his early forties, several inches shorter than you are,
and stocky, with a shaved head.' In fact on first glance she
had thought the man more resembled a thug rather than
the richest and most powerful man in New York!

'That would be Dex.'

'Dex…?' she echoed doubtfully.

'Mmm.' The man beside her nodded unconcernedly.
'He takes his duties as my bodyguard very seriously—to
the point that he always insists upon entering a room before I do. I'm not sure why,' he mused. 'Perhaps he expects
there to be an assassin on the other side of every door…'

Thia felt a sinking sensation in the pit of her stomach as

she heard the amused dismissal in this man's—in Lucien Steele's?—voice. Moistening her lips with the tip of tongue before speaking, she said, 'And where is Dex now...?'

'Probably standing guard on the other side of those French doors.' He nodded down the balcony to the same doorway Thia had escaped through minutes ago.

And was Dex making sure that no one came outside, or was he ensuring that Thia couldn't return inside until this man wished her to...?

She gave another frown as she looked up searchingly at the man now standing so near to her she could feel the heat emanating from his body on the bareness of her shoulders and arms. Once again she took note of that inborn air of power, arrogance, she had sensed in him from the first.

For all the world as if he was *used* to people licking his highly polished handmade Italian leather shoes...

Lucien continued to hold Cyn's now trembling hand and waited in silence for her to gather her breath as she looked up at him between long and silky lashes with eyes a dark and mysterious cobalt blue.

Those eyes became shadowed with apprehension as she gave another nervous flick of her little pink tongue over the moist fullness of her perfectly shaped lips. 'The same Lucien Steele who owns Steele Technology, Steele Media, Steele Atlantic Airline *and* Steele Industries, as well as all those other Steele Something-or-Others?' she murmured faintly.

He shrugged. 'It seemed like a good idea to diversify.'

She determinedly pulled her hand from his grasp before tightly gripping the top of the balustrade. 'The same Lucien Steele who's a zillionaire?'

'I believe you said that already...' Lucien nodded.

She drew in a deep breath, obviously completely unaware of how it tightened the material of her dress across her breasts and succeeded in outlining the fullness of those—aroused?—nipples. Nipples that were a delicate pink or a succulent rose? Whatever their colour, he was sure they would taste delicious. Sweet and juicy, and oh so ripe and responsive as he licked and suckled them.

He had noticed the woman he now knew to be Cynthia Hammond the moment he'd entered Felix and Simone Carew's penthouse apartment a short time ago. It had been impossible not to as she'd stood alone at the back of the opulent room, her hair a sleek and glossy unadorned black as it fell silkily to just below her shoulders, her eyes that deep cobalt blue in the beautiful pale delicacy of her face.

She wore a strapless ankle-length gown of that same deep blue, leaving the tops of her breasts, shoulders and arms completely bare. The smoothness of her skin was a beautiful pearly white unlike any other Lucien had ever seen: a pale ivory tinted lightly pink, luminescent. Smoothly delicate and pearly skin his fingers itched to touch and caress.

The simple style of that silky blue gown allowed it to cling to every curvaceous inch of her full breasts, slender waist and gently flaring hips, so much so that Lucien had questioned whether or not she wore anything beneath it.

He still questioned it…

But what had really made him take notice of her, even more than her natural beauty or the pearly perfection of her skin, was the fact that instead of moving towards him, as every other person in the room had done, this pale and delicately beautiful woman had instead taken advantage of his arrival to slip quietly from the room and go outside onto the balcony.

Nor had she returned by the time Lucien had finally managed to extract himself from the—what had she called it a few moments ago? The licking of his 'highly polished handmade Italian leather shoes'. His curiosity piqued— and very little piqued his jaded palate nowadays!—Lucien hadn't been able to resist coming out onto the balcony to look for her the moment he had managed to escape all that cloying attention.

She drew in another deep breath now before speaking, causing the fullness of her breasts to once again swell deliciously over the bodice of that clinging blue gown.

'I really do apologise for my rudeness, Mr Steele. It's no excuse, but I'm really not having a good evening—and my rudeness to you means that it has just got so much worse!' she conceded with another pained wince. 'But that is really no reason for me to have been rude about you—or to you.'

He quirked one dark brow. 'I don't think you know me well enough *as yet* to speak with any authority on whether or not I *deserve* for you to be rude to me or about me,' he drawled mockingly.

'Well…no…' She was obviously slightly unnerved by his emphasis on the words 'as yet'… 'But—' She gave a shake of her head, causing that silky and completely straight black hair to glide across the bareness of her shoulders and caress tantalisingly across the tops of her breasts. 'I still shouldn't have been so outspoken about someone I only know about from the media.'

'Especially when we all know how inaccurate the media can be?' he drawled wryly.

'Exactly!' She nodded enthusiastically before just as quickly pausing to eye him uncertainly. 'Don't you own something like ninety per cent of the worldwide media?'

'That would be contrary to monopoly regulations,' he drawled dismissively.

'Do zillionaires bother with little things like regulations?' she teased.

He chuckled huskily. 'They do if they don't want their zillionaire butts to end up in court!'

Thia felt what was becoming a familiar quiver down the length of her spine at the sound of this man's throaty laughter. As she also acknowledged that, for all this man unnerved her, she was actually enjoying herself—possibly for the first time since arriving in New York.

'Are you cold?'

Thia had no chance to confirm or deny that she was before Lucien Steele removed his evening jacket and placed it about the bareness of her shoulders. It reached almost down to her knees and smelt of the freshness of those lemons as his warmth surrounded her, and of the more insidious and earthy smell of the man himself.

'No, really—'

'Leave it.' Both his hands came down onto the shoulders of the jacket as she would have reached up and removed it.

Thia shivered anew as she felt the warmth of those long and elegant hands even through the material of his jacket. A shiver entirely due to the presence of this overwhelming man—also the reason for her earlier shiver—rather than any chill in the warm evening air…

His hands left her shoulders reluctantly as he moved to stand beside her once again, that pale gaze—silver?— once again intent on her face. The snug fit of his evening shirt revealed that his shoulders really were that wide, his chest muscled, his waist slender above lean hips and long legs; obviously Lucien Steele didn't spend *all* of his days sitting in boardrooms and adding to his billions.

'Why aren't you having a good evening?' he prompted softly.

Why? Because this visit to New York hadn't turned out to be anything like Thia had imagined it would be. Because she had once again been brought to a party and then quickly abandoned by—well, Jonathan certainly wasn't her boyfriend, but she had certainly thought of him as a friend. A friend who had disappeared with their hostess within minutes of their arrival, leaving her to the untender mercies of New York's finest.

Latterly she wasn't having a good evening because she was far too aware of the man standing beside her—of the way the warmth and seductive smell of Lucien Steele's tailored jacket made her feel as if she was surrounded by the man himself.

And lastly because Thia had no idea how to deal with the unprecedented arousal now coursing through her body!

She gave a shrug. 'I don't enjoy parties like this one.'

'Why not?'

She grimaced, taking care not to insult this man for a second time this evening. 'It's just a personal choice.'

He nodded. 'And where do you fit in with this crowd? Are you an actress?'

'Heavens, no!'

'A wannabe?'

'I beg your pardon…?'

He shrugged those impossibly wide shoulders. 'Do you wannabe an actress?'

'Oh, I see.' Thia gave a rueful smile. 'No, I have no interest in becoming an actress, either.'

'A model?'

She snorted. 'Hardly, when I'm only five feet two inches in my bare feet!'

'You aren't being very helpful, Cyn.' There was an underlying impatience in that amused tone. Thia had seen far too much of the reaction of New York's elite these past four days not to know they had absolutely no interest in cultivating the company of a student and a waitress. Lucien Steele would have no further interest in her, either, once he knew. Which might not be a bad thing…

Her chin rose determinedly. 'I'm just a nobody on a visit to New York.'

Lucien totally disagreed with at least part of that statement. Cynthia Hammond was certainly somebody. Somebody—a woman—whose beauty and conversation he found just as intriguing as he had hoped he might…

She quirked dark brows. 'I believe that's your cue to politely excuse yourself?'

His eyes narrowed. 'And why would I wish to do that?'

She shrugged her shoulders beneath his jacket. 'It's what everyone else I've met in New York has done once they realise I'm of use to them.'

Yes, Lucien could imagine, knowing New York society as well as he did, that its members would have felt no hesitation whatsoever in making their lack of interest known. 'I believe I've already stated that I prefer not to be like everyone else.'

'Ain't that the truth? I mean—' A delicious blush now coloured those pale ivory cheeks as she briefly closed her eyes before looking up at him apologetically. 'I apologise once again. I'm really *not* having a good evening!' She sighed.

He nodded. 'Would you like to leave? We could go somewhere quiet and have a drink together?'

Cyn blinked those long lashes. 'I beg your pardon…?'

Lucien gave a hard, humourless smile. 'I hate parties like this one too.'

'But you're the guest of honour!'

He grimaced. 'I especially hate parties where I'm the guest of honour.'

Thia looked up at him searchingly, not sure whether or not Lucien Steele was playing with her. Not sure why he was bothering, if that should be the case!

The steady regard of those pale eyes and the grimness of his expression told her that this was a man who rarely, if ever, played.

He was seriously asking her to leave the Carews' party with him…

CHAPTER TWO

THIA GAVE A rueful shake of her head as she smiled. 'That really wouldn't be a good idea.'

'Why not?'

'Are you always this persistent?' She frowned.

He seemed to give the idea some thought before answering. 'When I want something badly enough, yes,' he finally murmured, without apology.

The intensity in that silver gaze as he looked down at Thia told her all too clearly that right now Lucien Steele wanted *her*.

Badly.

Wickedly!

She repressed another shiver of awareness just at the thought of how those chiselled lips and strong hands might feel as they sought out all the secret dips and hollows of her body.

'I really think it's time I went back inside.' She was slightly flustered as she slipped his jacket from about her shoulders and held it out to him. 'Please take it,' she urged when he made no effort to do so.

He looked down at her searchingly for several seconds before slowly taking the jacket and placing it dismissively over the balustrade in front of him—as if it *hadn't* cost as much as Thia might earn in a year as a waitress including tips!

'Cyn...'

He wasn't even touching her, and yet he managed to hold her mesmerised just by the way he murmured his own unique name for her in that deeply seductive voice, sending more rivulets of awareness down Thia's spine and causing a return of that tingling sensation in her breasts, accompanied by an unaccustomed warmth between her thighs.

'Yes...?' she answered breathlessly.

'I *really* want you to leave with me.'

'I can't.' She groaned in protest at the compulsion in the huskiness of his voice, sure that this man—a man who was not only sinfully handsome but rich as Creosus—rarely, if ever, asked for anything from anyone. He just took.

'Why not?'

'I just— What colour are your eyes, exactly...?' Whatever colour they were, they held Thia captive by their sheer intensity!

He blinked at the unexpectedness of the question. 'My eyes...?'

'Yes.'

His mouth twisted in a rueful smile. 'I believe it says grey on my passport.'

Thia gave a shake of her head. 'They're silver,' she corrected, barely able to breathe now, even knowing this was madness—that she was so totally aware of Lucien Steele, her skin so sensitised by the intensity of that glittering silver gaze fixed on her so intently, that she could feel the brush of each individual strand of her hair as it caressed lightly, silkily, across her shoulders and the tops of her breasts.

A totally unexpected and unprecedented reaction.

To any man. Goodness knew Jonathan was handsome enough, with his overlong blond hair, laughing blue eyes and lean masculinity, but for some reason she had just never found him attractive in *that* way. Just looking at Lucien Steele, knowing she was aware of everything about him, of all that underlying and leashed power, she knew that she never would be attracted to Jonathan—that Lucien Steele was so overpowering he ruined a woman's appreciation for any other man.

'Grey…silver…they can be whatever the hell colour you want them to be if you'll only leave with me now,' Lucien Steele urged again, with that same intensity.

She was tempted—Lord, was Thia tempted!—but it wouldn't do. No matter how distracted and inattentive Jonathan might choose to be, she couldn't arrive at a party with him and then leave with another man. Especially a man she found as disturbing as she did Lucien Steele!

A man who was over six feet of lean and compelling muscle. A man who was too handsome for his own good. A man who was just too…too intense—too much of everything—and whom she had discovered she found so mouthwateringly tempting.

Thia straightened her spine determinedly. 'I came here with someone.'

Those silver eyes narrowed with displeasure. 'A male someone?'

'Yes.'

His gaze moved to her left hand. 'You aren't wearing any rings.'

Thia gave a shake of her head. 'He isn't that sort of friend.'

'Then who is he?'

'I don't think that's any of your business—'

'And if I choose to make it so?'

'He's just a friend,' she dismissed impatiently, not sure even that was true any longer. Jonathan had made it obviously he inhabited a different world from her now—a world she had no inclination or desire ever to become a part of.

Lucien Steele's expression was grim as he shook his head. 'He can't be that much of a friend if he brought you here and then just left you to your own devices.'

This was the same conclusion Thia had come to over the past four days! 'I'm an adult and perfectly capable of looking after myself, thank you very much,' she assured him tartly.

Lucien Steele raised dark brows. 'So much so that you came out here alone rather than remain at the party?'

She felt stung by the mockery in his tone. 'Maybe I just wanted to get away from all that boot-licking?' she challenged.

'Handmade Italian leather shoes,' he corrected dryly.

'Whatever,' Thia dismissed impatiently. 'I'm sure you didn't come here alone tonight, either…' She vaguely recalled Jonathan mentioning something about Lucien Steele currently being involved with the supermodel Lyndsay Turner. A woman who, six feet tall and blond, couldn't be any more Thia's opposite!

Lucien's mouth thinned as he recalled the scene that had taken place with Lyndsay a week ago. A scene in which the supermodel had seriously overestimated his feelings for her and that had resulted in the end of their month-long relationship. Hell, he didn't *do* promises—let alone engagement and wedding rings.

He grimaced. 'As it happens, I did. And I want to leave with *you*,' he added determinedly, knowing it had been a long time since he had wanted anything as much as he now wanted to spend time alone with Cynthia Hammond.

'You don't know the first thing about me,' she dismissed exasperatedly.

'Which is precisely the reason I want the two of us to go somewhere quiet and talk—so that I can get to know you better,' he pushed insistently. The more this woman resisted him the more determined he became to leave the party with her this evening. At which time he intended to find out exactly which of Felix Carew's male guests was the friend Cyn had mentioned…

She attempted to tease. 'Has no one ever told you that it isn't possible to have *everything* you want?'

'No.' A nerve pulsed in Lucien's tightly clenched jaw.

'Because you're so rich and powerful no one would ever dare to tell you otherwise?' she asked softly, reminding him of his earlier comment.

'No doubt.' Again he answered unapologetically.

Thia gave an exasperated laugh at this man's unrelenting arrogance; she really had never met a man quite like him before! 'Then I shall have the distinction of being the first to do so! It's been…*interesting* meeting you, Mr Steele, but I really should go back inside and— What are you doing…?' She gasped softly as his gaze continued to hold hers captive even as his head slowly descended towards her, the warmth of his breath as light as a caress against her cheeks and lips.

'I want—I'd *like* to kiss you,' he corrected huskily, his lips just centimetres away from her own. 'Are you going to let me?'

'No…' Thia was aware her protest sounded half-hearted and she found herself unable to look away from those mesmerising silver eyes.

'Say yes, Cyn.' He moved slightly, his lips a hot and brief caress against the heat of her cheek before he raised his head and looked at her once again, not touching her with anything but the intensity of that glittering gaze.

She couldn't breathe, couldn't move so much as a muscle, as she continued to be held captive by the intensity of those eyes. Much like a deer caught in the headlights of an oncoming car. Or a freight train. Either of which was capable of flattening whatever stood in their way. As Lucien Steele's brand of seduction was capable of crushing both Thia and her resistance...

She drew in a shaky breath before stepping back and away from him. 'Thank you for the invitation, Mr Steele, but no.'

'Lucien.'

She shook her head. 'I believe I would prefer to continue calling you Mr Steele. Not that we'll ever meet again after this evening. But even so—'

'Why not?'

Thia gave a lightly dismissive laugh at the sharpness of his tone. 'Because you inhabit this world and I—I inhabit another one.'

'And yet here you are...?'

'Yes, here I am.' And she wouldn't be coming back again if she could help it! 'I really do have to go back inside now—'

'And look for your *friend?*' he prompted harshly.

'Yes.' Thia grimaced, very much afraid that she and that 'friend' were going to have words before the evening was over. Certainly she had no intention of letting Jonathan get away with bringing her to another party like this one and then leaving her to go off somewhere with the beautiful Simone. Jonathan's habit of just forgetting Thia's existence the moment they arrived at one of these parties was becoming tedious as well as a complete waste of her time, when she really didn't enjoy being here.

'Who is he?'

'It's really none of your business,' Thia snapped in irritation at Lucien Steele's persistence.

Those silver eyes narrowed, his jaw tightening. 'At least tell me where you're staying in New York.'

She gave an exasperated grimace. 'That's even less your business! Now, if you'll excuse me…' Thia didn't wait for him to reply before turning on her four-inch-heeled shoes and walking away, her head held determinedly high as she forced herself not to hurry, not to reveal how desperately she needed to get away from Lucien Steele's disturbingly compelling presence.

Even if she *was* completely aware of that silver gaze as a sensual caress across the bareness of her shoulders and down the length of her spine and the slender curve of her hips!

Lucien Steele was without doubt the most disturbingly sexual man she had ever—

'Where the *hell* have you been?' Jonathan demanded the moment she stepped back into the Carews' huge sitting room. The expression on his boyishly handsome face was accusing as he took a rough hold of her arm.

An entirely unfair accusation, in Thia's estimation, considering *he* was the one who had gone missing with their hostess for almost an hour, leaving her to be approached by Lucien Steele!

'Can we talk about this somewhere less…public, Jonathan?' She glared at him, very aware of the silent—listening?—presence of Lucien Steele's bodyguard, Dex, just feet away from the two of them. 'Preferably in the privacy of your car, once we've *left*,' she added pointedly.

Jonathan looked less than pleased by her last comment. 'You know damned well I can't leave yet,' he dismissed impatiently, even as he physically dragged her over to a quieter corner of the room.

'Could that possibly be because you haven't yet had a chance to say hello to Lucien Steele?' Thia felt stung into taunting him as she rubbed the top of her arm where Jonathan's fingers had dug so painfully into her flesh that she would probably have bruises to show for it tomorrow. 'I noticed you and our beautiful hostess were noticeably absent when he arrived.'

'What does *that* mean?' he glowered darkly. 'And what the hell's got into you, talking to me like that?'

'Nothing's got into me.' She gave a weary sigh, knowing that not all of her frustration with this evening was Jonathan's fault. Her nerves were still rattled from that encounter with Lucien Steele on the balcony—to a degree that she could still feel the seductive brush of those chiselled lips against her cheek and the warmth of his breath brushing against her skin… 'I just want to leave, that's all.' She grimaced.

'I've told you that I can't go just yet.' Jonathan scowled down at her.

'Then I'll just have to go downstairs and get a taxi—'

'It's a cab,' he corrected impatiently. 'And you aren't going anywhere until I say you can,' he added determinedly.

Thia looked at him searchingly, noting the reckless brightness of his eyes and the unaccustomed flush to his cheeks. 'Have you been drinking…?'

'It's a party. Of course I've been drinking!' Jonathan eyed her impatiently.

'In that case I'm definitely taking a cab back to your apartment,' Thia stated firmly.

'I said you'll leave when I *say* you can!' His eyes glittered.

Thia's cheeks warmed as she stared at him incredulously. 'Who do you think you are to talk to me like that?' she gasped.

Jonathan's expression darkened. 'I think I'm the man who paid for you to come to New York!'

Her eyes widened incredulously. 'And you believe that gives you the right to tell me what I can and can't do?'

'I think it gives me the right to do with you whatever the hell I feel like doing!' he sneered.

Thia felt the colour drain from her cheeks at the unmistakable threat in his voice. 'I don't know what's got into you, Jonathan.' Her voice shook as she tried to hold back tears of hurt. 'But I do know I don't like you like this. You're obviously drunk. Or something.' She wasn't a hundred per cent certain that reckless brightness in his eyes and the flush to his cheeks had been caused by alcohol alone...

Jonathan certainly wasn't behaving this evening— hadn't been for the past four days, if she was completely honest—like the charming and uncomplicated friend she had known in England...

She drew in a deep breath. 'I think it's best if I leave now, Jonathan. We can talk later. Or tomorrow—'

'You're staying put, damn it.' He reached out and grasped the top of her arm once again, the fingers of his other hand like a vice about her wrist as he twisted painfully.

Thia gave a gasp at the pain he was deliberately—viciously—inflicting on both her arm and her wrist. 'You're hurting me, Jonathan,' she breathed, very much aware of the other guests in the room and the curious sideways glances that were now being sent their way.

'Then stop being so damned difficult! I've said you aren't going anywhere and that's an end to it—' Jonathan broke off abruptly, his gaze moving past Thia and over her left shoulder and his eyes widening before he abruptly released her arm and wrist and forced a charmingly boyish smile to his lips.

Thia's spine stiffened as she guessed from the sudden pause in the conversation around them, the expectant stillness in the air and the way her skin tingled in awareness, exactly who was standing behind her.

Only one man had the power to cause such awe in New York's elite and the ability to possess the very air about him…

The same man who exuded such sexual attraction that it caused every nerve-ending in Thia's body to react and strain towards the pull of that raw sensuality!

Lucien Steele…

Lucien had remained out on the balcony for several more minutes after Cynthia Hammond had walked away from him, giving the hardness of his arousal time to subside even as he pondered the unexpected fierceness of his physical reaction to her.

Her skin—that pearly, luminescent skin—had been as soft and perfect to the light caress of his lips against her cheek as he had imagined it would be, and he could still smell her perfume…something lightly floral along with underlying warmly desirable woman. The same warmth that had surrounded him, enveloped him, as he'd shrugged back into his evening jacket ready for returning to the Carews' party as if the woman herself were wrapped around him.

Lucien couldn't remember the last time he'd had such a visceral reaction to a woman that he wanted to take her right here and right now. If he ever had...

All the more surprising because Cynthia Hammond, at little over five feet tall, ebony-haired and probably only twenty or so, wasn't the type of woman he usually found himself attracted to. He had always preferred tall, leggy blondes, and women nearer to his own age of thirty-five. Women who knew and accepted that his interest in them was purely physical, and that it would be fleeting.

Cynthia Hammond looked too young, too inexperienced to accept the intensity of passion Lucien would demand from her even for the brief time that his interest lasted. And it would be brief—a week or two, a month at the most—before Lucien once again found himself feeling restless, bored with having the same woman in his bed.

No, better by far, he had decided, that he stay well away from the too-young and too-inexperienced Cynthia Hammond.

And he would have done so if, when he had finally stepped back into the Carews' apartment, Dex hadn't felt it necessary to take him to one side and inform him of the way Jonathan Miller had verbally berated Cynthia Hammond the moment she'd returned to the party, before physically dragging her away.

Did that mean that Jonathan Miller, the star of one of the television series currently airing on Lucien's own network, was the friend Cyn had come to the party with?

Watching the couple as they'd stood together on the opposite side of the room, talking softly but obviously heatedly, Lucien had been unable to stop the narrowing of his eyes when he saw the way Cyn suddenly paled. His fists had clenched at his sides as he'd realised that Miller had a painful grip on her arm and his other hand was twisting her wrist, despite Cyn's obvious efforts to free herself. The thought of a single bruise marring the pearly perfection of her skin had been enough to send Lucien striding forcefully across the room.

Jonathan Miller was one of the reasons Lucien was back in New York at the moment. The actor's behaviour this past few months had become a definite cause for concern and required that Lucien intervene personally after receiving information that the verbal warning he had given Miller six weeks ago, about his drug habit and the affair he was having with his married co-star—the wife of the show's director—had made little difference to the other man's behaviour.

Another private meeting with Jonathan Miller would have to wait until tomorrow. At the moment Lucien was more concerned with the aggressive way the younger man was currently behaving towards Cyn. No matter how intense or demanding Lucien's own physical needs might be, he would never deliberately hurt a woman—he much preferred to give pleasure rather than pain—and he wouldn't tolerate another man behaving in that way in his presence, either.

His gaze settled on Cyn as she stood with her bared shoulders turned towards him. 'Are you ready to leave now…?' he prompted huskily.

Thia's heart leapt into her throat as Lucien Steele reiterated his invitation to leave the party with him, as he offered to take her away from this nightmare. Away from Jonathan. A Jonathan who was becoming unrecognisable as the charming man she had met two years ago—a man she had thought was her friend.

But friends didn't deliberately hurt each other, and the top of her arm still ached from where Jonathan's fingers had dug so painfully into her flesh just seconds ago, and her wrist was sore from where he had twisted it so viciously. Not only had he hurt her, but he had frightened her too when he had spoken to her so threateningly. And it shamed her, embarrassed her, to think that Lucien Steele might have witnessed that physical and verbal attack.

'Cyn...?'

She could see the confusion in Jonathan's eyes and he was the one to answer the other man lightly. 'I think you've made a mistake, Mr Steele. This is Thia Hammond, my—'

'Cyn...?'

Long, elegant fingers slipped possessively, gently beneath her elbow and Lucien Steele continued to ignore the other man as he came to stand beside her. Thia felt that now familiar shiver down the length of her spine just at the touch of those possessive fingers against her skin, accompanied by the compulsion in Lucien Steele's husky voice. She could actually *feel* that compulsion as that voice willed her to look up at him.

She turned slowly, much like a marionette whose strings were being pulled, her lids widening, pupils expanding, and all the air suddenly sucked from her lungs as she took her first clear look at Lucien Steele in the glare of light from the chandeliers above them.

Oh. My. God.

She had thought him mesmerising, compelling, as they

had stood outside together in the moonlight, but that was as nothing compared to the intensity of the magnetism he exuded in the brightly lit sitting room of the Carews' apartment. So much so that even this huge room, the size of a tennis court, seemed too small to hold all that raw and savage power.

His hair was so deep a black it appeared almost blue beneath the lights of the chandelier, and his bronzed face was beautifully sculptured. His high, intelligent brow, the sharp blade of a nose between high cheekbones, and his mouth—oh, God, his mouth!—were sinfully, decadently chiseled. His top lip was slightly fuller than the bottom—an indication of the sensuality he had exuded when they were outside together on the balcony?—and his jaw was square and determined, darkened by the shadow of a dark stubble.

It was the face of a warrior, a marauder, a man who took what he wanted and to hell with whoever or whatever stood in his way.

As if that savagely beautiful face wasn't enough, his perfectly tailored evening suit—had Thia *really* had that gorgeous jacket wrapped about her just minutes ago?—and white silk shirt showed the perfection of his widely muscled shoulders and chest, his tapered waist, powerful thighs and long, lean legs encased in matching black trousers above those soft Italian leather shoes she had referred to so scathingly such a short time ago.

All the trappings of urbanity, in fact—an urbanity that was dispelled the moment she looked at that handsomely savage face!

A face that was dominated by those amazing and compelling silver eyes surrounded by long and silky dark lashes.

Those same compelling silver eyes now held Thia's own gaze captive, hostage, and refused to release her until she acquiesced, surrendered to that raw and demanding power...

CHAPTER THREE

'CYN…?' LUCIEN QUESTIONED for the third and last time—and that was twice more than he would have allowed any other woman.

If Cyn Hammond ignored him for a third time then he would take it that she was a willing participant in Miller's abusive treatment. It wasn't to Lucien's personal taste, but that was Cyn's business—not his. No matter how much he might desire her himself…

'Thia?' Jonathan Miller looked totally confused by this whole encounter.

Lucien's eyes moved past Cyn to the other man, hardening to steel as he pinned Miller with his razor-sharp gaze. Bruises were already forming on Cyn's arm where Miller had held her too tightly just minutes ago, and her wrist looked red and sore. An unforgivable assault, as far as Lucien was concerned, on the perfection of that pearly unblemished skin.

'You hurt her, Miller,' he rasped harshly, his own fingers curling reassuringly about Cyn's elbow as he felt the way she still trembled. An indication that she really *wasn't* happy about Miller's rough treatment of her…

The other man's face flushed with anger—an emotion he quickly masked behind the boyishly charming smile that was currently holding American television audiences so enrapt, but succeeded only in leaving Lucien cold.

'Thia and I have had a slight misunderstanding, that's all—'

'It was *your* misunderstanding, Jonathan, not mine.' Cyn was the one to answer coldly and Lucien felt her straighten determinedly. 'Mr Steele has very kindly offered to drive me home, and I've decided to accept his offer.'

There were two things wrong with that statement as far as Lucien was concerned. One, he knew he was far from kind. Two, he had offered to take Cyn for a drink somewhere quieter than the Carews' apartment—not to drive her home. Especially if that 'home' should also happen to be Miller's apartment…

But the details could be sorted out later. For the moment Lucien just wanted to get Cyn away from here. He could still feel the slight trembling of her slender but curvaceous body. Those cobalt blue eyes were dark, there was an enticing flush to her cheeks, her pouting lips were moist and parted, and those deliciously full breasts were once again swelling temptingly against the bodice of her gown as she breathed.

And Lucien could think of a much better use for all that pent up emotion than anger…

'How do the two of you even know each other?' Jonathan Miller scowled darkly.

'If you'll excuse us, Miller?' Lucien didn't spare the other man so much as a glance, let alone answer him, as he turned to give Dex a slight nod of his head. He held Cyn to his side by a light but firm grasp of her elbow as he walked away, the other guests immediately clearing a pathway for them to cross the room to the Carews' private elevator in the hallway.

'What the hell is going on—?'

Lucien gave a cold smile of satisfaction as he heard Miller's protest cut short, knowing that Dex would have responded to his silent instruction and, in his own inimitable and deadly style, prevented the actor from attempting to follow the two of them. Lucien's smile hardened, his eyes chilling to ice as he thought of the conversation he was going to have with Jonathan Miller tomorrow. A conversation that would now include a discussion on the other man's treatment of the delicately lovely woman at his side...

Thia had no idea what she was doing, agreeing to leave the Carews' party with the dangerously compelling Lucien Steele, of all people. Especially when he had made his physical interest in her so obvious during the time the two of them had been outside on the balcony together!

She just wanted to get away from here. From a Jonathan she no longer recognised. And from the curious glances of all the other guests as they observed the tension between the three of them—some surreptitiously, some blatantly.

But was leaving with the dangerously attractive Lucien Steele, a man who was so arrogant she wasn't sure she even liked him, really the answer...?

'Shouldn't we say goodbye to the Carews before we leave?' she prompted hesitantly as Lucien Steele pressed a button and the lift doors opened.

'Dex will deal with it,' he dismissed unconcernedly.

'I—then shouldn't we at least wait for him...?' Thia made no move to enter the lift, her nervousness increasing the longer she spent in this man's compelling company.

'He'll make his own way down.' Lucien Steele released her elbow as he indicated she should enter the lift ahead of him.

Thia still hesitated. She wanted to get away from Jonathan, yes, but she now realised she felt no safer with Lucien Steele—if for a totally different reason!

'Changed your mind…?' he drawled mockingly.

Her chin rose at the taunt. 'No.' She stepped determinedly into the lift, her gaze averted as Lucien Steele stepped in beside her and pressed the button for the mirror-walled lift to descend.

Thia shot him several nervous glances from beneath her lashes as he stood broodingly on the other side of the lift, feeling that now familiar quiver trembling down her spine as she found herself surrounded by numerous mirrored images of him. This man was impressive under any circumstances, but she stood no chance of remaining immune to him in the confines of a lift.

Lucien Steele was sin incarnate, right from the top of his glossy hair—so much blacker than Thia's own, like shiny blue-black silk, the sort of tousled, overlong hair that made Thia's fingers itch to thread their way through it—to the soles of those Italian leather shoes.

He was a man so totally out of Thia's league that she had no business being there with him at all, let alone imagining threading her fingers through that delicious blue-black hair.

'Ask.'

Thia's startled gaze moved from that silky dark hair to the sculptured perfection of his face. Once again she felt that jolt of physical awareness as she found herself ensnared by the piercing intensity of those silver eyes. 'Um—sorry?'

He shrugged. 'You have a question you want to ask me.'

'I do…?'

His mouth twisted ruefully. 'You do.'

She chewed briefly on her bottom lip. 'Your hair—it's beautiful. I—I've never seen hair quite that blue-black colour before…?'

He raised a brow equally as dark. 'Are you sure you want *that* to be your one question?'

Thia blinked. 'My one question?'

He gave an abrupt inclination of his head. 'Yes.'

She frowned slightly. Surely he wasn't serious…? 'I've just never seen hair that colour before…' she repeated nervously. 'It's the colour of a starless night sky.'

His mouth twisted derisively. 'That was a statement, not a question.'

Yes, it was. But this man unnerved Thia to such a degree she couldn't think straight.

Lucien Steele sighed. 'Somewhere way back in my ancestry—a couple of hundred years or so ago—my great-great-grandfather is reputed to have been an Apache Indian who carried off a rancher's wife before impregnating her,' he dismissed derisively. 'The black hair has appeared in several generations since.'

Dear Lord, this man really was a warrior! Not an axe-wielding, fur-covered Viking, or a kilt-wearing, claymore-brandishing Celt, but a clout-covered, bow-and-arrow-carrying, bareback horse-riding Native American Indian!

It was far too easy for Thia to picture him as such—with that inky-black hair a long waterfall down his back, his muscled and gleaming chest and shoulders bare, just that clout-cloth between him and the horse he rode, the bareness of his long muscled legs gripping—

'Surely I haven't shocked you into silence?' he taunted.

Thia knew by his mocking expression that he wanted her to be shocked, that Lucien Steele was deliberately trying to unnerve her with tales of Apache warriors carrying off innocent women for the sole purpose of ravishing them.

In the same way he was doing the modern equivalent of carrying her off? Also for ravishment…?

Her chin rose. 'Not in the least.'

Those silver eyes continued to mock her. 'My father is a native New Yorker, but my mother is French—hence I was given the name Lucien. My turn now,' he added softly.

She gave a wary start. 'Your turn to do what…?' she prompted huskily.

Those chiselled lips curled into a derisive smile as he obviously heard the tremble in her voice. 'Ask you a question.'

She moistened dry lips. 'Which is…?'

'Cyn, if you don't stop looking at me like that then I'm going to have to stop the elevator and take you right now.'

As if to back up his statement he pressed a button and halted the lift's descent, before crossing the floor with all the grace of the predator he undoubtedly was and standing just inches in front of her.

Thia's eyes had widened, both at his actions and at the raw desire she could hear beneath the harshness of his tone. 'I—you can't just stop the lift like that…!'

'I believe I already did,' he dismissed arrogantly.

Thia found herself totally unable to look away from the intensity of that glittering silver gaze as Lucien looked down at her from between narrowed lids, her cheeks flushed, her heart beating wildly—apprehensively?—in her chest. 'I—that wasn't a question, either.'

'No.'

She winced. 'How was I looking at you…?'

'As if you'd like to rip my clothes from my body before wrapping your legs about my waist as I push you up against the wall and take you!' His voice was a low and urgent rasp.

Thia's breath caught in her throat as she imagined herself doing any or all of those things, her cheeks flushing, burning. 'I don't think—'

'It's probably better if you don't.'

Lucien Steele's gaze continued to hold hers captive.

She stepped away instinctively, only to feel her back pressing up against the mirrored wall. Lucien Steele dogged her steps until he again stood mere inches away from her and slowly raised his hands to place them on the mirror either side of her head. Lowering his head, he stared down at her with those compelling silver eyes, causing Thia to once again moisten her lips with the tip of her tongue.

'I advise you not to do that again unless you're willing to take the consequences!' he rasped harshly.

Thia's tongue froze on her parted lips as she was once again beset by the feeling of being trapped in the headlights of a car—or, more accurately, the glittering compulsion of Lucien Steele's gaze.

Her throat moved as she swallowed before speaking. 'Consequences?'

He nodded abruptly. 'I'd be more than willing to participate in your fantasy.' His jaw was tight, and desire gleamed in his eyes.

It was a depth of desire Thia had never encountered before, and one that caused her breath to hitch in her throat and her skin to flush with heat: a single-minded depth of desire that made her feel like running for the hills!

'What's Miller to you?' Lucien Steele prompted abruptly.

She blinked long dark lashes. 'Is that your question?'

He bared his teeth in a parody of a smile as he nodded. 'Contrary to my Apache ancestor, I make it a rule never to take another man's woman.'

"Take another man's'—!' She frowned. 'You really *are* something of a barbarian, aren't you?'

Rather than feeling insulted at the accusation, as she had intended, Lucien Steele instead bared his teeth in a wolfish smile. 'You have no idea.'

Oh, yes, Thia definitely had an idea. More than an idea. And her response to this man's raw sexuality terrified the life out of her. Almost as much as it aroused her...

'Cyn?' Lucien pressed forcefully.

She shrugged bare shoulders, those ivory breasts swelling invitingly against her gown. 'I already told you—Jonathan is just a friend—'

'A friend who had no hesitation in hurting you?' Lucien glared his displeasure as he looked down to where dark smudges were already appearing on the smooth paleness of her arm. Her wrist was still slightly red too. 'Who left his mark on you?' he added harshly as he gave in to the temptation to brush his fingertips gently over those darkening smudges.

'Yes...' Her bottom lip trembled, as if she were on the verge of crying. 'I've never seen him behave like that before. He was out of control...' She gave a dazed shake of her head. 'He's never behaved aggressively with me before,' she insisted dully.

'That's something, I suppose.' Lucien nodded abruptly.

'I—would you please restart the lift now...?' Those

tears were trembling on the tips of her long dark lashes, threatening to overflow.

He was *scaring* her, damn it!

Because this—his coming on to her so strongly—was too much, too soon after Miller's earlier aggression.

Or just maybe, despite what she might claim to the contrary, her relationship with Miller wasn't as innocent as she claimed it to be…?

In Lucien's experience no woman was as ingenuous as Cyn Hammond appeared to be. Her ingenuousness had encouraged him to reveal more about himself and his family in the last five minutes than he had told anyone for a very long time. Not that Lucien was ashamed of his heritage—it was what it was. It was his private life in general that he preferred to keep exactly that—private.

He straightened abruptly before stepping back. 'A word of advice, Cyn—you should stay well away from Miller in future. He's bad news.'

Her expression sharpened. 'What do you mean?'

'I believe you've more than used up your quota of questions for one evening.' His expression was grim.

'But you seem to know something I don't—'

'I'm sure I know a lot of things you don't, Cyn,' he rasped with finality, before turning to press the button to restart the elevator.

'Thank you,' Cyn breathed softly as it resumed its soundless descent.

'I didn't do it for you.' Lucien gave a hard, dismissive smile. 'The elevator has been stopped between floors for so long now Dex is probably imagining you've assassinated me.'

Thia frowned. 'Is it a defence mechanism, or are you really this arrogant and rude?'

His gaze was hooded as he answered her. 'Quite a bit of the latter and a whole lot of the former.'

'That's what I thought.' She nodded, able to breathe a little easier now that he wasn't standing quite so close to her. Well…perhaps not easier. Lucien Steele's presence was still so overpowering that Thia challenged anyone, man or woman, to be completely relaxed in his company.

He put his hand beneath her elbow again as the lift came to a stop, the doors opening and allowing the two of them to step out into the marble foyer of the luxurious Manhattan apartment building.

Thia's eyes widened as she saw Dex was already there, waiting for them. 'How did you…?'

'Service elevator,' the man supplied tersely, dismissively, his censorious glance fixed on his employer.

'Stop looking so disapproving, Dex,' Lucien Steele drawled. 'I checked before getting in the elevator: there's absolutely nowhere that Miss Hammond could hide a knife or a gun beneath that figure-hugging gown.'

Thia felt the colour warm her cheeks. 'Definitely a *lot* of the latter,' she muttered, in reference to their previous conversation and heard Lucien Steele chuckle huskily beside her even as she turned to give the still frowning Dex a smile. 'Mr Steele does like to have his little joke.'

There was no answering smile from the bodyguard as he opened the door for them to leave. 'I've had the car brought round to the front entrance.'

'Good,' Lucien Steele bit out shortly, his hand still beneath Thia's elbow as he strode towards the black limousine parked beside the pavement, its engine purring softly into life even as Dex moved forward to open the back door for them to get inside.

'I can get a taxi—a cab—from here,' Thia assured

Lucien Steele quickly. His behaviour in the lift wasn't conducive to her wanting to get into the back of a limousine with him.

'Get in.'

That compelling expression was back on Lucien Steele's face as he raised one black brow, standing to one side as he waited for her to get into the back of the limousine ahead of him.

Thia gave a pained frown. 'I appreciate your help earlier, but I'd really rather just get a cab from here…'

He didn't speak again, just continued to look down at her compellingly. Because he was so used to everyone doing exactly as he wished them to, whenever he wished it, he had no doubt Thia was going to get into the limousine.

'I could always just pick you up and put you inside…?' Lucien Steele raised dark brows.

'And I could always scream if you tried to do that.'

'You could, yes.' He smiled confidently.

'Or not,' Thia muttered as she saw the inflexibility in his challenging gaze.

Sighing, she finally climbed awkwardly into the back of the limousine. She barely had enough time to slide across the other side of the seat before Lucien Steele got in beside her. Dex closed the door behind them before getting into the front of the car beside the driver and the car moved off smoothly into the steady flow of evening traffic.

'I don't like being ordered about,' Thia informed Lucien tightly.

'No?'

'No!' She glared her irritation across the dim interior of the car. The windows were of smoked glass, as was the partition between the front and back of the car. 'Any more than I suspect you do.' Once again he was intimidating in the close confines of the car, so big and dark, and she could smell his lemon scent again, the insidious musk of the man himself, all mixed together with the expensive smell of the leather interior of the car.

'That would depend on the circumstances and on what I was being ordered to do,' he drawled.

Her irritation deepened along with the blush in her cheeks. 'Do you think you could get your mind out of the bedroom for two minutes?'

He turned, his thigh pressing against hers as he draped his arm along the back of the seat behind her. 'There's no need for a bedroom when this part of the car is completely private and soundproofed.'

'How convenient for you.'

'For *us*,' he corrected huskily.

Thia's throat moved as she swallowed nervously. 'Unless it's escaped your notice, I'm really not in the mood to play sexual cat-and-mouse games.' She moved her thigh from the warmth of his and edged further along the seat towards the door. 'You offered to drive me home—not seduce me in the back of your car.'

'I believe my original offer was to take you for a quiet drink somewhere,' he reminded her softly.

She gave a shake of her head. 'I'm not in the mood for a drink, either,' she added determinedly.

He smiled slightly in the darkness. 'Then what *are* you in the mood for?'

Thia ignored the innuendo in his voice and instead thought of Jonathan's brutish and insulting behaviour this evening—that reckless glitter in his eyes—all of which told her that it wouldn't be a good idea for her to go back to his apartment tonight. In fact after tonight she believed it would better for both of them if she moved out of Jonathan's apartment altogether and into a hotel, until she flew back to London in a couple of days' time.

Not that she could really afford to do that, but the thought of being any more beholden to Jonathan was no longer an option after the way he had spoken to her earlier. She was also going to repay the cost of the airfare to him as soon as she was able. She was definitely going to have bruises on the top of her arm from where he had gripped her so tightly. It was—

'Cyn?'

She turned sharply to look at Lucien Steele, flicking her tongue out to moisten the dryness of her lips—only to freeze in the action as that glittering silver gaze followed the movement, reminding her all too forcefully of his earlier threat. 'I—could you drop me off at a hotel? An inexpensive one,' she added, very aware of the small amount of money left in her bank account.

This situation would have been funny if Thia hadn't felt quite so much like crying. Here she was, seated in the back of a chauffeur-driven limousine, with reputedly the richest and most powerful man in New York, and she barely had enough money in her bank account to cover next month's rent on her bedsit, let alone an 'inexpensive' hotel!

Lucien Steele pressed the intercom button on the door beside him. 'Steele Heights, please, Paul,' he instructed the driver.

'Will do, Mr Steele,' the disembodied voice came back immediately.

'I totally forgot about the worldwide Steele Hotels earlier in my list of Steele Something-or-Others…' Thia frowned. 'But I'm guessing that none of your hotels are inexpensive…?'

The man beside her gave a tight smile. 'You'll be staying as my guest, obviously.'

'*No!* No…' she repeated, more calmly. 'Thank you. I always make a point of paying my own way.'

Her cheeks paled as she recalled that the one time she hadn't it had been thrown back in her face. She certainly had no intention of being beholden to a man as dangerous as Lucien Steele.

Unfortunately she was barely keeping her head above water now on the money she earned working evening shifts at the restaurant. That would change, she hoped, once she had finished her dissertation in a few months' time and hopefully acquired her Masters degree a couple of months after that. She could then at last go out and get a full-time job relevant to her qualifications. But for the moment she had to watch every penny in order to be able to pay her tuition fees and bills, let alone eat.

A concept she realised the man at her side, with all his millions, couldn't even begin to comprehend…

'Why the smile…?' Lucien prompted curiously.

Cyn gave a shake of her head, that silky dark hair cascading over her shoulders. 'You wouldn't understand.'

'Try me,' he invited harshly, having guessed from her request to go to a hotel that she had indeed been staying at Miller's apartment with him. Lucien had meant it when he'd said he didn't poach another man's woman. *Ever.*

His own parents' marriage had been ripped apart under just those circumstances, with his mother having been seduced away from her husband and son by a much older and even wealthier man than his father. They were divorced now, and had been for almost twenty years, but the acrimony of their separation had taken its toll on Lucien. To a degree that he had complete contempt for any man or woman who intruded on an existing relationship.

The fact that Cyn Hammond claimed she and Jonathan Miller were only friends didn't change the fact that she was obviously staying at the other man's apartment with him. Or at least had been until his aggression this evening...

She gave a grimace as she answered his question. 'I'm a student working as a waitress to support myself through uni. *Now* do you believe you inhabit a different world from me? One where you would think nothing of staying at a prestigious hotel like Steele Heights. I've seen the Steele Hotel in London, and I don't think I could afford to pay the rent on a broom cupboard!'

'I've already stated you will be staying as my guest.'

'And I've refused the offer! Sorry.' She grimaced at her sharpness. 'It's very kind of you, Lucien, but no. Thank you,' she added less caustically. 'As I said, I pay my own way.'

He looked at her through narrowed lids. 'How old are you?'

'Why do you want to know?' She looked puzzled by the question.

'Humour me.'

She shrugged. 'I'm twenty-three—nearly twenty-four.'

'And your parents aren't helping you through university?'

'I'm sure they would have if they were still alive.' She smiled sadly. 'They were both killed in a car crash when I was seventeen, almost eighteen,' she explained at his questioning look. 'I've been on my own ever since,' she dismissed lightly.

The lightness didn't fool Lucien for a single moment; his own parents had divorced when he was sixteen, so he knew exactly how it felt, how gut-wrenching it was to have the foundations of your life ripped apart at such a sensitive age. And Cyn's loss had been so much more severe than his own. At least his parents were both still alive, even if they were now married to other people.

The things Cyn had told him went a long way to explaining the reason for her earlier smile, though; Lucien had more money than he knew what to do with and Cyn obviously had none at all.

'I can relate to that,' he murmured huskily.

'Sorry?'

'My own parents parted and divorced when I was sixteen. Obviously it isn't quite the same, but the result was just as devastating,' he bit out harshly.

'Is that why you're so driven?'

'Maybe.' Lucien scowled; he really had talked far too much about his personal life to this woman.

'It was tough for me, after the accident, but I've managed okay,' she added brightly. 'Obviously not as okay as you, but even so… I worked for a couple of years to get my basic tuition fees together, so now I just work to pay the bills.'

He frowned. 'There was no money after your parents died?'

Cyn smiled as she shook her head. 'Not a lot, no. We lived in rented accommodation that was far too big for me once I was on my own,' she dismissed without rancour. 'I've almost finished my course now, anyway,' she added briskly. 'And then I can get myself a real job.'

It all sounded like another world to Lucien. 'As what?'

She shrugged her bare shoulders. 'My degree will be in English Literature, so maybe something in teaching or publishing.'

He frowned. 'It so happens that one of those other Steele Something-or-Others is Steele Publishing, with offices in New York, London and Sydney.'

She smiled ruefully. 'I haven't finished my degree yet. Nor would I aim so high as a job at Steele Publishing once I have,' she added with a frown.

Lucien found himself questioning the sincerity of her refusal. It wouldn't be the first time a woman had down-played the importance of his wealth in order to try and trap him into a relationship.

Thia had no idea why she had confided in Lucien Steele, of all people, about her parents' death and her financial struggles since then. Maybe as a response to his admis-sion of his own parents' divorce?

She *did* know as she watched the expressions flit-ting across his for once readable face, noting impatience quickly followed by wariness, that he had obviously drawn his own conclusions—completely wrong ones!—about her reason for having done so!

She turned to look out of the window beside her, stung in spite of herself. 'Just ask your driver to drop me off any-where here,' she instructed stiffly. 'There are a couple of cheap hotels nearby.'

'I have no intention of dropping you off anywhere!' Lucien Steele rasped. 'This is New York, Cyn,' he added as she turned to protest. 'You can't just walk about the streets at night alone. Especially dressed like that.'

Thia felt the blush in her cheeks as she looked down at her revealing evening gown, acknowledging he was right. She would be leaving herself open to all sorts of trouble if she got out of the car looking like this. 'Then *you* sug-gest somewhere,' she prompted awkwardly.

'We'll be at Steele Heights in a couple of minutes, at which time I *suggest* you put aside any idea of false pride—'

'There's nothing false about my pride!' Thia turned on him indignantly. 'It's been hard-won, I can assure you.'

'It *is* false pride when you're endangering yourself because of it,' he insisted harshly. 'Now, stop being so damned stubborn and just accept the help being offered to you.'

'No.'

'Don't make me force you, Cyn.'

'I'd like to see you try!' She could feel the heat of her anger in her cheeks.

'Would you?' he challenged softly. 'Is that what all this is about, Cyn? Do you enjoy it…get off on it…when a man bends you to his will, as Miller did earlier?'

'How dare you—?'

'Cyn—'

'My name is *Thia,* damn it!' Her eyes glittered hotly even as she grappled with the door handle beside her, only to find it was locked.

'Tell Paul to stop the car and unlock this damned door. *Now,*' she instructed through gritted teeth.

'There's no need for—'

'Now, Lucien!' Thia breathed deeply in her fury, not sure she had ever been this angry in her life before.

He sighed deeply. 'Aren't you being a little melodramatic?'

'I'm being a *lot* melodramatic,' she correctly hotly. 'But then you were a lot insulting. I don't— Ah, Paul.' She had at last managed to find what she sincerely hoped was the button for the intercom.

'Miss Hammond…?' the driver answered uncertainly.

'I would like you to stop the car right now, Paul, and unlock the back doors, please,' she requested tightly.

There was a brief pause before he responded. 'Mr Steele...?'

Thia looked across at Lucien challengingly, daring him to contradict her request. She was so furious with him and his insulting arrogance she was likely to resort to hitting him if he even attempted to do so.

He looked at her for several more minutes before answering his driver. 'Stop the car as soon as it's convenient, Paul. Miss Hammond has decided to leave us here,' he added, and he turned to look out of the window beside him uninterestedly.

As if she were a petulant child, Thia acknowledged. As if he hadn't just insulted her, accused her of—of— She didn't even want to think about what he had accused her of!

She kept her face turned away from him for the short time it took Paul to find a place to safely park the limousine, her anger turning into heated tears. Tears she had no intention of allowing the cynical and insulting Lucien Steele the satisfaction of seeing fall.

'Thank you,' she muttered stiffly, once the car was parked and Paul had got out to open the door beside her. She kept her face averted as she stepped out onto the pavement before walking away, head held high, without so much as a backward glance.

'Mr Steele...?' Dex prompted beside him uncertainly.

Lucien had uncurled himself from the back of the car to stand on the pavement, his expression grim as he watched Cynthia Hammond stride determinedly along the crowded street in her revealing evening gown, seemingly unaware—or simply uncaring?—of the leering looks being directed at her by the majority of the men and the disapproving ones by the women.

'Go,' Lucien instructed the other man tightly; if Cyn—Thia—had so little concern for her own safety then someone else would have to have it for her.

CHAPTER FOUR

A REALLY UNPLEASANT thing about waking up in a strange hotel room was the initial feeling of panic caused by not knowing exactly where you were. Even more unpleasant was noticing that the less-than-salubrious room still smelt of the previous occupant's body odour and cigarette smoke.

But the worst thing—the *very* worst thing—was returning to that disgusting-smelling hotel bedroom after taking a lukewarm shower in the adjoining uncleaned bathroom and realising that you had no clothes to leave in other than the ankle-length blue evening gown you had worn the night before, along with a pair of minuscule blue panties and four-inch-heeled take-me-to-bed shoes.

All of which became all too apparent to Thia within minutes of her waking up in that awful hotel bedroom and taking that shower!

She had been too angry and upset the evening before— too furious with the arrogantly insulting Lucien Steele—to notice how faded and worn the furniture and décor in this hotel room was, how threadbare and discoloured the towel wrapped about her naked body, let alone the view outside the grimy window of a rusted fire escape and a brick wall.

Thia had been sensible enough the night before, after

the lone night porter on duty had openly leered at her when she'd booked in, to at least lock and secure the chain on the flimsy door, plus push a chair under and against the door handle, before crawling between the cold sheets and thin blankets on the bed.

Not that it had helped her to fall asleep—she'd still been too angry at the things Lucien Steele had said to be able to relax enough to sleep.

She dropped down heavily onto the bed now and surveyed what that anger had brought her to. A seedy hotel and a horrible-smelling room that was probably usually let by the hour rather than all night. God, no wonder the night porter had leered at her; he had probably thought she was a hooker, waiting for her next paying customer to arrive.

At the moment she *felt* like a hooker waiting for her next paying customer to arrive!

How was she even going to get out of this awful hotel when she didn't even have any suitable clothes to wear?

Thia tensed sharply as a knock sounded on the flimsy door, turning to eye it warily. 'Yes…?'

'Miss Hammond?'

She rose slowly, cautiously, to her feet. 'Dex, is that you…?' she prompted disbelievingly.

'Yes, Miss Hammond.'

How on earth had Lucien Steele's bodyguard even known where to find her…? More to the point, *why* had he bothered to find her?

At that moment Thia didn't care how or why Dex was here. She was just relieved to know he was standing outside in the hallway. She hurried across the room to remove the chair from under the door handle, slide the safety chain across, before unlocking the door itself and flinging it open.

'Oh, thank God, Dex!' She launched herself into his arms as she allowed the tears to fall hotly down her cheeks.

'Er—Miss Hammond...?' he prompted several minutes later, when her tears showed no signs of stopping. His discomfort was obvious in his hesitant tone and the stiffness of his body as he patted her back awkwardly.

Well, of *course* Dex was uncomfortable, Thia acknowledged as she drew herself up straight before backing off self-consciously. What man wouldn't be uncomfortable when a deranged woman launched herself into his arms and started crying? Moreover a deranged woman wearing only a threadbare bathtowel that was barely wide enough to cover her naked breasts and backside!

'I'm so sorry for crying all over you, Dex,' she choked, on the edge of hysterical laughter now, as she started to see the humour of the situation rather than only the embarrassment. 'I was just so relieved to see a familiar face!'

'You—do you think we might go into your room for a moment?' Dex shifted uncomfortably as a man emerged from a room further down the hallway, eyeing Thia's nakedness suggestively as he lingered over locking his door.

'Of course.' Thia felt the blush in her cheeks as she stepped back into the room. 'I—is that my suitcase...?' She looked down at the lime-green suitcase Dex had brought in with him; it was so distinctive in its ugliness that she was sure it must be the same one she had picked up for next to nothing in a sale before coming to New York. The same suitcase that she had intended collecting, along with her clothes, from Jonathan's apartment later this morning... 'How did you get it?' She looked at Dex suspiciously.

He returned that gaze unblinkingly. 'Mr Steele obtained it from Mr Miller's apartment this morning.'

'Mr Steele did…?' Thia repeated stupidly. 'Earlier this morning? But it's only eight-thirty now…'

Dex nodded abruptly. 'It was an early appointment.'

She doubted that Jonathan would have appreciated that, considering he hadn't emerged from his bedroom before twelve o'clock on a single morning since her arrival in New York. 'And Lu—Mr Steele just asked him for my things and Jonathan handed them over?'

Dex's mouth thinned. 'Yes.'

Thia looked at him closely. 'It wasn't quite as simple as that, was it?' she guessed heavily.

He shrugged broad shoulders. 'I believe there may have been a…a certain reluctance on Mr Miller's part to co-operate.'

Thia would just bet there had. Jonathan had been so angry with her yesterday evening that she had been expecting him to refuse to hand over her things when she went to his apartment for them later. An unpleasant confrontation that Lucien Steele had circumvented for her by making that visit himself. She could almost feel sorry for Jonathan as she imagined how that particular meeting would have panned out. Almost. She was still too disgusted with Jonathan's unpleasant behaviour the previous evening to be able to rouse too much sympathy for him.

But she was surprised at Lucien Steele having bothered himself to go to Jonathan's apartment himself to collect her things; Lucien had let her leave easily enough last night, and he didn't give the impression he was a man who would inconvenience himself by chasing after a woman who had walked away from him as Thia had.

She drew a shaky breath. 'No one was hurt, I hope?'

'I wasn't there, so I wouldn't know,' Dex dismissed evenly.

'I had the impression you accompanied Mr Steele everywhere?' Thia frowned her puzzlement.

'Normally I do.' His mouth flattened. 'I spent last night standing guard in the hallway outside this room, Miss Hammond.' He answered her question before she had even asked it.

Thia took a step back in surprise, only to have to clutch at the front of the meagre towel in order to stop it from falling off completely. Her cheeks blushed a furious red as she tried to hold on to her modesty as well as her dignity. 'I—I had no idea you were out there...' Maybe if she had she wouldn't have spent half the night terrified that someone—that dodgy night porter, for one!—might try to force the flimsy lock on the door and break in.

A suitable punishment, Lucien Steele would no doubt believe, for the way in which she had walked away from him last night! Because there was no way that Dex had spent the night guarding the door to her hotel room without the full knowledge, and instruction of his arrogant employer...

'I doubt you would have been too happy about it if you had.' Dex bared his teeth in a knowing smile before reaching into the breast pocket of his jacket and pulling out an expensive-looking cream vellum envelope with her name scrawled boldly across the front of it. 'Mr Steele had Paul deliver your suitcase here a short time ago, along with this.'

Thia stared at the envelope as if it were a snake about to bite her, knowing that it had to be Lucien Steele's own bold handwriting on the front of it and dreading reading what he had written inside.

At the same time she felt a warmth, a feeling of being

protected, just knowing that Lucien had cared enough to ensure her safety last night in spite of herself…

'A Miss Hammond is downstairs in Reception, asking to see you, Mr Steele. She doesn't have an appointment, of course,' Ben, his PA, continued lightly, 'but she seems quite determined. I wasn't quite sure what I should do about her.'

Lucien looked up to scowl his displeasure at Ben as he stood enquiringly on the other side of the glass-topped desk that dominated this spacious thirtieth-floor office. Lucien wasn't sure himself what to do about Cynthia Hammond.

She was so damned stubborn, as well as ridiculously proud, that Lucien hadn't even been able to guess what her reaction might be to his having had her things delivered to her at that disgustingly downbeat hotel in which she had chosen to stay the night rather than accept his offer of a room at Steele Heights. He certainly hadn't expected that she would actually pay him a visit at his office in Steele Tower.

And he should have done—Cynthia Hammond was nothing if not predictably unpredictable. 'How determined is she, Ben?' He sighed wearily, already far too familiar with Cyn's stubbornness.

'Very.' His PA's mouth twitched, as if he were holding back a smile.

The wisest thing to do—the *safest* thing to do for Lucien's own peace of mind, which would be best served by never seeing the beautiful Cynthia Hammond again—would be to instruct Security to show her the door…as if she didn't already know exactly where it was! But if Cyn was determined enough to see him, then Lucien didn't doubt that she'd just sit there and wait until it was time for him to leave at the end of the day.

He pulled back the cuff on his shirt and glanced at the plain gold watch on his wrist. 'I don't leave for my next appointment for ten minutes, right?'

'Correct, Mr Steele.'

He nodded abruptly. 'Have Security show her up.'

Lucien leant back in his high-backed white leather chair as Ben left the office, knowing this was probably a mistake. He already knew, on just their few minutes' acquaintance the evening before, that Cynthia Hammond was trouble.

Enough to have caused him a night full of dreams of caressing that pearly skin, of making love to her in every position possible—so much so that he had woken this morning with an arousal that had refused to go down until he'd stood under the spray of an ice-cold shower!

He had even had Paul drive by the hotel where he knew she had spent the night on his way to visit Jonathan Miller's apartment this morning. The neighbourhood was bad enough—full of drug addicts and hookers—but the hotel itself was beyond description, and fully explained Dex's concern when he had telephoned Lucien the night before to tell him exactly which hotel Cyn had checked into and to ask what he should do about it. What the hell had possessed her to stay in such a disreputable hovel?

Money. Lucien answered his own question. He knew from his conversation earlier that morning with Jonathan Miller that Cyn really was exactly what she had said she was: a student working as a waitress to put herself through university, and just over here for a week's visit.

Her finances were not Lucien's problem, of course, but he had been infuriated all over again just looking at the outside of that disgusting hotel earlier, imagining that vulnerable loveliness protected only by the flimsy door Dex had described to him. Dex had been so worried about the situation Lucien believed the other man would have decided to stand guard over her for the night whether Lucien had instructed him to do so or not!

Just another example of the trouble Cynthia Hammond caused with her—

'*Wow!* This is a beautiful building, Lucien! And this office is just incredible!'

Lucien also gave a *wow,* but inwardly, as he glanced across the room to where Cynthia Hammond had just breezily entered his office. A Cynthia Hammond whose black hair was once again a straight curtain swaying silkily to just below her shoulders. The beautiful delicacy of her face appeared free of make-up apart from a coral-coloured lipgloss and the glow of those electric blue eyes. She was dressed in a violent pink cropped sleeveless top that left her shoulders and arms bare and revealed at least six inches of her bare and slender midriff—as well as the fact that she wore no bra beneath it. And below that bare midriff was the tightest pair of skinny low-rider blue denims Lucien had ever seen in his life. So tight that he wondered whether Cyn wore any underwear beneath...

And that was just the front view. Ben's admiring glance, as he lingered in the doorway long enough to watch Cyn stroll across the spacious office, was evidence that the back view was just as sexily enticing!

Cyn did casual elegance well—so much so that Lucien felt decidedly overdressed in his perfectly tailored black suit, navy blue silk shirt and black silk tie. 'Don't you have some work to do, Ben?' he prompted harshly as he stood up—and then sat down again as he realised his arousal had sprung back to instant and eager attention. The benefits of his icy cold shower earlier this morning obviously had no effect when once again faced with the enticing Cynthia Hammond.

Trouble with a capital T!

'Thanks, Ben.' Thia turned to smile at the PA before he closed the door on his way out, then returned her gaze to the impressive office rather than the man seated behind the desk, putting off the moment when she would have to face the disturbing Lucien Steele. Just a brief glance in his direction as she had entered the cavernous office had been enough for her to feel as if all the air had been sucked from her lungs, and her nerve-endings were all tingling on high alert.

This black and chrome office was not only beautiful, it was *huge*. Carpeted completely in black, it had an area set aside for two white leather sofas and a bar serving coffee as well as alcohol, and another area with a glass and marble conference table, as well as Lucien Steele's own huge desk, bookshelves lining the wall behind him, and an outer wall completely in glass, giving a panoramic view of the New York skyline.

It really was the biggest office Thia had ever seen, but even so her gaze was drawn as if by a magnet inevitably back to the man seated behind the chrome and black marble desk. The office was easily big enough to accommodate half a dozen executive offices, and yet somehow—by sheer force of will, Thia suspected—Lucien Steele still managed to dominate, to *possess*, all the space around him.

As he did Thia?

Maybe she should have power-dressed for this meeting rather than deciding to go casual? She did have one slim black skirt and a white blouse with her—they would certainly have blended in with the stark black, white and chrome décor of his office. Much more so than her shockingly pink cropped top.

Oh, well, it was too late to worry about that now. She would have to work with what she had.

'Say what you have to say, Cyn, and then go,' Lucien Steele bit out coldly. 'I have to leave for another appointment in five minutes.'

Her breath caught in her throat as she looked at Lucien. A Lucien who was just as knee-tremblingly gorgeous this morning as the previous night. Thia had convinced herself during her restless night of half-sleep that no one could possibly be that magnetically handsome, that she must have drunk too much of the Carews' champagne and imagined all that leashed sexual power.

She had been wrong. Lucien Steele was even more overpoweringly attractive in the clear light of day, with the sun shining in through the floor-to-ceiling windows turning his hair that amazing blue-black, his bronzed face dominated by those silver eyes, and his features so hard and chiselled an artist would weep over his male beauty. And as for the width of those muscled shoulders—!

Time for her to stop drooling! 'Nice to see that you're still living up to my previous description of you as being arrogant and rude,' she greeted with saccharine sweetness.

He continued to look at her coldly with those steel-grey eyes. 'I doubt you want to hear my opinion of *you* after the stunt you pulled last night.'

She felt the colour warm her cheeks and knew he had to be referring to the hotel in which she had spent the night, which Dex would no doubt have described to his employer in graphic detail. 'I didn't have the funds to stay anywhere else.'

'You wouldn't have needed any funds if you had just accepted the room I offered you at Steele Towers,' Lucien reminded her harshly.

'Accepting the room you offered me at Steele Towers would have put me under obligation to you,' she came back, just as forcefully.

Lucien stilled, eyes narrowing to steely slits. 'Are you telling me,' he asked softly, 'that the reason you refused my offer last night was because you believed I would expect to share that bedroom with you for the night as payment?'

'Well, you can't blame me for thinking that after the way you came on to me outside on the balcony and then again in the lift!'

Lucien raised dark brows. 'I can't *blame* you for thinking that?'

'Well…no…' Cyn eyed him, obviously slightly nervous of his quiet tone and the calmness of his expression.

And she was wise to be! Because inwardly Lucien was seething, furious—more furious than he remembered being for a very long time, if ever. Even during the visit he had paid to Jonathan Miller's apartment earlier this morning he had remained totally in control—coldly and dangerously so. But just a few minutes spent in the infuriating Cynthia Hammond's company and Lucien was ready to put his hands about her throat and throttle her!

If it weren't for the fact that he knew he would much rather put his hands on another part of her anatomy, starting with that tantalisingly bare and silky midriff, and stroke her instead…

Thia took a step back as Lucien Steele stood up and moved round to the front of his desk. His proximity, and the flat canvas shoes she was wearing, meant she had to tilt her head back in order to be able to look him in the face. A face that made her wish she were an artist. What joy, what satisfaction, to commit those hard and mesmerising features to canvas. Especially if Lucien could be persuaded into posing in traditional Apache clout cloth, with oil rubbed into the bare bronzed skin of his chest and arms, emphasising all the dips and hollows of those sleek muscles—

'What are you thinking about, Cyn?'

She looked up guiltily as she realised her appreciative gaze had actually wandered down to that muscled chest as she imagined him bare from the waist up—. 'I—you—nice suit.' She gave him a falsely bright smile.

Lucien Steele's mouth tilted sceptically, as if he knew exactly what she had been thinking. 'Thanks,' he drawled derisively. 'But I believe we were discussing your reckless behaviour last night and your reasons for it?' His voice hardened and all humour left his expression. 'Do you have any idea what could have happened to you if Dex hadn't stayed outside your room all night?'

She had a pretty good idea, yes. 'It was stupid of me. I accept that.'

'Do you?' he bit out harshly.

She nodded. 'That's why I'm here, actually. I wanted to thank you.' She grimaced. 'For allowing Dex to stand guard last night. For having my things delivered to the hotel this morning. And for sending that keycard, in the envelope Dex gave me, for a suite at Steele Heights.'

For all her expectations of what Lucien Steele *might* have put in that vellum envelope Dex had handed her this morning, there had been nothing in it but a keycard for a suite at Steele Heights, which he had obviously booked for her.

Thia had wrestled with her pride over accepting, of course, along with that old adage about accepting sweets from strangers. This was a different sort of suite, of course, but she told herself it was still sensible to be wary. But pride and wariness weren't going to put a roof over her head tonight, and she couldn't possibly go back to Jonathan's.

Lucien leant back against his desk and seemed to guess some of her thoughts. 'I trust you've overcome your scruples and moved in there now?'

'Yes.' Thia grimaced. Just the thought of that luxurious suite—the sitting room, bedroom and equally beautiful adjoining bathroom—was enough for her to know she had done the right thing. It might take her a while, but she fully intended to reimburse Lucien for his generosity.

He quirked one dark brow. 'Does that mean you no longer mind feeling under obligation to me?'

Thia looked up at him sharply, unable to read anything from his mocking expression. 'I think the question should be do *you* believe I'm under any obligation to you?'

'Let me see...' He crossed his elegantly clad legs at the ankles as he studied her consideringly. 'I left a perfectly good party last night because I thought we were going on somewhere to have a drink together. A drink that never happened. You flounced off in a snit after I offered to drive you somewhere, which greatly inconvenienced me as Dex was then forced to stand guard over your room all night. And I was put to the trouble this morning of asking your ex-boyfriend to pack up your belongings in that hideous lime-green suitcase before having my driver deliver it to that seedy hotel.' He gave a glance at the slender gold watch on his wrist. 'Your unexpected visit here this morning means I am now already three minutes late leaving for my next appointment. So what do *you* think, Cyn? *Are* you obligated to me?'

Well, when he put it like that… 'Maybe,' Thia allowed with a pained wince.

'I would say there's no *maybe* about it.' He slowly straightened to his full height of several inches over six feet, that silver gaze fixed on her unblinkingly as he took a step forward.

Thia took a step back as she was once again overwhelmed by the unique lemon and musk scent of Lucien Steele. 'What are you doing?'

'What does it look as if I'm doing?'

He was standing so close now she could feel the warmth he exuded from his body against the bareness of her midriff and arms. His face—mouth—only was inches away from her own as he lowered his head slightly.

She moistened her lips with the tip of her tongue. 'It looks to me as if you're trying to intimidate me!'

He gave a slow and mocking smile as he regarded her through narrowed lids. 'Am I succeeding?'

'You must know that you intimidate everyone.'

'I'm not interested in everyone, Cyn, just you.'

Thia's heart was beating such a loud tattoo in her chest that she thought Lucien must be able to hear it. Or at least see the way her breasts were quickly rising and falling as she tried to drag air into her starved lungs. 'You're standing far too close to me,' she protested weakly.

He tilted his head, bringing those chiselled lips even closer to hers. 'I like standing close to you.'

She realised she liked standing close to Lucien too. That she liked him. That she wanted to do so much more than stand close to him. She wanted Lucien to pull her into his arms and kiss her. To make love to her.

Which was strange when she had never felt the least inclination to make love with any man before now. But Lucien wasn't just any man. He was dark and dangerous and overpoweringly, mesmerisingly, sexually attractive— a combination Thia had never come across before now. She knew her breasts had swelled, the nipples hard nubs, pressing against her cropped top, and between her thighs she was damp, aching. For Lucien Steele's touch!

As if he was able to read that hunger in her face, Lucien's pupils dilated and his head slowly lowered, until those beautiful sculptured lips laid gentle but hungry siege to hers.

Thia felt as if she had been jolted with several thousand volts of electricity. And heat. Such burning heat coursing through her. She stepped in closer to that hard, unyield- ing body and her arms moved up and over Lucien's wide shoulders as if of their own volition. The warmth of his strong hands spanned the slenderness of her bare waist as her fingers became entangled in that silky black hair at his nape, her lips parting as she lost herself in the heat of his kiss.

Trouble…

Oh, yes, Cyn Hammond, with her black hair, electric- blue eyes, beautiful face and deliciously enticing body, was definitely Trouble with a capital T…

But at this moment, with the softness of her responsive lips parted beneath his, his hands caressing, enjoying the feel of the soft perfection of her bare midriff, Lucien didn't give a damn about that.

Nothing had changed since last night. If anything he wanted her more than he had then.

Again. Right here.

And right now!

Lucien deepened the kiss even as he moulded her slender curves against his own much harder ones, intoxicated, lost in Cyn's taste as he ran his tongue along the pouting softness of her bottom lip. Groaning low in his throat, he let his tongue caress past those addictive lips and into the heat beneath, plunging, possessing that heat as his hands moved restlessly, caressingly, down the length of her spine. Soon Lucien was able to cup that shapely bottom and pull her snugly into and against the pulsing length of his arousal.

The softness of her thighs felt so good against his, so hot and welcoming. He shifted, the hardness of his shaft now cupped and cushioned in that softness, and moved one of his hands to cup her breast through her T-shirt. It was a perfect fit into the palm of his hand, the nipple hard as an unripe berry as Lucien brushed the soft pad of his thumb across it and heard Cyn's gasp of pleasure, felt her back arching, pressing her breast harder into his cupping hand in a silent plea.

Her skin felt as smooth as silk beneath Lucien's fingertips as he slipped his hand beneath the bottom of her top to cup her bare breast—

Thia wrenched her mouth from Lucien's and pulled out of his arms before taking a stumbling step backwards—as if those few inches in any way nullified Lucien's sexual potency, or the devastation wrought upon her senses by that hungry kiss and those caressing hands!

'No...' she breathed shakily, her cheeks ablaze with embarrassed colour as she attempted to straighten her top over breasts that pulsed and ached for the pleasure she had just denied them.

Lucien's gaze was hooded. There was a flush across those high cheekbones, a nerve pulsing in his clenched jaw. 'No?'

'No,' Thia repeated more firmly. 'This is—I don't do this.'

'"This" being…?'

'Seduction in a zillionaire's office!'

He arched one dark brow. 'How many zillionaires do you know?'

Her cheeks warmed. 'Just the one.'

He nodded. 'That's what I thought.' He crossed his arms in front of his chest and he looked at her from between narrowed lids. 'Just what did you think was going to happen, Cyn, when you came to my office dressed—or rather undressed—like that?' That glittering silver gaze swept appreciatively over her breasts, naked beneath the crop top, her bare midriff and hip-hugging denims.

She hadn't allowed herself to think before coming here—had just acted on impulse, knowing she had to thank Lucien Steele for his help some time today and just wanting to get it over with. But, yes, now that he mentioned it she wasn't exactly dressed for repelling advances. Deliberately if subconsciously so? Lord, she hoped not!

'Stop calling me Cyn,' she snapped defensively.

'But that's what you are to me… Sin and all that word implies.' He all but purred. 'You have all the temptation of a candy bar in that shocking pink top. One that I want to lick all over.'

Thia felt heat in her already blushing cheeks at the provocative imagines that statement conjured in her mind. 'You—I don't—didn't—' She gave a shake of her head. 'Could we get back to our earlier conversation?' *Please,* she added silently, knowing she would have plenty of time later today to think about and to remember with embarrassment the touch of Lucien's lips and hands on her body. 'For one thing, Jonathan was only ever my friend,' she continued determinedly.

'Not any more he isn't.' Lucien nodded with grim satisfaction. 'He made it clear before I left his apartment earlier this morning that he was feeling decidedly less than charitable towards you,' he explained dryly.

Thia's eyes widened. 'What did you say to him?'

'About you?' He shrugged. 'As you have neither a father nor brother to protect you, I thought it necessary that someone should warn Miller against laying so much as a finger on you with the intention of hurting you ever again.'

She gasped. 'I can look after myself!'

'Is that why you spent the night at a less-than-reputable hotel? Why you have bruises on your arm?' Lucien's expression darkened with displeasure as his glittering silver gaze moved to the purple-black smudges at the top of her left arm. 'If I had known the extent of your bruising I would have inflicted a few of my own on him this morning, rather than just firing his ass!'

Thia gasped even as she looked up searchingly into that ruthlessly handsome face, totally unnerved by the dangerous glitter in Lucien's eyes as he continued to glower at the bruises on her arms. 'You fired Jonathan from *Network?*'

He looked up into her face as he gave a humourless smile of satisfaction. 'Oh, yes.'

Oh, good grief...

CHAPTER FIVE

LUCIEN'S HUMOURLESS SMILE became a grimace as he saw the expression of horror on Cyn's face. 'Don't worry. My decision to fire Miller wasn't because of anything he did or said to you. Although that was certainly a side issue in the amount of satisfaction I felt doing it.'

'Then why did you fire him?' She looked totally bewildered.

Lucien gave another impatient glance at his wristwatch. 'Look, can we continue this conversation later? Possibly over dinner? I really do have to leave for my appointment now.' He moved around his desk to pick up the file he needed for his meeting before putting it inside his black leather briefcase and snapping it shut. 'Cyn?' he prompted irritably as she stood as still as an Easter Island statue.

He was more than a little irritated with himself for having suggested the two of them have dinner together when he knew that the best thing for both of them was not be alone together again. His response to Cyn—as he had proved a short time ago!—was so different than to any other woman he had ever met. She was so different from those preening, self-centred, high-maintenance women he usually dated...

'Hmm?' She looked across at him blankly.

'Dinner? Tonight?' he repeated shortly.

'I—no.' She shook her head from side to side. 'You've been very kind to me, but—'

'You consider my almost making love to you just now as being *kind* to you…?' Lucien bit out derisively.

Her cheeks flushed a fiery red. 'No, of course not—'

'Dinner. Tonight,' he said impatiently. He couldn't remember the last time he had been late for a business appointment. Business always came first with him, pleasure second. And making love to Cyn just now had been pure pleasure. 'We can eat at the hotel if that would make you feel…*safer?*' he taunted.

Thia easily heard the mockery in Lucien's voice. A mockery she knew she deserved.

So Lucien had kissed her. More than kissed her. She wasn't a child, for goodness' sake, but a twenty-three-year-old woman, and just because this was the first time that anything like this had happened to her it was no reason for her to go off at the deep end as if she were some scandalised Victorian heroine!

Besides which, it was obvious Lucien wasn't going to tell her any more now about why he had fired Jonathan, and she desperately wanted to know.

Was it even possible for him to dismiss Jonathan so arbitrarily? Admittedly this was Lucien Steele she was talking about—a man who had already proved how much he liked having his own way—but surely Jonathan had a contract that would safeguard him from something like this happening. Besides which, *Network* was the most popular series being shown on US television at the moment; sacking its English star would be nothing short of suicide for both the series *and* Steele Media. And Lucien *was* Steele Media.

'Fine, we'll eat at Steele Heights,' she bit out abruptly. 'What time and which restaurant?' There were three of them, but obviously Cyn hadn't eaten at any.

Lucien moved briskly from behind his desk, briefcase in hand, and took hold of her elbow with the other hand. 'We can talk about that in the car before I drop you off at the hotel.'

'I'm not going back to the hotel just yet.' Thia dug her heels in at being managed again, even as she recognised that familiar tingling warmth where Lucien's fingers now lightly touched her arm. 'I'm going to the Empire State Building this afternoon.'

He raised dark brows. 'Why?'

'What do you mean, *why?*' She looked up at him irritably. 'It's a famous New York landmark, and I've been here five days already and not managed to go to the top of it yet.'

Lucien's mouth twisted derisively. 'I was born in New York, have lived here most of my thirty-five years, and I can honestly say I've never been even to the top of the Empire State Building.'

'You could always come with me—' Thia broke off as she realised the ridiculousness of her suggestion. Of course Lucien Steele, zillionaire entrepreneur, didn't want to do something as mundane as go with her to the top of the Empire State Building any more than Thia really wanted him to accompany her. Did she...? No, of course she didn't. She had succumbed to this man's sexual magnetism enough for one day—made a fool of herself enough for one day— thank you very much.

'Forget it,' she dismissed, with a lightness she was far

from feeling. She wasn't one hundred per cent sure *what* she was feeling at the moment, or thinking. She was too tremblingly aware of Lucien having kissed her just minutes ago to be able to put two coherent thoughts together. 'You said you had a meeting to get to?' she reminded him.

Yes, he did. But strangely, just for a few seconds, Lucien had actually been considering cancelling his business meeting and going with Cyn to visit the Empire State building instead. Unbelievable.

Zillionaires didn't get to be or stay zillionaires, by playing hooky from work to go off and play tourist with a visitor from England. Even if—*especially* if—that visitor was Cyn Hammond. A woman who apparently had the ability to make Lucien forget everything but his desire to be with her and make love to her.

Something that had definitely not happened to him before today.

But, damn it, Cyn really did look like a tempting stick of candy in that pink top… And it took no effort at all on Lucien's part to imagine the pleasure of licking his tongue over every inch of that soft and silky flesh…

He nodded abruptly. 'I can drop you off at the Empire State Building on my way.'

'It's such a lovely day I think I'd rather walk,' she refused lightly, lifting a hand in parting to Ben as they passed through his office and out into the hallway before stepping into the private elevator together.

Just the thought of Cyn wandering the streets of New York dressed in nothing more than that skimpy pink top and those body-hugging denims was enough to bring a dark scowl back to Lucien's brow. 'Do you have *any* sense of self-preservation at all?' he rasped harshly as he released her elbow to press the button for the elevator to take them down to the ground floor.

'It's the middle of the day, for goodness' sake!' She glanced at him with those cobalt blue eyes through lushly dark lashes.

Lucien eyed her impatiently. 'Remind me to tell you later tonight about the statistics for daytime muggings and shootings in New York.'

She chewed on her bottom lip. 'You still have to tell me what time I'm meeting you this evening, and at which restaurant in the hotel,' she said firmly.

'Eight o'clock.' He frowned. 'Go down to the ground floor. I'll have someone waiting to show you to the private elevator that will bring you directly up to the penthouse apartment.'

Her eyes widened. 'The penthouse? You live in an apartment at the top of the Steele Heights Hotel?' Thia was too surprised not to gape at him incredulously.

He gave a smile of satisfaction at her reaction. 'I occupy the whole of the fiftieth floor of Steele Heights when I'm in New York.'

'The whole floor?' she gasped. 'What do you have up there? A tennis court?'

'Not quite.' Lucien smiled tightly. 'There is a full-sized gym, though. A small pool and a sauna. And a games room. A small private cinema for twenty people.' He quirked a dark brow as Cyn gaped at him. 'Changed your mind about having dinner with me at the hotel this evening?' Those silver eyes mocked her.

It didn't take too much effort on Thia's part to realise Lucien was challenging her, daring her. He expected her to baulk at agreeing to have dinner with him now that she knew they would be completely alone in his penthouse apartment. And good sense told Thia that it would be a wise move on her part *not* to rise to this particular challenge, to just withdraw and concede Lucien as being the winner.

Unfortunately Thia had never backed down from a challenge in her life. She wouldn't have been able to survive the death of her parents or worked as a waitress for the past five years in order to support herself through uni if that was the case. And she had no intention of backing down now, either.

Even if she did suspect that Lucien wasn't just challenging her by inviting her to his apartment and that the main reason he wanted them to dine in the privacy of his apartment was because he didn't want to be seen out with her in public.

She knew enough about Lucien Steele to know he was a man the media loved to photograph, invariably entering some famous restaurant or club, and always with a beautiful model or actress on his arm. Being seen with a waitress student from London hardly fitted in with that image.

'Fine.' She nodded abruptly. 'Eight o'clock. Your apartment.'

'No need to dress formally,' Lucien told her dismissively. 'Although perhaps something a little less revealing than what you're currently wearing might be more appropriate,' he added dryly.

'It's a crop top, Lucien. All women are wearing them nowadays.'

'None of the women *I've* escorted have ever done so,' he assured her decisively.

'That's your loss!' Thia felt stung by Lucien's casual mention of those women he'd escorted. Which was ridiculous of her. The fact that they were eating dinner at

his apartment told her that this wasn't a date, just a convenient way for the two of them to be able to finish their
conversation in private. Well away from the public eye…

'Yes.' He bared his teeth in a wolfish smile as the two
of them stepped out of the lift together, causing Thia to
blush as he reached out to grasp one of her hands lightly
in his before raising it to skim his lips across her knuckles. 'Until later, Cyn.'

Thia snatched her hand from within his grasp, aware
of the stares being directed their way by the other people milling about in the lobby of Steele Tower even if he
wasn't. 'I hope you're enjoying yourself,' she hissed, even
as she did her best to ignore the tingling sensation now
coursing the length of her arm. And beyond…

'It has its moments.' His eyes glittered with satisfied
amusement as he looked down at her.

Thia glared right back at him. 'You could have told me
your reason for firing Jonathan in the time we've been
talking together.'

'I do things my own way in my own time, Cyn,' he bit
out tersely. 'If you have a problem with that, then I suggest—'

'I didn't say I had a problem with it,' she snapped irritably. 'Only that—oh, never mind!' Lucien had the ability
to rob her of her good sense, along with any possibility of
withstanding his lethal attraction.

A lethal attraction that affected every other woman
in his vicinity, if the adoring glances of the receptionists
were any indication, as well as those of the power-dressed
businesswomen going in and out of the building.

All of them, without exception, had swept a contemptuous gaze over the casually dressed Thia—no doubt wondering what a man like Lucien Steele was doing even

wasting his time talking to someone like her—before returning that gaze longingly, invitingly, to the man at Thia's
side. One poor woman had almost walked into a potted
plant because she had been so preoccupied with eating
Lucien up with her eyes!

It was a longing Thia knew she was also guilty of.

Challenge or no challenge, she really shouldn't have
agreed to have dinner alone with him in his apartment
this evening…

Thia looked in dismay at the chaos that was her bedroom
in the suite on the tenth floor of the Steele Heights Hotel.
Clothes were strewn all over the bed after she had hastily
tried them on and then as quickly discarded them. Finding
exactly the right casual outfit to wear to have dinner with
the dangerously seductive Lucien Steele in—oh, hell—
fifteen minutes' time was proving much more difficult
than she had thought it would. And she hadn't dried her
hair yet, or applied any make-up.

She had been late getting back to the hotel as the long
queues at the Empire State Building had meant she'd had
to wait in line for a long time before getting to the top.
It had been worth the wait when she finally got there, of
course, but by that time it had been starting to get late.

She'd also had the strangest feeling all afternoon that
she was being followed…

Lucien's warnings earlier had made her paranoid. That
was more than a possibility. Whatever the reason, Thia
had felt so uncomfortable by the time she'd come down
from the top of the Empire State Building and stepped
back out into the street that she had decided to treat herself and take a taxi back to the hotel.

She had taken out her laptop and gone online for half

an hour once she was back in the hotel suite, determined to know at least a little more about the enigmatic Lucien Steele before they met again this evening.

Unfortunately the moment she'd come offline and lain back on the bed she had fallen asleep, tired from her outing, and also exhausted from the previous sleepless night she had spent at that awful hotel. No surprise, then, that she hadn't woken up again until almost seven-thirty!

Which now meant she was seriously in danger of being late—and she still hadn't found anything to wear that she thought suitable for having dinner with a man like Lucien Steele!

Oh, to hell with it. Black denims and a fitted blouse the same colour blue as her eyes would have to do; she simply didn't have any more time to waste angsting over what she should or shouldn't wear to have dinner with a zillionaire. And the blue blouse also had the benefit of having elbow-length sleeves, meaning those bruises Jonathan had inflicted on her arm the previous evening, which had so angered Lucien earlier, would be safely hidden from his piercing gaze.

Jonathan....

If she concentrated on the fact that it was only because she wanted to know exactly why Lucien had decided to fire Jonathan from *Network* that she had agreed to have dinner with Lucien—even if she no longer believed that!— then maybe she would be able to get through this evening.

The butterflies fluttering about in her stomach didn't seem to be listening to her assurances as she stood alone in the private lift minutes later, on her way up to the penthouse apartment. Her hair still wasn't completely dry and her face felt flushed. No doubt it looked it too, despite her application of a light foundation.

The manager of the hotel himself had been waiting on the ground floor to show her into the private coded lift. The sheer opulence of the lift in which she was now whizzing up fifty floors to the penthouse apartment—black carpet, plush bench seat along one mirrored wall, a couple of pot plants—and the thought of the overwhelmingly sexy man who would be waiting up there for her were so far beyond what was normal for Thia, was it any wonder she was so nervous she felt nauseous?

Or maybe it was just the thought of being alone with Lucien again that was making her feel that way... Her online snooping about him earlier had informed her that he was thirty-five years old—something Lucien had already told her—and the only child of New Yorker Howard Steele and Parisian Francine Maynard. Educated at private school and then Harvard, he had attained a law degree and in his spare time designed a new gaming console and graphics for many computer games, enabling him to make his first million—or possibly billion?—before he was twenty-one. That was something else Lucien had already told her. He had taken full advantage of this success by diversifying those millions into any number of other successful businesses.

There had also, depressingly, been dozens of photographs of him with dozens of the women he had escorted at some time or other during the past fifteen years: socialites, actresses, models. All of them, without exception, were extremely beautiful, as well as being tall and blond.

And this was the man that Thia, five-foot-two, raven-haired and merely pretty, had agreed to have dinner alone with this evening...

Knowing she simply wasn't his type should have made her feel less nervous about the evening ahead. Should have.

But it didn't. How could it when she only had to think of the way Lucien had kissed her so intensely this afternoon, of his caressing hands on her bare midriff—and higher!—to know that he had felt desire for her then, even if she *was* five-foot-two and raven-haired!

After all her apprehension, the man who had caused all those butterflies in her stomach was nowhere to be seen when Thia stepped out of the lift into the penthouse apartment seconds later. The apartment itself was everything she had thought it would be—white marble floors, original artwork displayed on ivory walls. She walked tentatively down the hallway to the sitting room in search of Lucien. It was a spaciously elegant room, with the same minimalist white, black and chrome décor of Lucien's office. Had the man never heard of any other colours but white, black and chrome?

The view from the floor-to-ceiling windows was even more spectacular than the one from the Carews' apartment—

'I'm sorry I wasn't here to greet you when you arrived, Cyn. My meeting ran much later than I had anticipated and I only got back a few minutes ago.'

Thia turned almost guiltily at the sound of Lucien's voice, very aware of the fact that she had just walked into his private apartment and made herself at home, only to stand and stare, her mouth falling open, blue eyes wide and unblinking, as she took in his rakishly disheveled and practically nude appearance.

Lucien had obviously just taken a shower. His black hair was still damp and tousled, a towel was draped about his shoulders, and he wore only a pair of faded blue denims sitting low down on the leanness of his hips, leaving that glistening bronzed chest and shoulders—the same ones

Thia had fantasised about earlier this afternoon!—openly on view. Revealing he was just as deliciously muscled as she had imagined he would be. His nipples were the size and colour of two dark bronze coins amongst the dusting of dark hair that dipped and then disappeared beneath the waistband of his denims.

If Lucien had wanted to lick her all over this afternoon then Thia now wanted to do the same to him... Dressed in those low-slung denims, with his bronzed shoulders and chest bare, overlong blue-black hair sexily dishevelled, his bare feet long and elegant, Lucien definitely looked good enough to eat!

'Cyn...?' Lucien eyed her questioningly as she made no response.

Or perhaps she did...

She was wearing another pair of those snug-fitting denims this evening—black this time—with a fitted blouse the same electric blue colour as her sooty-lashed eyes. The material of the blouse was so sheer it was possible for Lucien to see that she wore no bra beneath it. Her breasts were a pert shadow, nipples plump as berries as they pressed against the soft gauzy material. Hard and aroused berries...

'I—er—shouldn't you go and finish dressing...?'

Lucien dragged his gaze slowly, reluctantly away from admiring those plump, nipple-crested breasts to look up into Cyn's face, instantly noting the flush to her cheeks and the almost fevered glitter to her eyes as she shifted uncomfortably from one booted foot to the other. As if her breasts weren't the only part of her body that was swollen with arousal...

Instead of doing as she suggested Lucien stepped further into the sitting room. 'I'll get you a drink first.' He threw the damp towel down onto a chair as he strolled over to the bar in the corner of the room. 'Bottled water, white wine, red wine...something stronger...?' He arched a questioning brow.

Was Lucien strutting his bare, bronzed stuff deliberately? Thia wondered. As a way of disconcerting her? If he was then he was succeeding. She had never felt so uncomfortably aware of a man in her life as she was now by all his warm naked flesh. Or so aroused!

The man should have a public health warning stamped on his chest. Something along the lines of 'Danger to all women with a pulse' ought to do it. And Thia was the only woman with a pulse presently in Lucien Steele's disturbing vicinity! Her throat felt as if it had closed up completely, and her chest was so tight she could barely breathe, let alone speak.

She cleared her throat before even attempting it. 'Red wine would be lovely, thank you,' she finally managed to squeak, in a voice that sounded absolutely nothing like her own, only to draw a hissing breath into her starved lungs as Lucien turned away from her. The muscles shifted in his back beneath that smooth bronzed skin as he bent to take a bottle of wine from the rack beside the bar, and even more muscles flexed in his arms as he straightened to open it, the twin dips at the base of his spine clearly visible above the low-riding denims.

Twin dips Thia longed to stroke her tongue over, to taste, before working her way slowly up the length of that deliciously muscled back...!

'Here you go.' Lucien strolled unconcernedly across the room carrying two glasses of red wine—one obviously meant for Thia, the other for himself.

Evidence that he didn't have any intention of putting any more clothes on in the immediate future? And why should he? This was his home, after all!

His close proximity now meant that Thia was instantly overwhelmed by that smell of lemons and the musky male scent she now associated only with this man, and her hand was trembling slightly as she reached out to take one of the wine glasses from him—only to spill some of the wine over the top of the glass as a jolt of electricity shot up her arm the moment her fingers came into contact with his.

'Sorry,' she mumbled self-consciously, passing the glass quickly into her other hand with the intention of licking the spilt wine dripping from her fingers.

'Let me…' Lucien reached out to catch her hand in his before it reached her parted lips, his gaze easily holding hers as he carried her fingers to his own mouth before lapping up the wine with a slow and deliberate rasp of his tongue. 'Mmm, delicious.' He licked his lips. 'Perhaps I should consider always drinking wine this way…?' His shaft certainly thought it was a good idea as it rose up hard and demanding inside his denims!

'Lucien—'

'Hmm?' He continued to lick the slenderness of Cyn's silky fingers even after all the wine had gone, enjoying the way her hand was trembling in his and watching the slow rise and fall of those plumped breasts and aroused nipples, his erection now almost painful in its intensity.

She snatched her hand away from his to glare up at him. 'Are you doing this on purpose?'

'Doing what…?'

Her eyes narrowed. 'Would you please go and put some clothes on?'

Lucien straightened slowly to look at her from between

narrowed lids. 'You seem a little…tense this evening, Cyn. Didn't the Empire State live up to your expectations?'

'The Empire State was every bit as wonderful as I always imagined it would be. And I'm not in the least tense!' She moved away jerkily until she stood apart from him.

Far enough that she thought she had put a safe distance between them.

Lucien was so aroused right now he didn't think the other side of the world would be far enough away to keep Cyn safe from him…

His meeting that afternoon had not gone well. No, that wasn't accurate. It hadn't been the meeting that was responsible for his feelings of impatience and dissatisfaction all afternoon. That had been due to the intrusive thoughts he'd had of Cyn all through that lengthy meeting—not just the silkiness of her skin, her responsive breasts, the delicious taste of her mouth, but also the fact that he *liked* her…her sense of humour, the way she answered him back, everything about her, damn it! It had caused Lucien to finally call a halt to negotiations and reschedule the meeting for another day next week.

Needless to say he had not been best pleased that he had allowed the distraction of those thoughts of Cyn to infringe on his business meeting, but one look at her tonight, dressed in those snug-fitting black denims and the delicate blue blouse, with the silky darkness of her hair loose about her shoulders, and his earlier feeling of irritated dissatisfaction had instantly been replaced by desire.

'I thought that I had been invited up here for dinner,' she snapped now. 'Not to witness a male strip show!'

Lucien made no effort to hold back his grin of satisfaction at her obvious discomfort at seeing his bare chest. It seemed only fair when he had thought of her all afternoon.

When his shaft was now an uncomfortable, painful throb against his denims. 'I'm wearing more now than I would be on a beach,' he reasoned.

'Unless you haven't noticed, we don't happen to *be* on a beach.' She frowned. 'And I do not have any intention of providing your amusement for the evening.'

He eyed her mockingly. 'Oh, I haven't even begun to be amused yet, Cyn.'

'And as far as I'm concerned you aren't going to be, either!' She placed her glass down noisily on the coffee table before straightening and turning, with the obvious intention of walking out on him.

Lucien reached out and grasped her arm as she would have stormed past him—only to ease up on the pressure of that grasp as he saw the way she winced. 'Are your wrist and arm still hurting you?' he rasped.

'No. I—they're fine.' She gave a dismissive shake of her head, her eyes avoiding meeting his piercingly questioning gaze. 'You just caught me unawares, that's all.'

'I don't believe you.'

She sighed her impatience. 'I don't care whether or not— What are you doing?' she demanded as Lucien released her arm before moving his hands to the front of her blouse, his fingers unfastening the tiny blue buttons. 'Lucien? Stop it!' She slapped ineffectually at his hands.

'I don't trust your version of "fine", Cyn. I intend to see for myself,' Lucien muttered grimly as he continued unfastening those buttons.

'Stop it, I said!' She pulled sharply away from him—a move immediately followed by a delicate ripping sound as Lucien refused to release his hold. The gauzy blouse ripped completely away from the last remaining buttons, leaving Cyn's breasts completely bared to his heated gaze.

Full and beautifully sloping breasts…tipped by two perfect rosy-red nipples…those nipples were plumping and hardening in tempting arousal as Lucien continued to look down at them appreciatively.

CHAPTER SIX

'I CAN'T BELIEVE you just did that!' Thia was the first to recover enough to speak, staring accusingly at Lucien even as her shaking hands scrabbled desperately to pull the two sides of her blouse together over her bared breasts, feeling mortified by her nakedness in front of a man she already found far too overpoweringly attractive for comfort.

Her knees had once again turned to the consistency of jelly at the heat she saw in those silver eyes…!

'I believe, if you think about it, you'll find that *we* just did that,' Lucien drawled hardly. 'You pulled away. I didn't let go.' He shrugged.

Thia bristled indignantly, clutching on to anger as a means of hiding her embarrassment—and arousal—at the continued heat in Lucien's gaze. 'You shouldn't have been unbuttoning my blouse in the first place!'

'I wanted to see your bruises. I still want to see them,' he added determinedly.

'You saw a lot more than my bruises!' she snapped. 'And I believe we've already had one discussion about my feelings concerning what you do or don't want. In this instance what you wanted resulted in the ruination of a blouse I was rather fond of and saved for weeks to buy.'

'I'll replace it for you tomorrow.'

'Oh, won't that be just wonderful?' She huffed her exasperation. 'I can hear your telephone conversation with the woman in the shop now—*Send a blue blouse round to Miss Hammond's suite at Steele Heights Hotel. I ripped the last one off her!*' She attempted to mimic his deep tones. 'Are you laughing at me, Lucien?' Thia eyed him suspiciously and she thought—was *sure*!—she saw his lips twitch.

He chuckled softly. 'Admiring the way you sounded so much like me.'

'Well, I certainly can't stay and have dinner with you *now*.'

'Why not?' All amusement fled and his expression darkened.

'Hello?' She gave him a pitying look. 'Ripped blouse and no bra?'

'I noticed that.' Lucien nodded, silver eyes once again gleaming with laughter even if his expression remained hard and unyielding. 'We've met three times now, and on none of those occasions have you been wearing a bra,' he added curiously.

Thia's cheeks blushed a fiery red as she thought of the revealing gown she had been wearing last night—no way could she have been wearing a bra beneath *that*. And the intimacy of Lucien's caresses in his office earlier today had shown him that she hadn't been wearing a bra under her pink crop top, either. As for ripping her blouse just now and baring her breasts...!

'I—the uniform I have to wear when I'm working at the restaurant is of some heavy material that makes me really hot, so I usually go without one and it's just become a habit,' she explained defensively.

'Don't get me wrong. I'm not complaining.'

'Why am I not surprised?' If she were honest, Thia's
initial shock and anger were already fading and she now
felt a little like laughing herself—slightly hysterically—at
this farcical situation. Hearing her blouse rip, seeing the
initial shock on Lucien's face, had been like something
out of a sitcom. Except Thia didn't intend letting him off
the hook quite that easily...

Oh, she had no doubt that ripping her blouse had been
an accident, and that she was as much to blame for it as
Lucien was. But if he hadn't been behaving quite so badly
by insisting on having his own way—again!—he would
never have been in a position to rip her blouse in the first
place. Or to bare her breasts. And that really had been embarrassing rather than funny.

Besides, she really did find Lucien far too disturbing
when he was only wearing a pair of faded denims and
showing lots of bare, muscled flesh. Her ripped blouse
was the perfect excuse for her to cry off having dinner
with him this evening.

'We haven't talked about the Jonathan Miller situation yet.'

Lucien had just—deliberately?—said the one thing
guaranteed to ensure Thia stayed exactly where she was!

Lucien had found himself scowling at the idea of Thia
working in a public restaurant night after night, wearing
no bra, with those delicious breasts jiggling beneath her
uniform for all her male customers to see and ogle.

Just as it now displeased him that Cyn was so obviously
rethinking her decision about not having dinner with him
only because he had mentioned the Jonathan Miller situation.

The other man had physically hurt her, was responsible for her having had nowhere to sleep last night other

than that disreputable hotel, and yet Miller hadn't given a damn what had happened to her when he'd thrown her belongings haphazardly into a suitcase this morning and handed them over to Lucien.

Worst of all, Lucien now knew, from his conversation with Miller, that the other man had been using Cyn for his own purposes. He had believed—wrongly, as it happened—that her presence in his apartment in New York would give the impression that his affair with Simone Carew, was over. Something Cyn was still totally unaware of...

'Well?' he rasped harshly.

She gave a pained frown. 'Perhaps you have a T-shirt I could wear? And maybe you could find one for yourself while you're at it?' she added hopefully.

How did this woman manage to deflate his temper, to make him want to smile, when just seconds ago he had been in a less than agreeable mood at how distracted he had been all afternoon? Because of this woman...

But smile he did as he crossed his arms in front of his chest. 'It really bothers you, doesn't it?'

'All that naked manly chest stuff? Yes, it does.' She nodded. 'And it isn't polite, either.'

'That was a rebuke worthy of my mother!' Lucien was no longer just smiling. He was chuckling softly.

'And?'

'And far be it from me to disobey any woman who can scold like my mother!'

'You're so funny.' She eyed him irritably.

He gave an unconcerned shrug. 'I'll get you one of my T-shirts.' No doubt Cyn would look sexy as hell in one of his over-large tops!

Her eyes narrowed suspiciously. 'You're being very obliging all of a sudden.'

Lucien quirked a dark brow. 'As opposed to…?'

'As opposed to your usual bossy and domineering self—' She broke off to eye Lucien warily as he dropped his arms back to his sides before stepping closer to her.

'You know, Cyn,' he murmured softly, 'it really isn't a good idea to insult your dinner host.'

'Would that be the same dinner host who almost ripped my blouse off me a few minutes ago?'

The very same dinner host who would enjoy nothing more than ripping the rest of that blouse from her body! The realisation made Lucien scowl again.

This woman—too young for him in years and experience, and far too outspoken for her own good—made him forget all his own rules about the women in his life—namely, only older, experienced women, who knew exactly what they were getting—or rather what they were not going to get from him, such as marriage and for ever—when they entered into a relationship with him.

He'd had little time even for the *idea* of marriage after his parents had separated and then divorced so acrimoniously, and making his own fortune before he was even twenty-one had quickly opened his eyes to the fact that most women saw only dollar signs when they looked at him, not the man behind those billions of dollars.

So far in their acquaintance Cyn Hammond had resisted all his offers of help, financial or otherwise, and that pride and independence just made him like her more.

'Good point.' He straightened abruptly. 'I'll be back in a few minutes.'

Thia admired Lucien's loose-limbed walk as he left the room, only able to breathe again once she knew she was alone. She knew from that determined glitter in Lucien's eyes just now that she had only barely—literally!—man-aged to avert a possibly physically explosive situation. Just as she knew she wasn't sure if she had the strength of will to resist another one...

The truth was her breasts tingled and she grew damp between her thighs every time she so much as dared a glance at all that fascinating naked and bronzed flesh!

Lucien was without doubt the most nerve-sizzling and gorgeous man Thia had ever seen. His whole body was muscled and toned but not too much so, in that muscle-bound and unattractive way some men were. And as for the strength and beauty of that perfectly chiselled face...!

All that wealth and power, and the man also had a face and body that would make poets of both sexes wax lyrical. Hell, *she* was writing a sonnet in her head about him!

And now she was completely alone with him, in his fif-tieth floor apartment, with her tattered and ripped blouse pulled tightly across her bare breasts...

She should have kept to her earlier decision to leave. Should have made her escape as quickly and as—

'Here you go—what is it?' Lucien questioned sharply, having come back into the room and seen how pale Cyn's face had become in his absence. Her eyes were dark and troubled smudges between those sooty lashes. 'Cyn?' he prompted again concernedly as she only continued to look at him nervously, with eyes so dark they appeared navy blue.

Her creamy throat moved as she swallowed before speaking. 'I think it would be better if I left now, after all...'

Lucien frowned. 'What have you eaten today?'

She looked puzzled by the change of subject. 'No breakfast, but I bought a hot-dog from a street vendor on the way to the Empire State Building for lunch.'

'Then you need to eat. Put this T-shirt on and then we'll go into the kitchen and see what Dex has provided us with to cook for dinner.' He held out the white T-shirt he had brought back for her to wear, having pulled on a black short-sleeved polo shirt over his own naked chest. A naked chest that had seemed to bother her as much as she bothered him...

Her eyes widened. 'Does Dex do your food shopping for you, too?'

'When necessary, yes.'

'What else does he do for you...?'

'Many, many things,' Lucien drawled derisively.

'You probably wouldn't know how to go about buying your own groceries anyway,' she dismissed ruefully.

'Probably not,' he acknowledged easily. 'Does it bother you that we're eating here?'

Cyn shrugged. 'I just assumed you would be ordering hotel room service this evening.'

'Most of the time I do.' He nodded.

'But you decided tonight would be an exception?' she said knowingly.

'I just thought you would prefer to eat here. Don't tell me.' He grimaced. 'You don't know how to cook?'

'Of course I know how to—' She broke off, eyes narrowing suspiciously. 'You're challenging me to get your own way again, aren't you?'

He quirked a brow. 'Is it working?'

Some of the tension eased from her expression. 'Yes.'

He nodded. 'Then that's exactly what I'm doing.'

Cyn eyed him frustratedly. 'Why are you so determined to keep me here?'

Lucien had absolutely no idea! Especially when he had initially made the suggestion of dinner in his apartment just to see what Cyn's reaction would be. Boy, had *that* backfired on him! 'Why are you so determined to leave?' he came back challengingly.

'Yep, the face of an angel and the wiles of the devil...'

Lucien heard her mutter the words irritably. 'Sorry?' he said. He knew exactly what Cyn had said—he just wanted to see if he could get her to say it again. Especially the part where she said he had the face of an angel...

'Nothing.' Cyn refused to humour him and gave a rueful shake of her head. 'Okay, give me the T-shirt.' She took it out of his outstretched hand before holding it up defensively in front of her breasts. 'Why don't you just disappear off into the kitchen while I slip off my blouse and put this on?' she prompted as he made no effort to leave.

'And if I'd rather stay here and watch you slip off your blouse...'

He enjoyed the flush that instantly coloured her cheeks. Enjoyed teasing Cyn, full-stop. So much so that, despite her being so disruptive and stubborn, teasing her was fast becoming one of Lucien's favourite pastimes. Exclusively so.

'Life is just full of little disappointments!' she came back, with insincere sweetness.

'Oh, it wouldn't be a *little* disappointment, Cyn,' he assured her huskily. And it wouldn't be; Lucien could imagine nothing he would enjoy more than to see Cyn strip out of her blouse, allowing him to look his fill of those pert little breasts and plump, rose-coloured nipples.

'Go,' she instructed firmly.

'And you accuse *me* of being bossy...'

'You've made a fine art of it. I'm just doing it out of self-defence.'

Lucien gave a wicked 'wiles of the devil' grin. 'Do you need defending from me?'

She eyed him irritably. 'Now you're deliberately twisting my words.'

He shrugged. 'Maybe that's because you're trying to spoil my fun.'

She gasped. 'Because I won't let you stand there and gawp at me while I change my blouse?'

'I never *gawp,* Cyn,' he drawled derisively. 'If I stayed I would just stand here quietly and appreciate.'

Her face warmed. 'You aren't staying.'

Lucien gave another appreciative grin; she really was cute when she got her dander up.

Cute? He had never found a woman *cute* in his life!

Until now…

Because Cyn, all hot and bothered and clutching his T-shirt tightly to her as if it were her only defence, was most definitely cute.

'Okay, I'll leave you to change,' he murmured dryly. 'I'll take the bottle of wine and glasses through with me.'

'Fine.' She nodded distractedly.

Anything to get him out of the room while she changed her top, Lucien acknowledged ruefully as he collected up the bottle of wine and glasses before leaving. As if such a flimsy barrier—*any* barrier!—could have stopped him if he had decided he wanted her naked!

'Did you have Dex follow me today…?' Thia prompted huskily when she entered the kitchen.

Lucien turned from taking food out of the huge chrome refrigerator that took up half the space of one wall in what was a beautiful kitchen—white marble floors again, extensive kitchen units a pale grey, a black wooden work table in the middle of the vast room, silver cooking utensils hanging from a rack next to a grey and white cooker. No doubt there was a dishwasher built into one of those cabinets, too.

He hadn't answered her question yet…

'Lucien?' she said softly as she lifted her replenished glass from the table and took a sip of red wine.

'I got so distracted by how sexy you look in my T-shirt that I've forgotten what the question was,' he came back dryly.

No, he hadn't. This man didn't forget anything. *Ever.* And his prevarication was answer enough. He *had* instructed Dex to follow her this afternoon. And Thia wasn't sure how she felt about that. Annoyed that he had dared to have her followed at all, but also concerned as to why he continued to feel it necessary…

And sexy was the last thing she looked in Lucien's white T-shirt. The shoulder seams hung halfway down her arms, meaning that the short sleeves finished below her elbows, and it was so wide across the chest it hung on her like a sack, so long it reached almost to her knees. Well…it didn't hang *completely* like a sack, Thia realised as she glanced down. Colour once again warmed her cheeks as she saw the way the T-shirt skimmed across the tips of her breasts. Across the hard, aroused thrust of her nipples!

Even so, *ridiculous* was the word Thia would have used to describe her current appearance, not sexy.

'*Did* you have Dex follow me today?' she repeated determinedly.

'I did, yes.'

'Can I ask why?' she prompted warily.

'You can if you can make salad and ask at the same time.' Lucien seemed totally relaxed as he placed the makings of a salad down on the kitchen table before returning to the fridge for steaks.

Thia rolled her eyes. 'I'm a woman, Lucien. Multitasking is what we do best.' She took the salad vegetables out of the bags and put them in the sink to wash them.

'That sounds…interesting.' He turned to arch mocked brows.

She was utterly charmed by this man when he became temptingly playful. And she shouldn't allow herself to be.

It wasn't just those twelve years in age that separated them, it was what Lucien had done in those twelve years that set them so far apart—as evidenced by all those photographs of him online, taken with the multitude of women he had briefly shared his life with. Or, more accurately, his bed.

And at the grand age of twenty-three Thia was still a virgin. Not deliberately. Not even consciously as in 'saving herself' for the man she loved and wanted to marry.

She had just been too busy keeping her life together since her parents died to do more than accept the occasional date, and very rarely a second from the same man. Jonathan had been the exception, but even he had become just a friend rather than a boyfriend. Thia had never been even slightly tempted to deepen their relationship into something more.

And yet in the twenty-four hours she had known Lucien Steele she seemed to have thought of nothing else but how it would feel to go to bed with him. To make love with him.

Weird.

Dangerous!

Because Lucien might desire her, but he didn't do fall-ing in love and long-term relationships. And why should he when he could have any woman—as many women as he wanted? Except…

'What are you thinking about so deeply that it's mak-ing you frown…?' he asked huskily.

Thia snapped herself out of imagining how it would feel to have Lucien Steele fall in love with her. A ridiculous thought when she so obviously wasn't his type.

And yet here she was, in this apartment, with a relaxed and charming Lucien, and the two of them intended to cook dinner together just like any other couple spending the evening at home together.

She took another sip of wine before answering him. 'Nothing of any importance,' she dismissed brightly as she put the wine glass down to drain the vegetables. 'Do you have any dressing to go with the salad or shall I make some?'

'Can you do that?'

Thia gave him a scathing glance as she crossed the room to open the vast refrigerator and look inside for in-gredients for a dressing. 'I'm a waitress, remember?'

'You're a student, working as a waitress in your spare time,' he corrected lightly.

She straightened slowly. 'No, I'm actually a waitress who's working for a degree in my spare time,' she in-sisted firmly. 'And you still haven't answered my origi-nal question.'

'Which was…?'

'Why did you have Dex follow me today?' she repeated determinedly, knowing that Lucien was once again trying to avoid answering one of her questions.

He shrugged. 'Dex suggested it was necessary. I agreed with him.'

'What does that mean?'

'It means that he was obviously as concerned about your walking about New York on your own as I was. You might have been robbed or attacked. Speaking of which…' Lucien strolled across the kitchen, checking her wrist first, which was only slightly reddened from where Jonathan's fingers had twisted it, before gently peeling back the sleeve of the white T-shirt. He drew in a hissing breath as he saw the livid black and blue bruises on the top of her arm.

'They look worse than they feel.' Thia pulled out of his grasp before turning to take down a chopping board and starting to dice vegetables for the salad. 'Isn't it time you started cooking the steaks…?' she prompted dryly.

'Deflection is only a delaying tactic, Cyn. Sooner or later we're going to talk about those bruises,' he assured her grimly.

'Then let's make it later,' she dismissed. 'Steaks, Lucien?' she repeated pointedly when she turned to find him still watching her from between narrowed lids.

He gave a deep sigh. 'Okay, Cyn, we'll do this your way for now,' he conceded. 'We'll eat first and then we'll talk.'

'It really is true what they say—men don't multi-task!' She smiled teasingly.

'Maybe we just prefer to do one thing at a time and ensure that we do it really, really well?' Lucien murmured huskily, suggestively, and made a determined effort to damp down the renewed anger he felt at seeing those bruises on Cyn's delicately lovely skin.

Colour washed over her cheeks. 'You're obviously wasting your talents as an entrepreneur, Lucien; you should have been a comedian.'

But what Lucien was actually doing was mirroring her own deflection...

Because he was once again so angry after seeing Cyn's bruises—bruises inflicted by Miller—that he didn't want to have to answer her question as to why he'd had Dex follow her on her outing this afternoon just yet.

Oh, he accepted that he would have to answer it some time—just not yet. Talking about the reason Dex had followed her to the Empire State Building earlier, and how his concern was directly linked to Jonathan Miller, was not conducive to the two of them being able to enjoy cooking and eating a meal together. And, despite Lucien's earlier irritation, he was totally enjoying Cyn's company.

'How do you like your steak?' he prompted as he moved to turn up the heat beneath the griddle, hoping he remembered how to cook steaks. Cyn's assumption earlier had been a correct one: it had been years since Lucien had cooked for himself or anyone else.

'Medium rare, please,' she answered distractedly as she put the salad into a wooden bowl. 'Are we eating in here or in the dining room?'

'Which would you prefer?'

Her brows rose. 'You're actually asking for my opinion about something now?'

Lucien turned to lean back against one of the kitchen cabinets. 'Smart-mouthed young ladies are likely to get their bottoms spanked!'

Her eyes widened. 'Dinner hosts who threaten their female guests are likely to get cayenne pepper sprinkled on their half of the salad dressing. What is it?' she questioned curiously as Lucien began to chuckle. 'You aren't used to being teased like this, are you?' she realised slowly.

'No, I'm not,' he conceded ruefully, unable to remember the last time anyone had dared to tease him, let alone argue with him in the way that Cyn so often did. 'My mother does it occasionally, just to keep it real, but only mom/son stuff.' He shrugged.

Cyn eyed him wistfully. 'Have you remained close to both your parents?'

He nodded. 'I don't see either of them as often as I could or should—but, yeah, I've stayed close to both of them.'

'That's nice.'

Lucien looked at her searchingly. 'Don't you have any family of your own?'

'None close, no.' She grimaced. 'Don't feel sorry for me, Lucien,' she added lightly as he still frowned. 'I had great parents. I lost them a little earlier than I would have wished or wanted, but I still count myself lucky to have had them to love and be loved by for seventeen years.'

The more Lucien came to know about Cynthia Hammond, the more he came to appreciate that she really was unlike any other woman he had ever known. So obviously beautiful—inside as well as out. And that outward beauty she could so easily have used to her advantage these past six years, if she had wanted to, by snaring herself a rich husband to support her. Instead she had chosen independence.

No feeling sorry for herself at the premature death of her parents. She was just grateful to have had them for as long as she had. And instead of bitching about the necessity to fend for herself after their deaths she had picked herself up and started working her way through university. And instead of bemoaning the fact that Jonathan Miller, a man she had believed to be her friend, had let her down royally since she'd come to New York she had done all she could to remain loyal to him.

It was fast becoming an irresistible combination to Lucien when coupled with the fact that she was so bright and bubbly she made him laugh, was mouthwateringly beautiful, and obviously intelligent.

She also, Lucien discovered a short time later—once the two of them were seated opposite each other at the small candlelit table in the window of the dining room, where they could look out over the city—ate with such passionate relish that he found himself enjoying watching her, devouring her with his eyes rather than eating his own food.

The expression of pleasure on her face as she took her first forkful of dessert—a New York cheesecake from a famous deli in the city—was almost orgasmic. Her eyes were closed, cheeks flushed, pouting lips slightly moist as she licked her tongue across them.

Lucien groaned inwardly as his erection, having remained painfully hard and throbbing inside his denims during the whole of dinner, rose even higher, seeming to take on a life of its own. To such a degree that he had to shift on his seat in order to make himself more comfortable!

Not that he was complaining. No, not at all. His thoughts had turned to the possibility of taking Cyn to his bed, of making love to her until he saw that same look on her face over and over again as he pleasured her to orgasm after orgasm.

'That was…indescribably good.' Thia sighed her pleasure as she placed her fork down on her empty dessert plate. 'Aren't you going to eat yours…?' She hadn't realised until now that Lucien was watching her rather than eating his own cheesecake.

Dinner with Lucien Steele had been far more enjoyable than she had thought it would be. The food had been good, and the conversation even more so as they'd discussed their eclectic tastes in books, films, television and art. Surprisingly, their opinions on a lot of those subjects had been the same, and the times when they hadn't been they had argued teasingly rather than forcefully. Thia liked this more relaxed Lucien. Too much so!

Lucien pushed his untouched dessert plate across the table towards her. 'You have it.'

'I couldn't eat another bite,' Thia refused, before chuckling huskily. 'I bet you're doubly glad now not to be seen out in public with me. I've realised since I've been here that it isn't really the done thing in New York for a woman to actually *enjoy* eating. We're supposed to just pick at the food on our plate before pushing it away uninterestedly. I've always enjoyed my food too much to be able to do that.' She gave a rueful shake of her head. 'Besides, it's rude not to eat when someone has taken you out for a meal or cooked for you. And I've enjoyed this much more than going out, anyway. Cooking dinner is probably the first normal thing I've done since coming to New York! Do you think…?' Her voice trailed off as she realised that Lucien had gone very quiet.

An unusual occurrence for him, when he seemed to have something to say on so many other subjects!

'Lucien…?' Thia eyed him warily as she saw the way his eyes glittered across at her with that intense silver light. His mouth had thinned, his jaw tensed—all signs, she recognised, of his displeasure.

What had she said to annoy him? Perhaps he hadn't

liked her comment on the expectations of New York society? After all, he was a member of that society.

Whatever she had said, Lucien obviously wasn't happy about it...

CHAPTER SEVEN

THERE WAS A cold weight of anger in Lucien's chest, making it difficult for him to breathe, let alone speak. Cyn actually thought—she believed that he—

Lucien stood up abruptly, noisily, from the table, thrusting his hands into his pockets as he turned to look sightlessly out of the window, breathing deeply through his nose in an effort to control that anger. If he said anything now he was only going to make the situation worse than it already was.

'Lucien?'

The uncertainty, hesitation in Cyn's voice succeeded in annoying him all over again. Just minutes ago they had been talking so comfortably together—occasionally arguing light-heartedly about a book, a film or a painting they had both read or seen, but for the most part finding they shared a lot of the same likes and dislikes.

That easy conversation, coupled with Cyn's obvious enjoyment of the food they had prepared, had resulted in Lucien feeling relaxed in her company in a way he never had with any other woman. Not completely relaxed. He was too aware of everything about her for that: her silky midnight hair, those beautiful glowing cobalt blue eyes, her flushed cheeks, the moist pout of her lips, the way his borrowed T-shirt hugged the delicious uptilting curve of her breasts whenever she moved her arms to emphasise a point in conversation… But Cyn's complete lack of awareness of Lucien's appreciation of those things had been another part of his enjoyment of the evening. There had been none of the overt flirting that he experienced with so many other women, or the flaunting of her sexuality in an effort to impress him. Cyn had just been her usual outspoken self. An outspoken self that he found totally enticing…

And now this!

He drew a deep breath into his starved lungs before turning back to face her, his own face slightly in shadow as he stood out of the full glow of the flickering candlelight. 'You believe I made a conscious decision not to take you out to a restaurant for dinner this evening because I didn't want to be seen publicly in your company?'

Ah. That was the comment that had annoyed him…

Thia gave a dismissive shrug. 'It's no big deal, Lucien. Believe me, I've seen photos of the women you usually escort, and I don't even come close—'

'Seen how?' he prompted suspiciously.

She gave a self-conscious grimace. 'I—er—checked you out online earlier this evening,' she admitted reluctantly, wishing Lucien wasn't standing in the shadows so that she could see the expression on his face.

'Why did you do that?'

'Because I wanted to know more about the man I had agreed to have dinner with, alone in his apartment,' she came back defensively. 'I was using that sense of self-preservation you seem to think I have so little of.'

He gave a terse inclination of his head. 'And after reading about me online, seeing photographs of the women I usually escort, you came to the conclusion I was deliberately keeping you hidden away in my apartment this evening because I didn't want to be seen out in public with you?'

'Oh, no. I decided that after you made the invitation earlier today,' Thia dismissed easily.

His brows rose. 'Can I ask why?'

She sighed heavily. 'When was the last time you cooked dinner for a woman in your apartment?'

'What does that—?'

'Just answer the question, please, Lucien,' she cajoled teasingly.

He shrugged. 'I think tonight is the first time I've cooked dinner in my apartment at all—let alone for or with a woman.'

'Exactly.' Thia had noticed earlier that none of the state-of-the-art equipment in the kitchen looked as if it had ever been used.

His mouth thinned. 'If you must know, I made the invitation initially because I suspected your having dinner alone with me here would throw you into something of a panic, and I wanted to see what you would do.'

'And I called your bluff and accepted.' She gave a rueful shake of her head.

'Yes, you did.' He nodded slowly.

'Probably best not to challenge me again, hmm?'

'I don't regret a single moment of this evening.'

Thia's cheeks bloomed with heated colour as she recalled the earlier part of the evening, when Lucien had ripped her blouse. 'You were also aware, because I told you so last night, that New York society has absolutely no interest in furthering its acquaintance with a waitress from

London. Just think how shocked they would have been to see Lucien Steele in a restaurant with *me!*'

He breathed his impatience. 'I don't give a damn what anyone else thinks.'

'I'm really not in the least offended by any of this, Lucien.' Thia smiled. 'I had a good time this evening. As for New York society…I don't enjoy their company either, so why should it bother me what any of them think of me?'

'Do you have so little interest in what *I* might think of you?' he prompted softly.

That was a difficult question to answer. Thia was so attracted to Lucien that of course it mattered to her whether or not he liked her—just as it mattered what he thought of her. But by the same token it also didn't. Because they wouldn't ever see each other again after tonight. Even the money for the suite, which Thia was so determined to pay back to him, no matter how long it took her to do so, could be sent to his office at Steele Tower when the time came. They had no reason to see each other again once she left here this evening. Which, although disappointing, was just a fact of life. Their totally different lives…

'I like to think I'm a realist, Lucien,' she answered lightly. 'Zillionaire Lucien Steele—' she pointed to him '—and Cynthia Hammond, waitress/student, living from payday to payday.' She pointed to her own chest. 'Not exactly a basis for friendship.'

'I have no interest in being your *friend!*' he rasped with harsh dismissal.

She flinched at the starkness of his statement. 'I believe I just said that—'

'I have no interest in being your friend because I want to be your lover. Touch me.' Lucien stepped forward to grasp her hand impatiently in his before lifting it to the bulge at the front of his denims.

Evidence of an arousal that Thia had been completely unaware of until that moment. She couldn't possibly remain unaware of it now—not when she could feel the long, hard length of Lucien's swollen shaft, the heat of it burning her fingertips as she stroked them tentatively against him. Her eyes widened as she felt the jolt, the throb, of that arousal in response to her slightest caress.

She moistened her lips with the tip of her tongue and looked up at Lucien. 'Does one preclude the other…?'

His mouth twisted derisively. 'In my experience, yes.'

In Thia's limited experience too…

She'd only dated maybe half a dozen times these past six years, and had always ended up being friends with those men rather than lovers. Including Jonathan. Although she suspected that their friendship had ceased after his behaviour yesterday, and yet again this morning, when he had packed her belongings into her suitcase and handed it over to Lucien seemingly without a second thought as to where or how she was.

'Stop thinking about Miller,' Lucien rasped.

She blinked. 'How did you know—?'

'I think I'm intelligent enough to know when the woman I'm with is thinking about another man,' he bit out harshly, having known from the way Cyn's gaze had become slightly unfocused that her attention was no longer completely here with him. Which, considering her hand was currently pressed against his pulsing erection, was less than flattering.

She gave a rueful smile. 'I sincerely doubt it's happened to you often enough for that to be true.'

'It's never happened to me before, as far as I'm aware,' he grated.

He lifted her hand away impatiently before pulling her to her feet, so that she now stood just inches in front of him. His other hand moved beneath her chin to raise her face, so that she had no choice but to look up at him. 'And, yes, I was challenging you earlier. I wanted to unnerve you a little by inviting you to my apartment. But I did *not* have dinner with you here as a way of hiding you away. I'm insulted that you should ever have thought that I did.' He was more than insulted—he actually felt hurt that Cyn could believe him capable of behaving in that way where she was concerned...

Thia could see that he was. His eyes glittered danger-ously, there was angry colour along those high cheekbones, his lips had thinned and his jaw thrust forward forcefully.

'I apologise if I was mistaken.'

'You were,' he bit out. 'You still are.'

She nodded; Lucien was too upset not to be telling her the truth.

'Have I succeeded in ruining the evening?' She looked up at him through long dark lashes.

Lucien eyed her impatiently. 'I have absolutely no idea.'

She drew in a shaky breath. 'How about we clear away in here while you decide?'

His eyes narrowed. 'Are you humouring me, Thia?'

The fact that Lucien had called her Thia for the first time was indicative of how upset he was. 'Is it working?' she deliberately used the same phrase he had to her ear-lier, when she had challenged him about always wanting his own way.

Some of the tension left his shoulders. 'Maybe a little,' he conceded dryly. 'And we can just blow out the candles in here and leave all this for housekeeping to clear away in the morning.' He indicated the dinner table beside them.

Thia's stomach did a somersault. 'Oh...'

He gave a rueful shake of his head. 'I have no idea how you do that...'

'Do what?' She looked up at him curiously.

'Make me want to laugh when just seconds ago I was so angry with you I wanted to kiss you senseless!' He gave a self-disgusted shake of his head as the last of his earlier tension eased from his expression.

'Senseless, hmm?' Thia eyed him teasingly. 'According to you, that wouldn't be too difficult!'

'See?' Lucien chuckled wryly, shaking his head.

The sudden hunger in Lucien's gaze told Thia this was the ideal time for her to suggest she return to her own suite in the hotel, to thank Lucien for dinner, and his company and conversation, and then leave, never to see or hear from him again.

It was the latter part of that plan that stopped her from doing any of those things... 'Does one preclude the other?' she repeated provocatively, daringly.

'You *want* me to kiss you senseless...?' he prompted gruffly.

She drew in a sharp breath, knowing this was a moment of truth. 'Even more than I enjoy watching you laugh,' she acknowledged shyly.

Lucien's piercing gaze narrowed on her searchingly. 'Be very sure about this, Thia,' he finally warned her. 'I want you so badly that once I have you in my bed I'm unlikely to let you out of it again until I've made love to you at least half a dozen times.'

Thia's heart leapt as he jumped from kissing her senseless to taking her to his bed. Her heart pounded loudly in her chest at the thought of all that currently leashed but promised passion. Of having this man—having *Lucien Steele!*—want to make love to her with such an intensity of feeling. It was an intensity of passion she didn't know, in her inexperience, that she could even begin to match...

But she would at least like to the opportunity to try!

'Can you do that? I thought that men needed to...to rest for a while...recuperate before...well, you know...'

He arched dark brows. 'Let's give it a try, shall we? Besides, I don't recall giving any time limit for making love to you those half a dozen times.'

No, he hadn't, had he? Thia acknowledged even as her cheeks burned. In embarrassment or excitement? She really wasn't sure! 'I only have one more full day left before I leave New York, and don't you have to go to work tomorrow?'

'Not if I have you in my bed, no,' Lucien assured her softly.

Thia's heart was now beating a wild tattoo in her chest and she breathed shallowly, feeling as if she were standing on the edge of a precipice: behind her was the safety of returning to her own hotel suite, in front of her the unknown of sharing Lucien's bed for the night.

She drew in a shaky breath. 'Well, then...'

Lucien's control was now so tightly stretched that he felt as if the slightest provocation from Cyn would make it snap. That *he* would snap, and simply rip that T-shirt off her in the same way he had her blouse earlier.

It was an uncomfortable feeling for a man who never lost control. Of any situation and especially of himself. But this woman—barely tall enough to reach his shoulders, so slender he felt as if he might crush her if he held her too tightly—had thrown him off balance from the moment he first saw her.

Just twenty-four admittedly eventful hours ago…!

'Well, then…what…?' he prompted slowly.

The slenderness of Cyn's throat moved as she swallowed before answering him. 'Let's go to bed.'

'No more arguments or questions? Just "Let's go to bed"?' He raised dark brows.

She moistened her lips with the tip of her tongue before replying huskily. 'I—if that's okay with you, yes.'

If it was okay with him?

If Cyn only knew how much he wanted to rip her clothes off right now, before laying her down on the carpet and just taking her, right here and right now, plunging into the warmth of her again and again, then she would be probably be shocked out of her mind. *He* was out of his mind—for this woman.

Which was the reason Lucien was going to do none of those things. He was balanced on the edge of his self-control right now, and needed to slow things down. For Cyn's sake rather than his own. Because he didn't want to frighten her with the intensity of the desire she aroused in him.

'It's more than okay with me, Cyn,' he assured her gruffly, blowing out the candles on the table and throwing the room into darkness before putting his arm about the slenderness of her waist as he guided her out of the dining room and down the hallway towards his bedroom.

Thia's nervousness deepened with each step she took down the hallway towards sharing Lucien's bed. To sharing Lucien Steele's bed!

Those other women—the ones she had seen online,

photographed with Lucien—had all looked sophisticated and confident, and they no doubt had the physical experience, the confidence in their sexuality, to go with those looks. Whereas she—

For goodness' sake, she was twenty-three years old and she was going to lose her virginity some time—so why not with Lucien, a man she found as physically exciting as she did knee-meltingly attractive. A man who made her feel safe and protected as well as desired.

Was that *all* she felt for Lucien?

Or was she already a little—more than a little!—in love with him?

And wouldn't that be the biggest mistake of her life—in love with a man whose relationships never seemed to last longer than a month?

'Cyn?'

She blinked as she realised that while she had been so lost in thought they had already entered what must be the master bedroom—Lucien's bedroom. A huge four-poster bed dominated the shadowed room, and those shadows made it impossible for her to tell whether the black, white and chrome décor Lucien seemed to prefer had spilt over into his bedroom. The carpet beneath her feet was certainly dark, as were the curtains and the satin cover and cushions piled on the bed, but the actual colours eluded her in the darkness...

'Say now if you're feeling...less than sure about this,' Lucien prompted gruffly, his hands resting lightly on her waist as he turned her so that she was looking up at him.

The one thing Thia was totally sure about was that she wanted Lucien. Her body ached with that longing; her breasts were swollen and tingling, nipples hard and aroused, and there was a heated dampness between her thighs. At the same time she *so* didn't want to be a disappointment to him!

It would have been better if he had just made love to her right there in the dining room. If he hadn't given her time to think, to become so nervous.

But this was Lucien Steele, a man of sophistication and control. He wasn't the type of man to be so desperate for a woman he would rip her clothes off—well, apart from Thia's blouse earlier. But that had been an accident rather than passion! Or the type of man to make wild and desperate love to her.

Thia chewed worriedly on her bottom lip as she looked up into his hard and shadowed face, at those pale eyes glittering down at her intently in the darkness. 'I am a little nervous,' she admitted softly. 'I'm not as experienced as you are, and there have been all those other women for you—' She broke off as he placed silencing fingertips against her lips.

'I'm clean medically, if that's what's bothering you.'

'It isn't,' she assured him hastily, her cheeks blushing a fiery-red. 'And I—I'm—er—clean too.' How could she be anything else when she had never been to bed with anyone?

He nodded abruptly. 'And that's the last time I want to talk about other people for either of us.'

'But—'

'Cyn, neither of us is experienced when it comes to each other.' He moved his hand to gently cup her cheek. 'Half the fun will be in learning which caress or touch pleases the other,' he added huskily.

Fun? Going to bed with a man, making love with him, was *fun*? Thia had never thought of it in quite that light before, but she had no reason to doubt what Lucien said. He had always been totally, bluntly honest when he spoke to her.

'You're right.' She shook off her feelings of nervousness and straightened determinedly. 'Is it okay if I just use the bathroom?'

'Of course.' Lucien released her before stepping back. 'Don't be long,' he added huskily as he opened the door to the adjoining bathroom and switched on the light for her.

Thia leant back weakly against the door the moment it closed behind her and she was alone in the bathroom, her legs shaking so badly she could no longer stand without that support at her back.

Lucien stared at that closed bathroom door for several seconds after Cyn had closed it so firmly behind her, a frown darkening his brow as he considered her behaviour just now. She was more than just nervous. She seemed almost afraid. Just of him? Or of any man?

Why? Had something happened to her in the past? Maybe even with Miller? Something to make her nervous about going to bed with another man? It seemed highly possible, when she'd admitted she *had* been thinking of the other man when he'd called her on it a few minutes ago. It made Lucien wish now that he had given in to the impulse he'd had this morning to punch the other man in the face as Miller threw Cyn's belongings into her suitcase without so much as a thought or a question as to what was going to happen to her.

Whatever the reason for Cyn's nervousness, Lucien didn't intend adding to it. He was glad now that he had shown such restraint a few minutes ago. He wanted to make slow and leisurely love to her, no matter the cost to his own self-control. Wanted to touch and pleasure Cyn until she could think of nothing else, no one else, but him and their lovemaking—

Lovemaking? Was he actually falling in love with Cyn?

It was an emotion he had always avoided in the past, and his choice of women—experienced and self-absorbed—was probably a reflection of that decision. Until now. Cyn was like no other woman he had ever known. And, yes, she was slipping—already *had* slipped?—beneath his defences.

None of which he wanted to explore too deeply right now.

Lucien crossed the bedroom to turn on the bedside lamp before turning back the bedcovers and quickly removing his clothes. His shaft bobbed achingly now that it was free of the confines of his denims.

He lingered beside the bed, looking down at the black silk bedsheets as he imagined how right Cyn would look lying there, with that beautiful, pale, luminescent body spread out before him like a feast he wanted to gorge himself on. Just the thought of it was enough to cause his aching erection to throb eagerly, releasing pre-cum onto the bulbous tip before it spilt over and dripped slowly down his length.

Sweet heaven!

Lucien grasped his length before smoothing that liquid over it with the soft pad of his thumb, knowing he had never been this aroused before, this needy of any woman. Not in the way he now needed—desired—Cyn…

Thia studied herself critically in the mirror over the bathroom sink once she had taken her clothes off. Her face was pale, eyes fever-bright, her hair a silky black curtain across her bared shoulders. Her skin was smooth and unblemished, breasts firm and uptilting, tipped by engorged rosy-red nipples. Her waist was slender, hips flaring gently around the dark thatch of curls between her thighs, her legs long and slender.

She was as ready as she was ever going to be to walk out of here and go to bed with Lucien!

That courage didn't include walking out stark naked, though, and quickly she pulled on the black silk robe she had found hanging behind the bathroom door, tying the belt of what was obviously Lucien's own bathrobe tightly about the slenderness of her waist before taking a deep breath and opening the bathroom door, switching off the light…

Only to come to an abrupt halt in that doorway as she realised that Lucien had turned on a single lamp on the bedside table, allowing her to see that the bedroom was indeed decorated in those black, white and chrome colours Lucien favoured. Lucien himself was already lying in the bed, that bronzed chest bare, only a black silk sheet draped over him and concealing his lower body.

She had thought they would make love in the darkness—had imagined slipping almost anonymously beneath the bedcovers and then—

'Take off the robe, Cyn.'

She raised a startled gaze to Lucien and saw he was leaning up on his elbow, causing the muscles to bulge in his arm, as he looked across at her with those glittering silver eyes. The darkness of his overlong hair was now tousled and falling rakishly over his forehead, probably after he had removed his T-shirt.

He was utterly beautiful in the same way that a deadly predator was beautiful—with all the power in that sleek and muscled body just waiting to be unleashed.

'I want to look at you,' he encouraged gruffly.

Thia's throat had gone so dry she could barely speak. 'Doesn't that work both ways?'

'Sure.' The intensity of his gaze never left hers as he slowly kicked down the black silk sheet.

Thia's breath caught in her throat and she could only stand and stare. At the width of his shoulders. At his muscled chest covered in that misting of dark hair. She could now see that it trailed down over his navel and grew thicker at the base of his arousal.

Oh. Good. Grief.

That was never going to fit inside her!

Lucien was a tall man, several inches over six feet and his bronze-skinned body was deeply muscled, so it was no surprise that his aroused shaft was in perfect proportion to the rest of him—at least nine, possibly ten inches long, and so thick and wide Thia doubted her fingers would meet if she were to clasp them around it as she so longed, ached to do. Just as she longed to caress, to touch and become familiar with every perfect inch of him!

Even so, her wide gaze moved back unerringly to the heavy thrust of his arousal.

Maybe it was like those 'one size fits all' pairs of socks or gloves you could buy? Hadn't she read somewhere, in one of those sophisticated women's magazines often left lying around in a dentist's waiting room, that if a woman was prepared properly, with lots of foreplay, she was capable of stretching *down there,* accommodating any length or thickness—

'Cyn?'

Her startled gaze moved back up to Lucien's face and, her cheeks flamed with colour as she met the heat in his eyes. He looked across at her expectantly, his hand held out to her invitingly, obviously waiting for her to unfasten the robe and remove it completely before joining him in the bed...

CHAPTER EIGHT

LUCIEN TAMPED DOWN the urgency he felt to get out of bed
and go to Cyn and instead waited patiently, allowing Cyn
to take her time, to adjust. Allowing her to be the one to
come *to* him.

They had all night—hours and hours for him to pleasure her into coming *for* him!

Right now her face was so pale that her ivory skin appeared almost translucent. Blue veins showed at the delicacy of her temples and her cobalt-blue eyes were dark
and shadowed as she continued to look across at him,
cheeks pale, her lips slightly parted, as if she were having trouble breathing.

'I'm starting to get a complex, Cyn,' he murmured ruefully.

Her startled gaze was quickly raised to his. 'You are…?
But you're beautiful, Lucien,' she murmured huskily.

'So are you.' Lucien slowly lifted his arm to hold out his
hand to her again, holding his breath as the nervousness in
Cyn's gaze told him that she might turn tail and run if he
made any sort of hasty move in her direction. Something
he found surprisingly endearing rather than irritating.

Cyn was so different from the women he had been with
in the past. Beautiful women, certainly, but it was usu-

ally a pampered and sometimes enhanced beauty, after hours spent at beauty salons and spas or beneath a plastic surgeon's knife. And all those women, without exception, had been confident of their perfectly toned bodies, of their sexual appeal.

Cyn, on the other hand, obviously had no time or money to spend at beauty salons or spas. The sleekness of her body was just as nature had intended it, as was her breathtaking beauty. A beauty that was all the more appealing because Cyn seemed so completely unaware of it, of its effect on him and every other man she came into contact with. The women in New York society might have no interest in furthering the acquaintance of student/waitress Cynthia Hammond from England, but Lucien very much doubted the men felt the same way!

And Lucien was the lucky man who had her all to himself—for tonight, at least...

Thia was frozen in place—couldn't move, couldn't speak, could only continue to stand in the bathroom doorway as she stared across at Lucien in mute appeal, inwardly cursing herself for her gauche behaviour but unable to do anything about it.

'Please, Cyn!' he said gruffly.

It was the aching need that deepened Lucien's voice to a growl which finally broke her out of that icy cage, causing Thia to take one step forward, and then another, until she finally stood beside the bed, allowing Lucien to reach out and enfold one of her trembling hands in his much warmer one.

He lifted it slowly to his lips, his gaze still holding hers as those lips grazed the back of her knuckles, tongue rasping, tasting. 'You are so very beautiful, Cyn.'

The warmth of his breath brushed lightly against her over-sensitised skin. She swallowed. 'I believe you'll find the saying is *Beautiful as sin...*'

'Nothing could be as beautiful as you.' He gave a slow shake of his head.

At this moment in time, Thia finished ruefully inside her head. Right here and right now she had Lucien's complete attention. But tomorrow it would be different—

Oh, to hell with tomorrow!

For once in her carefully constructed life she was going to take not what was safe, or what she could afford, but what she *wanted.*

And tonight she so very much wanted to be here with Lucien.

She lowered her lashes and pulled her hand gently from his grasp, before moving to unfasten the belt of the robe, shrugging the black silk from her shoulders and hearing Lucien's breath catching in his throat as she allowed the robe to slide down her arms to fall onto the carpet at her feet. She was completely naked in front of him as she finally raised her lashes to look at him.

'You're exquisite,' Lucien groaned, taking the time to admire each and every curve and dip and hollow of her naked body before moving smoothly up onto his knees at the edge of the bed, nullifying the difference in their heights, putting his face on a level with hers as his arms moved about the slenderness of her waist.

Her hands moved up to clasp onto his shoulders as he pulled her in closer to him. Her skin felt so soft and she was so slender Lucien felt as if he could wrap his arms about her twice. His palms spread, fingers splayed across her shapely bottom, as he settled those slender curves into his much harder ones before touching his mouth lightly against hers.

Lucien moved his lips across her creamy soft cheek to the softness beneath her ear, along the column of her throat. The rasp of his tongue tasted the shady hollows at the base of her throat as one of his hands curled about the gentle thrust of her breast, the soft pad of his thumb unerringly finding, stroking the aroused nipple.

'Look at the two of us, Cyn,' he groaned throatily. 'See how beautiful we are together,' he encouraged as she looked down to where his hand cupped her breast. He looked at that contrast himself. Ivory and bronze…

Her skin looked so white against the natural bronze tone of Lucien's. Ice and fire. And fire invariably melted ice, didn't it?

Thia's inhibitions were melting, and her earlier apprehension along with it, as she twined her arms over those strong, muscled shoulders, her fingers becoming entangled in silky dark hair as she initiated a kiss between them this time—gentle at first, and then deeper, hungrier, as their passion flared out of control.

Lucien continued to kiss her even as Thia felt his arms move beneath her knees and about her shoulders. He lifted her easily up and onto the bed, lying her down almost reverently onto the black silk sheets before stretching his long length beside her, his gaze holding hers before his head lowered, lashes falling down against those hard cheekbones, and his lips parted. He drew her nipple into his mouth, gently suckling, licking that aroused nub, even as his hands caressed the ribcage beneath her breasts, the slender curve of her waist, before moving lower still.

Thia arched into his caresses as her nervousness faded completely and pleasure coursed through her—building,

building, until she moved restlessly against him, needing more, wanting more. She was groaning low in her throat as she felt Lucien's fingers against the silky curls between her thighs, seeking and finding the nubbin hidden there and moving lower still, to where the slickness of her juices had made her wet, so very wet, circling, moistening her swollen lips.

His thumb pressed delicately against the nubbin above and still she wanted more, needed more. She felt as if she were poised on the edge of a precipice, one that burned. Flames were licking up and through her body, sensitising her to every touch of Lucien's hands, to every sweep of his tongue across the swollen hardness of her nipples, as he divided his attentions between the two, first licking, then suckling. Each lick and suck seemed to increase the volcanic pleasure rising between her thighs.

'Please, Lucien!' Her fingers tightened in his hair and she pulled his head up, forced him to look at her with eyes that glittered pure silver. His lips were swollen and moist. 'Please…!' she groaned beseechingly. 'Lucien…'

He moved so swiftly, so urgently, that Thia barely had time to realise he now lay between her parted thighs.

'You are so beautiful *here,* Cyn,' he murmured. His breath was a warm caress as the soft pads of his thumbs slicked her juices over those plump folds and the sensitive knot of flesh above. 'Look at us, Cyn,' he encouraged gruffly. 'Move up onto your elbows and show me those pretty breasts.'

Thia would have done anything Lucien asked of her at that moment. Her cheeks were flushed, eyes fever-bright, as she looked down at him, at his hair midnight-black against the paleness of her skin, bronzed back long and muscled, buttocks taut.

His gaze held hers as he cupped his hands beneath her bottom and held her up and open to him. 'I'm going to eat you up, Cyn,' he promised, and his head lowered and his tongue swept, rasped against her slick folds.

Over and over again he lapped her gently, and then harder, until Thia was no longer able to hold herself up on her elbows as the pleasure grew and grew inside her. Lucien's fingers were digging almost painfully into the globes of her bottom as he thrust a tongue deep inside her slick channel, sending her over that volcanic edge as the pleasure surged and swelled, surged and swelled again and again, taking Thia into the magic of her first ever climax.

It was the first of many. Lucien continued to pleasure her, taking her up to that plateau again and again, each time ensuring that he took her over the edge and into the maelstrom of pleasure on the other side, until Thia's throat felt ragged and sore from the sobbing cries of each climax. Her body was becoming completely boneless as those releases came swifter and fiercer each time, and Lucien's arms were looped beneath her thighs now, holding her wider to allow for the ministrations of his lips and tongue, increasing her pleasure each and every time she came.

'No more, Lucien!' Thia finally gasped, her fingers digging into his muscled shoulders. Blackness had begun to creep into the edges of her vision and she knew she couldn't take any more. There was foreplay and then there was hurtling over the edge into unconsciousness. Which was exactly what was going to happen if her body was racked by one more incredible climax! 'Please, Lucien. I just can't...' She looked at him pleadingly as he raised his head to look at her, his cheeks flushed, lips swollen and moist.

'I'm sorry—I got carried away. Are you okay?' He gave a shake of his head.

'Yes…'

'You just taste so delicious…' He groaned achingly as he moved up beside her, his hands shaking slightly as he cupped the heat of her cheek. 'Like the finest, rarest brandy. I just couldn't stop drinking your sweet essence. Taste yourself, Cyn,' he encouraged huskily, and brushed his lips lightly against hers.

The taste was sweet and slightly salty, with an underlying musk. Thia's cheeks blazed with colour at the knowledge that Lucien now knew her body inside and out, more intimately than she did. That he—

She tensed to stillness as the telephone began to ring on the bedside table. Lucien scowled his displeasure and didn't even glance at the telephone. 'Ignore it,' he rasped.

'But—'

'Nothing and no one is going to intrude on the two of us being together tonight. I won't allow it,' he stated determinedly.

'But it could be important—'

'Obviously not,' he murmured in satisfaction as the telephone fell quiet after the sixth ring, allowing him to reach out and remove the receiver to prevent it from ringing and disturbing them again.

He rolled onto his back, hands firm on Cyn's hips, and lifted her up and over him. Her thighs now straddled his, and the dampness of her folds pressed against the hardness of his shaft as she sat upright, the swell of her breasts, tipped by strawberry-ripe nipples, peeping through the dark swathe of her hair.

'Do you have birth control, Cyn?'

'I didn't think...' she groaned. 'I—no, I don't.' Her cheeks were fiery red. 'Do you?'

Lucien would have preferred there to be nothing between him and Cyn the first time he entered her, but at the same time he liked that her lack of protection indicated she wasn't involved sexually with any other man right now.

He reached out and opened a drawer on the side table before taking out a silver foil packet and opening it. 'Would you...?' he invited huskily.

'Me?' Her eyes were wide.

'Perhaps not.' Lucien chuckled softly before quickly dealing with it himself. 'I want to be inside you now, Cyn...' he said huskily. 'In fact if I don't get inside you soon I think I'm going to spontaneously combust.' He settled her above him. 'I promise I'll go slower next time, but for the moment I just need—'

'Next time...?' Cyn squeaked.

'You said earlier that you would stay with me until I had made love to you half a dozen times, remember?' Lucien gave a hard, satisfied smile.

She gasped. 'But I—I already—I've lost count of how many times I've already—'

'Foreplay doesn't count,' he dismissed. 'When I'm inside you and we climax together—something I'm greatly looking forward to, by the way—that's when it counts. And I want you so badly this time I'm not going to last,' he acknowledged.

He knew it was true. His liking for Cyn, his enjoyment of her company as well as her body, had enhanced their lovemaking to a pitch he had never known before...

Thia gasped. All those incredible, mind-blowing climaxes didn't *count*? He couldn't truly think that she was going to be able to repeat this past hour—or however long it had been since Lucien had started making love to her. She had completely lost track of time! If they did she wouldn't just lose consciousness, she would surely die. And wouldn't that look great on her headstone—*Here lies Cynthia Hammond, dead from too much pleasure!*

But what a wonderful way to go...

Emotion—love...?—swelled in Thia's chest as she looked down at the man sprawled beneath her on the bed. Lucien really was the most gorgeous, sexy man she had ever met—breathtakingly handsome, elegantly muscled and loose-limbed. And he was all hers.

For the moment, that taunting little voice whispered again inside her head.

This moment was all that mattered. Because it was all there was for her and Lucien. They had no tomorrow. No future. Just here and now.

And she wanted it. Wanted Lucien.

She held that silver gaze with her own and eased up on her knees before reaching down between them, fingers light, as she guided his sheathed length to the slickness of her channel—only to freeze in place as she suddenly heard the unexpected sound of Mozart's *Requiem* playing!

'It's my mobile,' Lucien explained impatiently when he saw Cyn's dazed expression. 'Damn, it!' His hands slapped down forcefully onto the mattress beside him. He should have turned the damn thing off before making love with Cyn. Should have—

'You need to answer it, Lucien.' A frown marred Cyn's brow. 'It must be something important for someone to call again so quickly—and on your mobile this time.'

Nothing was more important at this moment than his need to make love with Cyn. *Nothing!*

'Lucien…?' she prompted huskily as his damned mobile just kept on playing Mozart's *Requiem*.

Which, in the circumstances, was very apt…

Talk about killing the moment! One interruption was bad enough. Lucien had managed to save the situation the first time, but he doubted he would be able to do so a second time.

A sentiment Cyn obviously echoed as she slid off and away from him, over to the side of the bed, before bending down to pick up the black silk robe from the floor. Her back was long and slender, ivory skin gleaming pale and oh-so-beautiful in the glow of the lamp, before she slipped her arms into the robe, pulling it about herself and then standing up to fasten the belt. She turned to face him.

'You have to answer the call, Lucien.' Her gaze remained firmly fixed on his face rather than lower, where he was still hard and wanting.

Oh, yes, there was no doubting he had to answer the call—and whoever was on the other end of it was going to feel the full force of his displeasure!

He slid to the side of the bed before reaching for his denims and taking his mobile out of the pocket to take the call. 'Steele,' he rasped harshly.

Thia winced at the coldness of Lucien's voice, feeling sorry for whoever was on the other end of that line. At the same time she couldn't help but admire the play of muscles across the broad width of Lucien's shoulders and back beneath that bronzed skin as he sat on the other side of the bed, his black hair rakishly tousled from her fingers earlier.

Earlier…

Her cheeks warmed as she thought of those earlier intimacies. Lucien's hands, lips and tongue caressing her, touching her everywhere. Giving pleasure wherever they touched. Taking her to climax again and again.

Her legs trembled just at remembering that pleasure—

'I'll be down in five minutes,' Lucien grated harshly, before abruptly ending the call and standing up decisively to cross the room and collect up the clothes he had taken off earlier, his eyes cold, his expression grimly discouraging.

Thia looked at him dazedly. He seemed almost unaware of her presence. 'Lucien…?'

He was scowling darkly as he turned to look at her. 'That was Dex,' he bit out economically. 'It appears that your ex-boyfriend is downstairs in Reception and he's been making a damned exhibition of himself!'

She gasped. 'Jonathan?'

Lucien nodded sharply. 'Unless you have any other ex-boyfriends in New York?'

She gave a pained wince at the harsh anger she heard in his tone. Misdirected anger, in her opinion. 'I told you— Jonathan was never my boyfriend. And isn't it more likely he's making an exhibition of himself in *your* hotel because you fired him from *Network* this morning?'

It was a valid, reasoned argument, Lucien acknowledged impatiently—but at the same time he knew he was just too tense at the moment to be reasoned with. Even by Cyn.

He had enjoyed this evening with her more than he had enjoyed being with a woman for a very long time—if ever. Not just making love to her, but cooking dinner with her, talking freely about everything and nothing, when usually he was careful of how much he revealed about himself to the women he was involved with—a self-defence reflex that simply hadn't existed with Cyn from the beginning.

And now *this*.

His mouth thinned with his displeasure. 'I apologise for being grouchy. I just—' He ran his hand through the dark thickness of his hair. 'I'll get dressed and go down and sort this situation out. I shouldn't be long. What are you doing...?' He frowned as Cyn turned towards the bathroom.

'Getting dressed so that I can come with you.'

'You aren't coming downstairs with me.'

'Oh, but I am,' she assured him.

'No—'

'Yes,' she bit out firmly, her hands resting on her hips as she raised challenging brows.

Lucien's nostrils flared. 'My hotel. My problem.'

'Your hotel, certainly. But we don't know yet whose problem it is,' she insisted stubbornly.

His jaw clenched. 'Look, Cyn, there are some things about Miller I don't believe you're aware of—'

'What sort of things?' She looked at him sharply.

'Things,' Lucien bit out tersely. This evening had already gone to hell in a handbasket. Cyn did not need to know about all of Jonathan Miller's behaviour, or the reason the other man had been using her, which was sure to come out if Miller was as belligerent as Dex had said he was. 'In the circumstances, the best thing you can do is—'

'Please don't tell me that the best thing I can do is to stay up here and make coffee, like a good little woman, and wait until the Mighty Hunter returns!' Her eyes glowed deeply cobalt.

Apart from the good little woman and Mighty Hunter crack, that was exactly what Lucien had been about to say. 'Well...maybe you could forget the coffee,' he said dryly.

'And maybe I can forget the whole scenario—because

it isn't going to happen!' She thrust her hands into the pockets of his silk robe.

Lucien noted that it was far too big for her; it was wrapped about her almost twice, with the sleeves turned up to the slenderness of her wrists, and the length reached down to her calves—altogether making her look like a little girl trying to play grown-up.

'Dex has managed to take Miller to a secure room for the moment, but it could get nasty, Cyn.'

'I've been a waitress for six years; believe me, I know how to deal with *nasty,*' she assured him dryly.

Lucien was starting to notice that Cyn seemed to use the waitress angle as a defence mechanism. As if in constant reminder to herself, and more probably Lucien, of who and what she was...

Who she was to Lucien was Cynthia Hammond—a beautiful and independent young woman whom he admired and desired.

What she was to Lucien was also Cynthia Hammond—a beautiful and independent young woman whom Lucien admired as well as desired.

The rest, he realised, had become totally unimportant to him—was just background noise and of no consequence.

Not true of Cyn, obviously...

He drew in a deep breath. 'I would really rather you didn't do this.'

'Your opinion is noted.' She nodded.

'But ignored?'

'But ignored.'

'Fine,' he bit out between clenched teeth, knowing he couldn't like Cyn's independence of spirit on the one hand and then expect her not to do exactly as she pleased on the other. 'I'll be leaving in about two minutes. If you aren't ready—'

'I'll be ready.'

She hurried into the bathroom and closed the door behind her.

Lucien drew in several controlling breaths as he glared at that closed bathroom door, knowing that the next few minutes' conversation with Miller would in all probability put an end to Lucien and Cyn spending the rest of the night together...

CHAPTER NINE

'MAKING AN EXHIBITION of himself how?' Thia prompted softly.

Lucien was scowling broodingly where he stood on the other side of the private lift as it descended to the ground floor.

He was once again dressed in those casual denims and black T-shirt, although the heavy darkness of his hair was still tousled—from Thia's own fingers earlier, and also Lucien's own now as he ran his hands through it in impatient frustration. Probably because of her stubbornness in insisting on accompanying him downstairs rather than Jonathan's behaviour, Thia acknowledged ruefully.

Silver eyes glittered through narrowed lids. 'He came in and demanded to see me. According to Dex, once both the receptionist and the manager had told him I wasn't available this evening, Miller then decided to start shouting and hurling the potted plants about. When that failed to get him what he wanted he resorted to smashing up the furniture, which was when Security arrived and took charge of the situation.'

'How...?'

'Two of them lifted him up and carried him away to a secure room before calling Dex,' Lucien explained grimly.

Thia winced as she pictured the scene. 'I can imagine Jonathan might be upset after what happened this morning, but surely this isn't normal behaviour?'

Lucien gave her an irritated frowning glance. 'Cyn, have you *really* not noticed anything different about him since you came to New York?'

Well…she *had* noticed that Jonathan was more self-absorbed than he'd used to be. That he slept the mornings away and barely spoke when he did emerge, sleepy-eyed and unkempt, from his bedroom. And he had insisted on the two of them attending those awful parties together every night, at which he usually abandoned her shortly after they had arrived. And he had been extremely aggressive at the Carews' party last night—she had the sore wrist and the bruises on her arms to prove that!

She chewed on her bottom lip. 'Maybe he's a little more…into himself than he used to be.'

'That's one way of describing it, I suppose.' Lucien nodded grimly, standing back as the lift came to a halt and allowing her to step out into the marbled hallway first.

Thia eyed him guardedly as she walked along the hallway beside him; Lucien obviously knew which room Jonathan had been secured in. 'How would *you* describe it?'

Lucien's mouth thinned. 'As the classic behaviour of an addict.'

She drew in a sharp breath as she came to an abrupt halt in the hallway. 'Are you saying that Jonathan is—that he's taking drugs?'

'Amongst other things.' Lucien scowled.

'He's drinking too?'

'Not that I know of, no.'

'Then what "other things" are you talking about…?' Thia felt dazed, disorientated, at Lucien's revelation about

Jonathan. Admittedly Jonathan hadn't seemed quite himself since she arrived in New York, but she had put that down to reaction to his sudden stardom. It must be difficult coping with being so suddenly thrust into the limelight, finding himself so much in demand, as well as having so many beautiful women throwing themselves at him.

Lucien grimaced. 'This is not a good time for me to discuss this with you.'

'It's exactly the time you should discuss this with me,' Thia insisted impatiently. 'Maybe if someone had thought to discuss it with me earlier I might have been able to talk to him about it—perhaps persuaded him to seek help.' She gave a shake of her head. 'As things now stand he's not only messed up his career, but the rest of his life as well!'

Lucien frowned as he heard the underlying criticism in her tone. 'Damn it, Cyn, do *not* turn this around on me. Miller was given a warning about his behaviour weeks ago. In fact he's been given two warnings.'

'When, exactly?'

'The first was two months ago. And again about five weeks ago, when it became obvious he had taken no notice of the first warning. I have a strict no-drugs policy on all contracts,' he added grimly.

'What sort of warn—? Did you say *five weeks* ago...?' she prompted guardedly.

Lucien quirked dark brows. 'Mean something to you?'

'Jonathan visited me in London a month ago...' She chewed on her bottom lip. 'I hadn't seen him for almost three months, and he had only telephoned me a couple of times since he'd left for New York, and then he—he just turned up one weekend.'

Lucien nodded. 'And subsequently invited you to come and stay with him in New York?'

'How do you know that?'

He scowled. 'I just did the math, Cyn.'

'I don't understand…'

Lucien didn't see why he should be the one to explain Miller's behaviour, either. Cyn already considered him callous for firing Miller. He wasn't going to be the one to tell her that Miller had only invited her to New York as a cover for his affair with another—married!—woman!

The fact that Cyn was with him now would probably be enough for Miller to realise she must have been with Lucien in his apartment when Dex telephoned a short time ago. Add that to the fact that she was so obviously wearing a man's oversized T-shirt and Miller was sure to add two and two together and come up with the correct answer of four!

Which was precisely the reason Lucien hadn't wanted Cyn with him during this confrontation. Well, okay, it wasn't the whole reason. He really would have preferred it that Cyn stayed in his apartment, made coffee, like the good little woman, and waited for the Mighty Hunter to return. He wanted to protect her from herself, if necessary. As it was, he somehow doubted that Cyn would be returning to his apartment tonight at all…

'Could we get a move on, do you think?' Lucien snapped tersely, giving a pointed glance at his wristwatch. 'I told Dex I'd be there in five minutes and it's been over ten.'

Cyn blinked at his vehemence. 'Of course. Sorry.'

She grimaced as she once again fell into step beside him, leaving Lucien feeling as if he had just delivered a kick to an already abused and defenceless animal.

Not that he thought of Cyn as defenceless—she was too independent, too determined ever to be completely that.

But he had no doubt that Miller's real reason for inviting her to come to New York was going to upset her.

It was hard to believe, considering the tension between them now, that the two of them had been making love just minutes ago—that he now knew Cyn's body intimately, and exactly how to give her pleasure.

On the plus side, his erection had got the message that the night of pleasure was over and had deflated back to normal proportions. Not that it would take much to revive his desire…just a sultry look from cobalt blue eyes, the merest touch of Cyn's hand anywhere on his body. Which Lucien already knew wasn't going to happen in the immediate future. If ever again.

Another reason for Lucien to be displeased at Miller's increasingly erratic behaviour. If he needed another reason. Which he didn't. Forget the drugs and the affair with Simone Carew; the man was an out-and-out bastard for attempting to use Cyn as a shield for that affair. Not that the ruse had worked, but that didn't excuse Miller's callous behaviour towards a woman who had thought he was her friend. Or the fact that the other man had held Cyn so roughly the evening before he had succeeded in badly bruising her.

And Cyn was annoyed with *him*, because he had fired Miller for blatant and continuous breach of contract!

'Dex.' He greeted the other man grimly as they turned a corner and he saw his bodyguard standing outside a door to the right of the hallway. 'He's in there?' He nodded to the closed door.

Dex scowled. 'Yes.'

'And has he quietened down?'

'Some.' Dex nodded grimly before shooting Cyn a frowning glance. 'I don't think it's a good idea for Miss

Hammond to go in with you. Miller is violent, and he's also throwing out all sorts of accusations,' he warned with a pointed glance at Lucien.

'I'm going in,' Cyn informed them both stubbornly.

Lucien's mouth tightened. 'As you can see, Dex, Miss Hammond insists on accompanying me.'

'It's really not a good idea, Miss Hammond,' Dex warned her gently.

It was a gentleness Lucien hadn't even known the other man was capable of. No doubt Dex found Cyn's beauty and her air of fragility appealing—but the fragility was deceptive. There was a toughness beneath that fragile exterior that made Lucien think Cyn would be capable of stopping a Humber in its tracks if she chose to do so! Hopefully Dex was concerned in a fatherly sort of way, because Lucien knew he wouldn't be at all happy with his bodyguard having a crush on the woman he—

The woman he what…? Was falling in love with? Was already in love with?

Now was hardly the time for Lucien to think about what he might or might not be feeling for Cyn. Damn it, they had met precisely three times now, and shared one evening together. Admittedly it had been the most enjoyable—and arousing!—evening Lucien had ever spent with a woman…

The depth of his desire for Cyn was unprecedented—to the point that Lucien really had thought he was going to come just at the taste of her on his tongue.

And for the early part of the evening she had believed him to have deliberately hidden her away in his apartment because he didn't want to be seen in public with her. She may still believe that, for all he had denied it.

Damn it, he should have tanned her backside earlier rather than making love to her!

'I appreciate your concern, Dex.' Thia answered the older man softly. 'But Jonathan is my friend—'

'No. He really isn't,' Lucien rasped harshly.

'And I have every intention of speaking with him to-night,' she continued firmly, at the same time giving Lucien a reproving frown.

'I agree with Mr Steele,' Dex murmured regretfully. 'Mr Miller's behaviour earlier was…out of control,' he added.

Thia had come to like and trust this man over the past couple of days—how could she *not* like and trust a man who had stood guard all night outside her bedroom in that awful hotel in order to ensure she came to no harm from any of the staff or other guests staying there? In fact she felt slightly guilty now, for thinking Dex looked like a thug the first time she had seen him. He might look tough, but she didn't doubt there was a heart of gold under that hard exterior.

And she valued his advice now—as she did Lucien's. Although his scowling expression indicated he thought otherwise! She just didn't feel she could abandon Jonathan when he so obviously needed all the friends he could get. She had no doubt that all those shallow people who had been all over Jonathan at those celebrity parties would drift away the moment they knew he had been dropped as the star of *Network*.

'I appreciate your concern, Dex.' She smiled her gratitude as she placed a hand lightly on his muscled forearm. 'I really do.'

'But she's going to ignore it,' Lucien said knowingly.

Her smile faded as she turned to face him, knowing

how displeased he was with her by the coldness in his eyes as he looked down the length of his nose at her, but unable to do anything about it.

She accepted, despite that interruption to their love-making, that Lucien had become her lover this evening—was closer to her and now knew her more intimately than any other man ever had. But by the same token she had been friends with Jonathan for two years now, and she didn't desert her friends. Especially when one of those friends was so obviously in trouble.

She drew in a deep, steadying breath. 'Yes, I'm afraid I am.'

Lucien had known she would. She had to be the most ir-ritatingly stubborn woman he had ever known!

As well as being the most beautiful—inside as well as out. And the funniest. Her comments were sometimes to-tally outrageous. She was also the sexiest woman Lucien had ever known. And definitely the most responsive!

That in itself was such a turn-on—an aphrodisiac. Lucien was an accomplished lover, and had certainly never had any complaints about his sexual technique, his ability to bring a woman to climax, or in finding his own release. But with Cyn there had been no need for that measured and deliberate technique—just pure pleasure as, after her initial shyness, she had held absolutely nothing back and responded to his lightest touch, at the same time height-ening his own pleasure and arousal.

To such an extent that Lucien knew Cyn was fast be-coming his own addiction...

And yet here they were at loggerheads again, just min-utes later—and over Jonathan Miller, of all people. A man

Lucien didn't consider as being good enough to lick Cyn's boots, let alone to deserve her loyalty and friendship.

'Fine,' he bit out harshly before turning away. 'You had better unlock the door and let us in, then, Dex. The sooner we get this over and done with the better for all of us,' he added grimly.

'Lucien…?' Cyn prompted almost pleadingly.

'You've made your decision, Cyn.' He rounded on her angrily, hands clenching at his sides. 'I only hope you don't live to regret it. No, damn it, I *know* you're going to regret it!' He glared down at her.

Thia had a sinking feeling she would too… Both Dex and Lucien seemed convinced of it, and she had no reason to distrust the opinion of either man.

Yes, Jonathan had been less than a polite host since she'd arrived in New York—to the point where his behaviour the previous evening meant she'd had no choice but to move out of his apartment. She just couldn't quite bring herself to turn her back on him if he needed a friend.

Lucien followed Dex into the room, the two of them blocking her view of Jonathan until they moved aside and Thia finally saw him where he stood silhouetted against the darkness of the window. He looked a mess: his denims were covered in soil—from the pot plants he had thrown about the hotel reception?—his T-shirt was ragged and torn, but it was the bruises on his face and the cut over one eye that dismayed her the most.

His lips curled back into a sneer as he saw the shocked expression on her face. 'You should see the other guy!'

'The "other guy" is at the hospital, having stitches put in the gash to the head he received when you smashed a lamp over him,' Lucien rasped harshly.

Jonathan turned that sneering expression onto the older man. 'He shouldn't have got in my way.'

'Watch your mouth, Miller. Unless you want him to press charges for assault,' Lucien warned grimly.

Thia paled at the knowledge that Jonathan had attacked another man with a lamp, necessitating that man needing to go to the hospital for stitches. 'You're just making the situation worse, Jonathan—'

'Exactly what are *you* doing here, Thia?' Jonathan turned on her, eyeing her speculatively as he took in the whole of her appearance in one sweeping glance. 'You look as if you just fell out of bed. Oh. My. God.' He gave a harsh laugh as he turned that speculative gaze on Lucien and then back to Thia. 'You just fell out of *his* bed! How priceless is that—'

She winced. 'Jonathan, don't.'

'Shut up, Miller,' Lucien bit out coldly at the same time.

'The prudish Thia Hammond and the almighty Lucien Steele!' Jonathan ignored them both as he laughed all the harder at a joke obviously only he appreciated.

Thia felt numb. Lucien was obviously icily furious. Dex remained stoically silent.

Jonathan's humour was so derisive and scathing Thia felt about two inches high—as he no doubt intended her to do. 'You aren't helping, Jonathan.'

'I have nothing left to lose,' he assured her scornfully as he gave a shake of his head. 'You stupid little fool—don't you know that he's just using you to get back at me?' He looked at Thia pityingly.

'You're the one who used her, Miller,' Lucien scorned icily.

Jonathan glared. 'I tried to convince you that Thia and I were involved, yes. In the futile hope of getting you off my back. But what you've done tonight—seducing Thia—is ten times worse than anything I did!' He gave a disgusted shake of his head before turning to Thia with accusing eyes. 'Damn it, Thia, we actually dated for a while two years ago—until you made it obvious you weren't interested in me in that way. And yet you only met Steele yesterday and already you've been to bed with him! Unbloody-believable!' He eyed her incredulously.

When he put it like that it *was* pretty incredible, Thia acknowledged with an inner wince. Not that she and Lucien had completely consummated their lovemaking, but that was pure semantics. After the number of times Lucien had brought her to sobbing orgasm he was definitely her lover. A man, as Jonathan had just pointed out, she had only known for twenty-four hours...

Lucien had heard enough—seen enough. Cyn's face was tinged slightly green and she was swaying slightly, as if she was about to pass out! 'I suggest we talk about this again tomorrow, Miller,' he snapped icily. 'When you've had a chance to...calm down.' He eyed the other man disgustedly, knowing by Miller's flushed cheeks and overbright eyes that he was high on something—something he needed to sleep off overnight. Preferably with Dex keeping a sharp eye on him to ensure he didn't take anything else.

'You would no doubt prefer it if Thia didn't hear all the sordid details?' the younger man taunted.

Lucien shrugged. 'They're your sordid details.'

'Not all of them,' Miller challenged. 'Something I'm pretty sure you won't have shared with Thia either.'

Lucien's mouth tightened. 'Not only do your empty threats carry no weight with me, but they could be decidedly dangerous. To your future career,' he added softly.

'You don't think Thia has a right to know that the *real*

reason you've been trying to break my contract the last couple of months—the reason for your being with her tonight—is because I've been having an affair with the woman I seduced out of *your* bed?'

'We both know that isn't true, Miller.' Lucien's teeth were clenched so tightly his jaw ached.

'Do we?'

'Yes!' he rasped. 'Something I will discuss with you in more detail tomorrow,' he added determinedly.

'And will you also fill me in on all the juicy details of how you succeeded in seducing and deflowering the Virgin Queen?' Miller came back tauntingly.

'What the hell...?' Lucien muttered.

'It's what I've always called Thia in my mind.' The other man grinned unrepentantly.

Lucien stilled as all thought of Miller's accusations fled his mind. Barely breathing, he felt his heart pounding loudly in his chest as he gave Cyn a brief disbelieving glance—just long enough to show him that she had somehow managed to go even paler. Her cheeks were now paper-white.

The Virgin Queen?

Was it possible that on this subject at least Miller might be telling the truth and Cyn had been a virgin? Correction: she was still technically a virgin—despite the intensity of their lovemaking earlier.

Had Lucien taken a virgin to his bed and not even known it? Would he only have realised it the moment he ripped through that delicate barrier?

Lucien was the one who now felt nauseous. Sick to his stomach, in fact, at how close he had come to taking Cyn's innocence without even realising until it was too late.

Perhaps he should have known.

He had noted that disingenuous air about her the first time they met. There had also been her shyness earlier, in regard to her own nudity as much as his. Her confusion when he had assured her he had a clean bill of health and her hesitant confirmation that she did too. And the glaringly obvious fact that Cyn wasn't on any birth control.

Because she was a virgin.

Even during the wildness of his youth Lucien had never taken a virgin to his bed—had stayed well away from any female who looked as if she might still be one. A woman's virginity was something to be valued—a gift—not something to be thrown away on a casual relationship, and Lucien had never felt enough for any of the women he had been involved with to want to take a relationship any further.

What had Cyn been thinking earlier?

Maybe she hadn't been thinking at all? Lucien knew he certainly hadn't. He had been too aroused, too caught up in the intensity of his desire for Cyn—of his growing addiction to her—to be able to connect up the dots of her behaviour and their conversation and realise exactly how innocent she was. As it was, he had been on the point of thrusting into her, of taking her innocence, when the ringtone of his mobile had interrupted them.

Sweet, merciful heaven…!

CHAPTER TEN

'LUCIEN—'

'Not now, Thia.'

She almost had to run to keep up with Lucien's much longer strides, and Jonathan's mocking laughter followed them as they walked down the deserted marble hallway towards where the main lifts were situated, in the reception area of the hotel. The lifts Thia would need to use if she was returning to her suite on the tenth floor. Which it seemed she was about to do...

'Is Dex going to stay with Jonathan tonight?' Thia hadn't been able to hear all the softly spoken conversation that had taken place between Lucien and Dex before Lucien had taken a firm hold of her arm and escorted her from the room, but she had gathered that Dex intended taking Jonathan out of the back entrance of the hotel and then driving him to his apartment.

Lucien nodded abruptly. 'If only to make sure he stays out of trouble for the rest of the night.'

She winced. 'Is the drug thing really that bad?'

'Yes,' he answered grimly.

Thia frowned. 'Lucien, what did Jonathan mean? He seemed to be implying that there was a woman involved in your decision to fire him from *Network*?'

Lucien turned to look down at her with icy silver eyes. 'I don't think that's the conversation we should be having right now, Thia.'

The fact that he kept calling her Thia in that icily clipped tone was far from reassuring... Not that she wasn't totally aware of the reason for Lucien's coldness. It was as if an arctic chill had taken over the room the moment Jonathan had so baldly announced her virginity. Lucien's shocked reaction to that statement had been unmistakable. As if she had a disease, or something equally as unpleasant! Good grief, he had been a virgin himself once upon a time—many years ago now, no doubt, but still...

'I don't understand why you're so annoyed.' She frowned. 'It's my virginity, and as such I can choose to lose it when I damn well please. It's no big deal.'

'I'm guessing that's why you've waited twenty-three years to even think about doing so?'

Thia smarted at his scathing tone. 'It isn't the first time I've considered it—and that's my bruised arm, Lucien!' she complained, when his fingers tightly grasped the top of her arm as he came to a halt in the deserted hallway before swinging her round to face him.

He released her as abruptly, glaring down at her, nostrils flaring as he breathed deeply. 'What the hell were you thinking, Thia? What were you doing going alone to a man's apartment at all?'

'Accepting an invitation to dinner in a man's apartment isn't saying *Here I am—take me to bed!*'

'It's been my experience that that depends on the woman and her reasons for accepting the invitation.'

She bristled. 'I don't think I like the accusation in your tone.'

'Well, that's just too bad,' he bit out harshly. 'Because

my tone isn't going to change until I know exactly why you went to bed with me earlier this evening!'

Her cheeks blazed with colour. 'I thought I was making love with a man whom I desired and who also desired me!'

His jaw tightened. 'Not good enough, Thia—'

'Well, it's the only explanation I have. And stop calling me that!' Tears stung her eyes.

'It's your name,' he dismissed curtly.

'But *you've* never called me by it.' She blinked back those heated tears. 'And I—I liked it that only you had ever called me Cyn,' she admitted huskily, realising it was the truth. She had found Lucien's unique name for her irritating at first, but had very quickly come to like that uniqueness.

His nostrils flared in his impatience. 'Answer the damned question, Thia!'

'Which one?' she came back just as angrily. He'd called her that name again. 'Why did I decide to have dinner alone with you in your apartment this evening? Or why did I choose you as the man to whom I wanted to lose my virginity? Or perhaps to you they're one and the same question?' she challenged scornfully. 'You obviously think that I had pre-planned going to bed with you this evening! That I was attempting to—to entrap you into—into *what,* exactly?' Thia looked at him sharply.

Lucien was still too stunned at the knowledge of Cyn's virginity—at the thought of her never having been with anyone else—to be able to reason this situation out with his usually controlled logic. As a consequence he was talking without thinking about what he was saying, uncharacteristically shooting straight from the hip. But, damn it, if his mobile had rung even a few seconds later—!

'Damned if I know,' he muttered exasperatedly.

'Oh, I think you *do* know, Lucien.' Cyn's voice shook with anger. 'I think you've decided—that you believe—I deliberately set out to seduce you this evening.'

'I believe *I* was the one who did the seducing—'

'Ah, but what if I'm clever enough to let you *think* you did the seducing?' she taunted, eyes glittering darkly.

He gave a rueful shake of his head. 'You aren't—'

'It's a pity you asked about birth control, really,' she continued without pause. 'Otherwise I might even have discovered I was pregnant in a few weeks' time. And wouldn't that have been wonderful? I can see the head-lines in the newspapers now—*I had Lucien Steele's love-child!* Except we aren't in love with each other, and there isn't ever going to be a child—'

'Stop it, Cyn!' he rasped sharply, reaching up to grasp her by the shoulders before shaking her. 'Just *stop* it!'

'Let me go, Lucien,' she choked. 'I don't like you very much at the moment.' Tears fell unchecked down the pale-ness of her cheeks, her eyes dark blue pools of misery.

Lucien didn't like himself very much at the moment ei-ther. And it was really no excuse that he was still in shock from Miller's 'Virgin Queen' comment. His knee-jerk angry comments had now made Cyn think—believe—that he was angry about her virginity. When in actual fact he felt like getting down on his knees and worshipping at her beautiful feet. A woman's virginity was a gift. A gift Cyn had been about to give to *him* this evening. The truth was he was in total awe at the measure of that gift.

And he had made her cry. That was just unacceptable.

He released her shoulders before pulling her into his arms—a move she instantly fought against as she tried to push him away, before beating her fists against his chest when she failed to release herself.

'I said, let me go, Lucien!' She glared up at him as he still held her tightly against his chest.

'Let me explain, Cyn—'

'I have questions I want answered too, Lucien. And so far you've refused to answer any of them. Including explaining about this woman Jonathan reputedly stole from you—'

'I don't consider Miller's fantasies as being relevant to our present conversation!' He scowled darkly.

'And I disagree with that opinion. Jonathan said that the two of us making love together this evening was deliberate on your part—that you seduced me to get back at him—'

'Does that *really* sound like something I would do?' he grated, jaw clenched.

'Any more than entrapment sounds like something I would do?' she came back tauntingly. 'I don't really know you, Lucien…'

'Oh, you know me, Cyn,' Lucien assured her softly. 'In just a few short days I've allowed you to know me better than anyone else ever has. And the conversation we need to have is about what happened between the two of us this evening.'

'I think we—you, certainly—have already said more than enough on that subject!' she assured him firmly.

'Because I was understandably stunned at learning of your—your innocence?'

'Was that you being stunned? It looked more like shock to me!'

'You're being unreasonable, Cyn—'

'Probably because I *feel* unreasonable!' Cyn gave another push against his chest with her bent elbows, those tears still dampening her cheeks. 'So much has happened this evening that I—Lucien, if you don't release me I'm going to start screaming, and I think the other guests staying at the hotel have already witnessed enough of a scene for one evening!'

'You're upset—'

'Of *course* I'm upset!' Cyn stilled to look up at him incredulously. 'I've just learnt that the friend I came to New York to visit has not only become involved in taking drugs, but has also been using me to hide his affair with another woman. Add to that the fact that the man I had dinner with and made love with earlier this evening also seems to have been involved with that woman—'

'I'm not involved with anyone but you.'

'I think that gives me the right to be upset, don't you?' she continued determinedly.

Lucien frowned his own frustration with the situation as he released her, before allowing his arms to drop slowly back to his sides, knowing he had handled this situation badly, that his first instinct—to kneel and worship at Cyn's feet—was the one he should have taken.

'I apologise. It— I— It isn't every day a man learns that the woman he has just made love with is a virgin.'

'No, I believe we're becoming something of an endangered species.' She nodded abruptly. 'Thank you for the fun of cooking dinner together this evening, Lucien. I enjoyed it. The sex too. The rest of the evening… Not quite so much.' She stepped back. 'I'll make sure I have your T-shirt laundered and returned to you before I leave on Saturday—'

'Do you think I give a damn about my T-shirt?' he bit out in his frustration with her determination to leave him.

'Probably not.' She grimaced. 'I'm sure you have dozens of others just like it. Or you could *buy* another dozen like it! I would just feel better if I had this one laundered and returned to you.'

So that she didn't even have *that* as a reminder of him once she had returned to her life in London, Lucien guessed heavily.

Lucien wouldn't need anything to remind him of Cyn once she had gone.

He had spoken the truth when he'd told her that he had been more open, more relaxed in her company, than he ever had with any other woman.

As for the sex…!

He'd had good sex in his life, pleasurable sex, and very occasionally mechanical sex, when mutual sexual release had been the only objective, but he'd never had such mind-blowing and compatible sex as he'd enjoyed tonight with Cyn, where the slightest touch, every caress, gave them both unimagined pleasure.

He had always believed that sort of sex had to be worked at, with the two people involved having a rapport that went beyond the physical to the emotional.

He and Cyn had something between them beyond the physical. Lucien had known Cyn a matter of days, and yet the two of them had instinctively found that rapport. In and out of bed. Only to have it all come crashing down about their heads the moment Dex rang to tell them of Miller's presence downstairs in the hotel reception area.

Not only that, but Cyn was a virgin, and now that Lucien knew that he realised that her shyness earlier was an indication that she was an inexperienced virgin. A *very* inexperienced virgin, who had climaxed half a dozen times in his arms. Which was surely unusual—and perhaps an indication that she felt more for him than just physical attraction?

Or was that just wishful thinking on his part…?

Lucien didn't know any more. Had somehow lost his perspective. On everything. A loss that necessitated in him needing time and space in which to consider exactly what he felt for Cyn. Time the mutinously angry expression on Cyn's face now told him he simply didn't have!

'Fine.' He tersely accepted her suggestion about returning the T-shirt. 'But I'll see you again before you leave—'

'I don't think that's a good idea.' She backed up another step, putting even more distance between the two of them.

Lucien scowled darkly across that distance. 'You're being unreasonable—'

'Outraged virgin unreasonable? Or just normal female unreasonable?' she taunted with insincere sweetness.

'Just unreasonable,' he grated between clenched teeth, not wanting to lose his temper and say something else he would have cause to regret. The fact that he was in danger of losing his temper at all was troubling. He *never* lost his control—let alone his temper. Tonight, with Cyn, he had certainly lost his control, and his temper was now seriously in danger of following it. 'You're putting words into my mouth now, Cyn,' he continued evenly. 'And we *will* see each other again before you leave. I'll make sure of it.'

She raised midnight brows. 'I'd be interested to know how.'

Lucien gave a humourless smile. 'I believe, ironically, that you're travelling back to London on Saturday on the Steele Atlantic Airline.'

'How on earth did you know that?' She stared at him incredulously.

'I checked.' He shrugged. 'I thought it would be a nice gesture to bump your seat up to First Class. Miller was a cheapskate for not booking you into First Class in the first place!'

'He did,' she snapped. 'I'm the one who insisted he change it to Economy.'

'No doubt because you have every intention of paying the money back to him.' Lucien sighed, only too well aware of Cyn's fierce independence. It was a knowledge that made his earlier comments—accusations!—even more ridiculous. And unforgivable.

'Of course.' She tilted her chin proudly.

Lucien nodded. 'Nevertheless, if you avoid seeing me again before you leave for the airport on Saturday, one telephone call from me and the flight gets delayed...or cancelled altogether.'

Cyn gasped. 'You wouldn't seriously do that?'

He raised a mocking brow. 'What do you think?'

'I think you're way way out of line on this—that is what I *think*!' she hissed forcefully.

He shrugged. 'Your choice.'

'You—you egomaniac!' Thia glared at him. Arrogant, manipulative, *impossible* ego-maniac!

Lucien gave a hard, humourless smile. 'As I said, it's up to you. We either talk again before you leave or you don't leave.'

'There are other airlines.'

He shrugged. 'I will ensure that none are available to you.'

She gasped. 'You can't do that—'

'Oh, but I can.'

Her eyes widened. 'You would really stop me from leaving New York until we've spoken again...?'

His mouth thinned. 'You aren't giving me any alternative.'

'We all have choices, Lucien.' She gave a shake of her

head. 'And your overbearing behaviour now is leaving *me* with no choice but to dislike you intensely.'

He sighed. 'Well, at least it's *intensely;* I would hate it to be anything so insipid as just mediocre dislike! Look, I'm not enjoying backing you into a corner, Cyn,' he reasoned grimly as she glared at him. 'All I'm asking for is that we both sleep on this situation and then have a conversation tomorrow. Is that too much to ask?'

Was it? Could Thia even bear to be alone with him again after all that had been said?

Oh, she accepted that Lucien had been shocked at the way Jonathan had just blurted out her physical innocence. But Lucien's response to that knowledge had been—damned painful. That was what it had been!

'Okay, we'll talk again tomorrow.' She spoke in measured tones. 'But in a public place. With the agreement that I can get up and leave any time I want to.'

His eyes narrowed. 'I'm not sure I like your implication…'

'And my answer to that is pretty much the same as the one you gave me a few minutes ago—that's just too bad!' She looked at him challengingly.

Lucien gave a slow shake of his head. 'How the hell did we get into this situation, Cyn? One minute I have my mouth and my hands all over you, and the next—'

'You don't,' she snapped, the finality of her tone implying he never would again.

Except…it was impossible for Lucien not to see the outline of her nipples pouting hard as berries against the soft material of his T-shirt. Or not to note the way an aroused flush now coloured her throat and up into her cheeks. Or see the feverish glitter in the deep blue of her eyes.

Cyn was angry with him right now—and justifiably so

after his own train-wreck of a conversation just now—but that hadn't stopped her from remembering the fierceness of the desire that had flared between them earlier, or prevented the reaction of her body to those memories.

'Tomorrow, Cyn?' he encouraged huskily. 'Let's both just take a night to calm down.'

She frowned. 'It's my last day and I'd planned on taking a boat ride to see the Statue of Liberty. Don't tell me!' She grimaced as she obviously saw his expression. 'You've never been there, either!'

He smiled slightly. 'You live in London—have *you* ever been to the Tower of London and Buckingham Palace?'

'The Palace, yes. The Tower, no.' She shrugged. 'Okay, point taken. But tomorrow really is my last chance to take that boat trip...'

'Then we'll arrange to meet up in the evening.' Lucien shrugged.

Cyn eyed him warily. 'You're being very obliging all of a sudden.'

He grimaced. 'Maybe I'm trying to score points in the hope of making up for behaving like such a jackass earlier?'

'And maybe you just like having your own way,' she said knowingly. 'Okay, Lucien, we'll meet again tomorrow evening. But I'll be out most of the day, so leave a message for me at the front desk as to where we're supposed to meet up.'

He grimaced. 'Not the most gracious acceptance of an invitation I've ever received, but considering the jackass circumstances I'll happily take it.'

'This isn't a date, Lucien.' Cyn snapped her impatience.

She was doing it again—making him want to laugh when the situation, the strain that now existed between the two of them, should have meant he didn't find any of this in the least amusing! Besides which, Lucien had no doubt that if he *did* dare to laugh Cyn would be the one throwing potted plants around the hotel's reception—in an attempt to hit him with one of them!

Just thinking of Miller's behaviour earlier tonight was enough to dampen Lucien's amusement. 'I want your word. I would *like* your word,' he amended impatiently, bearing in mind Cyn's scathing comment earlier about his always wanting to have his own way, 'that you will stay away from Miller's apartment tomorrow.'

'I thought I might just—'

'I would really rather you didn't,' Lucien said frustratedly. 'You saw what he was like this evening, Cyn. His behaviour is currently unpredictable at best, violent at worst. You could get hurt. Far worse than just those bruises on your arm,' he added grimly.

She looked pained as she shook her head. 'Jonathan's life is in such a mess right now—'

'And it's a self-inflicted mess. Damn it, Cyn.' He scowled. 'He's already admitted he was only using you as a shield for his affair with another woman when he invited you to stay with him in New York!'

'Even so, it doesn't seem right—my just leaving without seeing him again.' She gave a sad shake of her head. 'I would feel as if I were abandoning him... Not everyone is as capable of handling sudden fame and fortune as you were,' she defended, when Lucien looked unimpressed.

'Damn it, Cyn.' He rasped his impatience with her continued concern for a man who didn't deserve it. 'Okay, if I see what can be done about getting Miller to accept help, maybe even going to a rehab facility, will you give me your promise not to go to his apartment tomorrow?'

'And you'll reconsider firing him from *Network*?'

'Don't push your luck, Cyn,' Lucien warned softly.

To his surprise, she gave a rueful grin. 'Okay, but it was worth a try, don't you think, as you're in such an amenable mood?'

Some of the tension eased from Lucien's shoulders as he looked at her admiringly. 'You are one gutsy lady, Cynthia Hammond!'

Thia was feeling far from gutsy at the moment. In fact reaction seemed to be setting in and she suddenly felt very tired, her legs less than steady. A reaction no doubt due to that fierceness of passion between herself and Lucien earlier as much as Jonathan's erratic, and...yes, she admitted *dangerously* unbalanced behaviour.

She was willing to concede that Lucien was right about that, at least; she had hardly recognised Jonathan this evening as the man she had known for two years.

But there were still so many questions that remained unanswered. The most burning question of all, for Thia, being the name of the woman Jonathan claimed to have seduced out of Lucien's bed.

Mainly because Thia simply couldn't believe that any woman would be stupid enough ever to prefer Jonathan over Lucien...

CHAPTER ELEVEN

'YOU JUST NEVER listen, do you? Never heed advice when it's given, even when it's for your own safety!'

Lucien's expression was as dark as thunder as he strode past Thia and into her hotel suite early the following evening, impressively handsome in a perfectly tailored black evening suit with a snowy white shirt and red silk bow-tie—making it obvious he had obviously only called to see her on his way out somewhere.

'Do come in, Lucien,' she invited dryly, and she slowly closed the door behind him before following him through to her sitting room. Her hair was pulled back in a high ponytail and she was wearing a pale blue fitted T-shirt and low-rider denims. 'Make yourself at home,' she continued as he dropped a large box down onto the coffee table before sitting down in one of the armchairs. 'And do please help yourself to a drink,' she invited.

He bounced restlessly back onto his feet a second later to cross the room and open the mini-bar, taking out one of the miniature bottles of whisky and pouring it into a glass before throwing it to the back of his throat and downing the fiery contents in one long swallow.

'Feeling better?'

Lucien turned, silver eyes spearing her from across

the room. 'Not in the least,' he grated harshly, taking out another miniature bottle of whisky before opening it and pouring it into the empty glass.

'What's wrong, Lucien?' Thia frowned.

His eyes narrowed to glittering silver slits. 'You gave me your word last night that you wouldn't see Miller today—'

'I believe I said that I wouldn't go to his apartment,' she corrected with a self-conscious grimace, knowing exactly where this conversation was going now.

'So you invited him to come here instead?'

Thia sighed. 'I didn't *invite* him anywhere, Lucien. Jonathan turned up outside my door. You only just missed him, in fact...'

His jaw tightened. 'I'm well aware of that!'

She arched a brow. 'Dex?'

Lucien's eyes narrowed. 'It was totally irresponsible of you to be completely alone with Miller in your suite—'

'But I wasn't completely alone with him, was I?' Thia said knowingly. 'I'm pretty sure Dex followed me to the docks today, and that he was standing guard outside the door to this suite earlier. And no doubt he ratted me out by telephoning you and telling you Jonathan was here.'

Lucien's eyes glittered a warning. 'Dex worries about your safety almost as much as I do.'

'Who's watching your back while Dex is busy watching mine?'

'I can take care of myself.'

'So can I!'

Lucien gave a disgusted snort. 'I discovered the first grey hair at my temple when I looked in the mirror to shave earlier—I'm damned sure it's appeared since yesterday.'

'Very distinguished,' she mocked. 'But there is absolutely no need for either you or Dex to worry about me,' she dismissed lightly. 'Jonathan only came by to apologise for the way he's behaved these past few weeks. He also said that when the two of you spoke earlier today you offered to give him another chance on *Network* if he agrees to go to rehab.'

'An offer I am seriously rethinking.'

She sighed. 'Don't be petty, Lucien.'

An angry flush darkened his cheeks. 'I made the offer because you asked me to, Cyn. Not for Miller's sake.'

'And because you know it makes good business sense,' she pointed out ruefully. 'It would be indescribably bad business for you to sack the star of *Network* when the programme—and Jonathan—are obviously both so popular.'

Lucien's mouth thinned. 'And you seriously think losing a few dollars actually *matters* to me?'

Thia slipped her hands into the back pockets of her denims so that Lucien wouldn't see that they were shaking slightly—evidence that she wasn't feeling as blasé about this conversation and Jonathan's visit earlier as she wished to give the impression of being.

She had seen Lucien in a variety of moods these past few days: the confident seducer on the evening they met, the focused billionaire businessman at his office the following day, playful and then seductive in his apartment yesterday evening, before he became cold and dismissive towards Jonathan, and then a total enigma to her after Jonathan deliberately dropped the bombshell of her virginity into the conversation.

But Lucien's mood this evening—a mixture of anger and concern—was as unpredictable as the man himself.

Her chin rose. 'I thought we had agreed to meet in a public place this evening?'

'I decided to come here after Dex called up to the penthouse and informed me of Miller's visit.'

'You could have just telephoned.'

'I could have *just* done a lot of things—and, believe me, my immediate response was to do what I've threatened to do several times before and put you over my knee for having behaved so damned irresponsibly,' he bit out harshly.

Thia frowned. 'Correct me if I'm wrong, but shouldn't *I* be the one who's feeling angry and upset?' she challenged.

Lucien's expression became wary. 'About what?'

'About *everything!*' she burst out.

He stilled. 'What else did Miller tell you earlier?' Lucien's expression was enigmatic as he picked up the whisky glass and moved to stand in the middle of the room—a move that instantly dominated the space.

'Nothing I hadn't already worked out for myself,' Thia answered heavily. She had realised last night, as she'd lain alone in her bed, unable to sleep, exactly who the woman involved in the triangle must be. There had been only one obvious answer—only one woman Jonathan had spent any amount of time alone with over the past few days. And it wasn't a triangle but a square. Because Simone Carew, Jonathan's co-star in *Network,* also had a husband...

And if, as Jonathan claimed, he had seduced Simone away from Lucien's bed several months ago, then Jonathan's assertion that Lucien, believing Thia was Jonathan's English lover, had seduced her as a way of getting back at Jonathan, it all made complete sense.

Painfully so.

Perhaps it was as well she would be leaving New York tomorrow, with no intentions of seeing Lucien or Jonathan ever again.

Not seeing Jonathan again didn't bother her in the

slightest—they had said all they had to say to each other earlier.

Not seeing Lucien again—that was something else entirely.

Because Thia had realised something else as she'd lain alone in her bed the previous night. Something so huge, so devastating, that she had no idea how she was going to survive it.

She was in love with Lucien Steele.

Thia had heard of love at first sight, of course. Of how the sound of a particular voice could send shivers of awareness down the spine. How the first sight of that person's face could affect you so badly that breathing became difficult. Of how their touch could turn your legs to jelly and their kisses make you forget everything else but being with them.

Yes, Thia had heard of things like that happening—and now she realised that was exactly what had happened to her!

The worst of it was that the man she was in love with was Lucien Steele—a man who might or might not have been deliberately using her but who certainly wasn't in love with her.

'Such as?' Lucien prompted harshly as he saw the pained look on Cyn's face. 'Damn it, Cyn, even the condemned man is given an opportunity to defend himself!' he said as she remained silent.

She looked up, focusing on him with effort. 'You're far from being a condemned man, Lucien.' She gave a rueful shake of her head. 'And I think it's for the best if we forget about all of this and just move on.'

'Move on to where?' he prompted huskily.

She gave a pained frown. 'Well, Jonathan to rehab,

hopefully. Me back to England. And you—well, you to whatever it is you usually do before moving on to another relationship. Not that we actually *had* a relationship,' she added hurriedly. 'I didn't mean to imply that—'

'You're waffling, Cyn.'

'What I'm doing is trying to allow both of us to walk away from this situation with a little dignity.' Her eyes flashed a deep dark blue.

'I don't remember saying I wanted to walk away.' He quirked one dark brow.

She gave a shake of her head. 'I know the truth now, Lucien. I worked out most of it for myself—Simone Carew. Jonathan filled in the bits I didn't know, so let's just stop pretending, shall we? The condensed version of what happened is that you gave Jonathan two separate verbal warnings, about Simone and the drugs, he invited me over here in an attempt to mislead you about his continuing relationship with Simone at least, and you—you flirted with me to get back at him for taking Simone from you. End of story.'

'That's only Miller's version of the story, Cyn...' Lucien murmured softly as he placed his whisky glass carefully, deliberately, down on the coffee table before straightening.

His deliberation obviously didn't fool Cyn for a moment, as she now looked across at him warily. 'I told you—some of it I worked out for myself and the rest... It really isn't that important, Lucien.' She gave a dismissive shake of her head.

'Maybe not to you,' he bit out harshly. 'I, on the other hand, have no intention of allowing you to continue believing I have ever been involved with a married woman. It goes against every code I've ever lived by.' He drew in a sharp breath. 'My parents' marriage ended because my mother left my father for someone else,' he stated flatly.

'I would never put another man through the pain my father went through after she left him.'

Cyn's eyes widened. 'I didn't realise… Did your relationship with Simone happen *before* she married Felix?'

Lucien gave an exasperated sigh. 'It never happened at all!'

She winced at his vehemence. 'Then why did Jonathan say that it did…?'

'I can only assume because that's what Simone told him—probably as a way of piquing his interest.'

'I— But— *Why?* No, strike that question.' Cyn gave an impatiently disgusted shake of her head. 'I've met Simone Carew a few times over the past few days and she's a very silly, very vain woman. So, yes, I can well believe she's capable of telling Jonathan something like that just for the kudos. It isn't enough that she's married to one of the most influential directors in television—she also had to claim to having had a relationship with the richest and most powerful man in New York!'

Lucien gave a humourless smile. 'I knew you would get there in the end!'

'This isn't the time for your sarcasm, Lucien.' Cyn glared. 'And if you knew she was going around telling such lies why didn't you stop her?'

'Because I didn't know about it until Miller blurted it out to me a few weeks ago.' He scowled. 'And once I did know it didn't seem particularly important—'

'Simone Carew was going around telling anyone who would listen that the two of you'd had an affair, and it didn't seem particularly important to you?' Cyn stared at him incredulously. 'What about her poor husband?'

Lucien gave a weary sigh. 'Felix is thirty years older than Simone and he knew exactly what he was getting into when he married her. As a result, he chooses to look the other way when she has one of her little extra-marital flings.'

'Big of him.'

'Not really.' Lucien grimaced. 'He happens to be in love with her. And there are always rumours circulating in New York about everyone—most of them untrue or exaggerations of the truth. So why would I have bothered denying the ones about Simone and me? Have you never heard people say the more you deny something the more likely people are to believe it's the truth?'

'I wouldn't have!'

'That's because *you* are nothing like anyone else I have ever met,' Lucien dismissed huskily.

Thia didn't know what to say in answer to that comment. Didn't know what to say, full-stop.

Oh, she believed Lucien when he said he hadn't ever had an affair with Simone—why wouldn't she believe him when he had no reason to bother lying to her? It was totally unimportant to Lucien what *she* believed!

It did, however, raise the question as to why Lucien had pursued *her* so determinedly...

'What's in the box, Lucien?' Thia deliberately changed the subject as she looked down at the box Lucien had dropped down onto the coffee table when he first entered the suite.

'End of subject?'

She avoided meeting his exasperated gaze. 'I can't see any point in talking about it further. It's—I apologise if I misjudged you.' She gave a shake of her head. 'Obviously I'm not equipped—I don't understand the behind-the-scenes machinations and silly games of your world.'

'None of that is *my* world, Cyn. It's an inevitable part of it, granted, but not something I have ever chosen to involve myself in,' he assured her softly. 'As for what's in the box…why don't you open it up and see?'

Thia eyed the box as if it were a bomb about to go off, having no idea what could possibly be inside.

'It's a replacement for the blouse that was ripped!' she realised with some relief, her cheeks warming as she recalled exactly how and when her blouse had been ripped. And what had followed.

She couldn't think about that now! *Wouldn't* think about that now. There would be time enough for thinking about making love with Lucien, of being in love with him, in all the months and years of her life yet to come…

'Open it up, Cyn,' Lucien encouraged gruffly as he moved to sit down on the sofa beside the coffee table.

'Before I forget—I had your T-shirt laundered today—'

'Will you stop delaying and open the damned box, Cyn?'

'I can do it later,' she dismissed. 'You're obviously on your way out somewhere.' She gave a pointed look at his evening clothes. 'I wouldn't want to delay you any more than I have already—'

'You aren't delaying me.'

'But—'

'What is so difficult about opening the box, Cyn?' He barked his impatience with her prevarication.

Thia worried her bottom lip between her teeth. 'I just— I'm sorry if I'm being less than gracious. I'm just a little out of practice at receiving gifts…'

Lucien's scowl deepened as he realised the reason for that: Cyn's parents had died six years ago and she'd admitted to having no other family. And her relationship with Miller obviously hadn't been of the gift-giving variety—he was a taker, not a giver!

'It isn't a gift, Cyn,' Lucien assured softly. 'I ruined your blouse. I'm simply replacing it.'

A delicate blush warmed the ivory of her cheeks, emphasising the dark shadows under those cobalt blue eyes. Because Cyn hadn't slept well the night before?

Neither had Lucien. His thoughts had chased round and round on themselves as he'd tried to make sense, to use his normal cold logic, to explain and dissect his feelings for Cyn. In the end he had been forced to acknowledge, to accept, that there was no sense or reason to any of it. It just was.

There was now a dull ache in his chest at the realisation he wanted to shower Cyn with gifts, to give her anything and everything she had ever wanted or desired. At the same as he knew that her fierce independence would no doubt compel her to throw his generosity back in his face!

Lucien was totally at a loss to know what to do about this intriguing woman. Was currently following a previously untrodden path—one that had no signs or indications to tell him where to go or what he should do next. Except he knew he wasn't going to allow her to just walk out of his life tomorrow.

He took heart from the blush that now coloured her cheeks at the mention of her blouse ripping the night before. 'I would like to know if you approve of the replacement blouse, Cyn,' he encouraged gruffly.

'I would love to have been a fly on your office wall during *that* telephone conversation!' she teased as she finally moved forward to loosen the lid of the box before removing it completely.

'I went to the store this morning and picked out the blouse myself, Cyn.'

She gave him a startled look. 'You did?'

'I did,' he confirmed gruffly.

'I— But— Why…?'

He shrugged. 'I didn't trust a store assistant to pick out a blouse that was an exact match in colour for your eyes.'

'Oh…'

'Yes…oh…' Lucien echoed softly as he looked into, held captive, those beautiful cobalt blue eyes. 'Do you like it?' he prompted huskily as she folded back the tissue paper and down looked at the blouse he had chosen for her.

Did Thia *like* it?

Even if she hadn't this blouse would have been special to her, because Lucien had picked it out for her personally. As it was, Thia had never seen or touched such a beautiful blouse before. The colour indeed a perfect match for her eyes, and the material softer, silkier, than anything else she had ever owned.

Tears stung her eyes as she looked up. 'It's beautiful, Lucien,' she breathed softly. 'Far too expensive, of course. But don't worry,' she added as a frown reappeared between his eyes, 'I'm not going to insult you by refusing to accept it!'

'Good, because it certainly isn't going back to the store, and it really isn't my size or colour.'

'Very funny.' Thia picked up the blouse carefully, not sure when she would ever find the opportunity to wear something so beautiful—and expensive!—but loving it anyway. 'I—there appears to be something else in the box…' she breathed softly as she realised the blouse had been hiding the fact that there was another article wrapped in tissue beneath it. 'Lucien?' She looked up at him uncertainly.

'Ah. Yes.' He looked less than his usual confident self as he gave a self-conscious grimace. 'That's for you to wear this evening—unless you already have something you would prefer. You looked lovely in the gown you were wearing the evening we met, for example, although you might feel happier wearing something new.'

Thia eyed him warily. 'And where am I going this evening that I would need to wear something new?'

'To a charity ball.' He stood up restlessly, instantly dwarfing the room—and Thia—with the sheer power of his personality. 'With me. It's the reason I'm dressed like this.' He indicated his formal evening clothes.

'A charity ball...?' Thia echoed softly.

He nodded. 'I thought we could spend a couple of hours at the ball and then leave when you've had enough.'

She looked at him sharply. 'Is this because of what I said to you last night?'

He grimaced. 'You said a lot of things to me last night, Cyn.'

Yes, she had—and quite a lot of them had been insulting. Most especially the part where she had suggested Lucien was hiding her away because he didn't want to be seen in public with a waitress student from London... 'There's really no need for you to do this, Lucien. I was out of line, saying what I did, and I apologise for misjudging you—'

'You apologised for that last night,' he dismissed briskly. 'Tonight we're going out to a charity ball. Most, if not all of New York society will be there too.' Lucien met her gaze unblinkingly.

'Exactly how much per ticket is this charity ball?' Thia

had seen several of these glittering affairs televised, and knew that they cost thousands of dollars to attend.

'What the hell does that have to do with—?'

'Please, Lucien.'

His mouth thinned. 'Ten thousand dollars.'

'For *both*?' she squeaked.

'Per ticket.'

'Ten thous…?' Thia couldn't even finish the sentence—could only gape at him.

He shrugged. 'The proceeds from the evening go towards the care of abused children.'

Even so… Ten thousand dollars a ticket! It was—'I can't allow you to spend that sort of money on me.' She gave a determined shake of her head.

'It isn't for you. It's for abused children. And I've already bought the tickets, whether we attend or not, so why not use them?'

'Because—because I—' She gave a pained wince. 'Why don't you just take whoever you were originally going to take?'

'I bought the extra ticket today, Cyn. You *are* the person I was originally going to take.' His gaze was compelling in its intensity.

Maybe so, but that didn't mean Thia had to go to the charity ball with him.

Did it…?

CHAPTER TWELVE

'THAT WASN'T SO bad, was it…?' Lucien turned to look at Cyn as the two of them sat in the back of the limousine, driven by Paul, with Dex seated beside him, and they left the charity ball shortly before midnight.

'It wasn't bad at all. Everyone was so…nice.' She looked at him from beneath silky dark lashes.

'They can be.' Lucien nodded.

'It probably helped that I was being escorted by the richest and most powerful man in New York!'

'I didn't notice any pitying glances being directed my way,' he teased huskily.

'If there were, they were kept well hidden!'

Lucien reached across the distance between them to lift up one of her hands before intertwining his fingers with hers—ivory and bronze. 'Will you come up to my apartment for a nightcap when we get back to the hotel?' he invited gruffly.

Thia gave him a shy glance in the dimly lit confines of the back of the limousine. The privacy partition was up between them and the front of the car. To her surprise, she had enjoyed the evening much more than she had thought she would, meeting so many more people than just the celebrity side of New York society. Such was the force of

Lucien's personality that all of them had accepted her place at his side without so much as a raised eyebrow.

The only moment of awkwardness for Thia had been when they had spoken briefly to Felix and Simone Carew. The older woman had avoided meeting Thia's gaze—that fact alone telling Thia that Jonathan must have spoken to the actress today, and that Simone knew Thia now knew about the two of them.

Lucien's manner had been extremely cool towards the other woman, and his arm had stayed possessively about Thia's waist as he spoke exclusively to Felix, before making their excuses so that he could introduce Thia to some friends of his across the room. That arm had remained firmly about her waist for the rest of the evening.

She had even worn the gown Lucien had selected and bought for her. A bright red figure-hugging, ankle-length dress that left her shoulders and the swell of her breasts bare. And she had secured the darkness of her hair at her crown. The appreciation in Lucien's eyes when she'd rejoined him in the sitting room of her suite had been enough to tell her that he approved of her appearance.

She moistened her lips with the tip of her tongue now. 'Is that a good idea?'

His fingers tightened about hers. 'We can go to your suite if you would prefer it?'

'I've had a lovely time this evening, Lucien, but—'

'This sounds suspiciously like a brush-off to me.' He had tensed beside her.

Thia gave a shake of her head. 'I'm leaving in the morning, Lucien. Let's not make things complicated.'

His eyes glowed in the dim light. 'What if I want to complicate the hell out of things?'

She smiled sadly. 'We both know that isn't a good idea. I'm…what I am, and you're…what you are.'

'And didn't tonight prove to you that I don't give a damn about the waitress/student/billionaire/businessman thing?'

Thia chuckled huskily. 'The difference between us I was referring to was actually the virgin and the man of experience thing!'

'Ah.'

'Yes—*ah*. A difference that horrified you last night,' she reminded him huskily.

'It didn't horrify me. I was just surprised,' he amended impatiently. 'But I'm over the surprise now, and—'

'And you want to continue where we left off last night?' Thia arched her brows.

'You know, Cyn, when—if—I've ever thought of proposing marriage to a woman, I certainly didn't envisage it would be in the back of a car. Even if that car *is* a limousine! But if that's how it has to be, then I guess—'

'Did you say you're proposing marriage…?' Thia turned fully on the leather seat to look at him with wide disbelieving eyes. Lucien couldn't really mean he was proposing marriage to *her*!

'Well, no,' he answered predictably. 'Because I haven't actually got around to asking you yet,' he added dryly. 'I believe I need to get down on one knee for that, and although the back of this car is plenty big enough I think you would prefer that Paul and Dex didn't make their own assumptions as to exactly what I'm doing when I drop down onto my knees in front of you!'

Thia felt the warm rush of colour that heated her cheeks just at the thought of what the other two men might think about seeing their employer falling to his knees in the back of the car.

She snatched her hand out of his. 'Stop teasing me, Lucien— What are you doing?' she gasped as he moved down onto his knees in front of her after all, before taking both of her hands in his. 'Lucien!'

What *was* he doing?

How the hell did Lucien know? He was still travelling that untrodden path with no signs or indications to guide him.

Thia had obviously enjoyed herself this evening, and he could only hope part of that enjoyment had been his own company.

She looked so beautiful tonight Lucien hadn't been able to take his eyes off her. The fact that other men had also looked at her covetously had been enough for Lucien to keep his arm possessively about her waist all evening, rather than just accepting the glances of admiration his dates usually merited. He didn't want any other man admiring Thia but him.

He knew it was probably too soon for Cyn. That the two of them had only known each other a couple of days. But what a couple of days they had been!

That first evening, when he had literally looked across a crowded room and seen her for the first time, she'd been so beautiful she had taken his breath away. And he had felt as if she had punched him in the chest later on, when she'd preferred to walk away from him, in the middle of a crowded New York street, rather than accompany him to Steele Heights Hotel. The following morning, when he had seen the disreputable hotel where she had spent the night, he'd actually had palpitations! And when she had arrived at his office later that afternoon, wearing that cropped pink T-shirt and those figure-hugging low-rider denims, his physical reaction had been so wonderfully different...!

Cooking dinner last night with Cyn had been fun, and their conversation stimulating, while at the same time Lucien had felt more comfortable, more at ease in her company than he had ever been before. And she had looked so cute in his over-sized T-shirt. He had even enjoyed shopping for the blouse and gown for her earlier today. As for making love with her last night... How Cyn had responded, the way she had given herself to him totally, only for him to learn later that she was inexperienced, an innocent, had literally brought him to his knees.

And he had been on his knees ever since.

He was on his knees again now...

'I'm really not insane, Cyn.' His hands tightened about hers as he looked up intently into her beautiful pale face. 'I am, however, currently shaking in those handmade Italian leather shoes you mentioned at our first meeting,' he admitted ruefully.

She blinked. 'Why?'

'I've never proposed to a woman before, and the thought of having you refuse is enough to make any man shake.'

Cyn gave a pained frown. 'I don't—this is just—'

'Too soon? Too sudden? I know all that, Cyn.' He grimaced. 'I've been telling myself the same thing all day. But none of it changes the fact that I've fallen in love with you—that the thought of you going back to London tomorrow, of never seeing you again, is unacceptable to me. I don't just love you, Cyn, I adore you. I love your spirit, your teasing, your intelligence, your kindness, your loyalty, the way you give the whole of yourself, no matter what the situation. I had no idea how empty my life and heart were until I met you, but you've filled both of them in a way I could never have imagined. In a way I never want to live without,' he added huskily.

Thia stared at him incredulously. Had Lucien just said—? Had he really just told her that he loved her? He adored her?

Maybe she was the one who was insane—because he really couldn't have said those things. Not to *her*. Not Lucien Steele, American zillionaire, the richest and most powerful man in New York.

And yet there he was, on his knees in front of her, her hands held tightly in his as he gazed up at her with such a look of love Thia thought her heart had actually stuttered and then stilled in her chest.

'Hey, look…you don't have to answer me now.' He'd obviously mistaken her look of disbelief for one of panic. 'There's no rush. I realise that it's too much for me to expect you to know if you'll ever feel the same way about me, but we can spend as long as you like getting to know each other better. You'll want to go back to London anyway, to finish your degree. I'll buy an apartment there, or maybe a house, so that we can spend as much time together as you have free, and then, after a few months, if you—'

'Yes.'

'If you still don't think you could ever love me the way I love you, then I'll—'

'Yes.'

'I'll somehow have to learn to accept it, to live with that. I won't like it, but—'

'I said *yes,* Lucien.' Thia squeezed his hands to pull him up so that she could look directly into his face. 'I said yes, Lucien…' she repeated softly as he returned her gaze questioningly.

'Yes, what...?'

Her breath caught in her throat, tears stinging the backs of her eyes. But they were tears of happiness. Lucien loved her. He really loved her. He knew that she had struggled to finance her degree and understood she was determined to finish it. He was going to buy a home in London so that he could be close to her while she did so. He had asked her to *marry* him!

Yes, it was too soon.

For other people.

Not for Lucien and Thia.

Because they were a result of their past—people who had both lost the security of their parents in different ways, at a vulnerable time in their lives. As a result they were two people who didn't love or trust easily—and the fact that they had fallen in love with each other surely had to be fate's reward for all those previous years of loneliness.

Thia slid forward on the leather seat and then down onto her knees in the carpeted footwell beside him. 'I said yes, Lucien.' She raised her hands to cup each side of his beloved and handsome face. 'Yes, I love you, too. Yes, I'll marry you. Tomorrow, if you like.'

'I— But—'

'Or maybe we can wait a while, if that's too soon for you. Lucien!' She gasped as he pulled her tightly against him before his mouth claimed hers hungrily.

'I'll take that as a yes to us getting married, then,' Lucien murmured a long time later, when the two of them were cuddled up together on one of the sofas in the sitting room of his penthouse apartment at Steele Heights, with only a side lamp to illuminate the room.

Cyn stirred beside him. 'I still think you're mean to make me wait for you until our wedding night.'

'Shouldn't that be my line?' he came back indulgently, more relaxed, happier than he had ever been in his life before. How could he feel any other way when he had the woman he loved beside him?

'It should, yes.' She pouted up at him. 'But you're the one who's gone all "not until we're married" on me.'

Lucien chuckled softly, trailing her loosened hair like midnight silk over his fingers. 'That doesn't mean we can't...*be* together before then. I would just prefer that we left things the way they are for now. I can't wait to see you walk down the aisle to me, all dressed in white and all the time knowing that I'm going to undress you later that night and make love to you for the first time.'

When he put it like that...

Cyn moved up on her elbow to look down at him, loving how relaxed Lucien looked, how *loved* he looked. 'What do you mean, we can *be* together before then...?'

His mouth quirked seductively. 'You enjoyed what we did last night, didn't you?'

'Oh, yes.' Her cheeks grew hot at the memory of their lovemaking.

'Would you like to repeat it tonight?'

'That depends...'

His smile faded to a frown. 'On what?'

Thia gave a rueful smile. 'On whether or not you'll allow me to...reciprocate. You'll have to show me how, of course, but I'm sure I'll quickly get the hang of it—'

'Dear God...!' Lucien gave a pained groan and closed his eyes briefly, before opening them again, those same eyes narrowing as he saw how mischievously she returned his gaze. 'You're teasing me again!' he realised self-derisively.

'Only partly.' She wrinkled her nose at him. 'I know the mechanics, of course, but I'm guessing that doesn't mean a whole lot when it comes to the real thing?'

'Let's go and see for ourselves, shall we…?' Lucien stood up, bending down to lift her up into his arms and cradling her tenderly against his chest.

Thia wrapped her arms about his shoulders and gazed up at him adoringly. 'I could get used to this.'

'I very much hope that you do—because I intend spoiling and petting you for the rest of your life.' That same love glowed in Lucien's eyes as he looked down at her. 'I love you very much, Cynthia Hammond. Thank you for coming into my life.'

Her lips trembled with emotion. 'I love *you* very much, Lucien Steele. Thank *you* for coming into my life.'

It was everything.

Now.

Tomorrow.

Always.

* * * * *

RAPUNZEL IN NEW YORK

NIKKI LOGAN

To Carol and Marlon:
I hope my Viktoria is the kind of woman
you'd have wanted yours to grow into.

Nikki Logan lives next to a string of protected wetlands in Western Australia, with her long suffering partner and a menagerie of furred, feathered and scaly mates. She studied film and theatre at university, and worked for years in advertising and film distribution before finally settling down in the wildlife industry. Her romance with nature goes way back, and she considers her life charmed, given she works with wildlife by day and writes fiction by night—the perfect way to combine her two loves. Nikki believes that the passion and risk of falling in love are perfectly mirrored in the danger and beauty of wild places. Every romance she writes contains an element of nature, and if readers catch a waft of rich earth or the spray of wild ocean between the pages she knows her job is done. Visit Nikki online at www.nikkilogan.com.au

CHAPTER ONE

"YOU'D better get up here, Nathan. There's a woman about to jump from your building."

Two sentences.

That's all it took to tear Nathan Archer away from his Columbus Circle office and send him racing uptown. Ironic that the A-line was quicker than a cab or even his driver could get him up to Morningside, but the subway spilled him out just one block from the West 126th Street building he'd grown up in. Grown old in. Well before his time.

He pushed through the gathered throng, shaking his head at the impatient crowd. Was there a whole population of people who hovered in alleys and bars just waiting for some poor individual to be nudged too far in life? To climb out onto a bridge or a rooftop?

Or a ledge.

He followed their collective gaze upward. Sure enough, there she was. Not exactly preparing for a swan dive; more crouched than standing. She looked young, though it was hard to tell from this distance.

She was staring at the sky with an intensity strong enough to render her completely oblivious to the crowd gathering below. He lifted his eyes to the popcorn clouds. Was she praying? Or was she just in her own tormented world?

"The crisis team is mobilizing," a nearby cop said, turning back to stare uselessly up to the tenth floor. "ETA twenty minutes."

Twenty minutes? She'd already been out there at least the quarter hour it had taken him to get uptown. The chances of her lasting another twenty?

Not high.

He glanced around at the many spectators who were doing exactly nothing to rectify the situation and swallowed a groan. There was a reason he was more of a behind-the-scenes kind of guy. Behind the scenes had served him well his whole life. You got a lot done when you weren't wasting time as the center of attention. He paid people to do the limelight thing.

Unfortunately, none of them were here.

He was.

Nathan looked back up at the looming building and the woman perched precariously on it. Hadn't these old walls contained enough misery?

He muttered a curse and his legs started moving. Had nobody thought of doing this sooner? He pushed past a gaggle of onlookers and headed toward the building, counting windows as he went. It took him three minutes to get into his own building and up to the eighth floor, and he passed three residents on the stairs up to the tenth—they had no clue about the drama unfolding in their own building. If they saw it on the news tonight they'd be kicking themselves they missed it. Not that it was making the news tonight, or any night while he still breathed. His development didn't need the bad press. He hadn't worked on it all this time only to have it turned upside down by a woman with a blown psychiatric fuse.

Nate burst through the stairwell door and turned left, counting the windows he knew to be on the outside of the building. *Nine...ten...eleven...*On twelve, he paused for only a second before delivering a strategic kick right at the weak point in the door of apartment 10B. As fragile as the rest of the century old building, it exploded inwards in a shower of splinters.

Inside, the apartment was neat and carefully decorated but

small enough that he was able to check all the five rooms in less than thirty seconds, even with a limp from the jar that had just about snapped his ankle. Three rooms had outside windows that were sealed tight—safety measures. But, apparently back at the turn of the twentieth century some architect had considered that only grown men needed to be saved from themselves, because every apartment had one more window—small and awkwardly positioned above the toilet cistern, but just big enough for a slight woman to wiggle through. Or a young boy.

He knew that from experience.

This one stood wide open, its tasteful lemon curtains blowing gently in the breeze, providing access onto 10B's sheltered ledge.

Nathan's heart hammered from way more than the urgent sprint up two flights of stairs. He took a deep, tense breath, climbed onto the closed lid of the toilet and peered out the window, sickeningly prepared to find nothing but pigeon droppings and a swirl of air where a woman had just been.

But she was still out there, her back to him as she stretched out on the ledge on all fours, giving him a great view of her denim-clad behind...

...and the tangle of ropes and rigging that fixed her more than securely to the ledge.

Frustrated fury bubbled up deep inside. Of all the stupid-ass, time-wasting stunts... He boosted himself up and half through the window and barked to her butt, "Honey, you'd better be planning to jump, or I'm going to throw you off here myself."

Viktoria Morfitt spun so fast she nearly lost her careful balance on the ledge. Her reflexes were dulled through lack of use, but her muscle memory was still entirely intact, and it choreographed her muscles now to brace her more securely on the narrow stone shelf. Adrenaline pulsed through her bloodstream and her lungs sucked in an ache of cold air and then expelled it on a ripe curse as she spotted the man wedged in her bathroom window glaring at her like a maniac. His voice had drawn her attention, but his words whooshed away on the relentless New York sounds coming up from Morningside's streets.

What the—? She shuffled backward as far as the ledge allowed and knocked against the peregrine nest box she'd just been installing.

The stranger lurched farther forward, half hanging out the window, enormous hands stretched out toward her, and spoke more clearly. More slowly. "Easy, honey. Just a joke. How about you come back inside now?"

She wasn't fooled by those treacle tones for one moment. Or the intense eyes. Bad guys never turned up at your doorstep badly scarred, carrying violin cases and talking like Robert deNiro. They turned up like this: nice shirt, open collar, careless hair and designer stubble. Big, well-manicured hands. Good-looking. Exactly the sort of guy you'd think was okay to let inside your apartment.

Except that he'd already let himself in.

For one crazy second Tori considered leaping off the ledge. Her intruder could help himself to her stuff—whatever he wanted—and she could lower herself down to Barney's ledge. He'd be home for sure and his bathroom window was perpetually open so he could smoke out of it. Her hand slipped to the titanium fixings at her pelvis. Her rigging would hold. It always did.

A sharp pain gnawed deep and low. *Almost always.*

She raised her voice instead, hoping to alert a neighbour. "How about you get the heck out of my apartment!" Tension thumped out of her in waves that translated into quavers in her voice. Could he tell?

He reached forward again. "Look—"

Tori slid hard up against the corner of the building, clambering around the nest box. Dammit, any farther and she'd knock it off the ledge and have to start all over again. Well, that and possibly kill someone walking below…

She glanced easily over the ledge and met the intense stares of thirty or so passersby and a couple of NYPD officers. "Hey!"

she yelled down to the cops. "Get up here! There's a burglar in my apartment—10B!"

The stranger surged through the window and made a grab for her foot. She kicked it away, then stole a moment to glance back down. Two of the cops were running towards her building.

Heat poured off the contemptuous look he shot at her. "You know what? I have a meeting to get back to. So either go ahead and jump or get the hell back in here." With that, he disappeared back into her apartment.

Jump? She glanced back down at the crowd below, their expectant faces all peering up. *At her.*

Oh…no!

Heat surged up her throat. Someone must have called her in as a jumper when she was out on the ledge. *He* thought she was a jumper. But while most of them stood below waiting for the aerial show, only one had had the nerve to race up here and actually try to help her.

He deserved points for that.

"Wait!"

She scrabbled toward the now-vacant window and crouched to look inside. He was taller than he looked when he was squashed through her tiny window—broader, too—and he completely filled the doorway to her bathroom. Self-preservation made her pause. Him being good-looking didn't change the fact he was a stranger. And she wasn't much on strangers.

Tori peered in at him. "I'll come in when you're not there."

He rolled his eyes, then found hers again. "Fine. I'll be in the hall."

Then he was gone.

She swiveled on her bottom and slid her legs quickly through the tiny window, stretching down until her feet hit the toilet lid. Then she unclipped her brace-line with the ease of years of practice, clenched her abs, and brought her torso through in a twist that would have been right at home in Cirque du Soleil.

As good as his word, he'd moved out into the very public hallway. But between them lay a forest of timber shards.

"You kicked in my *door*?" She hit a pitch she usually heard only from the peregrine falcons that circled her building looking for somewhere to raise their chicks.

A frustrated breath shot from between his thin lips. "Apologies for assuming you were about to die."

He didn't look the slightest bit apologetic, but he did look stunningly well-dressed and gorgeous, despite the aloof arch of his eyebrows. Just then two uniformed officers exploded through the fire-escape doors and bolted toward them.

"He kicked in my door!" Tori repeated for their benefit.

Taller than either of the cops, he turned toward them easily, unconcerned. "Officers—"

They hit him like a subway car, slamming his considerable bulk up against the wall and forcing him into a frisk position. He winced at the discomfort and then squeezed his head sideways so that he could glare straight into her flared eyes.

Guilt gnawed wildly. He hadn't actually hurt her. Or even tried to.

He simmered while they roughly frisked him up and down, relieving him of his phone and wallet and tossing them roughly to the ground. He stared at her the whole time, as though this was her fault and not his. But that molten gaze was even more unsettling close up and so she bent to retrieve his property and busied herself dusting them carefully off while the police pressed his face to the wall.

"What are you doing here?" one asked.

"Same thing you are. Checking on a jumper."

"That's our job, sir," the second cop volunteered as he finished searching the stranger's pockets.

The man looked back over his shoulder at the first officer, his hands still carefully pressed out to both sides. "Didn't look like it was going to happen before nightfall."

"Protocols," the first cop muttered tightly, a flush rushing up his thick neck.

They shoved him back into the wall for good measure and Tori winced on his behalf. Okay, this had gone far enough.

"Are you responsible for this?" The taller cop spoke before she could, leaning around to have a good look at the gaping entrance to her apartment where the door hung from just one ancient, struggling hinge. "This is damage to private property."

"Actually I think you'll find it's my property," the man gritted out.

All three faces swiveled back to him. "Excuse me?" the taller cop asked.

The man slowly turned, his hands still in clear view. "My name is Nathan Archer. I own this building." He nodded at the wallet that Tori still held. "My identification's in there."

All sympathy for him vanished between breaths. "*You're* our landlord?" She held his property out numbly.

One of the officers pulled the man's driver's license from the wallet and confirmed his identification. "This confirms your name but not your ownership of this building."

He looked at Tori. "Who do you pay rent to?"

A money-hungry, capitalist corporate shark. Tori narrowed her eyes. "Sanmore Holdings."

The stranger looked back at the cop holding his wallet. "Back compartment."

The cop pulled out a crisp white business card. "Nathan Archer, Chief Executive, Sanmore Holdings."

The cops immediately eased their hold on him and he straightened.

Nathan Archer. The man responsible for the state of her building. Probably living below fifty-ninth himself, and way too busy and important to worry about elevators not working or torn carpet under their feet. She played the only card she had left and pleaded to the rapidly-losing-interest police.

"It's still my door. I must have rights?"

The second cop looked her over lazily while his partner answered for him. "I guess you could get him for trespass."

Archer immediately transferred the full force of his glare

onto the second officer. Insanely, Tori missed the searing ma-
levolence the moment it left her.

"Yes! Trespass. I didn't invite him in." She smiled trium-
phantly at her landlord for good measure.

That brought his eyes back to hers and her chest tightened
up fractionally.

"I was saving your life."

She shoved her hands on her hips and stood her ground. "My
life was just fine, thank you. I was fully rigged up."

"Not obvious from the street. Or from this side of the *locked*
door," he added pointedly, his blue, blue eyes simmering but no
longer furious. Not exactly. They flicked, lightning-fast, from
her head to her toes and back again, and the simmer morphed
into something a lot closer to interest—*sexual* interest. Breath
clogged her throat as he blazed his intensity in her direction,
every bit as naturally forceful as Niagara Falls.

In that moment the two cops ceased to exist.

It didn't help that a perky inner voice kept whispering over
her shoulder, seducing her with reason, weaving amongst the
subtle waves of his expensive scent and reminding her that he
had been trying to help. She didn't want to be seduced by any
part of this man. At all.

She wanted to be mad at him.

She straightened to her full height, shook off her conscience
and spoke slowly, in case one of those thumps his head had
taken at the hands of the local constabulary had dented his
greedy, corporate brain. "You broke my door!"

"I'll buy you a new door," he said, calm and completely
infuriating.

The police officers looked between them, bemused.

Tori glared up at him. "While you're buying stuff, how about
a new washer for the ancient laundry? Or a door buzzer that
works so we can quit calling messages up the stairwell."

The heat in his gaze swirled around her. He straightened and
narrowed his eyes. "Nothing in this building is below code."

"Nothing in this building is particularly above it, either.

You do just enough to make sure you meet the tenancy act. We have heat and water and electrics that aren't falling out of the ceiling, but that's about it. The elevator doesn't even go all the way to the top floor."

"It never has."

"So that's a good enough reason not to fix it now? The woman in 12C is eighty years old. She shouldn't be hiking it up four flights of stairs. And the fire code—"

His eyes glittered. "The fire code specifies that you use the stairs in an emergency. They work fine. I know because I just ran up them to save your life!"

She stepped closer, her chest heaving and dragged her eyes off his lips. This close she could practically feel the furnace of his anger. "Not if you're an octogenarian!"

"Then she should take an apartment on one of the lower floors."

Tall as he was, he had to lean down toward her to get in her face. It caused a riot in her pulse. She lifted her chin and leaned toward him. "Those apartments are full of *other* old people—"

The shorter cop growled behind them. "Would you two like some privacy? Or maybe a room?"

Tori snapped around to look at the cop and then back to the man in front of her. Sure enough, she was standing dangerously close to Nathan Archer and the hallway fairly sparkled with the live current swirling around the two of them.

"I have a room," she grumbled to the officer, though her eyes stayed on the tallest man in the hallway. "I just don't have a door."

Archer's deep voice rumbled through tight lips. A rich man's lips. Though she did wonder what they would look like if he smiled.

"I'll have that fixed by dinnertime."

Too bad if she wanted to take a nap or…relax…or something before then! "So you do have a maintenance team at your disposal. You wouldn't know it from the general condition of the building—"

"There you go," one officer cut in loudly. "Complete restitution. I think we're done here."

She spun back to him. "We're not done. What about the trespass?" The officer looked apologetically at Archer.

Oh, please... "Seriously? One waft of a fancy business card and now the rich guy is calling the shots?"

All three of them looked at her as if she was mad. Pretty much where she imagined they'd started an hour ago, back when she was up the ledge. "I want him charged with trespass. He entered my apartment without my permission."

Archer tried again. "Come on. I was trying to save your life."

She tossed her hair back. "Tell that to the judge."

"I guess I'll have to."

One officer reluctantly took her details while the other spoke quietly to Archer a few meters down the hall. He smiled while the cop shook his head and chuckled.

She wedged her hands to her hips again and spoke loudly. "When you're completely done with the testosterone bonding..."

Her cop took a deep breath and turned to the taller man. "You have the right to remain silent. Anything you say..."

As the Miranda unfolded, Tori handed Archer his cell phone and tried hard not to meet his eyes. She had a way of losing focus when she did that. But her fingers touched his as he wrapped them around his BlackBerry and she flinched away from the intimate brush of skin on skin.

Her pulse stumbled.

"...if you cannot afford an attorney..."

As if. He probably surrounded himself with attorneys. His fine white business shirt looked like it cost more than he spent on this building in a year.

The cops walked Archer back toward the stairs, finishing up their legal responsibilities. At some point someone decided handcuffs were overkill—*shame*—but Archer limped obediently between them anyway, speaking quietly into his phone and only half listening as his rights were fully enumerated.

As the cops sandwiched him through the door to the stairwell, he glanced back at her, a lock of dark hair falling across his forehead between those Hollywood eyes. He didn't look the slightest bit disturbed by the threat of legal action. For some reason, that only made her madder.

How often did this guy get arrested?

"Better save that single phone call they'll give you in lockup," she yelled down the hall to them. "You're going to need it to call someone about my door!"

CHAPTER TWO

"Your Honor—"

"Save it, Mr. Archer," the judge said, "I've made my ruling. I recognise that you meant well in going to the assistance of the plaintiff, however, the fact remains that you broke into her apartment and did material damage to her door and lock—"

"Which I fixed…"

The judge raised one hand and silenced him. "And that even though it was technically your own property, Ms Morfitt is afforded some protection under New York's Tenancy Protection Act, which makes her suit of trespass reasonable."

"If petty," Nate murmured. His attorney, business partner and best friend, Dean, counseled him to hold his tongue. Probably just as well or he'd end up behind bars for contempt. This whole thing was a ridiculous waste of his time—time that could have been better spent at his desk earning a bunch of zeroes for his company. All over a broken door that had been fixed the same day. If all his building's tenants were from the same planet as Viktoria Morfitt he'd be happy to see the back of them when he developed the site.

"I was trying to help her," he said flatly, for the hundredth time. No one but him seemed to care.

"Your file indicates that you specialize in Information Technology, is that correct?" the judge asked. She said that as though he was some kind of help-desk operator instead of the founder of one of the most successful young IT companies on the east coast.

Dean spoke just as Nate was about to educate her. "That is correct, Your Honor."

The judge didn't take her eyes off Nate's. Thinking. Plotting. "I'm going to commute your sentence, Mr. Archer, so that it doesn't haunt your record for the rest of your life. One hundred hours of community service to be undertaken within thirty days."

"Community service? Do you know what one hundred hours of my time *costs*?"

Dean swooped in to stop him saying more. "My client would be willing to pay financial compensation in lieu, Your Honor."

Willing was a stretch but he'd go with it.

The judge looked at Nate archly, and he stared solidly back at her. Then she dragged her eyes to his left. "No doubt, Counselor, but that's not on the table. The purpose of a service order is to give the defendant time to reflect. To learn. Not to make it all go away with the sweep of their assistant's pen." Nate could practically feel the order doubling in length. Or severity. She made some notes on the documentation in front of her, eyes narrowed. "Mr. Archer, I'm going to recommend you undertake your service on behalf of the plaintiff."

His stomach lurched. *Note to self: never upset a district judge.* "Are you serious?"

"Nate—" Dean just about choked in his haste to silence him, but then changed tack as the judge leaned as far forward as she could possibly go without tumbling from her lofty perch. "Thank you, Your Honor. We'll see that it happens."

But Nate spread his hands wide and tried one more time. "I was trying to help her, judge."

Dean's hand slid onto his forearm and gripped it hard. The judge's lips drew even tighter. "Which is why it's not a two-hundred-hour order, Mr. Archer. Counselor, please explain to your client that this is a judicial sentence, not a Wall Street negotiation."

Nate ignored that. "But what will I do for her?"

"Help her with her laundry? I really don't care. My order is set." She eyed the man by Nate's side. "Is that clear, Counselor?"

"It is, Your Honor, thank you." Dean whispered furiously in Nate's ear that a commuted service order was as good as invisible on his record.

"Easy for you to say," Nate growled. "That's not one hundred hours of *your* executive time." Spent in a building he preferred not to even think about.

The judge with super hearing lifted one arch brow. "I think you'll find that my time is just as valuable as yours, Mr. Archer, and you've taken up quite enough of it. Next!"

The gavel came down on any hope of someone seeing reason in all this lunacy.

Ten minutes later it was all over; Nate and Dean trod down the marble stairs of the justice building and shook hands. From an attorney's perspective it was a good outcome, but the idea of not only spending time in that building—with *her*...

Viktoria Morfitt's suit for trespass was ridiculous and everyone knew it. The cops. The judge. Even the woman herself, judging by the delicate little lines that had formed between her brows as the cops had escorted him from his own building.

But he'd spooked her out on the ledge and then made the tactical error of letting her know he was her landlord. If he'd kept his trap shut she probably would have let him off with the promise of restitution for the door. But no...He'd played the rare *do-you-know-who-I-am?* card, and she'd taken her first opportunity to let him know exactly what she thought about his building management.

Not very much.

And now he had a hundred hours of community service to think about how he might have done things differently.

"There's a morning we'll never get back," Dean grumbled

comfortably. "But don't worry about it, I'll get appeal paper-work straight off. Though you might have to do a few hours before that gets processed."

"When am I supposed to start this farce?"

"The judge's decree will be lodged after two-thirty today, but, reasonably, tomorrow will be fine. That'll give the public defender time to alert your jumper to the order."

"I'm sure she'll be thrilled."

"I'm sure she won't," his friend said, turning and trotting down the steps with a chuckle. "But the Archer charm hasn't failed you yet."

The fact that was true didn't really make things any better. One hundred hours with a human porcupine in a building he could barely stomach.

Great.

Tori filled her lungs behind her brand-new door and composed herself. The judge must have been having a badly hormonal day to task someone like Nathan Archer with community service. Either that or his smug confidence had got up Her Honor's nose as much as it had irritated *her* last week. Not hard to imagine.

Now or never… She pulled the door nice and wide and made a show of leaning on it. Showcasing it. "Mr. Archer."

The breath closest to her lips froze in its tracks at the sight of him filling her doorway and all her other breaths jammed up behind it in an oxygen pile-up.

Fortunately, he didn't notice as his blue eyes examined the door critically. "Could they have found anything less suitable?"

She looked at the modern, perfect door which was so out of place in a 1901 building. "I assumed you picked it specifically. But it locks, so I'm happy."

She'd forgotten how those eyes *really* felt when they rested on her. Like twin embers from a fire alighting on her skin.

Warm at first touch, but smoldering to an uncomfortable burn the longer they lingered.

"Well, one of us is, at least," he mumbled.

She couldn't stop the irritated sigh that escaped her. "I didn't ask for this community service, Mr. Archer. I'm no more thrilled than you are." The last thing she wanted was to be forced into the company of such a disagreeable stranger, with the uncomfortable responsibility of tasking him with chores.

Silence fell, and the only sound to interrupt it was 10A's television blaring out late afternoon *Sesame Street*.

He stared at her until finally saying, "May I come in?"

Heat broiled just below her collar. Leaving him standing in the hall... She stood back and let all six-foot-three of him into her home. "So how does this work?"

He shrugged those massive shoulders. "Search me, this is my first offence."

Tori winced, knowing that—truthfully—he'd done nothing more than try to help her. But one hundred hours was a small price to pay for how he'd neglected the building they both stood in. "Hey, service orders are the latest celebrity accessory. You can't buy that kind of street cred."

He turned and shot her a dark look from under perfectly manicured brows. Every glare he used was a glare wasted. She really didn't care whether or not he was happy. He was only her landlord.

She took his coat and turned to hang it on the back of her front door before remembering her new one didn't have a hook. She detoured via the sofa to drape it over the back. The contrast between the expensive fabric of his coat and the aged upholstery of her sofa couldn't have been more marked.

"Something's been bothering me," he said, turning those blue eyes on her. "About last week."

Only one thing? Quite a lot had been bothering her about it. Her reaction to his closeness not the least.

"What were you doing out on that ledge?" he continued.

"Not jumping."

"So I gathered."

She stared at him and then crossed to the large photo album on the coffee table. She spun it in his direction and flipped it open. "These are Wilma and Fred."

He leaned down to look at the range of photographs artfully displayed on the page. "Hawks?"

"Peregrine falcons. They live wild in this area."

Deep blue eyes lifted to hers. "And…?"

"And I was installing a nest box for them."

He blinked at her. "Out on the ledge?"

She clenched her teeth to avoid rolling her eyes. "I tried it in here, but it just didn't do as well." *Idiot.*

Archer grunted and Tori's arms stole round her midsection while he flicked through the various images in her album.

"These are good," he finally said. "Who took them?"

"I did."

His head came up. "Where from?"

She pulled back the breezy curtain from her living-room window to reveal spotless glass. "There's another window in the bedroom. Sometimes I use the roof. Mostly the ledge."

"So that wasn't your first dangerous foray out there?"

"It's not dangerous. I'm tethered at all times."

He lifted aristocratic eyebrows. "To a century-old building?"

A century-old building that's crumbling around you. He might as well have said it. It was perfectly evident to anyone who cared to look. The neglect wouldn't fly in Morningside proper, but being right on the border of West Harlem, he was getting away with it. Of course he was. Money talked around here.

"I pick the strongest point I can to fix to," she said.

He looked at the pictures again. "You must have some great equipment."

She shrugged. Let him believe that it was the camera that took the photo, not the person behind it. "I've always enjoyed wildlife photography." More than just enjoyed. She'd been on track to make a career out of it back when she'd graduated.

He reached the back pages of the album. "These ones weren't taken out your window." He flipped it her way and her heart gave a little lurch. An aerie with a stunning mountain vista stretching out in all directions behind it. An eagle in flight, its full wings spread three meters wide. Both taken from high points.

Really, *really* high points.

"I took those in the Appalachians and Cascades," she said, tightly, but then she forced the topic back to her city peregrines before he could ask any more questions. As far as she knew, this court order didn't come with the requirement for full disclosure about her past.

"Fred and Wilma turned up in our skies about three months ago, and then about four weeks ago they started visiting this building more and more. I made them a nest box for the coming breeding season so they don't have to perch precariously on a transformer or bridge or something."

So she could have a little bit of her old life here in her new one.

"Hawks..." He closed the album carefully and placed it gently back on the coffee table. Then he stood there not saying a word. Just thinking.

"So..." She cleared her throat. "Should we talk about how this is going to work? What you can do here for one hundred hours?"

His eyes bored into her and triggered a temperature spike. "I sense you've been giving it some thought?"

She crossed to the kitchen and took up the sheet of notepaper she'd prepared. "I made a list."

His lips twisted. "Really—of what?"

"Of all the things wrong with the building. Things that you can fix in one hundred hours."

The laundry. The elevator. The floors. The buzzer...

His eyebrows rose as he read down the page. "Long list."

"It's a bad building."

His long lashes practically obscured his eyes, they narrowed so far. "So why do you live here?"

Her stomach shriveled into a prune under his scrutiny. "Because I can afford it. Because it's close to the parks." Not that she'd visited those in a long time. But it was why she'd chosen this building originally.

He continued reading the list. "Just one problem."

"Why did I know there'd be a 'just'?"

He ignored her. "The judge's decree is firm on me not outsourcing any of this service. It has to be by my own hand. Most of this list calls for tradesmen."

She stared at him. "It hadn't occurred to me that you'd actually follow the order. You struck me as a corner-cutter."

"Not at all."

She matched his glare. "The front-door buzzer's still faulty."

"That's not about cutting corners—*or costs*," he said just as she was about to accuse him of precisely that.

"What is it, then?"

He folded his arms across his chest, highlighting its vast breadth. "It's asset strategy."

Her snort was unladylike in the extreme. "Is your strategy to let the building and everyone in it crumble to dust? If so, then you're right on target."

Was that the tiniest hint of color at his collar? He laid the list down on the table. "I've accepted the terms of the order. I'll see it through. My way."

"So what can you do? What *do* you do?"

His grunt was immediate. "I do a lot of paperwork. I sign things. Spend money."

"Just not here."

He ignored that. "I'm in the information industry."

Tori threw her hands up. "Well, what's that going to be useful for?"

It took the flare of his pupils to remind her how offensive

he might find that. And then she wondered why she cared all about offending him. "I mean, here…in my apartment."

"Actually, I have an idea. It relates to your birds."

"The falcons?"

"Urban raptors are a big deal on Manhattan. There are a number of webcams set up across the city, beaming out live images to the rest of the world. Kind of a virtual ecotourism. For those who are interested."

The way he said it made it perfectly clear of how little interest they were to him.

"I guess. I was just doing it for me." And in some ways she'd enjoyed keeping the peregrine falcon pair a special thing. A private thing. Which was probably selfish. The whole world should be able to see the beauty of nature. Wasn't that what her photography was all about? "A webcam, you think?"

"And a website. One's pointless without the other."

Flutters fizzed up inside her like champagne and the strangeness of it only made her realize how long it had been since something had really excited her. A website full of her images, full of her beautiful birds. For everyone to see. She knew about the other falcon locations in New York but hadn't thought for a moment she might ever be able to do something similar in Morningside.

"You can design a website?"

His expression darkened. "Sanmore's mailboy can design a simple website. As can half the fifth graders on Manhattan. It's no big deal."

Not for him, maybe. She turned her mind to the ledge. "I guess it wouldn't be too hard to set a camera up on the ledge, focused on the nest box. If anything of interest happens, it'll probably happen there."

"How can you be sure they'll use the box?" he asked.

"I can't. But I'm encouraging them down every day. So I'm optimistic."

His eyes narrowed. "Encouraging?"

Might as well tell it as it was. "Luring. They're usually

pigeon eaters, but mice are easier to trap. This building has no shortage."

His lips thinned. "All buildings have vermin."

Her laugh was raw. "Not this many."

He stared at her, considering. "Excuse me a moment." Then he stepped into her small kitchen and spoke in quiet tones into the cell phone she'd held for him the week before. When he returned, his expression was impassive. "You may need to find a new source of bird bait."

She frowned. "What did you just do?"

"I took care of the vermin problem."

"With one phone call?"

"I have good staff."

One phone call. It could have been solved so long before this. "Good staff but not residential agents, I'd say. We've been reporting the mice for eighteen months."

He thought about that. "I trust our agent to take care of code issues."

"This is the same agent you trusted with my door selection?"

His eyes shifted back to the hideously inappropriate door and she felt a mini rush of satisfaction that she'd finally scored a point. But snarking at him wasn't going to be a fun way to spend the next hundred hours. And as much as she'd like to make him suffer just a little bit for the torn carpet and clunky pipes and glacially slow elevator, she had to endure it, too. And she had a feeling he would give as good as he got.

"Anyway," she said. "I'm sure raw meat will suffice in the unlikely event I run out of fresh food."

"Then what? They'll just…come?"

She slid her hands onto her hips. "Is this interest? Or are you just being polite?"

His left eye twitched slightly. "I have a court order that says I should be interested, Ms. Morfitt. No offense."

She arched a single eyebrow. People like him had no idea how offensive their very existence was to people like her. To every tenant who scraped together the rent to live in his shabby building. To the people who went without every day so he could have another sportscar in his parking space.

Her birds had no way of making him money; therefore, they didn't rate for Nathan Archer.

"None taken." She wouldn't give him the satisfaction. "I'm planning on moving the mice to the nest box tomorrow, to see how the falcons respond to it."

"Might as well get the camera set up and operating straight-away, then," he said.

"You're assuming I've agreed?"

"Haven't you? Your eyes twinkled like the Manhattan sky-line when I suggested it."

It burned her that he could read her so easily. And it bothered her that he was paying that much attention to what her eyes were doing. Bothered and…something else. Her chest pressed in tighter.

She shook the rogue thought loose. "Can we use something small and unobtrusive? I don't want to scare them away just as they're starting to come close. It took me weeks to get them accustomed to visiting the ledge, and any day now they'll need to start laying."

He moved to the window and looked out, examining the wall material. "I can probably core out one of the stone blocks in the basement and fit the camera into it. They'll barely know it's there."

She smiled. "There you go, then. You're not totally without practical skills."

He opened his mouth to argue, but then seemed to think better of it. "I'll need your bathroom."

She flinched. That seemed a stupidly unsettling and intimate request—not that the dictatorial words in any way resembled a request. The man was going to be here for one hundred hours—of course he was going to need the facilities at some point.

She stepped back from the doorway. "You know the way."

One brow twitched. "You're not coming?"

Both her own shot upward. "Uh...no, you'll have to manage by yourself." Who knew, maybe the man had assistants for that, too.

"You're going to play hardball on this court order, aren't you? Well, don't come crying to me if I pull out something I shouldn't."

What? Tori frowned after his retreating figure. Then, as she heard the exaggerated *ziiip,* her frown doubled and she muttered, "What, Mr. Corporate America isn't a door-closer?"

Seconds later she heard another metallic *ziiip* and she realized her mistake. Heat flared up her throat. The man wasn't peeing. He was measuring—with a steel tape measure. Probably the ledge window.

Of course he was.

And she'd just come across as the biggest moron ever to breathe. Things were off to a great start.

Just fabulous.

Nathan turned out of West 126th Street onto St. Nicholas Avenue and wove his way through the late-afternoon pedestrian traffic heading for the subway. It didn't matter that it was nearly evening—activity levels at nearby Columbia University didn't drop until much later, which meant the streets around it were perpetually busy during class hours. Even a few blocks away. He'd spent a lot of time out on these streets as a kid—more than most—so he knew every square inch.

Something about Tori Morfitt really got his people antennae twitching. What was a young, beautiful woman—a wildlife photographer—doing living alone in his shabby building, with no job or family that he could discern, spending her time hanging out with birds?

In a world where he tended to attract compliant yes-men—and *oh-yes* women—encountering someone so wholly unconcerned about appropriateness, someone who wore their heart so dangerously on their sleeve was a refreshing change. When she forgot to be angry with him she was quite easygoing: bright, sharp, compassionate. And the immediate blaze of her eyes as he'd suggested the webcam had reached out, snared him by the intestines and slowly reeled him in.

No doubt his interest would waver the moment he uncovered her mysteries, but for now... There were worse ways of spending time—and community service—than with a lithe, healthy young woman who liked to spar verbally.

He pulled out his phone as he walked.

"Dean," he said the moment his attorney answered his call.

"Hey, Nate."

"Forget the appeal, will you?"

"Are you serious?" He could almost hear the frown in his friend's voice—a full two-eyebrow job. What he was really asking was, *Are you insane*? "I can get you off."

"I'd rather see it out, Dean. It's a principle thing."

"You sure you can afford the moral high ground right now? We have a lot on."

His friend's gentle censure merged with the noise of the traffic. "I'll fit everything in. You know that. It's been a long time since I had anyone to get home to." He jogged between cars across the street and joined the salmon-spawn crush on the subway stairs. "Who's going to care if I pull some late ones at the office?"

"You're superhuman, Nate, not invincible."

"I don't want to lawyer my way out of this. Call it strategy—a good chance to get a handle on the lay of the land at Morningside, tenant-wise."

A good chance to get a handle on one particular tenant, at least.

Dean took his time answering. "Wow. She must be something."

Nate instantly started feeling tetchy. If he had to face an inquisition he might as well go back to Tori's. "Who?"

"Your jumper."

"She wasn't jumping."

"Don't change the subject. This is about her, isn't it?"

Nate surged forward as he saw the subway car preparing to move off. "This is about me remembering where I came from. How things were done before the money."

Dean sobered immediately. "The building's getting to you, huh?"

Nate shouldered his way between closing subway doors and leaned on the glass partition. "I just don't want to buy my way out of this."

"So you keep saying. But I'm not convinced. You worked hard all your life precisely so that you could have access to the freedom money buys."

"Yeah, but I'll do my hundred hours and then walk away knowing I did it the right way." Knowing that *she* knew it.

Dean thought about that. "Your call, buddy."

"Thank you. You can withdraw the appeal?"

"Consider it done."

Nate signed off and slid his phone back into his pocket.

One hundred hours with Tori Morfitt and he got to keep the moral high ground. A win-win. His favorite type of outcome.

He had some guilt about the effort they were about to go to in setting up the webcam but, at the end of the day, it was his effort to waste. He'd be doing most of the work. And it wouldn't be totally pointless. His plans to redevelop the building site wouldn't kick off for months so they'd get one good season out of the webcam, at least.

Of course, it meant spending more hours in the building where he was born than he particularly wanted to, but he'd control that. He'd managed the feelings his whole childhood, how hard could it be now? Memories started to morph from the gray haze he usually maintained into more concrete shapes and sounds.

He went for his phone again and dialed his office rather than let them take root in his consciousness.

"Karin, I'm heading back. What have I missed?"

As always, work did a sensational job of shoving the

memories to one side. It had served him well for fifteen years and it didn't fail him now as the subway rattled him back downtown to his own world.

CHAPTER THREE

"ARE you sure this is safe?"

Twenty-four hours later, Nathan was hanging out Tori's window again, watching her fit the stone block he'd brought with him into the corner of the ledge opposite the nest box. It was artfully hollowed out, and comfortably housed a small black camera, the lens poking discreetly out the front. The peregrines would notice nothing unusual when they returned after an evening's hunting and the camera would be protected from New York's wilder weather.

"It's safe. I've been much higher than this," Tori said through tight lips, not because she was frightened, but because she didn't like to talk about climbing. Sometimes she didn't even like to *think* about climbing. It made her feel things she was better off suppressing. She shifted her weight, wedged her scaling boot more firmly in the corner, and slid the block fully back into position.

"Better you than me," he murmured.

"Not good with heights?" she teased lightly.

"I love heights. My company's forty floors up. It's falling to my death I'm not so wild about."

Tori's body responded instantly to his words, locking up hard, squeezing her lungs so hard they couldn't inflate. It took all her concentration to will them open again so that air could rush in. She faked busy work with the camera to buy a couple of recovery seconds.

When she could speak again, she said, "You seemed ready enough to lurch out here last week."

"I thought you were in trouble. I wasn't really thinking about myself."

Sure. And hell had an ice-hockey team. Her money was on him thinking very much about the bad publicity that goes with a jumper. She turned and gathered up some of the scattered substrate from the nesting box and returned it to where it could do the birds more good.

"Won't it all just blow out again?" he asked, watching her clean-up effort. "It's gusty up here."

"It's heavier than it looks, so it doesn't blow. The peregrines toss it all out while investigating the box. They'll probably just do it again but at least it will have started fully set up for their needs. It's all I can do. They seem to like it this way."

He shrugged and mumbled, "The hawk wants what the hawk wants."

Curiosity drew her gaze back to him. So he did have a sense of humor, albeit a reluctant one. "Well, if they'd *want* a little more tidily that would be great for me." She sat back on her haunches and examined the now-tidy box, then looked at the hidden camera. A thrill of excitement raced up her spine. Nothing like the adrenaline dump of her climbing days, but it was something. "Okay. I think we're done."

She scooted backwards and twisted through the window, taking care not to snag the new cable that draped through it, connecting the camera to the small temporary monitor set up in her bathroom. Nathan stood back and let her back in.

"When I come next I'll hook it up to your TV so you can watch it with the flick of a switch," he said, shifting his focus politely from the midriff she exposed as her T-shirt snagged on the window latch.

"If I have a couple of nesting peregrines to watch, I'm not going to be switching anywhere," she said. Having the nest visible via closed circuit television would be a vast improvement on leaning out her window every day. Less likely to disturb the birds, too.

She lifted her gaze to him as she stepped down off the toilet seat and killed her height advantage. "That would be great, thank you."

Neither of them moved from the cramped bathroom, but Archer clearly had no more idea what to do with genuine gratitude from her than she did. A tiny crease marred the perfectly groomed place between his eyebrows. Her breathing picked up pace as she stared up at him, and her lips fell open slightly. His sharp eyes followed every move. Then his own parted and Tori's breath caught.

A rapid tattoo on the door snapped them both from the awkward place where silent seconds had just passed. A subtle rush of disappointment abseiled through her veins. Her face turned toward her new front door and then the rest of her followed, almost reluctantly. "That will be Mr. Broswolowski."

She squeezed past Nate's body carefully, failing at total clearance, and twisted slightly to avoid rudely shouldering him in the chest. That only served to brush her front against him as she moved through into the living room. If she'd been stacked instead of athletic it would have been totally gratuitous. As it was, his tight jaw barely shifted and his eyes only flicked briefly downwards.

While her breath tightened unaccountably.

She flung the front door wide as soon as she got to it.

"Aren't you the Queen of Sheba," the elderly man standing in the hall said as he admired her spotless new door. "Need to get yourself a peephole, though. This isn't the upper west side, you know."

Tori laughed as he entered. "I knew you by your knock, Mr. Broswolowski."

The man dumped a large hamper of clean laundry on her coffee table and commenced his standard grumble. "This basket doesn't get any lighter coming up two flights of stairs. What use is an elevator if it can't go to all floors?" He straightened uncomfortably.

"I keep telling you to bring them to me dirty. I can launder them for you before I iron them. Save your spine."

"I'm not so old that I'm prepared to have a pretty girl go through my dirty linens. The stairs are fine. But that washer isn't getting any more efficient."

Nathan chose that moment to fully emerge from the direction of the bathroom. Mr. Broswolowski looked up then turned in surprise to Tori.

"Mr. Broswolowski, this is—" for no good reason she hesitated to sic her acerbic downstairs neighbor on their landlord "—a friend of mine. He's helping me with the falcons."

"Is that so?"

Tori held her breath and waited for the awkward comment to come; some observation to the effect that her neighbor had never seen her with a man, let alone had one wander out of her bathroom as if he owned the place. Which, of course, he did. Not that she was going to share the fact. *Her* giving Nathan Archer grief was one thing, but exposing him to the collective grizzles of all her neighbors…

"Just the usual, Mr. B?"

The older man might struggle with his eyes and his arthritis, but his mind was in perfect working order. He let his curiosity dissipate, which was uncharacteristic; heavy hints usually only spurred him on. But he glanced more than once at Nathan's imposing figure and Tori realized this was the first time she'd seen Mr. B outgunned.

"Bless you, yes. There's a few more than usual," he said. "I'm spring-cleaning."

She nudged him toward the door. "Cranes or peacocks?"

He let himself be bundled out into the hall. "In a hurry, Tori?"

"Time is money, Mr. B."

"Like either of us needs to worry about time." He chuckled, before adding, "Peacocks."

Tori returned his smile. He was so predictable. "Done. I'll have them to you by tomorrow afternoon."

"Yes, yes. I wouldn't want to interrupt your date…"

She clicked the door shut behind them pointedly as she followed the older man into the hall, to lessen the chance of Nathan hearing. "It's not a date. It's business."

"*Some* kind of business, anyway," Mr. B mumbled, turning away happily.

"None of yours, that's for sure," she called after him. His laugh ricocheted back towards her down the dim hallway. She turned and pushed the door to go back in, but it didn't budge. Her lashes fell closed. That's right…new door.

New *self-locking* door.

She took a deep breath and knocked, steeling herself for the inevitable questions. If she got lucky, Nathan would have gone back to work on the camera and not heard a word Mr. B had said. If she got lucky he'd not be the slightest bit interested in what she and her neighbors got up to.

But it had been a long time since she considered herself lucky

An old sorrow sliced through her.

"Come in," Nathan said with a satisfied mouth-twist as he opened her door. His eyes travelled to the basket overflowing with linens still sitting on the coffee table. "You do his laundry?"

She shifted the clean linen over to the service cupboard that served as a closet and lifted her chin. "He has arthritis. Ironing hurts him."

The frown deepened. "What was with the peacock?"

Awkwardness leached through her. Speaking of *none of your business*… But his question seemed genuine enough. To an outsider it probably did seem crazy. "I like to make it special. Fun. I do a sort of hot-steam origami with his linen. He likes the peacock fan for his sheets."

"Doesn't that defeat the purpose of ironing?"

She smiled. "He doesn't seem to mind. I did it one Christmas as a surprise and it's kind of…stuck."

"*One* Christmas? How long have you been doing it?"

She frowned. Wow. Had it really been four years? "A while."

"Does he pay you?"

Heat surged. Was everything about money for him? "Worried I'm operating a home business without a license?"

"No," he said. "Just curious."

He shoved his hands into deep pockets, lifting the hem of his expensive coat and flashing the line of his dark leather belt where a crisp white shirt tucked neatly into a narrow waist. It had been a long time since she'd been this close to someone in formal business wear. And a long time since she'd seen someone whom business wear suited quite so much. She immediately thought of her brother dressed up to the nines on his first day at his first Portland job. He'd been so overly pressed and so excited.

Her chest tightened. A lifetime ago.

"We have a kind of barter system going. Mr. Broswolowski was a stage producer and he's still got connections."

"You're an actor?"

Her laugh then was immediate. The idea of her standing on stage in front of hundreds of strangers… Her stomach knotted just from the image. "No. But Angel on three is, and Mr. Broswolowski throws her opportunities every now and again in return for me doing his laundry."

"Wait… You do his laundry and someone else reaps the benefit?"

"I benefit. Angel babysits the deCosta boy half a day a week as a thank you for Mr. B's inside information, and in return Mrs. deCosta brings me fresh groceries every Monday when she does her own run."

If he frowned any more his forehead was going to split down the middle. "Just how many people are involved in this scheme?" he asked.

"Across the whole building? Pretty much everyone, one way or another."

He gaped. "Thirty-six households?"

"Thirty-five. 8B's been empty for years. But pretty much everyone else gets involved in one way or another. It suits our needs. And it's economical. Doing Mr. B's ironing keeps my refrigerator stocked."

"What happens when the deCosta boy gets too old for babysitting?"

Tori blinked. Straight to the weak link in the supply chain. No wonder he was a squillionaire. "Laundry's not my only trade. I have other assets."

His laugh was more of a grunt. "A regular domestic portfolio."

She fought the prickles that begged to rise. "Hey, I didn't start it. Some poor kid with an entrepreneurial spirit came up with it in the eighties as a way of making ends meet. But it works for me."

Inexplicably his whole face tightened. His voice grew tight. "You do know you can have groceries delivered to your door?"

Tori blinked at him. "Sure. But who would do Mr. B's ironing?"

The Captain of Industry seemed to have no good answer for that. He stared at her, long and hard. "I guess you have a point."

She fought down her instinctive defensiveness. The man was just trying to make conversation. "It's not like it's against the law, it's just neighbors getting together to help each other out."

He turned back on a judgmental eyebrow-lift. "You're exchanging services for gratuities."

Heat blazed. "I do someone's *ironing*. You make it sound like I'm selling sexual favours in the hallway. That hasn't happened in this building for a decade."

He spun toward the television, but not before she saw the

way his face rapidly dumped its color. All of it. Every part of her wanted to apologise, but…what for? *He'd* insulted *her*.

She sighed. "How about we just stick to what we're here for." She took a deep breath. "Tell me about this CCTV jig."

He took a moment before emerging from behind her modest television. "This doesn't have the inputs I need. I'll bring you a new one."

"A new what?"

"A new television."

"You will not!"

He blinked at her. "This one won't work with the CCTV gear."

"I'm not accepting a gift like that from you to get you out of community service."

His eyes narrowed. "Have I asked you to let me off the service order?"

"I'm sure you're working up to it." She lifted her chin and absorbed the tiny adrenaline rush that came with sparring with him.

"You really don't have a very high opinion of me, do you?"

Tori frowned. "I've been entrusted with…I feel like there's an obligation there."

"To do what?"

"To sign your attendance. Properly."

"Like some kind of classroom roll call?" The stare he gave her went on forever. "And you wouldn't consider just signing it off to be rid of me?"

Oh, how she'd love to be rid of him. Except someone had forgotten to tell her skin that. The way it tingled when she opened the door to him this afternoon… The way it prickled even now, under his glare.

She shrugged. "They're trusting me."

"You don't know them."

"It doesn't matter. *I* would know."

"Well if you want me to do this by the book you're going

to need to take the television, otherwise there can be no webcam."

"I can't accept a television."

"Ms Morfitt—"

"Oh, for crying out loud, will you call me Viktoria? Or Tori. You make me feel like an aging spinster." And that likelihood was something she tried very hard not to think about. Living it later was going to be hard enough…

She stood and moved toward the kitchen. Toward her ever-bubbling coffeepot.

"Viktoria…"

Nathan frowned, not liking the formal sound of it on his lips and tried again as she moved away from him. "Tori. I run an IT empire; we have monitors and televisions littering my office. Giving you one is about as meaningful to me as giving you corporate stationery."

Her nostrils flared and he felt like a schmuck. She'd done the very best she could with the bare bones of this apartment but there was no disguising the absence of money in her world. Not surprising if she was living on a barter system. And here he was throwing around televisions as if they were nothing. Which—brutal truth be told—they were, in his world. But waving his worth around wasn't usually his style. Money had come hard to him, but he wasn't so far gone he forgot what it felt like to live the other way.

One minute back in this building and it was all too fresh. Uncomfortably so.

"Look. You'll need it to monitor the web feed. I need it to get this community service order signed off." She looked entirely unmoved. He searched around for inspiration.

It wasn't hard for him to get into the trading spirit. That junior entrepreneur she spoke of living in the building twenty years ago had been *him*. He'd had a raft of creative schemes going to try and make something from the nothing of his youth. Not that he was going to tell her that. "I'll trade you if I have to."

Her gray eyes scanned his body critically and a tingle of honeyed warmth trailed everywhere she looked. He'd never been more grateful that he kept in good shape under the designer suits. Which was ludicrous—just because *she* was in perfect shape. The way she'd twisted in through that window—

His whole body twitched.

"You don't look like someone who needs their ironing done," she said, carefully. "What am I going to trade you for?"

The spark of defiance and pride in her expression touched him somewhere down deep. Enough to ask her seriously, "What can you offer me?"

She frowned. "Photography?"

As good as her images were, did she truly think she had nothing else to offer? He wanted to push her. To show her otherwise. A good brain ticked away beneath those tumbling auburn locks. Never mind the fact this was a great chance to learn a little more about her. "I don't need it. I have a whole marketing department for that stuff."

Her delicate brows dipped. "Well…if we're talking something you *need*…"

Crap. He should have taken the photography.

"…how about I show you around your building?" she continued. "Introduce you to people. Show you the human face of this towering *asset*."

Nate's heart doubled in size and pressed hard against his lungs. Despite what he'd told Dean, getting to know his tenants was the last thing he wanted. Not when he was about to rip the building out from under them. But it did mean Tori would take the new television and that meant he'd get his life back ninety-five hours from now. And as a side bonus, he could get to know her better.

"Not that I can see how that actually benefits me, but I accept." Whatever it took. He'd just stall her indefinitely on her part of the bargain.

"Of course it benefits you. I'm sure you know your tenants

are an asset too. Some of them have lived here all their lives. You don't get more loyal customers than that."

...all their lives.

That meant some of them might have lived here back when *he* lived here. And when *she* lived here. His mother. Nate's skin tingled. Meeting those tenants was definitely out of the question. And therefore getting chummy with the natives was categorically not on his radar.

Except maybe this one. Surly or not, Tori grabbed his attention in a way no other woman had. A two-handed grab.

"I'll have the television delivered tomorrow," he cut in, shaking the image free. "Will you be home?"

"Yep."

"I haven't given you a time yet."

She shrugged. "I'll be home. I have a date with a *Battlestar Galactica* marathon and Mr. B's ironing, remember?"

For some reason, the thought of the same hands that took such artistic wildlife photos sweltering behind a steam iron all day made him uncomfortable. But what Viktoria Morfitt chose to do with her spare time was entirely her own business.

And her business was none of his business.

"Tori Morfitt, door!"

A man in a hemp beanie flung the front door wide and let Nate into the ground floor of his own building the next day, then hollered Tori's name up the stairwell. Somewhere upstairs, someone else echoed the call. And then someone else as the message passed up the building frontier-style.

"Buzzer doesn't work," the man finally said by way of awkward conversation and then turned back to scanning his mail.

Nate's smile was tight. What could he say? That was *his* buzzer doing such a bad job of providing security for his tenants. Fortunately, the neighbors had it covered—this guy wasn't letting him go anywhere until Tori appeared and vouched for him.

Security by proxy.

"She's jogging so she shouldn't be long," the guy eventually said, taking an exaggerated amount of time sorting through his post. Nate turned and looked outside, confused. He hadn't passed her in the street… Then again, Morningside was a campus district, full of people at all hours, and she might prefer the ease of the public parks. He turned more fully to watch the path that led up from the sidewalk to the foyer door.

Anyone would think he was looking forward to it.

The stairwell door burst open behind him, snapping his head back around. Tori came through flushed, sweating and kitted out in tight running gear. Her eyes flared as they hit him and she stumbled to a halt. "You're early."

Her chest rose and fell heavily with each breath. He concentrated extra hard on keeping his focus high, but it wasn't easy, given her training top was more bandage than clothing and her skin glistened with sweat along her breast line. "I had a meeting in Jersey. I figured there was no point going back downtown for only half an hour."

He took in the way she ran her palms down her tight-fitting workout gear. She looked as though she wanted to be anywhere else than here—with him. "Sorry. Is it a problem?"

"No. I just…" She pushed her fingers through damp hair. "Come on up."

As they turned, she threw a smile at beanie guy. "Thanks, Danny."

Danny gave her a keen smile and Nate immediately stood straighter as a surge of territoriality hit him out of nowhere. *Ridiculous.* As if she'd go for the half-washed hippie type anyway.

As he headed for the elevator, he realized he had no idea what type of guy she did go for. Not his type, judging by how quickly she took offense at just about everything he did.

"You're taking the stairs?" he said as she let him enter the elevator alone.

"I'll meet you up there," she said. "I'm nearly done with

my workout. And you really don't want to be locked in a small space with me right now. The rate that elevator moves I might even get there before you."

She turned and disappeared back through the door, leaving Nate to enter the elevator alone. As it happened, he couldn't think of anything better than being closed in a small space with Tori Morfitt—sweat or no sweat. Something about standing so close to all that radiating heat while he was buttoned up in his best three-piece… His subconscious slapped him for the pleasurable twinge that flicked through him, low and sharp.

She hadn't meant to get caught out in Lycra, all hot and bothered.

He pulled out his phone the moment the old doors slid shut and—as he had every time he got into this elevator—he picked a spot of carpet to focus on and kept his eyes glued there rather than look at himself in the age-speckled mirrors lining the walls. This little box held all kinds of memories for him—none of them good.

"Karin?" he greeted his assistant when she picked up. "I want you to get onto Tony Ciaccetti and have him sort out the door security at Morningside."

It was crazy that the residents of his building had to pass messages up the stairwell like a warfront. It was secure enough, just not convenient. Which hadn't really troubled him before, but now that he saw it in action he realized how difficult it could make things, especially for older residents. Even for Tori.

Just because he'd dreaded the knell of the buzzer as child didn't mean every tenant in the place had to suffer the consequences.

He lurched to a halt on the eighth floor and optimistically pressed Tori's floor again. The doors opened then closed, and for one hopeful moment he thought the elevator was going to rise. But no, the doors reopened impotently, as silently judging as Tori was every time she'd mention some failing part of the building.

"I'll see you tomorrow, Karin."

He stepped out into the hallway and disconnected his call, then turned with determination to the stairwell before daring to lift his eyes again. Today he just didn't need the shadows of the apartment where he grew up. In the relative silence of the stairwell his ears tuned in to the steady thump of feet coming closer. He trod the two flights and held open the door with her floor number painted on it in flaking blue.

A moment later Tori appeared, sprinting heavily up the final flight. She jogged straight past him onto the tenth floor. She didn't smell nearly as bad as she probably feared. Actually she smelled pretty good. An image of rumpled sheets twisted his gut, rough and distracting, before he shut it down.

"I'm sure someone would have told me if we'd installed a gym in the building."

She slowed to a walk and let him catch up and spoke between heavy puffs of breath. "I run the stairs every day."

He looked at her, frowning. Significant heat stained her perfect skin, but it didn't detract from the fine lines of her bone-structure. "All twelve floors?"

"Three times each."

His feet ground to a halt. Well, that explained her legs. "Why not run the streets? The parks? You have enough of them nearby."

Her lashes dropped. "I don't like to run alone, even during the day." She pulled a key from a chain that hung disguised in cleavage he wouldn't have expected to be there and opened her front door.

Nate closed it behind them. "It's just dawned on me that you've been very relaxed about having me in your home. Given you don't know me from Adam. And given your…interest…in security."

If by *interest* one meant *fixation*…

"Relaxed? No." Her smile was tight. "But you own the building. I figure if you had anything nefarious in mind you could get a key to any of our doors without any difficulty." The smile mellowed into a sweet twist. "Or just kick it right in."

His gut twanged. Here was he imagining her naked and meanwhile she was finally softening to him.

Schmuck.

"I'm not sure, but that sounded almost like…trust?"

"Or resignation to my fate."

Her husky laughter heightened the streak of color still high in her cheeks. She stood straighter to pat a towel down the bare, glistening parts of her body. His own tightened. Just slightly. It had been a long time since any woman got anything other than designer-sweaty in front of him. Exertion just wasn't in with the women in his social circles. Except one kind of exertion and even that was often carefully orchestrated. Yet that wasn't what was holding his attention—at least not entirely.

It was the warmth in Tori's eyes. He hadn't realized before that anything had been missing from her steady gaze, but seeing it now full of light and laughter, he knew he'd miss it terribly if it vanished again.

"I'll take trust," he said.

They fell to silence, standing awkwardly in her neat living room, staring at each other.

"I should…" She waved her hands at her state of dress, then glanced around nervously.

She wanted to take a shower, but not while he was in her home. So trust was a measured thing, then. He crossed to the giant box dumped in the middle of her floor. If he couldn't get absent, he'd get busy. "I'll get your TV hooked up while you're gone."

"I hope that's all box," she said, eyeing the monolith. "I probably can't afford the electricity for anything bigger."

Again the vast gulf between them came crashing home to him. He hadn't even thought about running costs for a big-screen plasma. So maybe he wasn't still as attuned to his roots as he liked to believe. "It's mostly packing foam. Don't worry."

At least he really, really hoped so.

She shifted nervously, then seemed to make a decision, and disappeared into her bedroom. He heard the spray of water and then the very definite snick of a lock being turned. At least she hadn't consigned him to the hall as she had that first day.

He'd spent enough time in hallways for one lifetime.

He took the opportunity to look around. The floor plan was identical to the apartment he'd grown up in, two floors down, and beneath the layer of bright, contemporary paint he still recognized the essential design. Tori's careful application of color and light helped to make this stock-standard apartment into a cozy, feminine home. Much nicer than the one he grew up in.

On the mantel, she'd displayed a number of framed photographs: a blissfully happy-looking gray-haired couple in front of a large RV named Freedom; a stunning print of a bald eagle in flight silhouetted against a blazing sky and one of Tori herself, fully kitted up in climbing gear but relaxed and pouring two mugs of steaming coffee from a campfire pot and laughing up at the camera, her cheeks flushed with cold and vibrant life.

Her parents. Her mountains. And, presumably, her life. The look of total comfort and adoration on her face as she looked at whoever was taking the photo—whoever the second cup of coffee was for—squirreled down deep into his soul.

A lover?

Again the slither of jealousy coiled low in his belly. What kind of a man would Tori Morfitt choose? Not the beanie guy, surely. She'd appreciate someone outdoorsy, not too precious to pitch a tent out in the woods somewhere. Maybe an alpha type. A smart guy? A rich guy?

He looked around again, frowning. No other evidence that anyone else lived here with her or ever had. No photos of a man. More important…why was a creature as intrinsically *wild* as Tori Morfitt living in a cruddy building in upper Manhattan?

And…why did he care?

Behind him the shower shut off, so Nate got busy tearing into the shipping box his firm had delivered. He wrestled the

TV from its container, said a tiny whisper of thanks that it truly was moderate in size and busied himself disconnecting the old one.

By the time Tori emerged from her shower, clean and fresh and feeling infinitely more respectable in a T-shirt and jeans, Nathan was tuning the new television. It was spectacular. Not enormous, but flat-screen, which made it far less obtrusive in her small apartment than its clunky predecessor, which presently dominated the coffee table. That had been her parents' before they'd sold up everything and committed themselves to a life roaming around North America in their mobile home. She'd been happy to take it, though. She'd had to replace everything when she moved in here with only the bare essentials five years ago.

It had been years since she'd had anything shiny and new in her apartment. Just the smell of the packaging was exciting.

Pathetic, Morfitt.

Nathan spun around as she cleared her throat and spoke. "Wow. I may also have to introduce you to the tenants in the next building over for a truly fair trade."

Not that she knew anyone in the next building or could even visualize it anymore. She frowned.

He picked up the remote control and crossed to stand beside her. "Ready for a show?"

He thumbed the remote and the screen filled with the vision-feed from her ledge—just like the image in the bathroom monitor but vastly larger. Her ledge—complete with side-opening nest box, scattered substrate and scrubbed clean of pigeon poop—filled her living room in glorious high definition. On-screen, a curl of residual steam from her shower drifted out the open bathroom window.

"I should have done this years ago," Tori whispered as she sank into her sofa, misty-eyed. "It's awesome."

As they watched, a heavily feathered, brown-and-black hawk appeared on the edge of the screen. Nathan sucked in a breath.

Tori leaned sideways as though it might improve the framing, then she scooted to the front of her sofa.

"Wilma, I think."

He slid down next to her, just as captivated. "How can you tell?"

"Her coloring is different and she's smaller."

"That's small?"

Tori laughed. "She looks huge on screen, but peregrines are smaller than most of the other birds of prey. Fred's a good deal bigger than her. He needs to be to provide for his family."

Wilma's patterned head turned close to 360 degrees as she scanned her environment relentlessly, but her clawed feet took her closer to the box. Step by cautious step.

"She's here to check it out," Tori whispered.

They watched in silence—as though the slightest noise from inside the apartment would somehow disturb Wilma's investigations—and she patrolled the ledge, inching ever closer to the box. She plucked what little substrate was left out of the box and then stepped into it, exploring it thoroughly but keeping a hawk eye on possible predators.

Left of screen another dark blur touched down.

"Fred!" Tori leaned even farther forward and Nathan was right beside her. His thigh pressed hard against hers, drawing her glance down for a heartbeat. But she forced it up to watch the screen.

The larger bird had alighted on the ledge blurrily close to the camera. But they could still make him out as he crossed back and forth in front of the camera lens, studying this foreign arrival while Wilma continued to toss substrate out of the box in the background. The camera stayed focused on the nest box.

"Easy buddy…" Nathan whispered as Fred pecked at the lens with his savage hooked beak and gnawed on the rubber surround. But the bird's curiosity soon waned and he turned his attention to his mate. Wilma stood in the nest box apparently satisfied with what she had found.

Tori held her breath. In her peripheral vision she saw Nathan turn to watch her face. But she couldn't take her own eyes off the screen.

"Come on...come on..."

Then it happened. Casually as you like, Wilma picked up a random piece of tossed substrate from the ledge and carried it back to the box. She tossed it straight out again the moment she put it down, but then went and selected another more acceptable to her.

"What's she doing?" Nathan asked.

Tori's throat was too thick to speak. She swallowed hard and then tried again. "Starting a nest."

It was the most beautiful thing she'd seen. Up in the mountains she'd seen majestic aeries but they'd all been fully formed. Renovations of last year's eroded nests. This was the first time she'd seen a bird choose and build a nest from scratch.

And they'd chosen *her* ledge. If not for Nathan and his television she wouldn't have seen any of this.

She turned her face to him as Wilma continued searching for exactly the right piece of substrate. "This is so special. I'm so sorry I've been such a pain in the butt about all of this. Thank you, Nathan."

His blue eyes were steady, but somehow they made her critically aware of how naked she'd been just moments before as water sluiced down over her hot skin while he worked just beyond her bathroom wall. And how naked she would be now if not for the thin layers of cotton-blend fabric separating them. Yet his eyes never so much as left hers.

He smiled. "You know, I've been here three times and that's the first time you've said my name. I was beginning to wonder if you knew what it was."

Heat rushed up her newly showered neck. "Of course I knew it. It's on your business card...Nathan..." She stumbled to a halt, cursing that just using his name should feel so intimate. But it did. As though she'd whispered it. "I mean... Yes, I knew it. I'm sorry."

"I'm not after an apology. I just like the way you say it."

The pulse in her throat started to thump. In her periphery, the birds continued exploring the ledge. But a pterodactyl touching down to join them couldn't have torn Tori's gaze from his.

"How do other people say it?"

"Most people call me Nate. Or Mr. Archer."

This is where she should make a flippant comment about him being accustomed to being called *sir*. But flippancy was beyond her. She murmured instead, "What would you like me to call you?"

He stared at her for an eternity and her breath thinned out to almost nothing. He licked his dry lips and the tiny motion transfixed her. The last of her breath evaporated.

"Nathan is perfect," he finally said, husky and low. "Unique to you."

His phone trilled and the two falcons on-screen took urgent flight at the sudden sound through the bathroom window. She and Nathan snapped their focus to the empty screen and, when Tori's drifted carefully back, his had lost all hint of the warm depth she'd briefly glimpsed.

He silenced the trilling. "Archer."

His brows immediately dropped as he held the phone to his ear and then his lips tightened. He turned away from her but not before his eyes drifted shut with what looked like pain. Or exquisite relief.

"Thank you, Karin," he said quietly before hanging up. "I'll come right back. Yes, let him know I'll be right down."

"Bad news?" Tori said brightly, trying to drag things back on a professional footing. Trying to regulate her pounding heart.

"No. The opposite. A business deal I've been waiting on has finally come through."

"Oh. Well… Yay business!" She tightened her hands in her lap. Was she more annoyed that the phone call had interrupted the strange moment they'd almost shared or that he was so easily yanked away from it?

"Anyway," he said, sliding his phone back into his coat pocket and clearing his throat, "Nathan it is. It seems awkward if I'm calling you Tori and you're calling me Mr. Archer."

Tori's stomach dropped away. *Awkward.*

Huh.

Just like this moment.

What had just happened? What had just ended before it began? There was no hint now in Nathan's body language of the momentary connection she'd felt. Or had she imagined it? Could she be that sad?

"Will they be back?" He nodded his head at the television.

The birds. That's right...the whole point of them being here together.

"I'll liberate some straw from Marco deCosta's gerbil," she said, as eager to move on as Nathan suddenly seemed to be. Maybe his eyes had dropped closed with sheer relief that they'd been interrupted by the phone call? "Hopefully Wilma will like that more than the substrate."

He stood, almost stumbling in his haste. "I need to cut today's visit short, I'm sorry. I'll see you tomorrow."

Tori shook her head back to full sensibility, reluctantly stepping free of the fine threads of attraction that had unexpectedly tangled around her feet.

It took him about fifteen seconds to gather himself together and disappear out the door, and Tori got the feeling if there'd been a big red eject button in her apartment he seriously would have thought about pressing it to get out of here more quickly. She held the door open for him and he was through it and gone before she could do more than hastily say goodbye.

Wow. The last time she'd had that effect on a man, she was eighteen and Rick had warned off one of her friends so badly he'd practically paled when she next spoke to him. And given that her overprotective brother wasn't around to scare off any man who looked sideways at her, she could only assume she'd managed to put Nathan Archer off all by herself.

Which was fine, since she wasn't keen to indulge the schoolgirl flutters she got whenever he was around, but still...

That took a particular breed of talent.

* * *

His car pulled up in front of the building and Nate leaped in, hoping that Tori wasn't watching out her window. He really didn't need any more rich-guy black marks from her this week.

"Mr. Archer," his driver said.

"Hi Simon. Back to the office, please."

He felt an indescribable fraud turning up at his childhood building in the company limo. Like some guy who'd spent a month's wages hiring the car for the day to make a good impression. Except he had another one just like it in Sanmore's parking garage and no one to make a good impression on, particularly.

If anything, it would have made a bad impression on Tori had she seen it. He'd never thought he'd be more self-conscious of having money than he ever was of not having it. But then he'd never thought he'd be hanging out in his old building again, either.

The streets of Morningside and then the Upper West Side cruised by as the limo headed downtown. Nate pulled up the document Karin had emailed him and read it through twice. Confirmation that his demolition strategy had finally been approved by the city. A year's worth of negotiations and compliance hoop-jumping in order that he could redevelop his building in Morningside. The building he'd grown up in. The building Tori and all her batty neighbors now lived in.

But not for long.

He'd bought the building because he could. It had been a suitably poetic use for his first bunch of profit zeros. More than cars or women or planes—to buy out the building that they'd been so poor in and know that no-one could ever take it away from them. And becoming his mother's landlord…

Stupidly gratifying.

He'd never before—or again—felt so valued by Darlene Archer as he had the day she'd realized she could hit him up for free rental. It was as though he'd finally been some good to her. After she took her last selfish breath, he'd closed up her apartment and focused one hundred percent of his attention on to growing Sanmore Holdings. It wasn't until Dean had quizzed him about this sole piece of real estate in his portfolio three years ago that he'd started to wonder what else he could put on this site. Something shiny and modern. Something with a future…

…and no past.

The practical demolition application had been easy enough to get through City Hall but recent changes to the Tenancy Act meant he had to give the thirty-five households in his building more notice than he wanted to once the idea of development had taken root. And now that he held the actual permissions in his hands he wasn't prepared to wait at all.

He'd rehouse all thirty-five families in the Ritz if it meant getting this building emptied faster. They could live out the final months of their lease elsewhere courtesy of Sanmore Holdings and he could get on with upgrading the site. The bomb it would cost was more than worth it.

The fact his memories would finally be exorcised from his soul…pure bonus.

Simon pulled the limo up in front of Nate's Columbus Circle office tower to let him out before driving off to do the complicated four-block double-back to access the building's rear car park. With the downtown traffic and the monolithic Trump Towers next door, Nate would be at his desk before Simon even started heading back this way.

Karin met him at the elevator, her handbag on her shoulder and a guilty expression on her face.

"Nice to see you were sticking around in case I needed anything," Nate said dryly.

"It's Friday night, Nathan Archer. Just because you have no life doesn't mean all of us want to work late. I have babies to feed."

She rattled off a few of the afternoon's highlights and thrust a document into his hands. "How did it go?" Her kind eyes knew him so well. "Hostilities ceased?"

Viktoria Morfitt.

"We don't have to be best friends, Karin. I'll just do my time and we'll be back to our regular programming at Sanmore."

Karin lifted a single brow. "Uh-huh."

He'd worked with his assistant long enough to know most of her nuances. She saved her best Harlem gestures for when she had a real point to make. He leaned forward and pushed the down button on the elevator for her. "It's going to be fine."

"You don't have time for this, Nate. You have the merger and the StarOne software trials coming up this month."

"Don't frown at me Karin. I'm the Good Samaritan on this one." He jiggled the elevator button again.

"So fight it. You have right on your side."

He still could. Dean had the appeal paperwork sitting in a file just in case. But standing in Viktoria Morfitt's apartment this afternoon as his body answered the call of all her post-workout pheromones he knew he wouldn't be changing his mind.

There was just something about her. Something he needed some time to figure out.

But arguing with Karin in the hallway wasn't going to get him that. "Okay, I'll go talk to Dean."

"Thank you," Karin said with all the righteousness of a mother of four who was right very often. Except not this time. "Have a good night. Don't stay too late."

She said that every night. And every night he said, "I won't."

But the amount of work he left for her in the mornings probably told her a whole different story.

Nate saw her safely into the elevator and then turned down the hall away from his own office and poked his head around the door of his best friend's.

Dean looked up from whatever legal tome he was reading. "Hey. You're back early."

"Can you have your team get onto something for me?" The two of them had a lot of history together, but their friendship worked so well because they both knew how to maintain clean lines between work and personal.

Dean snapped straight into employee mode. "Name it."

Nate rattled off his plan for rehoming his Morningside tenants to expedite the demolition. Paying out their lease and finding alternative accommodations for every one of them.

"Expensive," Dean murmured. In the circles they both moved in vast dollars didn't scare them but they were still noted.

Nate countered. "Worth it, though."

He watched the lawyer in Dean war with the friend in him. They'd been through so much together. Everything.

"Yeah, it probably is," Dean said with a sigh. "I'll take care of it."

Nate's shoulders instantly lightened up. "Thanks, buddy. I'll give you more information as I can. Good night. Go home and start your weekend."

Back in his own office, Nate signed off on the few things Karin had left for him and returned one quick phone call to an overseas banker. Someone had said "The world never sleeps' and it was never truer. There were half a dozen ways the world could get hold of Sanmore's CEO, 24/7—office phone, home phone, cell phone, email, text, Twitter, couriers—and often at the same time. There hadn't been such a thing as *silence* on this planet since the internet was first wrestled from the hands of the military and went public.

But since he was as responsible for that as everyone else involved in the online boom he really couldn't complain.

He moved over to his floor-to-ceiling windows and stared out at Columbus Circle, but it didn't take long for his eyes to track right...uptown towards Morningside. Towards Tori.

She was someone who would appreciate silence.

Lots of silence.

He could imagine her scaling the face of some mountain with nothing but the sounds of her own exertion and the wind in her ears. No phones. No email. No relentless accessibility.

What would that be like?

He could have a taste of it if he turned off his phone when he was at her place. If he took the subway instead of the car so no one knew where he was. It would be as close to invisible as he got. As close to private. Although being *private* with Tori Morfitt was not necessarily a good idea.

As tempting as it was.

CHAPTER FOUR

"SETTLE, GRETEL."

The humongous dog returned to her mat in Tori's living room and curled back up in a neat, gigantic heap.

"Good girl."

Gretel's big brown Great Dane eyes watched every move Tori made and blinked happily from time to time before finally closing for yet another doggie nap. Life would be so much easier if humans could get away with napping as much as dogs did.

"It's a rough life, kid," Tori murmured, working at her computer on her latest falcon images.

Thirteen out of fourteen days Gretel's owners, the Radcliffes, managed to coordinate their respective work so one of them was home to feed, love and walk their small horse of a dog during the day. Every second Saturday that was Tori's job. Except for the walking part, but Gretel didn't seem to mind the absence of exercise just that once. She happily traded it for pats and snacks on Tori's mat. And Tori traded Gretel's nurse mother, Tracey, for medical assistance, as she needed it. So far, she hadn't really required more than checkups, flu advice and the occasional herbal for when her insomnia was particularly bad. And for anything bigger there were house-call medical services.

Thank God for New York. A supplier for everything, no need too obscure. On call 24/7. The relentless, too-close noise of the city was a small price to pay for that kind of service.

She fiddled with the saturation on a particularly pretty digital shot of Wilma landing on the ledge, some tufts of feather and twig in her hooked beak during her first, aborted, nest-building phase. Nathan wanted lots of images for the website, to make it really special. Fortunately, although she lacked the technical expertise to make this website a reality, gorgeous photos she could definitely provide. In abundance.

Gretel let out a corker of a snore over on her mat.

"Nice, Gretel," Tori twisted her lips but didn't take her attention off screen. "Your dad teach you those manners?"

By midafternoon, she filed away the last of the images she'd selected for the website and glanced at her watch. Her heart gave a little lurch. Nathan would be here soon and her tranquil afternoon would be shot. He'd swan in, dominate her apartment, her time and generally take up clean air. Then he'd find some unique way of making her feel inadequate and remind her of how busy and important he was, and his work would be done!

And all the while she'd be mooning about how good he smelled or looked in a suit.

Crazy.

Tori snapped her attention away from the blank wall and forced it back onto the computer. She had time, maybe she could do a bit of Mrs. Arnold's memories album. Yet another trade. This one for clothing alterations. Most of the catalogue clothes she ordered fitted just fine around her hips but were a bit loose around her waist. She still had a small, hard, climber's midriff courtesy of the ab cruncher hooked to the base of her bedroom door—fabulous for fashion but not if you wanted your pants to stay up. Mrs. Arnold was a deft touch with a sewing machine and—thanks to her desire to have her memories captured digitally, which she was *not* a deft hand with—kept all Tori's pants politely in position by way of thanks.

She glanced at her watch again. *Screw it.* This was her Saturday, too…she wasn't going to wait around for someone to call up the stairwell to tell her Nathan had arrived. He wasn't the only one whose time was worth something. She fired up her image software and the screen peppered with Mrs. Arnold's long lifetime of scanned memories. But then, down in the corner of the screen, another folder displayed by default—her personal one—and Tori fought hard to ignore it. But the more she ignored, the more it seemed to pulse and grow. Begging her attention. Without taking her eyes off Mrs. Arnold's black-and-white wedding photos, her hand slid the cursor over to her personal folder and readied to shush it back to where it came from.

But her fingers didn't make the minute depression needed to click the file shut. They hovered anxiously over it instead. She glanced around the room as though someone would catch her looking and then, with tight breath, slid her wrist slightly to the left and clicked. The whole time frowning, knowing this wasn't smart. Knowing it was going to hurt.

But unable not to.

Mrs. Arnold's folder minimized, and Tori's personal images unpacked like a picnic on her screen. Her life in rich, high-res pixels. Tori as a child, dirty and bloody and having a fabulous time down some hole or another. Her school friends, always trying to turn Tori into the girl she resisted being. Images of her gray-haired parents sent from all over America, each one crazier than the one before, most of them featuring some over-sized monument on some long, busy interstate. The adventure of their lifetime. Love saturating each one.

Then Rick's folder. The one she tried to avoid but knew she wouldn't.

One click spilled her brother's beautiful face across her screen. Rick smiling. Rick on horseback. Rick looking back down to her from halfway up a rock face, the wind in his brown, tossed hair, the world in his bright, living eyes. So much like her own. The ache in her chest swelled out to encircle her lungs, too, stealing her breath. She'd taken all of these pictures. They'd spent so much time together and she'd captured so much of it by habit she literally had hundreds of photographs of her twin stored in her computer. But none in her apartment.

Losing him all over again in the waking moments of every day was hard enough without stretching it out across twelve hours. She liked to keep the memories contained.

She looked at them now, her mouse-finger clicking through all the different versions of her brother. Happy Rick. Frustrated Rick. Crazy Rick. Triumphant Rick. Rick in crisis. Rick in love. She'd grown up in his pocket and then shared a house with him until they were twenty-one—there wasn't an expression he had that she hadn't memorized.

Including the one in the split second when he'd realized he was going to die.

Behind her, something screeched and she jumped almost as high as Gretel who issued an urgent bark before galloping to the door. Heart thumping, she spun around and stared at her kitchen counter. Specifically at the great pile of cookbooks that were stacked there against the wall, against the—

The books buzzed again.

Tori quickly shifted the books and a vase of Mr. Chen's fresh-cut flowers away from the defunct intercom and stared at it as though it were alien technology. In so many ways it was. It had never worked in for five years here. Now it was making noise all of a sudden.

"Hello?" She pressed the blue button and shouted overly loud into the speaker. Alexander Bell couldn't have done better.

"Tori? It's Nate. Can you buzz me in?"

She blinked at the unit and muttered to herself. "I have no idea." She poked the blue button again and spoke loudly into the box. "Why is this working?"

His pause reeked with frustration. "I had it fixed." She heard him rattle the front door. "Try again."

She depressed the button marked with a bell and heard a clicking sound. He didn't call her back so she assumed he was in the building.

Her eyes went to the door where Gretel stood like a sentinel, eyeballs fixed on the shiny timber. It took her a few seconds to realise she was staring with the same vigilance, her heart pattering away in anticipation of Nate's brisk, confident knock.

"Do you have no pride?" she said to a tail wagging Gretel, but really it was for herself. She forced her attention back to her kitchen counter, now in disarray. Now that it was fully exposed, the intercom was really quite dusty so Tori quickly wiped it down and then set about making alternative space for her cookbook collection. She moved the flowers down to the coffee table.

First CCTV and now a working intercom. Way too much technological excitement for one week.

Gretel issued one of her booming barks and Tori snapped her head around to her apartment entrance as her heart burst into a furious thumping. She shoved her hip between the excited dog and the door and used her weight to force Gretel out of the way so she could open the door inwards, muttering to her, "It's not your parents, dopey. Too early."

Gretel's booming bark must have prewarned him, but still Nathan's eyebrows almost disappeared into the hair flopping over his forehead when he stepped into her apartment and saw the size of her other guest. He warily eyed the grinning, drooling monster that followed him in.

"I hope you get something amazing in return for that," he said, and then looked up at her. "What?"

Tori stared. He had exchanged his dark, tailored corporate clothes for a faded New York casual—well-loved jeans bunched around beaten boots, an earthy green hooded sweat, and a short suede jacket that matched the boots. His hair was finger-combed and loose, and free of whatever fifty-dollar-a-tube product usually kept it architecturally perfect. No doubt a lot of money went into making him look as though he'd just been throwing a ball for kids in the park. But it sure was well-spent.

For the first time, the gulf between them seemed to shrink. Monday-to-Friday Nathan screamed *hands off* in a way that made sidelining her hormones possible. But Saturday Nathan…

Her eyes tracked him into her tiny apartment. Breathless awareness surfed down her arteries, spreading a chaos of confusion to every cell in her body. She straightened self-consciously, just shy of giving Gretel a run for her money in the drool stakes.

…*this* Nathan was positively edible.

He courteously offered the dog the back of his hand, and Gretel swung around to give it an investigatory sniff, her muscled tail waving frantically. Tori snapped clear of her hormonal haze and dived for the coffee table just as the Dane's tail whipped the footing out from under the flowers she'd just moved there. In spite of her keen reflexes, the vase and its contents went flying. Water surged over the edge of the table and trickled onto the floor, but before she could do more than shout Gretel's name in exasperation, Nate tossed his jacket aside, hauled his sweater off and pressed it straight down into the spreading puddle, stemming the flow onto her carpet.

By the time Tori had wrestled an excited Gretel back to her mat and got her to drop and stay, Nate had the spill well and truly under control and three of the loose cut flowers in his hand. She joined him and picked up a few more from the floor. His sweatshirt was a ruined, soggy mess on the table, leaving him in just his T-shirt. Tori struggled not to appreciate the way the cotton fitted to his well-shaped torso and concentrated on plucking errant flower stalks from her sofa.

She'd hung out with climbers; buff torsos weren't anything new to her. Maybe it had just been a long time since she'd seen one. That's why her pulse was falling over itself suddenly.

That and the fact that he smelled different today. Killer cologne. She filled her lungs with his scent. Something…woodsy. She stared at him curiously. *Woodsy?* Why the change from his slick Fifth Avenue original?

"A dog like that should be out in the suburbs," Nathan said, breaking the silence she only just realized had stretched out.

"It was my fault. I shouldn't have put the flowers so low."

He straightened and stared at her. "Wow. I broke your door and you took me to court. Godzilla over there destroys your furniture and you give it full amnesty."

Heat threatened to peek over her collar. "*Gretel* didn't mean to do it."

"Excitement of the moment?"

Tori frowned, knowing exactly the same could be said for the day he broke her door down. "Okay, look. I'm sorry about everything that happened. You came lurching at me when I was out on the ledge. It freaked me out and I…" *I really don't like surprises.* "I may have overreacted a bit."

"Just a bit?"

"You have no idea how smug you were standing in that hallway with two cops eating out of your hand."

He glanced up at her. "Smug? Not something I was aware was in my professional repertoire."

"Seriously? No one's told you that before? You have this whole…lip-twist thing going on. It's extremely irritating."

Just like the tiny smile he gave her now. The way he saw right through her. His eyes sparkled. "Getting under your skin, Tori?"

Yes.

The toss of her head said the idea was laughable. "No. But you seem to be very accustomed to getting your own way. I don't like that in a person." God, she'd so nearly said *man*. Was his lumberjack cologne messing with her mind now, as well?

He studied her hard and finally spoke. "If I've railroaded you with anything, I apologize. Occupational hazard."

Should she tell him about that other annoying look he had— the whole innocent and earnest thing? Trouble was *that* look actually worked on her. Like right now. She thrust out her hand. "Give me your sweater, I'll wring it out."

"I'm here for a few hours. Hopefully it will dry out in that time."

In her north-facing windows? Not a chance. She wrung the

worst of the water out in her kitchen sink. "I'll take it up on to the roof—it'll get more sun there. Gretel needs a toilet stop anyway."

"You toilet the dog on the roof?" His cautious glance spoke volumes. "Is that hygienic?"

She had to laugh. "It's fine, Nathan. Wait and see."

It *was* fine. The roof was a mini haven for the residents of their building. One of the first things Tori had done when she moved in was install a big patch of turf alongside Mr. Chen's rooftop vegetable garden. Just turf—but a lush, large, elevated square. Mr. Chen let her piggyback off his reticulation and the Davidson kids' two pet rabbits kept the patch mowed with their daily visits and fertilized with their castings, so, while Gretel's fortnightly visits weren't great for it, it had plenty of recovery time in between.

"This is amazing," Nate said, looking around the crowded roof space. Tori's turf, Mr. Chen's veggies, a couple of deck-chairs, a small outdoor table, an empty wading pool, a washing line, and a rickety old telescope. It was a hive of activity—when it wasn't just the two of them.

Gretel crossed immediately to the grass, sniffed around briefly and did what she'd come for. While Nathan looked around, Tori carefully pegged his sweater on the sunny side of the washing-line to swing in the breeze.

"It wasn't like this when I liv—" He frowned darkly and flicked his eyes back to her. "When I bought the building."

Tori kicked off her shoes. "I wanted something to tend. I'd helped Mr. Chen build his vegetable garden so he helped me make this." She stepped onto the grass across from where Gretel had peed and sunk her bare toes into the thick green blades. Amazingly healthy given its containment. Although not given the massive amount of spoiling it got from Tori. It had to be the most expensive patch of lawn on Manhattan, inch-for-inch.

"I guess Gretel benefits," he smiled. "Of course, you know there's a park right at the end of the street?"

Her belly balled up tight and she frowned. "Right. But

Gretel's not mine and we weigh almost the same, I'd hate to lose her out in the street if something happened."

Nate's gaze narrowed but he accepted her word. "She seemed easy enough to handle on the stairs."

"That's because she was coming up. You wait till we have to take her back down."

Nate followed Tori's gaze to the dog and then upward to the telescope. He crossed to it and swung it around to look back toward lower Manhattan. "I'd forgotten what the view was like up here," he murmured.

"Not a patch on your office's outlook, I'm guessing."

He lifted his eyes and rested them on her. "Depends on what you value looking at."

For the life of her she couldn't tear her own eyes away. The air suddenly thinned like that on the highest mountain peaks and screws she barely knew she had began to tighten deep and low inside her. But then Gretel trotted over and saved the day, nudging Tori for a pat, providing the perfect, polite excuse to break the traction of Nathan's gaze.

"I prefer the rivers and parks," she said, slightly breathless. The upstate wilderness she hadn't visited since she'd lost Rick.

He swung the telescope around toward Riverside and picked out a few highlights to study. The rising arc of the telescope told her he'd spotted a hawk just before he asked "Why didn't you build your nest box up here?"

A tiny part of her mourned the return to the subject of the falcons. It only reminded her of the real reason he was standing with her on this roof. Duress. Couldn't they go on pretending they were just…friends…a little bit longer?

"Too exposed. They like cover on a couple of sides if they can. Also too much traffic up here."

He straightened. "Well, let's ease the congestion, shall we? Your website isn't going to design itself."

Tori sighed and followed him to the stairwell door, whistling for Gretel to follow. It took both of them to manhandle the dog back inside once she realized her rooftop visit was being cut unnaturally short, but she finally acquiesced.

On the tenth floor, Tori tossed her key to Nate.

"It's about time for me to drop her home," she said, her hand on the dogs smooth, warm head. "Let yourself in, I'll be right back."

Nate watched as she wrestled the small pony down the next flight of stairs. She hadn't been kidding when she'd spoken of the difficulty she'd have out in public if Gretel took it into her head to bolt. It was possible the dog actually *did* weigh more than its lithe human companion. She might have the taut array of climber's muscles, but Tori Morfitt was still half air.

And she blew as hot and cold as the most changeable winds. Today—lukewarm; he felt vaguely welcome. Maybe she mellowed on weekends? Maybe the presence of the dog chilled her out a bit? Whatever, standing on the roof with her was the first time he'd felt any kind of mutual respect between them. A reciprocal connection. Not the connection he kept stumbling over—the one he had no business feeling—but an intellectual one. Today he felt truly relaxed in her company.

He frowned and stumbled to a halt. *In this building.*

The residents had done something special up on that rooftop. Not complicated, not high-tech, but special. And clearly most of his tenants loved to spend some time up there. Just one more thing that would press on his conscience the day the demolition crew moved in.

Still, they were all on leases. Every single one of them knew nothing was forever.

Tori's door swung noiselessly inwards and Nate propped it open with a footstool, then poured himself a coffee from the simmering pot in the kitchen and made himself comfortable at Tori's computer ready for a long haul of web design. He was sure she had assumed he'd build the website in the comfort of his own home, on his own laptop, and then just upload it, finished, to her PC. That had been his plan, too, right up until the moment he found himself giving the doorman of his building a farewell salute this afternoon and turning left for the subway uptown. To Morningside. But, no. He was going to build the whole thing on her computer, downloading what he needed online, coding from scratch. The website he wanted to give Tori was old-school. Classic. Like her.

The long-forgotten rush of staring at a blank page of code hit him again now. Man, how long had he been out of his zone? Another thing he'd exchanged for success. He used to live on air and the thrill of programming back when he was starting out.

Nate wiggled the mouse to bring Tori's hibernating screen back to life and then sucked in a breath as he slowly sank back in his seat. Dozens of photos of the same man splayed out on the screen like a pack of cards. As if she'd just been poring over them in privacy. A good-looking, athletic man. A really happy man. A man literally on top of the world in some of the photographs.

A climber.

He flicked through them. Insanely, it had never seriously occurred to him that Tori might have a boyfriend. The absence of pictures in the apartment—of a man in the apartment— had given him a false sense of security. *Here* were the photos most girlfriends splashed all over their living rooms. Their phones. Their social networking accounts. The way the women he risked relationships with liked to carry him around like a social handbag.

A boyfriend. He'd been stupid to assume—

"What are you doing?

Her quiet, pained words brought him round sharply, as guilty as if he'd been caught digging through her underwear drawer. Heart thumping from way more than just the surprise of being caught.

Tori had a boyfriend.

"Sorry, were you working on something?"

The darkness of her gaze lifted slightly as she cleared her throat. "No. I was just…" She stepped forward and pressed slightly against him as she leaned in to close the file. The hairs right along that side of his body gravitated towards her. Her trembling hand missed the first attempt. But then the images sucked back into the file and disappeared into darkness. Which is exactly where she'd be hoping the subject could stay. He saw it in the way her eyes rested everywhere but on his.

He spun in the chair as she hurried into the kitchen to wash her hands. "Who was that, Tori?"

Her body stiffened and stumbled, but she forced her hands to reach for the simmering coffeepot.

He tried again. "Someone special?"

It had to be, the way she was going all out to pretend the images were of no consequence. She finished pouring her coffee and wiped down the spotless kitchen counter, then the coffeepot. Then a nonexistent mark on her refrigerator door. He watched her rinse the cloth thoroughly and lay it carefully over the edge of the sink to dry. He'd seen this kind of delay tactic in the boardroom; the corporate equivalent anyway. Silence was his best friend right now, he knew if he waited long enough she'd spill.

Eventually.

She turned to him, seemingly desperate for a task, and opened her mouth to ask him something, but her gaze fell on his still-steaming cup of coffee and the words dried up. But she was looking at him with speech trembling on her lips and he was steadily watching her. Waiting. She had to say something if she couldn't offer him a coffee.

She turned, reached into her tiny pastry, retrieved a packet of shortbread biscuits and placed a couple on a plate. Then, on still-bare feet, she brought him the offering and placed it silently next to him on her desk.

Still he waited.

The computer whirred, oblivious, in the awkward silence.

"My brother, Rick," she finally said.

Relief pumped through him in a steady, controlled feed. His eyes fell briefly shut. Not a boyfriend. Not a lover.

A brother.

Maybe all sisters kept hundreds of photos of their brothers. He wouldn't know, happy families were so far outside his field of experience.

He scrabbled around for something normal to fill the next silence. "Good-looking guy."

Pain flashed across her face in a hundred tiny muscle shifts and he knew, somehow, he'd said the wrong thing. Again.

"Yes."

"Good genes in your family."

The lameness of his words was only amplified by the silence with which they were met. *Christ, Archer, why don't you just ask her how she likes her eggs in the morning and be done with it...* He really was out of practice. How hard could it be to get someone to start talking about something more personal than the neighbors?

Attempt number two. "Where does he live?"

Tori stared at him, carefully neutral, then at the now-blank computer screen. Then she straightened and offered him a watered-down facsimile of a smile that barely twitched a cheek before speaking softly. "In my heart."

Nate's stomach sank. That explained the photos. "He's dead?"

She nodded.

When? How? And most importantly...*Are you okay?* But he only risked, "I'm sorry."

She lifted her coffee to her lips and her still-trembling fingers sloshed it in its cup. "Me, too."

"Were you close?"

She nodded again. Barely.

Okay, he was prepared to do this twenty-question fashion if he had to. The chance to peek inside Tori Morfitt's heart was too golden an opportunity to politely step back from. He scrabbled around for something lateral to ask.

"Did he teach you to climb?" Those photos that looked out over massive expanses of American landscape...

Tori's nostrils flared and she seemed to collapse in on herself like a tumbling building, walls of defense blocking him out. *Clang, clang, clang*...like the best system firewall, as the opportunities for him to advance slammed shut one by one. But he knew the best way through a crashing system was forward. Steady and unpanicked. Fewer mistakes that way.

"I taught him," she croaked.

Steady and unpanicked... "Did you both live in New York?"

"No. We're from Oregon." She was like a rusted piece of machinery oiled for the first time in thirty years. Slowly, painfully, her speech was coming more freely.

"Not from Manhattan?" he asked. Though he already knew the answer.

Her lips twisted and he almost heard the protesting squeak. "Most of Manhattan's not from Manhattan."

"I am." The words were out before he even knew they were forming.

Her almond eyes elongated and creased slightly at the corners. "I know. Your accent's a dead giveaway. Where did you grow up?"

His senses went on full alert. *Uh-uh. This is my inquisition, not yours.* "Not far from here. What part of Oregon?"

She leaned down over him and opened another photo album on the desktop. A heap of rugged wilderness shots scattered across the screen. Oregon, presumably.

"Medford, originally. Though Rick and I shared my grandmother's place on the edge of Portland when we moved out of home." Her conversation unwound along with some of the visible tension in her body.

"Good climbing district." He had no idea if that were true but she accepted it easily enough. "What brought you to New York?"

She stared long and hard. No longer tense but a million miles from relaxed. It only tweaked his instincts further. He wanted to tease the pain he could see right out of her, carefully and controlled. He wanted to see what she looked like without the perpetual shadow in her gaze.

"It wasn't Oregon."

He kept his smile light. "Florida would have been further."

"Geographically maybe."

Interesting. So what was she after by coming here? "Fresh start?"

"Something like that."

"Do you miss the wilderness?"

A sharp kind of pain flashed across her eyes, and then it was gone. "Every day."

"Why not go back?"

"There's nothing there for me now. After Rick… When he was gone, my parents sold up and hit the road. They're official Gray Nomads now."

"Was that their way of coping?"

A frown formed on her smooth brow. "It's their way of honoring Rick. By living their lives to the fullest."

"What's your way?"

The shutters dropped again. This time instant and entire. He'd pushed too far. But short of quizzing her on the finer details of how a healthy young man dies so young, he was going to have to ease back on trying to twist his way into her inner psyche. She'd tell him when she was ready.

Or not… Which would be quite telling in itself.

"They visited once but didn't like bringing the RV into Manhattan. We talk by phone all the time."

A spectacularly obvious change of subject but he let it go. "It's nice that you're close to your parents."

"Where's your family?"

Unprepared for the question, it took his defenses by surprise. A tiny thread of old pain took its chance and weaseled out between the cracks from the place he kept it carefully contained, tightening his whole body. "I'm all that's left."

Surprise lightened Tori's features, followed almost immedi-

ately by compassion. It was such a welcome change from the
shadows he'd caused her he forgot to be defensive about her
pity. "Really? I had imagined you as one in a big family of
successful Manhattan achievers."

His snort rivaled that of the half-dog-half-horse that had
just left. "No. I was born in the city but my mother wasn't. She
moved here back in the eighties to pursue…"

Wow. How was he going to put this…?

"Her dreams?" Tori stepped in.

He couldn't credit the woman he remembered with possibly
having aspirations and dreams. Certainly she'd never encouraged him to have any. "Her *job*. She never spoke of her family.
Or where she'd come from." Or where he had. Though he had
a pretty good idea about that.

"They're *your* family, too. You never asked about them?"

"All the time at the beginning. But my mother wasn't a
woman who believed in looking backwards." Plus she had no
idea at all which of dozens of men had actually fathered her
child.

Tori stared. "Huh. Not what I imagined at all," she said.

Uncomfortable, suddenly, with the false image she must have
had of his halcyon childhood in an up-market neighborhood
surrounded by opportunity and wealth and love, he shifted
decisively in the chair. He flicked casually through more of
her on-screen photographs, scrabbling for a subject change.

"Is that Potsdam?" he asked, enlarging one of her images
on-screen. It was a wilderness shot with a river twisting through
the background and a pretty village on its banks taken from
high up in a mountain range. "I went to school there. Clarkson.
Upstate, at the base of the Adirondack Mountains. That's definitely New York State."

She leaned in over him slightly to look at the image, and
her heat radiated deliciously. And her scent—lightly floral,
intensely seductive.

"That's where I took it. I climbed the Adirondacks with—"
She stumbled. "It looks like a beautiful place to go to school."

Six hundred acres on the banks of the Raquette River. "It was."

"Far from home." Her gray eyes slid sideways to search his. "Almost across the Canadian border."

"Almost across the universe. That's what I loved about it."

"You really weren't happy here. Why Clarkson?"

"Because they took me. I was early admission and on scholarship." *Hardship* scholarship seemed too pathetic to add.

"Early admission...? You must have been a bright kid."

"I studied and read relentlessly." And half the high-school faculty wanted him the heck out of his mother's orbit and, collectively, pulled every string they could to find him an opportunity.

"Then what happened?"

"I discovered the opposite sex." Those years at Clarkson were the first good years he'd ever had.

"And that was the end of the reading and the studying, I'm sure."

"Not at all. Every girl on campus wanted to take the young kid under their wing. They all thought I needed some kind of bridging tutoring. It was a great way to meet girls." A lot of girls. And volume meant he could keep them all at a nice, safe distance. Where they all belonged.

Tori laughed. "How early was your admission?"

"Only a year. But a year means a lot when you're seventeen. And I was happy not to let on that I was already aceing my classes."

Tori smiled. "My landlord, the player."

"Landlord?" He winced. "You make it sound like I have a paunch and a cardigan." It was more than just vanity that made him want that image of him stripped from her mind, permanently. He took a lot of pride in being a leader in the world's fastest-growing industry.

She backpedalled immediately. "Not at all. You're in great shape—"

The blush that stole up her neck only endeared her to him

more. Nate's lips twisted in exactly the way she hated. "Coming from a rock-climber that's quite a compliment."

"Ex rock-climber."

"You wouldn't know it. There's not an inch of fat on you."

Her eyes flew to his and flared as he watched. Okay, not his most subtle moment but totally worth it to see the dawning of awareness in her gray depths. Time slowed to molasses as he brushed his glance over every part of her face. The doe lashes. The smooth bridge of her nose with its peppering of freckles. The perfect shape of her mouth. Made for kissing…

As his focus lingered there, she sucked a corner of her bottom lip between pearly teeth, and tiny creases roosted in the corners of her eyes. Tiny, *anxious* creases.

He pushed away from the computer slightly, giving them both some much-needed oxygen. "How about you show me what you've pulled together for the website graphics and we'll start planning what kind of feel you want it to have? How we can bring the world into Morningside."

She regarded him thoughtfully, but then she crossed to the tiny dining alcove and selected one of two barely used chairs and brought it over to sit next to him. Close enough that her clothed arm pressed against his bare one, and her warmth radiated out and gently heated that part of him that was cold and empty from everything he'd not revealed.

A place where warmth seldom reached. Seldom survived.

He let the welcome glow soak in and did nothing to shift politely away. As she opened the computer file with her astounding falcon imagery he tried not to indulge the satisfaction of knowing that she hadn't moved away either.

She didn't like him smug.

CHAPTER FIVE

IN late afternoon, the stairwell spat Nate out on the eighth floor and, as he always did, he kept his eyes low and headed directly for the elevator, intentionally avoiding the far end of the hall. But as he drew close to the silver antique he slowed... wavered.

He should check. What if the place had been vandalized? What if a water pipe had burst? What if someone had been secretly living here the entire time it had been boarded up? Going back into his mother's apartment was not high on his list of favorite things to do, but it was probably necessary. Besides, how long could he hang out in this building and pretend apartment 8B didn't exist?

He wiped his damp palms on his jeans as he walked down the hall, fished the cluster of keys out of his pocket and then slid the tarnished bronze one carefully into the lock.

And then he stopped.

Hand poised. Lungs aching. Just staring at the tarnished letter B that hung crookedly on the outside of the door.

Every miserable memory of the woman—the men, the drinking, the wailing and moaning, the *other* moaning, the fighting—it all came back to him in a blinding, sickly rush. He recalled every reason he'd ever sealed up this door and not looked back.

He braced his hands on the door frame and let his head sag forward. If the pipes were damaged or the place was full of

vermin or squatters then that was going to have to be someone else's job to discover. He'd taken many risks in his life,
overcome many hurdles; he didn't consider himself lacking in
strength or courage, but nothing short of a force of nature was
getting him through that door.

He pulled his phone out to get Karin to arrange an
inspection.

"I think she's out," a quiet voice said behind him.

He turned to see a small, folded-over woman in a neat, faded
dress.

A violent rattle started up deep inside. "I'm just…uh…"

"She's probably gone for cigarettes. Smokes like a chimney,
that one." The old woman had a pruned smile, and bright,
vacant eyes. Kind and deep but…vacant. And disturbingly familiar. Nate's stomach coiled tighter.

"Nancy! There you are." Tori's head popped out of the stairwell and huffed with relief. "I just got a call to say you were
out. We've been looking for you all over the building."

The woman turned slowly. "I'm helping this delivery man.
He needs someone to sign for the parcel for 8B."

Tori looked at Nate curiously, then glanced around for a
delivery. There was no point denying it—that wouldn't help
the older woman's confusion. Nancy's ancient gaze drifted to
the phone he still held clutched in his hand. Clearly, she wasn't
moving until he had a signature.

"I'll take care of that," Tori said, putting her hand out for
the phone. She took it from him and pretended to sign it. The
old woman smiled again and stepped closer. Nate froze as the
complicated mix of smells reached out to him. Talcum powder.
Citrus. And old lady.

"Would you like to come on up with me?" she said to
him.

His chest clenched. Immediately. Painfully.

Conclusively.

"We'd love to, Nancy, thank you," Tori soothed. "It's a long
climb. Will you be okay?"

"The elevator's broken," she said, curling her arm for Tori to take.

His gut squeezed again. Something clearly was not right here.

"I know," Tori said. "But we'll help you. Wait a moment, Nancy, while I get the door." She moved down the hall. Nate took the older woman's arm.

"Miss Smith?" He hadn't meant to say it out loud and he barely did. The ancient ears certainly didn't hear him and neither did Tori. She was too busy propping the stairwell door open twenty feet away.

Would you like to come up?

It had become a regular offer when she'd step out of the lift on the eighth floor to swap to the stairwell and find Nate there, curled against the wall after school while his mother... worked. Nancy, according to Tori, but he'd only ever known her as Miss Smith. He spent the better part of most afternoons hanging out at her place—doing his homework, watching TV, watching her cook a meal. Occasionally he'd slept on her sofa when his mother went out all night and forgot to leave the key for him. Although he'd never eat with her no matter how hungry he was or how amazingly good her food smelled. Accepting sanctuary was one thing; accepting charity...

God, he hadn't thought about her in years. He hadn't let himself.

They were one long, exhausting flight up before she lifted her thin silver curls to look at Nate. "I should sign for that parcel."

"Perhaps when we get to your door," he said, lending her as much of his strength as he could and glancing over her head at Tori, who smiled tightly at him.

It took close to ten minutes to shuffle her up to the twelfth floor. Nate had long since realized that this was the eighty-something-year-old woman Tori had referred to on the first day they'd met. She was right. This climb would kill Miss Smith one day.

He held her arm tighter.

"Here we are," Tori smiled as they emerged on to the top floor of the twelve-story building. Nate's chest cramped up hard. God knows how the old lady's must be feeling. But his chest-squeeze was uncomfortable for way more than just his exertion, as twenty years in full tackle gear rushed headlong at him.

"You left your door open," Tori gently admonished as they stepped Nancy across the hall to 12C's entry.

He looked around. Nothing about this place had changed one bit. The furniture was even still where it had been two decades before. Like a museum display built to haunt him. But Miss Smith was changed. Had she always been this tiny? She made Tori seem positively robust. Or had he just grown so much?

In a building where everything felt as recent as last week, seeing Miss Smith so aged was a shock. A reminder that time actually had passed since that day when he was seventeen and he'd walked out of this building without a backward glance. He'd never even said goodbye to Miss Smith.

"Lemonade, dear?"

His head came up fast enough to give him whiplash, but she wasn't speaking to him. She was smiling at Tori, who closed the door carefully, properly, behind them.

That was straight out of his childhood, too. Miss Smith's lemonade. A sweet, tangy port in the relentless storm of his miserable childhood.

"I'd love some, Miss—" The words *Miss Smith* so nearly spilled from his lips until he remembered that he only knew her first name as far as Tori was concerned. "Nancy. Thank you."

Tori caught his eye apologetically as the older woman wandered into her kitchen. He split his frozen lips into something he hoped resembled a smile. But Tori's frown suggested maybe he hadn't quite pulled it off.

She dropped her voice. "I'm sorry Nathan. I hope this won't take long."

"She's got Alzheimer's?"

She glanced toward the kitchen. "Dementia. Mild enough she can still live on her own, but severe enough she might wander out of the building and forget where she lives. She's been stable for a few years, but it's been worse this past year. Inside her apartment she's generally okay. Or in the building. Everyone here looks out for her." Her eyes narrowed slightly. "You're extremely special. She would normally never invite a stranger up. Ever."

Nathan averted his eyes immediately and, grief welling, watched the tiny, blue-rinsed woman pottering in her kitchen. Miss Smith had given him shelter when he'd needed it—never a question asked—and he'd barely thought of her these past two decades. He remembered her as old twenty years ago, but logically she could only have been in her mid-sixties back then. Somewhere deep in his subconscious he'd convinced himself she'd have died by now. So to find her still living, but in such poor health… And all alone…

"Here you are, dear. No sugar." She reappeared and passed one of two tall glasses of home-squeezed lemonade to Tori, and then turned to him. "And extra for you."

Nate reeled as the soft, wrinkled hands extended a pebbled glass straight from his past. Extra sugar. Just how he'd always taken it. He glanced up between chest thumps but her pale eyes showed no recognition whatsoever. Whatever functioning part of her clouded brain remembered how he took his lemonade, it wasn't communicating with the part that would remember a face. Or a name. Or, God forbid, his circumstances.

She remembered him, but apparently she didn't.

His hand shook as he took the glass, and his eyes flicked to Tori.

She glanced openly and quizzically between him and Miss Smith. He didn't dare hold the older woman's gaze in case the spark of recognition should suddenly form. In case she'd re-member and blurt out what she knew. Instead, he took his lemonade and wandered over to the window to look out, keeping his back firmly to her.

The view didn't do much of a job of taking his mind off the imminent exposure that he risked by staying, but storming out now would only make it all more dramatic and obvious. The last thing he wanted or needed was for Tori to start asking questions about his childhood. He was as changed from the boy he'd been as Miss Smith was from the woman he remembered, but even through the haze of dementia she had recognized him on some unconscious level.

Tori sipped her lemonade and made quiet conversation with his old friend. Her tranquil goodness radiated outward and made him feel positively grimy for the kind of life he'd led here, for the decisions he'd made since leaving.

There was a reason he didn't like to go back into those feelings. They weren't productive.

The ice in his glass rattled and he realized how brutally he was holding his lemonade. He took a long, careful swig and half drained the contents, wincing. Memories flowed into him with the bittersweet liquid. The taste of citrus on his tongue as a boy, had become a balm against what he knew was going on downstairs, a psychological bridge to safety that he could cross as the drink crossed his lips, to enter Miss Smith's pillowed world. Somewhere normal. A thousand miles from the apartment four floors down where his mother sold her body to strangers three times a day.

Mission accomplished. These days he had money bursting out of metaphorical suitcases. More than any of them ever could have imagined. The life he lived now couldn't have been more different to the first two decades of his existence.

"Are you finished?" Tori's soft voice brought him around. She took his half-empty glass from his cold fingers. The warmth he'd admired earlier had completely vanished and a flat caution filled her expression instead. Understandable, given he'd been treating her to his back for the past ten minutes.

He nodded. "Let's get out of here." It was straight from his aching heart. From the part of him that still carried shame. But it visibly pierced her skin.

Her brows dropped and her eyes darkened. "I'm sorry to have kept you. But thank you for helping me get her back upstairs."

Disapproval leached through the tightness of her expression. She couldn't understand his haste, of course. She had no idea how many agonies it was for him, standing here, smelling these smells, reliving the memories. So unprepared.

In front of *her*.

"I'll start on the website tomorrow afternoon," he murmured. There was no way he could stay today.

"It's Sunday."

"Doesn't matter. The faster I get this done…" *The faster I get the hell out of this building.*

A dark shaft flashed across her face. "Right. Of course. Time is money."

He nodded his farewell, glanced at Miss Smith and hurried out into the relative silence of the hallway where his memories didn't shriek at him.

As he pushed open the stairwell door, he imagined Miss Smith's frail wrists trying to do it. Remembered how they'd had to proceeded slowly as a funeral cortège up the four flights from the eighth floor where she'd found him. He kept his eyes down as he switched from the stairs to the elevator, but then made himself raise them as he stepped in. He couldn't go on studying the carpet forever.

He glanced around at the aged inner furnishings and let himself go back where he seldom did. His sixteenth birthday. The cheaply dressed woman turning to him with a smile as fake as the nails that stalled the elevator in middescent. How he'd pressed his clenched fists to the polished glass throughout the whole encounter—wanting it and hating it at the same time—and stared into the reflection of his own anguished, fevered eyes until it was over.

But he never forgot it, nor forgave the woman who'd caused

it—not the stranger who'd popped the gum back into her mouth and tottered on high heels out of the elevator ahead of him, but her...his mother...the woman who'd gifted fifteen minutes of a fellow hooker's time to Nate for his sixteenth birthday. One of the rare times she'd given him anything.

And it had broken the final surviving fragment of his embittered young heart.

The next time he saw Darlene Archer was at her funeral. Dean's parents had offered him a no-questions-asked spare bed until his college scholarship kicked in. For months he'd been a model houseguest for them, so much so that Dean's mother had had to beg Nate not to do so much around the house. But he'd ignored her pleas; he was so desperate to stay. So damned desperate not to go back.

The lurch of the elevator snapped his thoughts back to the present. He shouldered his way through the aging doors and into the foyer before they were fully open, longing for fresh air all of a sudden. This was exactly why he'd locked those memories deep inside. It was bad enough growing up with the crippling lack of affection and interest from his mother. He didn't want to drag the anchors with him into his adult years.

And he hadn't. He'd stayed focused and on track right through college and into his career. That focus had brought him everything he wanted.

His mind threw up an image of the judgment leaching from perceptive gray eyes in Nancy Smith's apartment.

He pulled out his phone and dialed his office with unsteady fingers. "Karin," he said, and then cleared his voice so she could hear him more clearly. "Get someone to repair the elevator at Morningside, will you?"

Karin chose her words carefully. "That's not going to be cheap, Nathan. And you've just pressed the green light on demolition. Are you sure?"

It was unlike her to second-guess him, but then again, it was unlike him not to sound certain, to be reacting on emotion and not sound business sense. But his interest in making

Nancy Smith's day that little bit easier belonged one hundred percent in the past. His conscience and his judgment warred in a funnel of turbulent emotion deep inside. This was exactly why he never let emotion interfere with business.

He swore. "Get me three quotes, then. I'll see whether it's worth it." Then, because his assistant had been with him through thick and thin and because none of this was her fault, he softened his voice. "Thanks, Karin."

But somewhere deep inside he knew he'd do it. Or something better than fixing the elevator. He could make a difference for the woman who'd made such a difference to him, albeit years too late. He'd make sure she was re-housed somewhere better than his crappy old building—so she could be comfortable for the last years of her life.

It wasn't much of a thank-you, but it was something he could do.

CHAPTER SIX

"TORI, I'm sorry. Look at the time. I had no idea."

Tori straightened in her seat the following night and dropped her eyes to the computer's clock. How had four hours passed? One minute they were settling down to choose images and the next it was dark and Nathan's stomach had started vocalizing.

"Oh, wow. Me, neither. I got totally lost in the site."

She had. He'd used her images to start building a website that was elegant and clean, making stars of Fred and Wilma and building a simple text story around the two birds and the webcam. He did it in such a way that, later, when the birds bred, she'd be able to add their offspring easily. Tell a new generation of stories.

Though she had to admit he got visibly tense about the whole "future" part. Inexplicably.

But the moment passed and then so did the hours after it and now here they were, well after nine o'clock.

"Did you have plans?" she asked, mortified that some woman somewhere was tapping glossy acrylic nails on a counter top waiting for Nathan to appear.

"Nope." He finished a line of coding and turned to her, smiling with satisfaction. "You were my plans this evening."

That awkward pronouncement snapped her jaw shut audibly. She stared at him, speechless, a thick pleasure burbling upward.

I was?

"My goal was to finish this sucker tonight. A first draft, at least. No matter how long it took."

The broiling awareness thickened instantly to a hard, uncomfortable mass in her chest. He was going to stay up until all hours to get this project over with in the minimum amount of time. Her lips tightened. Of course he was. He had such a gift for making a girl feel *un*wanted.

"What if I'd had plans?" she asked, purely to be churlish.

His head came up. "Do you?"

No, but... "I might have."

He frowned at her prickly response. "Would you like me to go now? It's no problem."

Tori forced away the unexpected surge of defensiveness. She knew why he was here—the court order. Neither of them had pretended otherwise. Why the hell was she getting so offended by his haste? "No. Unless you want to? I'd understand."

It was ridiculous. Both of them stepping so carefully around the other's feelings.

Nathan chuckled first. "Let's start again." He sat up straighter. "Tori, it's late. Do you want to get some dinner?"

His smile melted her tension away to nothing. "Yes. Eating would be good."

"What do you like?"

"Anything but Portuguese chicken."

"What do you have against the Portuguese?"

"Nothing." She laughed. "Piri-Piri and I don't get along."

"I find it hard to imagine anyone or anything not getting along with you. You're very easy to be around."

More awkward silence. It was his color that rose this time, just slightly, in pinpricks high along his jaw. Tori scrabbled around for a distraction from just staring at him longer. "You wouldn't say that if you were with me right after I ingested Piri-Piri."

Oh, lord... The sort of thing you said around a campfire

after a long day climbing with your buddies, not around a hot man you couldn't stop staring at.

But Mr. Smooth took it in his stride. "Well, I've got a hankering for some Mexican. How about we clear our heads, take a walk and see if we can find somewhere with an outdoor table?"

Everything in her tightened up. She waved a carefully casual hand. "Why walk when we can dial? Eat in."

"Are you serious? We've been fixed in one position for four hours. We should probably be doing some yoga to unkink."

Immediately Tori thought of more collaborative ways of working the knots out of their muscles. A part of her longed to suggest it.

"Plus it's a beautiful night," he went on. "Come on, Tori, I'll take you to dinner. Somewhere with a view."

Again with the clenching muscles deep inside. What was going on with her? Was she really so out of touch with how this was done in normal circles? Not that anything was being done here tonight. This was just a practical necessity. They both had to eat.

"We've got one of the best views around right here," she said. "Why don't I set up the table on the roof while you pick up the takeout?"

The lines between his brows doubled. He shrugged. "Sure. Okay. Got any recommendations?"

Tori crossed to her fridge, relieved to be away from Nathan's scrutiny, and rifled through an enormous bundle of restaurant fliers pinned to its front.

"I should rephrase that," he said, deceptively light. "Any recommendations you *don't* have?"

She looked at the ridiculous wad in her hand and fought the bristle of discomfort at his gentle teasing. "I enjoy eating in."

"But not eating out?"

Her mouth dried up. She blinked at him urgently then stammered to speech. "W-wait till you've sat up there. You'll understand."

His eyes held hers while his brain ticked over. They nearly broiled with the intensity of his gaze. "You'd better make it special, then. Worth it."

And just like that it was a date.

What should have been a casual, convenient take-out meal had suddenly become a *special* tryst for two on the top of a New York building. He'd already seen the rooftop so she'd have to do more than just throw out a clean table cloth. And there was no electric light up there so they'd have to have candles.

Ugh…!

Not that a long-suppressed, girlie part of her wasn't thrilling at the idea of being on a date. After…how long? Even if it wasn't really a *date*-date. She hadn't sat across a dinner table from a man in five years. She wasn't even sure she remembered what people did on a date. Talked. Ate. Shared.

Kissed.

Her stomach flip-flopped. It was very telling that the idea of *sharing* with Nathan Archer was infinitely scarier than the idea of kissing him. Not that she'd given much thought to what it would be like to kiss him. Not truly. Okay, a few times…just casually wondering… Nothing serious.

Although now that the fantasy was in her head she had trouble shaking it.

"Yes." She thrust him the advertisement of the best TexMex in the area, just a few blocks over. "It'll be worth it."

Tori didn't take the word *special* any more lightly than the challenge she'd seen in Nathan's eyes as he headed out to buy the food. Whatever she did, she knew it had to be inspired.

Seven years ago she'd been hiking the Canadian Rockies and she'd had the best Mexican food she'd ever tasted in an Irish pub, of all places. They'd served sizzling meals on scorching hot tiles straight out of the fire, and margaritas in moonshine jars. Tonight she was desperate enough to recreate every part of that experience.

She'd loved it then, maybe Nathan would love it now.

She finished pouring margarita mix over a pitcher of hastily crushed ice, loaded up a couple of clean preserve jars and a crazy cowboy-hat candle her parents had sent her from Texas, and raced up the stairs. Then she came back down for the pizza stones she'd baked to blazing in her oven. She stacked them on top of each other and used the lifters to carry them carefully up the two flights of stairs. By the time she emerged, even her climbing arms were trembling from the strain.

She placed them carefully onto tiny terracotta blocks to protect the table. Then stood back to admire her handiwork.

Special. No denying it.

"Food's up," a deep voice said, behind her. She spun, still breathless from dashing around and kicking herself she hadn't dashed faster so she could have dedicated just sixty seconds to freshening up. So that, just once, he could see her at her best rather than her worst.

But then she remembered this wasn't a date-date. This was just dinner. "How did you get back in?"

"One of the perks of owning the building. I finally signed myself over a key."

Tori's heart fluttered. Just the idea that he could let himself in whenever he wanted… Was that uncertainty or excitement curling her stomach. Or was it just hunger?

She distracted herself with pouring slushy-ice margarita into the large empty jars while Nathan unloaded six containers of Mexico's finest. Then they both sat and got busy serving up rice, burritos, chili, tamales, stuffed peppers and skillet-fried fish onto their piping-hot stone tablets. The mouth-watering odors wafted around them. They loaded up their forks and sampled.

Nathan took a long, appreciative swallow from his moonshine jar to wash down the first mouthful of food and looked around before letting his contented eyes rest back on hers through the flicker of candlelight. "Okay, you win. This is without question the best way to eat Mexican *ever.*"

Tori waved a hand. "I do it like this all the time."

"You do not," he laughed. Though he looked as if he'd have believed her if she said she really did. "When you didn't want to come with me I wondered if I'd done something to..." He frowned. "But this is great. I appreciate the effort you've gone to."

She knew she'd offended him by not going with him to dinner. Not that she could explain why when she didn't even know herself. She'd just been listening to her body. And her body said stay. "You're welcome. It is nice, huh?"

To illustrate the point she took a big swig from her moonshine jar. Then she bit into a piping-hot tamale. "Okay, wow. That's better than..."

"Than?"

The spicy heaven filled her mouth with excited juices. She rolled her eyes with pleasure. "Everything."

He lifted one sexy eyebrow. "Not everything, surely?"

She sat back in her seat and chewed a tamale appreciatively. "I'm struggling to think of something better."

Nathan selected one from the tray, trying for himself. "It is good," he nodded slowly then his mouth split into a heart-stopping grin. "But not that good."

Tori smiled to cover the sudden pounding of her heart. What she wouldn't give just to lean forward and wipe the tamale grease right off his lips...with her own. Slowly and thoroughly. Lingering on the bottom one. Her tongue slipped out onto her own lips in sympathy. "Well, you'd know, I guess!"

"Meaning?"

She stiffened her back. "Meaning I imagine you've had a lot of...everything...to compare to."

He smiled. "You're talking about sex."

Thump, thump... "No, *you* were talking about sex. I was talking about everything else."

His narrowed gaze saw too much. "But not sex?"

It had to come up sooner or later. "If these tamales are like sex then I can understand what all the fuss is about."

Nathan stared at her and she took another healthy swig of margarita then finally met his eyes silently.

His blazed back at her. "You've never had sex?"

"Try and contain your disbelief. It's insulting." Her words would have been, too, if she hadn't punctuated them by casually popping another tamale between her tingling lips and smiling. Way more casually than she felt.

He seemed to shake himself free of his stupor. "I'm sorry. I'm having a hard time believing it."

"Why?"

The blue in his gaze boiled as furiously as a hot spring. "Have you seen yourself, Tori?"

She shrugged. "Maybe my body is my temple?"

He put down his fork and leaned forward. "Come on. Seriously?"

"Why do people who've had sex always find it inconceivable that someone else hasn't?" And on what planet did she sit across the table from a relative stranger talking about her nonexistent sex life?

Planet Nathan, apparently.

He considered that in silence. "You're right. I just…" He shook his head. "How old are you?"

That question had only just occurred to him? She'd looked him up on the internet him almost immediately after she'd met him to find out the essentials. Which had seemed stupid at the time. "I'm twenty-six."

"Huh." He shook his head.

"You're really struggling with this." Amazing. And insanely flattering. Her whole body tightened in response. "I was one of the boys at prep school, then I spent most of my teen years in sports clubs." And why the heck was she defending herself so vigorously? "Then on the peaks I was just one of the boys again. Maybe I missed my window of opportunity."

"Uh, no, Tori, that window is still *wide* open for you."

She stared at him as his lashes blinked, apparently at half speed. Or was everything around her just happening sluggishly?

Certainly the blood in her veins and what air was in her lungs were thickening up dangerously.

"All those climbers, Tori. All that testosterone…"

The glow dissipated just a bit. "The last person in the world you want to climb with is someone you're emotionally involved with." She topped up her rice and got stuck into it, hoping to change the subject.

"Why?"

Hoping in vain. "It's like brain surgery. You should never do it on someone you love. Makes it hard to stay objective."

"You climbed with your brother."

The food in her mouth congealed into a tasteless paste. She chewed it carefully then took care swallowing so that it stayed down. "We had rules. To keep things separate."

Mostly.

"What kind of rules?"

"We'd climb in groups and always partner someone else. If we were climbing together we'd only do novice peaks." That was the rule. But the moment they set it, they'd started breaking it. Incrementally. Which could only lead to one thing…

"Defeats the purpose, I would have thought," Nathan said.

"Not many people get that." She looked at him differently in that moment, but then she remembered in his own industry he was the risk-taker. The first one to the highest peaks. "So we'd try for groups whenever we could so we could really climb."

"And no-one wanted to…get closer?"

Some of the taste in her food returned and she smiled gently. "With them, Rick was like a rottweiler on patrol. I think he'd heard too many of their stories."

"Ah. Big brothers."

"Physically, definitely. He out-muscled all of them. But I was older than him by fifteen minutes."

That stilled the fork halfway to his mouth. "You and Rick were twins?"

Her chest ached. Five years meant nothing to the ball of pain still resident in her chest. "We were the full cliché. Finishing each other's sentences, being sensitive to each other, sharing a house…" She felt the darkness hovering and took a deep breath to stave it off. "I even wore his clothes until puberty hit and he shot up four sizes. It drove him nuts."

"He was lucky to have you." Blue eyes held hers as he got used to that idea. A chili-like warmth spread through her body and added to the sluggish mix. "So that explains how you stayed under the radar until you were twenty-one. You haven't met anyone since you came to Manhattan?"

Tori's muscles coordinated to squeeze the last bit of oxygen from her lungs. Okay, when the conversation started working its way around to him it was definitely time to stop talking about sex. She forced a chuckle. "Mr. B's not really my type and Marco deCosta isn't old enough yet."

He laughed. "You think you're joking. The day will come when that kid's not going to be able to look at you without a cushion in his lap."

Tori spluttered, surprised by the unfamiliar sound of her own full belly laugh, and intrigued by the sudden forked frown lines that appeared between Nathan's brows. She saw a chance to learn more about him. She took it.

"Was there someone like that for you?"

Almost definitely. A man as simmering as Nathan didn't wake up one day and discover he'd become sexy. That kind of charisma came from childhood. And people responded to charisma. No matter the shape or size or age. They just changed the manner of response. He probably didn't even know he had it.

He blinked three times. Rapidly. "What?"

She glanced down at her empty margarita glass leaned forward to refill it, smiling more comfortably now that the topic had moved on. "If there was ever a candidate for a *Graduate* moment, it's you. Was there some kind of older woman that excited you, Nathan Archer?"

His gaze darkened and his mouth formed a harsh, straight line. Tension radiated from him in angry ripples.

"No."

That one word was sharp and tight and sounded like the ugliest of curses. And just like that, all the joy sucked out of their beautiful, special meal.

And both of them knew it.

"I…" What could she say? She let her lips fall shut and shifted her eyes away from the sudden strain. And chivalry must have died because Nathan didn't swoop in and try to ease her discomfort. He just sat there, as awkward as she was.

When he did finally speak his voice wasn't seductive any more.

"Why don't you have a job, Tori?" he nearly sneered. "How do you make rent?"

If she'd thought he was asking because he was interested, she would have told him, even though it was a critically rude question to ask. But he wasn't. He was asking to strike back at her for whatever she'd said to offend. So Nathan had a mean streak. Good to know. But she'd learned a thing or two about independence since moving to New York, and about how the world worked. Men like him might run the world but *she* ran her part of it.

She took her napkin and dabbed carefully at her lips, then pushed her chair away from the rooftop table. "Goodnight Nathan. I'll email you the web files and you can finish the site at your own apartment."

Her legs took her nearly all the way to the door before she felt his warm hand on her shoulder. She shrugged it off.

"Tori, wait." He moved around in front of her.

She crossed her arms in front of her. "Get out of my way, Nathan."

"Tori. I'm sorry. That was a cheap shot."

He wasn't moving, though. She kept her muscles rigid. "If you want me to listen to you then I suggest you get out from between me and the only way off this roof."

He glanced behind him and cursed under his breath, then stepped back. "I'm not making this better, am I?"

She turned her eyes up to him, taking care to keep them neutral. Suddenly she regretted the jar-and-a-half of margarita. She'd rather do this with a full complement of faculties. "I understand privacy, Nathan, better than most people. But if there's something you don't want to talk about, just say so."

He blew his frustration out through clenched teeth. "I let my guard down. I wasn't prepared. You blindsided me."

"With a casual question about your childhood?"

He looked as confused as she felt. "Everyone has triggers, Tori. You just stumbled onto one of mine. A raw one."

"So you hit back?"

His face fell and the abject misery glowed as neon as the storefronts down on the street. It niggled at her conscience. "That was my poor attempt at changing the subject. But it was harsher than I'd meant. I'm really sorry, Tori."

She stared at him a moment longer. "I pay the rent from money I got when I sold our house in Oregon."

He held up a hand. "It's none of my business. You were right not to—"

"I have nothing to hide, Nathan." Not, strictly speaking, true, but that was an inner demon for another lifetime. "Rick left me his half of our grandmother's house in his will. I sold it to come here and the rent comes straight out of that bank account. I don't even see it."

His shoulders slumped as he nodded and he wedged his hands into his jeans pockets. An eternity passed silently and then Tori turned for the door. Just as she reached for the handle, he spoke. Flat. Strained.

"I grew up in a building...much like this one."

The surprise was enough to halt her fingers on the door handle. But she didn't turn.

He continued behind her. "I know you imagined me growing up in a brownstone with loving parents and a matched pair of retrievers but that's not how it was."

His tension brought her focus around to him.

"Money was a rare commodity in my world. It was just

my mother and me and she was always…occupied…with her work."

Tori frowned at that choice of phrase.

"So, no…my childhood really wasn't peppered with idyllic moments, and the sorts of people in my mother's industry were hardly the type to inspire thoughts of great romance in a young boy."

"What people?" The pain was so evident as it twisted his handsome face into a fierce scowl, but she needed to understand. Even if her heart beat hard enough to hurt. "What industry?"

He lifted bleak eyes. "She was in sales."

Something about the way he said it. Like it was a lie he'd been telling for so long it had started to sound like the truth. She had to push the words out of her tight throat as a whisper. "What did she sell?"

A moment ago her heart had hammered because of him. Now it pounded blood ruthlessly against the walls of her arteries *for* him. Every part of her wanted to spare him from the truth she could read between the pained lines of his face.

Don't say it. Don't say it…

He shrugged. "Whatever men were buying."

Years of controlled breathing in oxygen-deficient environments had trained her well. She swallowed the shocked gasp. "She was a prostitute."

"At least."

She let that sink in. Imagining what he'd seen. Empathy for the hurt little boy he must have been flowed through her. "I'm sure she was only doing it to—"

"Don't." His hand shot up, large and firm. "Do you think it hurts less thinking she was doing it to feed and clothe and educate me? That belief tore my soul to shards until I realized it wasn't true. I gave up defending her years ago."

The sounds of carousing down on 126th Street drifted up to them in the silence that followed and mingled with the dense cloud of pain suddenly hanging heavy on her rooftop.

What should you say to someone who'd just spilled their

soul at your feet? Exposed their deepest secrets. Should you thank them for their trust? Should you comfort them for their shame? Should you gloss over it and try to put things back to how they were five minutes before and wish you'd been a little more tolerant and a lot less reactive?

Tori stepped up to him and curled her fingers around his and did the only thing she would have wanted in his place.

She traded him.

"Rick died while he was climbing with me," she said, quietly. "I watched him fall."

CHAPTER SEVEN

THAT brought his eyes up sharply and drove the misery straight from them. They filled instead with clear, glinting compassion. "You saw your brother die?"

"I watched every last second until I lost sight of him." *As penance.*

"Christ, Tori…"

"I don't want your pity, Nathan. Any more than you want mine. But I wanted you to know that I do understand something about triggers. About the everyday little things that leap up and ambush you when you're not at all prepared." *You blindsided me.* "And how hard it can be to stay rational when those feelings swell up."

They stared at each other until she finally spoke again. "So, I believe you when you say you're sorry. And when you say you didn't mean to be harsh. But can I trust you not to do it again?"

He was recovering his composure by the second. But he still frowned, not entirely back to cool, calm and collected Nathan. "You can trust me to not want to. And to do my very best not to let it happen again."

She stared at him, long and hard. Could she have offered more in his place?

Probably not.

"Good enough," she said, as a shudder rippled through her. Nathan stripped off his coat and swung it around her bare shoulders then held it together at her throat. The warmth soaked immediately into her frigid skin.

"You guys were climbing together?" he asked, carefully.

Of course he was going to ask. No one would walk away from a pronouncement like that. And she'd pressed *him* for details. But her instinctive defenses came straight into play and locked up her muscles.

"We broke our own rule."

"You were climbing alone." She nodded. As usual his quick mind took him straight to the important part. He freed a hand to rub up and down her arm. "You had to deal with it alone. That must have been hell."

No one had ever asked her this. Amongst the many, many questions about Rick's death at the inquiry, about which peak they'd chosen and why, about how thoroughly they'd hammered in the cams, no one had asked her what it had felt like walking off that mountain without the brother she adored. The boy she'd shared a womb with.

She dropped her eyes. "I couldn't leave him at all for the first few hours. But I couldn't drag him out either, he was too big. And I had to get back into radio range." She straightened her shoulders and snuggled more deeply into the warmth of Nathan's jacket. "Leaving him behind was the hardest thing I've ever done."

Third-hardest. Lying back against the snow drift knowing that she lived when he'd died...

Infinitely worse.

And number one...

She shook her head and blinked back the tears that always came when she relived that day. The last thing she wanted to do was cry in front of Nathan. She cleared her thick throat.

He pulled her toward him and wrapped his arms around his own coat, speaking against the top of her hair. "Would Rick blame you?"

Would he? Given they'd both ended up in the same perilous situation? That it could just as easily have been her on the wrong side of the anchor. "No. He hated it when I pulled rank. He considered us equals."

"Then let yourself off the hook. You didn't cause his death."

Her gut flipped back on itself and then squeezed into a tiny fist. There's no way he could truly understand, any more than she could do more than graze the surface of empathy for a little boy growing up in Nathan's impossible situation.

But in a weird, hopelessly antisocial way, knowing he'd endured pain too actually helped her manage hers. Knowing he understood—the concept if not the detail. It made her feel closer to him—to any human being—than she'd been in years.

She pressed her forehead against his shoulder.

"Thank you for telling me," he murmured, still against her hair. "I know it can't have been easy."

She leaned into his hard body where her fists clenched the front of his coat shut. *Honey, you don't know the half of it.* Watching Rick fall was only part of her nightmare. But there were some things you never aired.

Ever.

"You're welcome," she mumbled into his broad shoulder, letting herself enjoy the gift of his heat.

"We make quite a pair, huh?" His chuckle was more about tension than humor.

A pair. It took that phrase to draw her attention finally to something startlingly obvious that she'd been missing. She was standing under the stars, wrapped up snugly in Nathan's coat, buried in his arms with her lips practically pressed against his shoulder. Pairs made her think of couples. And couples made her think of coupl*ing*. And coupling made her think of…

Desire pooled thick and low in her body as his scent worked its way right into the pores of her skin and brought her mind full circle.

…*Nathan.*

Wrapped in the arms of the sexiest man she knew. Close enough that she could feel his steady heartbeat. Close enough that she could feel the plane of a ridged pectoral muscle beneath her clenched fists through his light sweater. Close enough that she could die right now and happily spend eternity swilling in his scent.

Time to move.

But no sooner did her body warn her to withdraw thaw those strong arms tightened. Keeping her close. One hand slid around to her back and recommenced its hypnotic circling there. Tori fought the insane desire just to melt into him. To surrender... everything...for a moment and let someone else take all the weight.

For a few heavenly moments.

How long had it been since anyone had touched her, let alone a man? Let alone like this. She took her moments of bliss where she could find them.

She leaned more closely into his hard body and added a fistful of his sweater into her tight clutch to keep them close. Her eyes drifted shut. Somewhere a thousand miles off music tumbled out of a window, the ballad drifting up to them on the night air. He leaned a fraction to his left and she followed him, loath to lose his warmth and the connection so soon. Then he moved back slightly to the right, that magic hand going around and around against her spine the whole time. And she followed.

Step...after step. Swaying left then right.

The rocking motion soothed as much as it serrated her body against his in a delicious, subtle, unfamiliar friction.

"Tori..." he mumbled, after a lifetime of gentle movement "...are we dancing?"

She didn't lift her lashes. The real world wasn't welcome back just yet. She mumbled, "No, we're shuffling."

She felt him smile against her forehead. "Okay, then."

They swayed in silence for the rest of the song. Nathan gathered her more firmly to him and Tori burrowed happily into his hold. She'd worked hard on her ability to push unwanted thoughts out of her head and she prayed thanks for it now, for the toasty, naive glow that could fill her soul while she kept the hard, real world carefully separate.

Their feet slowed to a halt and Nathan rubbed his face down hers, nudging it out and up, while his hands stayed tightly locked around her body. The seductive graze of his prickled jaw against hers, the blazing tangle of his breath and the hammer of his chest against hers…all whipped her heartbeat into riot and sent her senses skittering wildly around them like a mini dervish. A ton-weight pressed in on her chest.

Oh, God, he's going to kiss me…

And if he didn't, she was going to kiss him.

Or possibly die from oxygen deficiency.

She lifted her heavy lids and glanced at him. This close, his blue eyes were as clear and deep as any glacial lake but fringed by dark, soft lashes and blazing the icy fire of a question unasked. Somewhere in their depths a cautious uncertainty did a lazy backstroke but it was overwhelmed by the bubbling energy and focus of the last thing she'd ever expected to see from him.

Desire.

The moment their gazes met, all the reasons this was a bad idea—how unprofessional it was, why she didn't deserve a moment like this and why he was totally unsuitable and unsafe for her—dissolved just like her caution when she was facing a new mountain for the first time. Something other than sense was ruling play here, surging through her bloodstream and setting fire to every cell it passed. Bringing them scorching to vivid life.

Baying for more.

She let her mouth follow her eyes and turned her head naturally into the heat of his, dropping her lips slightly open.

His focus flicked down to them a bare moment before he closed the gap with a whispered groan.

The moment Tori's lips met Nathan's soft, warm ones, her body lurched with the involuntary gasp of air that rushed in. He captured her parted mouth with his again. He tasted of tangy citrus and chili and something rarer, something indefinable. Something she'd never experienced but wanted, in that moment, to keep forever. Her blood pounded everywhere it came close to the surface and robbed her of strength. Her mouth slid against his—tasting, exploring, feeding—and her hands curled more tightly into his sweater to keep him close. He shifted one hand lower, to press her hips into him and the other higher, tangling in her hair and taking the weight of her head as she let it fall back to give him more access.

"Tori…" he gasped, as they both sucked in a desperate breath. But she closed the gap again, nowhere near done with learning the shape of his lips, the taste of his mouth, and the slide of his teeth. He met her with interest, tangling tongues the moment she invited him in and sending her mind spinning off with sensation.

She curled one arm around his bent neck, pulling him closer, and his hand abandoned her nape in favor of a slow, sensual slide down her shoulder around to her side and under his own coat that heated her like a sauna all of a sudden. He burrowed under her thin cotton blouse and curved big fingers around her waist, his skin blazing hot against hers.

"So soft… So tiny…" he murmured against her mouth.

Funny, exactly the opposite of what she'd just been thinking. *So hard. So male.* The sort of man to make a tomboy feel like a princess. Alone together on this towering rooftop, under the magical stars. Where anything goes…

That thought brought her crashing back into focus. Back to the place where she didn't deserve the pleasure that was threatening to make her sigh. Back to the reality of who she was and who he was. And the fact they'd both got way too carried away with a margarita-fuelled candlelight dinner under the handful of stars that the lights of Manhattan allowed.

She gently pulled back out of his grasp. He let her go reluctantly, those big man hands trailing across her midriff as she stepped clear of him on unsteady legs.

Her chest heaved as hard as his as she breathed out a wobbly exclamation. "Wow."

He shook his disheveled hair. "You sure don't kiss like a novice, Tori."

Given she could count the number of men she'd kissed on one hand—fingers, not thumb—it definitely wasn't from practice. She took a shaky breath and smiled, filled for the first time with some ancient goddess magic that made her feel invincible. And woman. And utterly, utterly sensual.

"Natural aptitude?"

His laugh was as rocky as the geysers at Yellowstone, releasing the tension built up inside on a hiss. What did other people do in situations like this? When you'd just been crawling inside the skin of someone you were supposed to be working with? When you barely knew each other?

"Nathan, I—"

"Please don't say you're sorry, Tori. Let's just call it a great way to end a truly enjoyable evening."

"The evening's over?" Was that her voice sounding so thin? So disappointed?

"I...think it has to be. That conversation was only going one place and I'm not about to take you there."

Conversation? Well, they *were* using their mouths.

She probably should have been all uptight about the implication of Nathan's words. But she was too muddled to do anything but take him perfectly literally. "Why not?"

"Trust me. You deserve better."

"Than what? Dirty rooftop sex. Or dirty rooftop sex with you, specifically?"

He reached out and readjusted his coat more firmly around her shoulders, avoiding the question and accidentally brushing one still tingling breast as he slipped a button through its eyelet. It screamed at her to argue the point.

"When you have sex for the first time Tori, it should be memorable for all the right reasons."

Will you be there, Nathan? But she couldn't ask that. Her courage only went so far.

He smoothed the sleeves of the coat down her arms and the move struck her as just a little bit too patronizing. It plucked away more of the golden strands that had lain so heavily over her usual defenses. Her eyes narrowed. "Shouldn't that be my decision?"

He stared at her and ran well-manicured fingers through his own hair to restore some order. "Tell you what, Tori. Tomorrow morning when you no longer have a belly full of Mexican food and margarita and lust, if you still think this is a good idea you just give me a call and I'll happily oblige. But tonight…it's goodnight."

Oblige. Like it would be some kind of civic duty. Part of his community service. Anger bubbled up. "What makes you think I don't have plans tomorrow?"

Wow, did rampant sexual frustration make everyone this irritable?

But it seemed to be catching. "You haven't had a single plan since I met you," he gritted.

That was too close to the truth, and she felt the boiling of sudden shame. To a man like him, staying at home a lot probably did seem like loser territory. Let alone all the time. She used the moments it took to shrug off his coat to master her brewing pique, and then folded the jacket carefully before handing it back to him.

She met his frown and threw him her best couldn't-careless smile. "Don't wait by the phone, Nathan. If it rings it won't be me."

CHAPTER EIGHT

THE phone did ring the following workday—many times—and it was never Tori.

Nathan stared up gridlocked Columbus Avenue toward Morningside. Again.

She'd said she wouldn't call. She would have come to her senses five minutes after coming down from that rooftop—from the amazing natural high of their kissing. Women like Viktoria Morfitt didn't belong with men like him. No matter how much tequila they'd ingested. She came from a good, wholesome family and he…just didn't.

But she'd know that now. After his extraordinary Dr. Phil full-confession moment by the stairs.

What the hell had he been thinking? No one but his most trusted circle knew about his mother. Dean and his parents, his school counselor who'd endorsed him for early admission, the financial aid registrar.

Okay so a few people knew. But he'd never imagined Tori would be one of them. And at his own admission. Desperate times, desperate measures—the way she'd stalked, so stiff-backed from the table. It had just tumbled from his lips rather than lose her and the beautiful evening she'd gone to such trouble to create. He would have said just about anything in that moment to keep her with him.

And then she'd trumped it. Well and truly.

She was there when her brother died. The *only* person there.

What kind of courage did it take to go for help and hold it all together until rescue arrived? Half a day on a mountain with a corpse that, just hours before, was the person you'd loved and teased and spent a life with.

Unimaginable.

But she'd endured it. Her eccentricities made a little bit more sense of that now. Something like that was bound to mess with your head. Change your priorities and the way you approached life. Even her folks had opted out and hit the road. Maybe this crazy existence she was living was the Tori equivalent of turning nomad.

Between the origami laundry, the tutoring, the crazy-dog minding, the photographs and the falcons—and there was undoubtedly a stack of things she was doing that he wasn't aware of—it was just as well Tori didn't have a job to be going to. She'd never have the time. She hadn't liked it when he rattled her about having no plans, but facts were facts. She was always home when he called, she was always home when he came for community service or when he dropped by with camera parts or televisions. As if she truly had nowhere else to be.

He frowned. Nor, apparently, did he.

An honest-to-goodness, New-York's-richest-list bachelor, struggling to find something better to do with his time than visit a beat-up century-old building uptown.

It wasn't until that moment—until he started counting up the visits—that he realized how much time he was spending at Tori's or on the phone to Tori. Or hunting down the perfect replacement apartment for Tori. Or thinking about Tori. Very little of it could be chalked up to a court order. There was something about her. Something unusually comfortable about being with her. Amazing when you consider how very *un*comfortable he was in that building. Yet here he was trying to come up with a good reason to go back, even now.

He glanced at his desk. And here he was finalizing the documents that would tumble the building to the ground. Even as he'd sat on the roof of it and eaten Mexican and kissed one of its inhabitants.

Guilt chewed like a dog on the rawhide of his conscience, but then reason kicked in. It was fine; Dean's team had already located alternative lease accommodation for twenty-eight of the thirty-five tenants—dog-friendly ones, kid-friendly ones, nana-friendly ones—and the remaining nine weren't far off being finalized. All within a twenty-block radius of the existing building or the tenants' workplaces. All with longish leases to give them time to make their own alternative arrangements. To see them right. He had something special in mind for Tori. Bigger and more comfortable than her modest little Morningside rental.

The phone rang and he reached for it absently. "Archer."

"I'm calling to apologise."

He dropped into his chair and then stood again—ridiculously—at the sound of Tori's breathless voice. For one crazy moment he thought she might be taking him up on his offer, tacky and ill-conceived as it had been. The absolute last thing he wanted to do was complicate things further by getting physical. Even if it was also the thing he wanted most.

But if he wanted to touch her, he'd have to tell her what was going on. About the demolition.

"Apologise for what?"

"I was supremely ungrateful last night. I never thanked you for all the work you did on the website. I was just looking at it again on my desktop. It really is amazing."

Apology accepted. As if he wouldn't. "Just a bit more to do and it will be ready to go."

"Thank you, Nathan."

God, he loved the way she said his name. That gentle west-coast accent, the breathlessness like light fingers trailing down his spine or the touch of her lips.

"And I wanted to make good on my part of the trade, at last," she went on.

Uh-oh...

"So I thought I could throw a small open house to celebrate the peregrine website going live. Give you a chance to meet some of your tenants. Give me a chance to get them excited about Wilma and Fred."

From her point of view it was a good idea to get the other tenants invested in her falcons. But it was a spectacularly bad one from his, for so many reasons. He still wasn't in a crashing hurry to meet anyone else from the building—anyone who might recognize him, or might see Darlene in Nathan's own dark coloring and do the math. Or simply recognize his surname. He had no idea how many of them had known his mother by anything other than her working name.

And somehow he thought it might be easier for them as tenants not to have met the man who was about to rehome them. To have shared coffee and cake with them, unawares. That felt more than a little wrong.

Like keeping the truth from Tori was starting to.

"So I was wondering if you could give me a realistic time frame on go-live day?"

Realistically? Today, if he pulled his finger out and got working on it instead of sitting around mooching about her. But the moment the website went live he'd have no more falcon project to work on and no more reason to see Tori.

And he really wanted to see her face when he showed her the new apartment. Personally. Frame by beautiful frame.

"Uh, how does Friday sound?"

"Friday would be great. That gives me a few days to plan. Will I—" she cleared her throat and spoke in a rush of words "—will you be coming around before then?"

"I have the code on my flash drive, so I can finish it here if you like. And I can do all the uploading and testing remotely." He paused, wondering if he was laying it on too thick when he really only wanted to know one thing. "I wasn't sure I'd be welcome."

Her sigh breathed down the phone. "I'm so sorry for

being snappish, Nathan. You didn't deserve that. We're both consenting adults. And it was just a kiss."

"Right…"

She didn't sound any more convinced about that than he did, but her remorse seemed entirely genuine. And, who knows, if she was as inexperienced as she made out then an unplanned, hot-and-heavy make-out session might have thrown her equilibrium. It threw his and he was much more used to casual contact. He specialized in casual. "Tensions were high. I imagine we both said more than we meant to."

"I guess it wasn't the usual after-dinner conversation," she murmured.

Hardly.

Dead brother. Hooker mother. *Another mint?*

"Tell you what. I'll finish the site from here and bring it round to you tomorrow evening. Will you be home?" It was almost pointless asking, but assuming—with her—would be relationship suicide.

He frowned. Relationship? Was that what they had? He didn't really do relationships, not with women. He saved those for the diminishing circle of friends he trusted. Relationships required emotional investment. Sex required nothing but time.

Why did he even care what she thought of him? But his body's response to the soft, low smile in her voice as she said, "Yes, I'll be home," made him realize he was starting to care. Inexplicably. And very much.

And that really wasn't a good idea.

She might be the virgin in a technical sense, but when it came to genuine, loving relationships she was miles ahead of him. She'd had a brother she'd loved with everything in her. Loving parents. Grandparents.

He simply had no point of reference at all.

When it came to love *he* was the virgin.

He shoved his hands deep into his trouser pockets. This really couldn't be about what he wanted. If it was he'd just call

Simon around to the front, get him to drop him at Morningside and not collect him until morning.

As he had so many times in so many other buildings in the city.

But Tori was different. He was drawn to her in a way he could barely understand.

Deep inside. Where he never, ever went.

Time to set up some boundaries.

"They have eggs!"

Tori launched herself at Nathan the moment he stepped through her door, her excitement driving away the residual discomfort at what a social klutz she had been two nights ago. Sure, it had been a while between kisses—a long while—but that was hardly Nathan's fault, hopefully he'd forgive her ridiculous overreaction. Her embarrassing and far too revealing *over-participation* in the kiss.

Or not, she realized, as he gently but firmly peeled her arms off him and set her away, keeping his focus safely elsewhere. A part of her wanted to shrivel at the careful neutrality of his expression, but the thrill surging like champagne bubbles through her blood couldn't care less about her blushes, and so she snagged his hand and dragged him to the television where the webcam showed a fabulous center-of-screen view of Wilma happily spread low in the nest box, patiently guarding something.

That got his attention. "Have you seen the eggs?" he asked.

"Nope. But she wouldn't be brooding if they weren't there." A strange, almost forgotten lightness filled her. It had been a long time between lightnesses, too. She turned her face up to him. "They've bred, Nathan!"

He wasn't looking at the screen anymore; his eyes were fixed firmly on her. And they were dark with something she thought was confusion. Or surprise. Or both. "You're radiant."

Heat raced into her cheeks. She'd made an effort to dress for him this time. Nothing flash, just her best, butt-hugging jeans and a simple shirt in the most flattering color she owned. She knew she had no real right to be this happy, but Nathan just noticing when she looked good added to her already erupting excitement about the falcons. "I'm sure it's not *that* unusual. I can be happy."

The expression settled into a frown. "It's good to see."

But then his focus flicked back to Wilma who looked comically uncertain about what her instincts were making her do. The she-falcon glanced anxiously around her, as if expecting more. Or some help. Tori hugged her arms around herself and worked hard not to bounce up and down.

Babies. Not the first she'd seen, but definitely the first she'd gone all squishy over.

"How long before the eggs hatch?" Beside her, Nathan's voice was measured but pleasingly rumbly.

"About a month."

"Then what happens?"

"Then Wilma and Fred raise the ones that survive. Teach them how to fly, hunt. How to be independent."

"How long does that take—until they're independent?"

Was he worried he wouldn't be around to see it? "About six weeks. You can watch it all on the webcam, Nathan."

Something finally dented the natural high she'd been on since switching on the webcam and seeing Wilma on the nest. Heck, since she'd drowned in Nathan's kiss on the rooftop. How sad that he wouldn't be here to see the hatching in person. That they'd go their separate ways any day now.

Sad for him.

Sadder for her.

Her heart squeezed hard. "We have to get this live as soon as possible," she mumbled, thrown by the sudden, intense ache. "People will want to see this part. How much time do you have this afternoon?"

His enigmatic eyes came back to hers, distracted by a visible uncertainty but then clearing as he seemed to make a decision. Their warmth reached out to her. "As much as you need."

Tuesday—Nathan had to be busy with work stuff today. No wonder he was distracted. The time he was giving her was so generous.

She took a deep breath.

"Well then, let's get to work."

They spent the whole afternoon and most of the night editing footage from the moment the webcam was powered up, hunting in fast forward for the best bits of footage and making a "What You Missed" archive for the website: Wilma and Fred checking out the box, visiting and revisiting, a short, solitary, X-rated Wilma and Fred, and then, finally, Mom on the nest and Dad hovering anxiously by, alert for interlopers.

If Tori had stuck her head out that bathroom window they would have been off, never to return. No question.

Wilma had laid during the night so it was almost impossible to see how many eggs there were, but peregrines usually produced three or four with the hope that at least one would survive to juvenile status. She'd have to feed eventually so perhaps there'd be a brief moment when Fred took over when Tori could catch a glimpse of how many eggs they'd made together. Would there be a Pebbles and BamBam, too?

She sighed. *Ah, reproduction, such a wonderful thing.*

And not just because she couldn't get her mind off the human equivalent lately; it was such a disturbingly short mental journey from Nathan to babies.

They worked through dinner, sharing ideas, compromising on differences, anticipating each other's thoughts, and celebrating the amazing footage and photos that the site brought together. Tori caught herself resting her gaze more on Nathan than the screen several times and had to force her focus back to proofreading the text content or making a decision on footage, only to catch herself doing it again a few minutes later.

He compelled her gaze toward him exactly the way her

climbing tools sometimes stuck to the natural magnetism of certain rock faces.

His own fault for being so good to look at. He was tall and built for endurance, where her climbing friends had been solid and built for bursts of massive full-body power, but she would have picked Nathan anyway. His brilliant mind would have ensnared her even amongst all their outdoorsy muscle. But the thickening stubble of beard he hadn't shaved off since Sunday night grew hard along his strong cheekbones and highlighted their strength. And she was way too aware of how his lips had felt on hers to worry whether they might be, technically, a little on the thin side by Hollywood standards. And every time she had an idea that he didn't like and he slid those deep-blue eyes sexily sideways at her in doubt...she just melted that little bit more.

She stared at him now, while his attention was thoroughly focused on the computer screen.

It couldn't hurt just to look, surely. To speculate.

All the excitement she felt now about the peregrine eggs only simmered in amongst the residual tingles from spending the last two nights reliving the feel of his mouth on hers. The strength of his arms pinning her to him. The feel of his hard planes under her hands. And creating endless, breathless scenarios about what would have happened if she hadn't pulled away from him back on the rooftop. If she'd heeded the raw, base call of a virile male. If she'd let the hungry ancient goddess in her respond.

Knowing how much she needed that.

Believing how little she deserved it.

"Coffee?"

She was on her feet and moving towards the kitchen before he could answer. She gulped down a glass of cold water and willed away the pheromones she could practically smell churning around her. They weren't helping her keep her mind on the job and the last thing she wanted was to be sitting so close to Nathan while practically radiating "take-me-now" vibes.

Rick had lost the chance of finding the right person for him; reaching out and grabbing what Nathan offered just didn't sit right with her.

Not that Nate had really offered anything. Nothing serious, anyway. Sex…if she wanted it. His offer to *oblige* might have been flippantly delivered, but Tori had the feeling that if she took him up on it he'd be as good as his word. And hopefully every bit as good as her fantasies. But that's it. A Manhattan-born captain of industry just didn't do more than slum it with maladjusted girls from Morningside.

Cinderella never would have actually ended up with the prince.

But she'd have had fun trying.

Tori dug down deep into her conscience to see how it felt about that? About a strictly physical experience. Exploring these feelings she'd pretty much given up on ever having. Not romance, not love—definitely not happy ever after—those were totally out of bounds. Just happy ever…now. A little more light-ness now that she'd been reminded of how good it felt. She held her breath better to hear her conscience's verdict.

Silence. Just the relentless thump of her tortured pulse. And that was as good as a yes.

She lifted her head and blazed molten fire at the broad back of the man in her living room. The reality of what to do next was almost crippling. She'd never seduced anyone in her life. Of those few paltry kisses she'd had, she'd only instigated one and that was stolen from a very unwilling Michael Toledo in fourth grade and it hadn't really ended all that well. He'd cried and she'd spent the afternoon in the Assistant Principal's office sharpening pencils.

The idea of walking up to Nathan and grabbing his square chin the way she'd done with Michael's round, pudgy one…

Not an option.

But neither was backing away from this decision now that she'd made it. Now that her conscience had, amazingly, ap-proved. It was far too rare a gift to give back.

"Have you got something stronger than coffee in that kitchen, Tori?" he asked, lightly, back over his shoulder.

If I had, I'd be drinking it right now. Heat simmered up from under her shirt as her whole body got in on the act of wanting him.

"Uh...no. Why?"

He turned and smiled one of his most knock out smiles. "Because unless there's anything new you've thought of, then we are officially done."

That stopped her cold. Every part of her.

The heat...

Her pulse...

Her tight breath.

Like the water sucking out to sea in advance of a tidal surge. If they truly were done, he had no good reason to be here anymore. The wave crashed back in over all the flipping fish of her emotions, carrying blind panic at the thought she wouldn't see him again.

Her voice shook as she risked speech. "The website's finished?"

"Yep. It'll take about three minutes to upload all the files and then your falcons are out there for the world to see."

Excitement and terror scrabbled and clawed for dominance. She'd been looking forward to this moment since Nathan had first put the idea of a webcam into her head. But for it to come now—just when she'd decided to throw herself at his feet...

Three minutes. That wasn't a lot of time for finesse.

She crossed out of the kitchen and moved towards him with purpose. "I've changed my mind."

He frowned at her. "You don't want to go live?"

Why hadn't she worn something more alluring than jeans and a T-shirt? Or brushed her teeth before answering the door? "I do want to go live. I've changed my mind about..." *Oh, God.* Her heart pounded hard enough to hear in her voice. "...about our conversation on Sunday night."

A cautious suspicion blinked to life in his eyes. "Which one?"

"The one in which you said you'd sleep with me if I still wanted to in the morning."

All six-foot-three of crafted muscle stiffened instantly. "Ah, Tori…"

She stepped up closer to him, hard against him and did her best to saturate her voice with confidence. "I still want to."

He slid his hands up her arms, but not to bring her closer. He forced an inch of sanity between them. "No, you don't. You're just excited the project's finished."

She used her upper-body strength to resist his gentle pressure. "I am excited that the website's finished, but not that our time together will be finished."

And there it was. Couldn't be plainer than that.

Take me, I'm yours.

He groaned and his tongue stole out to wet suddenly dry lips. Tori's eyes locked on it the way Fred and Wilma tracked pigeons. "Tori… You have terrible timing."

"Why?"

He looked around for inspiration. "It's 2:00 a.m. We've worked into the night."

Desperate measures. Nathan might be in denial, but she knew exactly what she wanted—for the first time in years. She slid one hand boldly under his shirt and rested it right over the hard warmth of his heart. It thumped powerfully against her fingers and he flinched backward on another deep groan.

She smiled to see him so affected. "I may not have been born in New York, but I'm pretty sure even here 2:00 a.m. is a perfectly good time for…"

The actual words evaporated.

"Sex?" His expression softened and he cupped his hands around hers through his fine shirt "You can't even say it comfortably—how were you planning on doing it?"

Heat roared up her neck. "I was hoping there wouldn't be

a whole lot of talking about it. I certainly wasn't expecting to have to beg."

She glanced away, but his silence brought her eyes back to him. "You wouldn't need to beg, Tori. I meant what I said the other night." His eyes flicked to the bedroom. "I would like nothing more than to carry you in there right now."

"Then *oblige* me." She threw the word intentionally back at him, her chest heaving.

He winced. "It wouldn't be fair on you, Tori. I can't offer you more than a good time."

"Okay." That tied in nicely with her own needs, anyway.

"It's not okay. You deserve someone who can care for you. Who can give you…more."

"I'm not asking for more."

He stroked her cheek with one finger. "You should be. You're worth someone's whole heart."

Rejection flamed wildly beneath her blood, whipping it into a bubbling frenzy. "Apparently not yours."

His lips tightened. "I should go."

If he went he wouldn't be back. She scrabbled for inspiration as he started to push away. "I'm asking you to be with me, Nathan. To teach me."

He swore under his breath and lifted pained blue eyes back to her. She wedged herself bodily into the chink she could suddenly see in his armor. He wanted to do this. He *did* want it. "Are you seriously going to walk away and leave me wondering?"

His gaze narrowed. "Wondering what?"

"How we'd be together."

His nostrils flared and his lips pressed together against something he wanted to say. His voice vibrated with tension when he said instead "You'll meet someone else." But he flinched slightly as he said those words and Tori's chin—and confidence—lifted.

She tossed her hair back. "You'd prefer to outsource this?"

Deep heat blazed dark and raw in his eyes, turning them

indigo. *No.* Everything in him said it. But outwardly he just repeated "I should go."

He swung around and checked the files had finished uploading, grabbed his coat and turned for the door. "Goodbye, Tori. I'll call in a few days and see how the site's going."

No!

Him leaving now was not an option. Not when she knew full well she'd never see him again. Not when she knew he wanted her as much as she wanted him.

"Nathan—"

He was out in the hall before she could pull enough salient words together. She shot out after him. "I'll ride down with you."

He didn't exactly protest, but he strode down the hall and into the stairwell without a word. His whole body was rigid as his long legs carried him down the stairs. She kept up easily, and her light jog matched her fevered thoughts perfectly. Neither of them spoke as they emerged onto the eighth floor. She noticed his glance didn't flick toward the empty 8B the way it usually did, then he palmed the elevator button.

The elevator car was still sitting at the top of its range and when the doors opened, she slipped in behind him and then stood in the same stony silence as him and stared at the faded light countdown that marked their interminable descent.

Confusion and mortification swirled in her addled mind.

He was really going to walk away from this! From her. Despite wanting her as much as she wanted him. The incredible buoyancy she'd been increasingly feeling since he'd turned up on her doorstep, court order in hand, came into crashing context.

He made her feel good. *He* brought lightness back into her world. *He* had her springing out of bed in the morning rather than crawling.

Nathan.

Not just any guy. And not just because he was good-looking. And not just because he was charming.

Because she was falling for him.

And as the momentousness of that sank like a stone into the pit of her stomach, Tori knew she was finished begging. Because him saying no now would mean so much more than him saying no five minutes ago, before she realized her heart was involved—the heart that was hammering hard enough to burst right open. But she couldn't just let him walk. Even if he was only in this for the short term.

She couldn't keep him forever—fine—but couldn't she have him for just a bit longer?

The elevator lurched to a halt on the ground floor and the old door started to groan open. *Only seconds now...* Nathan reached across to slide back the ornate outer door opening into the building's entry foyer. The move brought him closer to her for a bare moment and she swayed toward him instinctively. But then she squared her shoulders, lifted her eyes and spoke quietly past her wildly thumping pulse.

Not a plea, just a fact.

"Last chance, Nathan."

The corner of his eye twitched and his jaw tightened, but otherwise he kept his focus fixed on the door to the street—his escape—then stepped past her out the elevator door, and into the silent lobby...

...and was gone.

The acid of rejection burned high in her throat as the doors retracted agonizingly slowly across the elevator opening. Old, familiar pain burbled up from the place she'd worked so hard to bind it.

She should have known. Her conscience had set her up so thoroughly for this lesson in payback. It had seen what she, clearly, had not. That despite the dubious romance of a tequila-fuelled kiss, Nathan really wasn't all that interested in more from her. Not even casually. No matter what he said.

She kept her focus forward, her chin high until the moment the doors obscured her from his view should he look back.

But the second she couldn't see him—nor he, her—she

released the pain in a choked moan. She'd survived much worse, she knew she would survive this. But in that very moment it was impossible to imagine how.

Suddenly the door's slide yanked to a halt, and Tori lifted her face as it hauled open with more gusto than it had ever displayed, and Nathan surged back into the elevator. He swept her up in his tide and pushed her back against the rear of the tiny box, his mouth crushing down on hers while she was still sucking in an elated breath.

"This doesn't mean I care for you." He ground out the words against her lips.

Triumph exploded in every cell of her body. Her arms hooked instantly around his strong neck, her hands plunging their way deep into his dark hair, and she breathed a response in the half heartbeat he took to get a better angle on her mouth. "I don't want you to care for me."

God help her, it was the truth. And also the worst of lies.

Recognizing the truth was so exquisitely painful it was hard to separate it from the elation still surging through her blood. She didn't deserve someone like Nathan in her life forever. The only thing letting her have this moment for herself was the fact that there was no chance of it ending well for her beyond the priceless opportunity to feel this glorious man naked up against her. To steal something to remember him by. To remember lightness by—for when it was gone again.

He'd been crystal-clear. For now, not forever.

No wonder her conscience had been fine with it. It saw what a dead end lay ahead. It had nothing to lose.

Nathan groaned against her mouth and shuffled her sideways so that he could punch the up button on the elevator. She lurched against him as it began its creaking ascent, but he held on to her, sharing air, tangling tongues, grinding into her, their body temperatures rising with the elevator. Tori grew lightheaded from oxygen depletion and plain old sagging relief and she clung to him desperately.

There was a feverish quality to Nathan's kisses that hadn't

been there on the rooftop. An urgency that perfectly matched her own. He leaned her against the left side of the elevator and then a moment later pulled her back up into the centre, before shifting to the right. Every time they moved a different part of her throbbed with need, but no part of her was going to get satisfaction.

He was as restless as his hands...and as unsettled as she was beginning to feel. She tore her mouth free and gasped "What's wrong?"

His gaze ricocheted around the tiny space, hyper. "Nothing."

Tori frowned. She could be self-conscious, she could worry that he'd changed his mind or that she'd done something wrong. But something about the wild passion on his face as he'd forced his way back into her elevator forced the doubt to heel. This wasn't about her. And the fact it was about him worried her even more.

That was pain she could see in the shadows at the back of his eyes.

The elevator continued its torturous ascent, grumbling un-happily. She pulled her fingers out of his hair and slid them to either side of his flushed face, forcing him to look at her, and held his eyes steadily.

If he changed his mind now her life would be over, but at least she would know.

She stroked his jaw with her thumb. "Tell me."

Heat pumped off him and the wildness of his eyes took a moment to ease. Emotion flickered across his face until it finally resolved, taking the frown lines with it.

"Nothing's wrong." He took a deep breath and drank her in. Really looked at her. "Just a memory." A tiny smile broke free and he stooped to kiss her gently. "Something that doesn't belong here anymore."

He kissed her again—a different kind of kiss to his first ones, to the rooftop. It was a kiss full of light. Full of relief. She stretched up and kissed him back, taking care to strip it of any clue about how deeply her heart was involved. It was still a good kiss. Actually it was a fantastic kiss.

Which only made her wonder what it would be like to kiss him with love between them. Instead of...

Whatever it was they had.

The elevator hit the end of its reach and Tori led the way out to the stairwell, her heart hammering relentlessly against her ribs.

He must have picked up on her tension because he said, "You're sure?"

She stopped and looked back at him in the entry to the dim stairwell. One strong arm stretched up the door frame, hovering on the cusp between common sense and no return, equally willing to go with either. His concerned frown only drew her more to him.

"You thought I wouldn't be?" she murmured.

"You know what this is—between us?"

She thought about that long and hard. "I have no idea what this is. But I don't require promises, Nathan. Only honesty. I'm in no position to be asking for forever."

This might be as close to forever as she came.

She held out her hand towards him, steadier and more confident than she felt, and he pushed himself away from the door frame and was with her in a few easy steps, his eyes holding hers. His fingers dwarfed hers, stroking softly across her skin, and then folding through her own to form a sensual lifeline.

She led the way up two flights of stairs toward her bedroom—the one room he'd not been into—and gripped that human lifeline as tightly as any mountain rigging.

CHAPTER NINE

RIGHT up until the moment the cool of her bed linen kissed her naked back, Tori might have chickened out. But the moment she'd felt the touch of the safest *place* in the world within the safest *part* of her world in the arms of the safest *man* in her world, she knew this was one hundred-percent right. It wasn't forever—they both knew that—but it had been coming since the first moment she saw him.

Nathan's lips hadn't left hers since the two of them crashed through her new door, twisted up in each other's arms, stumbling in their rush to get each other naked. To know each other. To love each other.

Just for one night.

Now, his skin still radiated a blazing heat, lying half-sprawled on top of her, one sweaty leg thrown over her two, simmering blue holding her enraptured while her strained chest rose and fell heavily from the gymnastics of the past hour.

Of all the things she had secretly hoped to discover about making love for the first time—all the things she *did* discover—finding out she almost wasn't fit enough was not on her expected list.

"My chest is about to explode," she gasped. "You'd think being climbing-fit would have helped. How do normal people cope?"

Nathan chuckled close to her ear as his fingers traced lazily over the ridges of her brow, her nose, her lips. She bit gently at the fingers and heard the controlled heaving of his own lungs between his words. "I'm not sure most 'normal' people would have put quite that much effort into it."

Tori's flushed skin couldn't accommodate any more blood, so her blush had no purpose. "Really? Was I too…?"

Vigorous? Enthusiastic? *Trying too hard?*

Nathan's lips split wide in a dirty grin. "You were amazing." Then the smile sobered just slightly and he dragged his thumb over her bottom lip. "You *are* amazing."

Oh…

Moments like that made it hard to forget this was a one-off.

Moments like the one when he'd turned her blazing gaze to his and held it. When he'd gently stroked away the sneak of moisture that had escaped her eye after it all got too overwhelming. When he'd pulled her into his shoulder and murmured words of reassurance as she'd fragmented into a million shards of the sweetest diamond dust.

He hadn't made love to her like a man who didn't care.

And she hadn't responded like a woman who didn't want to be cared for.

Whoops on both their parts.

Not that there was any question about *whether* she cared. She wouldn't have risked—trusted—just anyone. Only Nathan. Arrogant, brave, wounded Nathan. But would she ever lie in her big bed again and not think of the wasted size of it? Would she ever touch her lips and not taste him there? Would she ever be the same? There were some consequences that a condom couldn't prevent.

The emotional ones.

Maybe she shouldn't have given in to her baser instincts and ripped open Pandora's box knowing she would never let herself keep what she found inside.

Not that he was offering. At all.

Even now.

Her eyes slid sideways again and collided with his electric-blue one. "Thank you, Nathan."

"This wasn't charity, Tori." His large hand slid around to tangle in her damp hair. "I've wanted to get you naked since the day you ratted me out to the cops."

She smiled. Was that only three weeks ago? "I'm still grateful. I'll always remember this."

When you're gone.

Nathan wiggled in harder against her and buried his lips somewhere near her ear. She was just as happy not to see that thought echoed back to her in his gaze. Her lashes drifted shut as his lips traced the outline of one lobe and she groaned her appreciation. As tired as she was it was a strange kind of exhaustion. The kind that could leave you ready for a repeat almost immediately. Not a bad system, really.

"There's still the launch party, remember?" he murmured, hot and damp against her ear.

Her eyes flew open. She spoke to the ceiling, virtually holding her breath. "You're going to come?"

"I figure I owe it to Wilma and Fred for invading their privacy so thoroughly yesterday."

Thoughts of the brief, frantic bird-sex they'd caught on the camera brought a smile to her lips. "Maybe they returned the favor just now."

He lifted his dark shaggy head and turned towards the window. Neither of them had bothered with the curtains so the whole bedroom stood exposed to the darkened ledge outside. The bed shook as Nathan laughed, deep and sexy.

It felt way too good to lie naked in his arms joking around. Dangerously comfortable.

Dangerously addictive.

She forced her thoughts onto something else. "I'm not sure how many people I should invite. It's not that big an apartment."

Beside her Nathan stilled. She could practically hear him thinking. Finally he spoke. "You'd like a bigger place?"

"Not especially, though it would be handy at a time like this." Not that throwing a party happened more than once every... five years. In fact, this would be her first.

Actually, a crazy dream of renting the apartment next door with its park-facing aspect and opening it up into one big apart-ment had occurred to her last year. Not that it was available, and not that she could afford it if it was.

Nathan rolled onto his back, dragging the light covers up and over both of them. He turned toward her on the pillow. "If you had a blank check, what improvements would you make?"

She frowned at him. "Is all post-coital conversation this suburban?"

He leaned over and kissed her—roughly, soundly. Fabulously. "I'm recharging. Humor me."

Tori's heart squeezed. After what they'd just done together how could a simple kiss still steal her breath? Yet it did.

"Ah, blank check...okay," she said as soon as she was able. "I guess I wouldn't mind making it a bit bigger. And actual park views instead of the glimpse I get right now. But I wouldn't want anything flash."

"Why not?"

Because there was something suitably monastic about living a simple life. Denying herself comforts. "I don't need it."

"You don't need a tantalizing Mexican spread on a rooftop either but you enjoyed it."

She had—a slip on her part. Maybe she'd become all-round too indulgent since meeting Nathan Archer.

He took her silence as reluctance and nudged her with his foot. "If you won't take pleasures, then what about conveniences?"

He really wanted to play this game. Okay. She turned to face him. "I guess a built-in laundry would be convenient. It would save me having to go to the basement."

"Balcony?"

She expelled a frustrated outburst on a small puff. "If we're going to totally redesign the building, sure!"

"Not here then. Anywhere. Anywhere in Manhattan."

She sat up straighter and threw him her best probing look. "Are you trying to seduce me with imagined spoils? Because… you know…I'm already naked, you really don't have to try that hard."

His smile turned sideways to fit her mouth better and he kissed her to silence. "Come on, Tori," he said when they finally came up for air. "Play the game. Anywhere at all on Manhattan."

Her eyes explored the room as though she'd find inspiration there. "Okay…if imaginary money truly is no object then let's talk park frontage."

"Central Park?"

Her laugh was immediate. "Don't be ridiculous. They don't make blank checks with enough space for all those zeroes. A more modest park will be just fine."

"That's what you'd like? A mid-sized place with a heap of facilities facing a park in a nice neighborhood?"

She sat up carefully, wondering how she could cut out the chit-chat and get back to the physical intimacy. Their best-before clock was ticking. She rolled fully over and met his eyes. "Yes, Nathan. That is my fantasy apartment."

And fantasy it would remain because not only did she have extremely limited income but, out here in the real world, moving was not even on her radar. She was more than happy where she was. Comfortably settled.

Entrenched.

In fact, the thought of shifting away from all the people she'd filled her life with, and her apartment with its soft colors and mismatched furnishings made her stomach positively lurch. "Where is all this going?"

"I'm just—" his expression grew cautious "—getting to know you better."

She shifted to her side and tucked the covers in more firmly around her. "Why? You'll be gone in a few days."

Somehow, through all the thick shields she usually kept

around her heart, she knew that his next words would really matter. Her heart set up an insistent thumping.

A scowl marred those beautiful eyes and he looked as though he was on the verge of saying something difficult. But then the moment passed, and he shifted more comfortably in the bed and when he lifted his face again his eyes glittered with speculation. "Got something other than conversation in mind for the few hours until breakfast?"

If she hadn't spent the past five years keeping her own secrets she wouldn't have so easily spotted his. But there it was, laid out on the bed in front of them, metaphorically shrouded so that she couldn't quite make out its shape. Not that she had any real desire to find out. Look what had happened last time he'd shared something with her. And she only had one secret left to trade him....

"We could sleep," she said lightly, knowing full-well that wasn't an option. If they only had one night she wasn't wasting a second of it on oblivion.

He gave her that smile again. The one that turned her insides to mush. The one that made her forget anything but him. "Is that what you'd like to do?" he murmured as he stirred against her.

She stretched out along his length. "Nope."

"What would you like to do?"

Be yours forever.

The force of her mind's whisper slammed the breath clean out of her and robbed her of speech. They didn't have forever. They had until morning. Until the launch party...max. She knew that.

She *knew* that.

Why was her subconscious taunting her with thoughts of forever—with what she hadn't earned? Was it still playing cruel games? Or, worse, had she done the unthinkable and fallen harder than she realized?

"Tori?" He sat up more fully as she sagged back against the pillows. "Are you okay?"

Her heart pounded. "I'm…um…" What could she say?

I think I love you, Nathan.

Surprise!

Instead, she did what she'd been doing so well for the past five years: she pushed the emotion deep down inside and slid the I'm-okay mask firmly into place. "I just realized we don't have any more protection."

Nathan's gaze instantly heated up and he lowered his smiling lips closer to hers, which seemed to tremble and swell in anticipation. "Well, then we'll just have to get creative." She wriggled down lower in the bed and willed a smile to her waiting lips. He swiped his mouth back and forth across hers and his hand slid resolutely down to hook under her knee. "Lucky you're athletic."

It took only a cluster of rapid heartbeats for his talented lips and hands to gather her fully back into his command, to finely tune her body back with his. Tori's chest made the transition from tight pain to lancing desire immediately, her tattoo-heart switching rhythm easily. It was far too possible to let herself sink into the swell of rising passion rather than face the reality of what her subconscious had just tossed up.

Love.

The one thing she absolutely, categorically could not have with him. Or anyone.

Love was something you earned.

CHAPTER TEN

"TAKE it easy, Tori, they'll come."

She knew by Nathan's narrowed gaze that she was completely failing to mask her nerves as she wiped down the coffee and dining tables for the third time. It would have been the tenth if not for his solid, reassuring presence that grounded her. As much as was possible.

It didn't matter that she knew everyone invited to the webcam launch tonight. It didn't matter that she liked everyone invited. This was the first time she'd brought her neighbors together in one place in the entire time she'd been resident in this building, and she was insanely, inexplicably nervous. She wasn't stressing that her guests weren't coming…

She was stressing that they *were*.

Ironic. The high school senior voted Medford's most likely to have a beer with a President, and she was nervous about serving her neighbors a bunch of finger food.

She balled the sponge into her tight fist and returned it to the immaculate kitchen, then mentally reviewed everything that was laid out on the counter. Again. Not surprisingly, it was all exactly the same as the last time she'd counted it.

"Tori…" Warm arms slipped around her and drew her into rock-solid strength, gently halting her frantic cleaning. "It's going to be fine. Everything looks great and we've catered for a football team."

We've…plural.

Double tension scored her subconscious. It was bad enough having a party—she had no one but herself to blame for that—but the end of the party technically signaled the end of something else. There was no good reason for Nathan to return after the last party guest walked through of her shiny new door. The gathering had bought her a few extra days—of the most blinding, pleasurable intimacy imaginable—but nothing more. Nothing else had changed.

There had been no talk of anything more. Despite Nathan's occasional slips into plural.

She had enough self-awareness to realise that the falcons weren't the whole reason she was throwing this ridiculous party. She wanted Nathan to meet her neighbors. To get to know them. She wanted them to get to know him, to like him. This motley group of New Yorkers was her de facto family and, on some deeply buried level, she wanted their approval.

Even though it was completely and utterly pointless.

"I don't know why I'm so nervous," she said, snuggling in more tightly against his strength and pressing her cheek over his heart so she could hear its reassuring beat.

He gathered her in and touched quiet lips to her hair. Was he counting down the kisses to their last one the way she was? The way she had been since their first one? "You're launching a webcam. It's a big deal."

She tipped her head back to look at him—her favorite angle, up along that tanned, rough throat and jaw—and frowned. "No it's not. These are my neighbors. This should be nothing."

His eyes clouded. "Is it because I'm here?"

"I don't think so. I want them to meet you."

His lips tightened. "You do?"

"Well… You know. Without you there would be no webcam project."

She wasn't fooling him any more than she fooled herself. Not only was she apparently too chicken to have her neighbors over for snacks, but she was too afraid to let him see how she felt about him.

Coward.

Then again, courage was something she'd said farewell to five years ago.

Behind them a sharp rap heralded the exact moment the clock switched over to six o'clock. Trust someone to be uber-prompt. She stiffened her back, pulled away from Nathan and turned for the door.

Game on.

Angel the actress was unfashionably on time, standing in the hall with a bottle in her hand and a curious smile on her face, but others weren't far behind. Tracey and Neville Radcliffe, then Mr. Broswolowski, the deCostas. Her neighbors from either side. Tony Diamond from the end of the hall—the only real magician she'd ever known—turned up a bit late, but he'd taken the time to escort Nancy Smith down from her top-floor apartment.

They and a handful of other neighbors were mingling fabulously and exclaiming how odd that they'd not had more parties like this—the high-rise equivalent of a street party—while Tori faked endless tasks in the kitchen as her heart hammered and her mouth ran clean out of saliva. It wasn't quite as awful as she'd worked herself up to believe, but it wasn't entirely comfortable either. Very crowded. Very oxygen-depleted. Even with the safety windows slid open. More than ever, she longed for the vast, open spaces and arctic winds of the high mountain ranges.

She closed her eyes and tried to remember what that had felt like buffeting against her skin.

"Tori?"

Nathan swung past her servery for the seventh time, bending to see under the overhead cupboards and snaring her gaze. He'd been his typical charming self, winning over her neighbors, circulating, working the room. Tori envied him the apparent ease with which he could speak with interest to anyone about anything and have them eating out of his hand. Angel Santos was just about ready to have his children and she didn't even know he was rich as sin.

Tori had told them he was a friend and they'd been working on a project together, but that was it. It was Nathan's call whether he wanted to out himself as their landlord. Or her lover. So far he'd chosen neither.

Though glancing at him across the room, seeing his smile and secretly knowing what that mouth had done for her just hours earlier was the only thing that effectively distracted her from her annoying anxiety. And judging by the twist of his lips, he remembered too.

Were all sexually active people this smug?

"Everyone's getting restless," he said now. "Could be time for the falcons?"

"Really? Now?" As excited as she was to be launching the website, the idea of standing in front of people and speaking formally suddenly brought a hint of bile to her mouth. She frowned, remembering how many presentations she'd done to climbing groups back in Oregon. How effortless they'd been. Talking about things she was passionate about had never been an issue. "Can't you chat to them a bit longer?"

Nathan's brows dropped. "These are *your* friends, Tori. I'm doing my best—" and it wasn't until that moment that she realized how strained he actually looked "—but it's not me they came to see."

He moved around into the kitchen, positioned himself against the counter in such a way that his body shielded her from the view of her guests as he said gently. "You've climbed mountains, Tori. Talking about these birds should be nothing."

Should be. "Then why isn't it?" Her pulse chattered rapidly.

She was hiding in her own kitchen. She'd left Nathan holding the bag for entertaining her friends. She would have happily crawled back into bed right now until every last one of them left.

Oh, that was not good.

Her head came up. She glanced at the people milling around her tiny living room. She tuned in to the hammering of her heart. Then she looked at Nathan—his handsome face filled with patience and rather a lot of confusion.

She could do this.

She sucked in a deep breath, lowered the bowl she'd been filling with yet more unnecessary snacks and turned to her living room.

"Okay. Let's start."

And if he noticed *her* unintentional plural, he didn't say a word.

The room came buzzing alive as Tori spoke to them about the peregrine webcam project and how, despite other parts of Manhattan having them, theirs would be Morningside's first wildlife webcam. Her use of *theirs* had to be intentional and Nate watched her enthusiasm wash over every one of her guests like a seductive wave, despite her stumbling nerves at the start. In return, their growing excitement cross-infected her and she grew louder and more confident as she got closer to the moment of switching on the webcam monitor.

Her eyes glittered, her smile beamed. This was more the Tori he'd expected tonight. This was the Tori he'd selfishly lost himself in the past few nights. Radiant, courageous, wild Tori.

Timid kitchen Tori was not a side of her he'd ever expected to see. It threw him, though he knew how much she liked to work within her comfort zone. It just reinforced how little he really knew about her. How not-real this whole *thing* between them was. And it really shouldn't matter because in a few hours their *thing* would be over. The project was finished.

Neither of them had spoken of more.

Coming here tonight had been a risk. His heart had been in his throat since that first knock on the door. Wondering if he'd be recognized. Wondering if he'd bump into someone he used to see taking out the trash a lifetime ago. Could he rely on the vast physical changes between seventeen-year-old Nate and the man he was now? Getting into discussions about the bad old days was really not his idea of a good time.

But as more guests arrived and minutes turned into hours and no one said a word or even looked askance at him—beyond the obvious speculation in most expressions as to what his relationship with Tori was really all about—he'd realized that no one *did* remember him. And the only one he recognized for certain was Miss Smith, who remembered nothing at all most of the time.

"Here they are, Wilma and Fred." Tori activated the plasma with a theatrical flourish and every person in the room craned forward to see it. The screen glowed to life and caught Wilma in the middle of her regular bath, that talon-like beak rifling through slick brown feathers, completely unaware that she was being watched. Thirty days on eggs. Thirty days barely leaving that ramshackle nest.

That took a special kind of bird.

Or person. The thought flitted across his mind that Tori would have that kind of focus. Especially if it involved thirty days indoors. She did love her apartment.

He frowned. She really did.

She pulled up the website on the monitor and talked everyone through the various parts of it, showing them her photography, the live webcam box, the species information. The links to New York's other urban raptor sites.

Marco deCosta was the first to jump on the computer mouse and start effortlessly navigating his way around the detailed site—it was a healthy reminder that the sorts of tools Sanmore had grown great on were just commonplace for kids now. Marco's parents followed and then, one by one, everyone else began to explore.

Tori chatted to Tracey and Neville Radcliffe—the owners of that mad mini-horse, Gretel—and her origami-laundry friend, the theatre producer. She showed them through her photo album of raptor images. They hung on her words as though they'd never seen or heard about Tori's background at all.

Maybe they hadn't. The way he'd had to pry it from her determined lips...

Yet her neighbors had become so fundamental to her life here in Morningside. Like a regular mini ecosystem with every person depending on every other for some aspect of day-to-day life. Most aspects, in Tori's case. She'd be lost without her portfolio of trades. Life would certainly cost her a whole lot more.

And, once again, his chest tightened at the very real necessity of moving everyone out of the building. Of splitting up friendships. Of displacing Tori.

He'd opened his mouth any number of times over the past few days to tell her what he had planned. But every time he'd even looked as though he might be working up to some serious conversation, Tori cut him off, distracted him with a question, an activity, a kiss. Almost as if she didn't want to get deep and meaningful with him.

At least not emotionally.

The more time he spent with her the more he realized how much structure her days had. Not that his corporate days had any less, and not that she wasn't willing to throw it all to the wind in order to spend hours with him under the sheets. It was just...rigid—compared to how he imagined her earlier years must have been as a nature-loving, mountaineering tomboy.

But then she'd lost her brother and had stopped doing all the things she loved. Maybe it had changed her. Which didn't mean she wasn't capable of changing back. She just needed the right incentive. And less structure.

He maneuvered himself through the throng and closer to her side and took a risk—did something unexpected. Scandalously unscheduled. He slid his hand around her waist and onto her hip and whispered in her ear, "Anything you need from me?"

Her startled look back over her shoulder pleased him and worried him in the same moment. He loved that he could get her pupils flaring like that just with a touch, but the immediate way she stepped clear of his hold—smiling beautifully the whole time so nothing looked amiss to her speculative neighbors—and firmly put him at a distance…she did it all too naturally and he noticed it way too much.

…for a guy who didn't plan on being here past morning.

His stomach rolled. It was Friday. His time with Tori was up.

Tick-tock, tick-tock…

That bothered him a heck of a lot more than it should. The last thing he wanted to do on their last night together was spend it talking business. Talking about the demolition. He'd tell her personally, but not here.

Not tonight.

It took another hour to get the last of them out the door. The magician had left early to head off to a gig somewhere, forgetting that he'd escorted Nancy down. That meant she was the last person left sitting on Tori's sofa, an embroidered cushion clutched in her parchment hands.

"I'm missing *Ellen*," she whispered as Nate sank down next to her.

She'd been a ferocious television addict when he was a boy. Watching seventies reruns on the box while he did his homework at her dining table. Not interfering, not parenting, just being a friend. He slid his hand over her bird-like one and years of gratitude leached through that one touch. And he remembered that, for all his childhood challenges, there was light too. And lemonade.

"The party's over, Miss Smith," he said softly. "Would you like to go home now?"

He glanced over his shoulder, saw that Tori was busy saying farewells to Mr. Broswolowski at the door and turned quickly back to Nancy. "It's not much of a thank-you for everything you did for me, I realise." Having this conversation was no risk. It was like speaking into a vacuum. "But I've chosen your new home carefully." And though she didn't yet know it, he'd committed to paying her way until the end.

That was something he could do for her. To approximate how much she'd done for him.

"Everything rolls to its appointed end."

He stared at her. That was what her muddled mind chose to hold onto—*William Bryant?*

"I still have that volume," she said, quietly, and her eyes lifted to his. Decisively. His pulse thundered and his breath sucked out of his lungs. Her lips split into a gentle smile. "You always did enjoy it particularly."

Every bit of saliva decamped from his mouth. "You remember me?"

She turned those vacant eyes on him and they did seem a little less…absent. "It takes me a bit more time these days…" She squeezed his hand. "But yes. Welcome home, Nathan."

Blood rushed in torrents past his ears, almost drowning her out.

"I'm pleased you did so well in life," she said. "I so wanted that for you."

His throat tightened, which didn't make swallowing what little moisture he'd managed to generate any easier. He practically croaked his response. "Thank you, Miss Smith. For everything."

She looked back down at the cushion in her hands, lifted her face again and looked around. "Whose house is this?"

What? "This is Tori's apartment."

"Tori?"

A sinking feeling hit him. "You came to her party."

Her smile was beatific. "I love parties." And then she started to hum an old waltz tune, smiling to herself. Lost in memory.

Lost—again—to him.

He slid his other hand over hers and blinked back emotion. He'd never let himself ask as a boy. A point of pride. But he could ask it now. "Miss Smith, may I come up?"

She turned her radiant, vacant, aged face up to his. "Oh, yes!"

It took him an age to get her up two flights of stairs and settled back into her own apartment. She barely even seemed to know she'd been out. But she knew her household routines and she slipped straight back into them in a way that made him feel more comfortable about leaving her alone. She made a cup of tea, swapped her good shoes for slippers, turned on *Ellen* and promptly began watching as though he'd ceased to exist.

She had as much daily structure as Tori and had obviously grown extra reliant on it. Clearly, in her own environment, she was infinitely more in control of her faculties.

And he was about to tear her out of that. Guilt nagged, despite all the nursing care he'd bought her for the rest of her waking days. And, inexplicably, his mind went straight back to Tori. To the other woman who loved things just the way they were.

Even when she didn't.

He took the stairs in pairs in his haste to get back to her. It was going to be tough for him to come up with any decent reason to keep seeing her now that the webcam and the launch party were over. They both knew this was temporary, they'd both enjoyed it enough to stretch it out all week. Whatever move he made now was either going to send the wrong message, or bring an end to their short relationship.

Neither of which he wanted.

What he wanted to do was send the *right* message and have her give him the *right* answer.

Stay.

But he wouldn't. He might have failed—abysmally—in his attempts not to let himself care for her, but the one thing he did have from growing up almost completely responsible for himself was killer self-discipline. He'd give her a final night she'd never forget, tell her about the redevelopment and the new place he'd found her, make sure she knew what an amazing woman she was and then kiss her one last time.

Before leaving her apartment forever, honoring the commitment he'd made himself.

Viktoria Morfitt could do so much better than a workaholic with a shame-filled past and no interest in committing. But she wasn't going to find better while he was around taking up space.

"So the place survived the onslaught?" He made light as he came back through the door into the now-spotless apartment, critically aware that they only had a few more hours together. Though, as Tori turned to him with a blazing smile and moved with her catlike grace across the room, his whole body rebelled at the very thought. How could he be a man of steel resolve one moment and have it melt to a molten metal puddle the moment she locked him in her focus?

Just one more reason to get out now. While he still could.

"Nathan, thank you for all your help. I seriously don't think I could have got through without you."

"Sure you could. At worst you would have had to cut up your own carrot sticks."

She stopped before him, below him, and peered up through those enormous gray eyes. His heart started thumping.

"Let me be grateful, Nathan. You did help me." A shadow flitted across her face and was gone. "In ways I wasn't expecting. I don't understand why I was so nervous."

The heart-thumps turned into painful squeezes and he dug around for a way to keep things from getting any heavier. Ironic, given it had been her keeping things comfortably undemanding for the past few days, but if she asked him to stay forever right now he'd have a hard time saying no. Not that he thought for a moment she actually would ask.

His hands slid up her arms and around under her shoulder blades. "You want to show gratitude?"

A deep light flared in her gray depths. "Another massage?"

"No. No massage." At least not just yet. "But we will need to be lying down for it. If you're that grateful…"

She smiled and stretched her arms up around his neck. "Extremely grateful…"

And then her lips were on his and he forgot everything but the feel and taste of her.

CHAPTER ELEVEN

TORI woke to the sound of someone rummaging around in the kitchen—singing—and her sleep-addled mind immediately lurched into tightness. Into the past.

Rick!

But a bare moment afterwards, reality intruded as it did every morning and she remembered. Not Rick. Not anymore. But instead of the deep sorrow she had grown accustomed to carrying around for the first minutes of every day, a warm gooey honey washed over her instead.

Nathan.

That was his terrible singing coming from the kitchen. She lay back against the pillow and let the sadness leach away under the fresh breeze of her smile. There was something supremely endearing about a man who couldn't sing but didn't care who knew it. Nathan had the casual confidence only fortune and success could bring and, clearly, he had no need or value for perfect pitch.

Which was really just as well. She'd have to tell Pavarotti to tone it down before he scared Wilma right off her nest.

She pulled the sheet up under her arms and trailed it behind her out of bed and into the kitchen. She stood silently behind him and watched the way his powerful body moved through her kitchen. Decisively. With confidence. And he was only making breakfast.

No wonder he made love with such proficiency.

"It's Saturday, why are you dressed for work?"

Inane, yes, but even after three days she still wasn't used to morning-after conversation. In fact, she was thoroughly out of practice with conversation at any time of the day if you didn't count Gretel. And after what they'd shared last night, he was lucky she could even form sentences.

Nathan had made love to her as though she was made of blown glass. Slow, tender, beautiful. Long into the night. In a way that made it so hard to remember he was leaving.

But she suspected, because of that.

He spun around to face her and patted his coat pocket, the bulging one. "A CEO's diary does not discriminate."

He moved towards her, slid one hand behind her head and dragged his lips back and forth across hers, sending her pulse into riots and shooting spurs of desire straight to her core. If she'd expected regret she wasn't going to get any. He looked pretty darned pleased with himself. And painfully gorgeous.

"There's that smug expression I was telling you about," she said, sagging slightly against her pantry door.

The smile twisted into a full-blown grin. "Sorry, can't help it. You draped in a sheet standing in the kitchen like some kind of Greek goddess is going to take a little getting used to."

Going to? Those weren't the words of man who was packing his bags. The part of her that knew better did a little happy dance and it just felt so foreign. She stepped closer and pulled his phone out of his coat pocket and slid it behind her back. "So…does this mean you can hang around for a few more hours before yielding to your non-discriminatory diary?"

Lord, she didn't want him to go just yet.

He pulled her into the circle of his arms. "Do you want me to?"

She weighed her words. No point in denying everything she'd said and done last night. But old fears died hard… "I don't want you *not* to."

His eyes darkened and flicked over the place between her

breasts where one hand clutched the sheet to her. Then they lifted back to hers. "I have a couple of things I need to do."

"Is one of them kissing me?"

His gaze was shadowed. "Several of them involve kissing you. But also some work stuff." His eyes flicked away and returned. Then he reached around behind her and liberated his phone. "I also want to talk to you about something."

Oh. Her stomach dropped as she saw the fleeting doom in his expression. *This was it.* She took a mini breath. "Okay…?"

"Do you want to get dressed?"

Her heart constricted. She stepped back from him and pulled the sheet tighter around her body. "Do I need to get dressed?"

"If you want me to concentrate, yes."

Either that was a monumental save, just as her demons were surging to the fore, or it was the truth. "Okay. I'll be right back."

He called behind her, "I'll have coffee ready."

He did. And honeyed toast. It was all disturbingly domestic and more than a little alarming. Either he was going to tell her their time together was officially over—a proposition she'd been in serious denial about this week—or…

Nope. She had no idea what else it could be. The demons did exuberant laps in her mind as her pulse rate picked up pace to match them.

"So, I've been thinking about something you said the night we were first together…"

Heat immediately climbed. God, she'd said so many things. And groaned some. And cried some. And whimpered some. Most of them embarrassing.

She cleared her throat. "About?"

"About how you value honesty."

The demons retreated to hover nearby just in case they were needed on short notice, and they made room for a breath, albeit a tight one. "Okay. How about you just spit it out?"

"Delicately put." His smile completely disarmed her, as

usual. He leaned forward. "Okay, here's the thing. I may have found you a new apartment."

She stared at him. Of the million things he might have said to her just then... "I don't want a new apartment."

"It has everything on your list. Space, park view, trees, built-in facilities, in a good area, closer to me, actually..."

What list? "Nathan, I don't need a new apartment. Why would you look for one?"

His eyes grew cautious. "I'm not a terrible landlord, Tori. There's a reason Sanmore hasn't spent more on this building."

"*Asset strategy*, you said." And she hoped her snort told him exactly what she thought about his strategy.

"Right. But there's more to it." He studied her closely. "What would you say if I told you I was planning renovations?"

She sat up straight in her chair. "Renovations! Fantastic. We're so overdue for some work."

"Extensive renovations."

Her bubble burst. She frowned. "How extensive?"

"Very."

A nasty, twisty bite took hold deep inside and her stomach curled up to protect itself. "'Very' as in days of inconvenience?"

His eyes were as blank as she'd ever seen them, in awful contrast to the fiery passion of last night. "'Very' as in weeks, possibly...longer."

From nowhere, a deep panic started to take hold. Breathlessness. Dry mouth. Fast heart. Exactly the sort of thing she'd had when she first started climbing. She curled her rapidly cooling fingers into her palms. "Why are you telling me specifically?"

"Because we... Because I don't want it to be between us. Going forward."

The anxiety stirred her anger though she didn't quite understand why she was feeling either. Wasn't he just being honest with her? "I was under the impression there would be no going forward?"

His face was cautious. "Is that what you want? To end things?"

"It's what we agreed."

"I didn't have all the facts then."

"What facts?"

"I had no idea who you were. What we'd be like together." He cleared his throat. "How you'd make me feel."

She stared at him, crystallizing ice racing along her veins. "And now you do, you're keen to bundle me up and throw me into an apartment closer to you so you can reduce the mileage on your booty calls, is that it?"

His head jerked. "It's not like that. You know it's not."

"Then explain it to me, Nathan."

"I respect you, Tori."

"And?"

"And this is your home. I thought you'd want to know first. So you can plan."

She swallowed but there was nothing in her mouth to swallow "So this is more FYI than community consultation?"

"Tori…"

Her heart pounded. "The renovations are a done deal?"

"More or less."

"What about everyone else, Nathan? There's thirty-five households in this building. Where will they go for weeks on end?"

"I'm going to find each of them alternative accommodations. And pay their rent."

Her nostrils flared. "A good financial deal, but what about their day-to-day lives?"

"I've had my best people working on this. Finding good matches. A place close to his brother for Mr. Browoslowski. A small loft in SoHo for Angel. One block back from Riverside for the Radcliffes—awesome Great Dane country…"

Tori watched his lips moving but struggled to take in his words. The blood was rushing past her ears way too fast.

"A three-bed right over the road from Marco's school for the deCostas, a wonderful place with 24/7 medical care for Nancy—"

"You're putting her in a home?"

"It's not a home, Tori. It's an independent aged-care apartment. With daily medical assistance."

"No, *this* is her home, Nathan. Here. Where she's lived her whole life." Panic rushed up into her stomach and bubbled there.

"She's not safe here, Tori. How much longer before she *has* to move anyway?"

She ignored his logic. "And the deCostas' apartment?"

"I thought the proximity to Marco's school made it perfect."

"And how do you know where Marco goes to school? How do you know where the Radcliffes like to walk Gretel? How do you know where Mr. B's crazy brother lives?"

"Tori..."

She pressed her lips together. "Were you mining me for information every time we were together?"

"No, I wasn't. But I remembered things you told me. You *wanted* me to get to know my tenants."

"Not so you could throw them out on the street!"

His eyes glittered dangerously. "Do you *know* how much I'm spending specifically so that I *don't* leave them high and dry?"

Her whole body physically shook. "Don't throw your money at me, Nathan Archer. Don't come in here and exploit my party and my friends the way you've exploited me."

He hissed his frustration. "I did *not* exploit you or your party. I *carried* your party while you went all Greta Garbo on us. I just listened to—"

She shoved away from the table and to her feet, and marched resolutely away from him into the room where they'd spent so many extraordinary, precious hours together, slamming the door shut on so much more than the conversation and hauling the pillow that had so recently cushioned his head across her chest. Confusion and anger and seething anxiety all raged within her and overwhelmed her senses. She'd worked so hard to numb herself internally over the past five years. To survive what had happened in her family.

Her stomach lurched. What had she imagined would happen if she opened the door to more sensation? To love. To desire.

To trust.

How her subconscious must be cackling. It would have seen exactly where this was going to end. She'd broken the golden rule—she'd let Nathan close and tried to have something for herself. Maybe she should count herself lucky it was only her heart this time.

Last time she broke a golden rule, someone she loved died.

The doorknob started to turn and Tori squared her shoulders and took a deep, shaky breath. Nathan's beautiful dark head peered around the door. It killed her that her wounded heart still gave a pathetic little lurch at seeing him.

"Can I come in?"

She shuddered full-body. The ache intensified into a sharp blade that slipped neatly through the muscles between her ribs and poised over her heart. Three weeks ago he'd kicked the door in, desperate to save a stranger. Or had he just been in the building anyway, measuring up for all these renovations?

She pressed her lips together. "Suit yourself. It's your apartment."

How easily it came back to her: the careless shrug, the vacant stare. She hadn't used them since the days following Rick's fall. Her soul had been collapsing in on itself then, too.

His shoulders sagged. "Tori...I didn't use you to get information on your neighbors."

"So you say."

"Are you seriously thinking that an officer of the court

colluded to place me here so that I could get a handful of not terribly interesting facts about the tenants in the building?"

Tori fought the frown birthed by that irritating bit of common sense. But she couldn't hide it completely.

"Right." Nathan stepped toward her, nodding. "So none of this was planned."

"Then you're just an opportunist?"

"Absolutely, I built my business on capitalizing on opportunity. But I wanted to do the right thing by everyone."

"The right thing would be finding a different way to do your renovations. Floor by floor. Without disrupting everyone."

A dark shadow crossed his face. "It's not that simple."

Panic started to well. "Why can't it be? Why do you have to throw everyone's lives into turmoil?"

My life.

"This is a good outcome for the tenants. Six months free rent will set them up with a deposit on a better place, or a foundation to keep renting the places we've found them if they want to stay. Or time to find somewhere new if they don't."

"Do you imagine Nancy will think about it that way?"

"I don't expect Nancy to think about this at all."

"She's eighty years old, Nathan. This building is a part of her. Just because she's drifting off doesn't mean she doesn't know her essential surroundings. Or the people around her. She runs her life by the strict order in her apartment, her routines and patterns." Her pulse rate started to skyrocket and tiny pricks of light exploded behind her eyes. "Have you even considered that? I know she's a stranger to you, but she's like family to us."

His nostrils flared. "Yes, I've considered that. I'm getting just a little bit tired of you assuming I'm this corporate ogre come to sack the village before torching it. Every one of you is on a lease, Tori, including Nancy. A lease with an end date. By your own choosing."

She didn't want to hear his logic. "Where's your loyalty to

some of the people who've been on those leases for decades—?"
To the woman whose body you were sharing.

Frustration hissed from his lips. "I've rewarded their loyalty tenfold. I sourced Nancy's new place personally and picked the best medical care I could find."

Everything began to spin and Tori couldn't grab all of the thoughts and images fast enough to force them into some kind of sense. She shook her head. "Why?"

"Because I—" He pinched his lips shut and changed tack. "Because she has no one else."

"What about the falcons? How do you think they're going to manage raising their young with the sounds of jackhammers pounding relentlessly behind them?"

"Seventy days, you said. To hatch, fledge and be independent. I've scheduled work to begin in seventy-five, so they should have moved on by then."

Her pulse began to hammer and dark spots flashed briefly across her eyes. She rubbed them and realized how damp her hands were. *Seventy-five days.* She had to be out in ten weeks. Hardly any time at all.

"You think they'll just fly away and come back next year? It doesn't work that way."

"According to your own fact sheet it does. Over generations. I can design the new building to be falcon-friendly. We'll have to trust that they return eventually."

Everything started to close in.

"Eventually?"

"You told me they're unlikely to breed again until their offspring move out into their own breeding territory."

Him being right didn't help. And him having thought a lot of things through carefully only boiled her blood more. She waved her hand out the bedroom door in the direction of the high tech monitoring gear. Her chest squeezed so hard it nearly stole the breath she needed to accuse him. She forced the words out.

"You knew the whole time you were installing everything,

designing the website, that it would barely get a few weeks of use? What a monumental waste of everyone's time."

His jaw clenched visibly. "It wasn't a waste. Look what it has achieved. The webcam wouldn't have had anything to show outside breeding season anyway. Just an empty box."

"Why didn't you just tell me about the renovations? We could have waited until after they were finished."

Nathan stared at her long and hard. "Because they won't be finished for some time."

Everything in her prickled at his tone. "How long?"

His eyes grew flinty. "Two years."

Her world lurched and tipped violently. "*Two years?* What the hell kind of renovations are you planning?"

"I wanted to talk to you about this, explain personally…"

"We're talking now. So explain."

His chest rose and fell on a controlled breath. Tori totally held hers. "I'm constructing a whole new building on this site."

Her blood froze over, her word barely more than a whisper. "What?"

"I'm demolishing this old building and erecting something new in its place. Something larger. More contemporary."

The knife poised between her ribs shifted trajectory and neatly pierced her lungs. All the air escaped in a pained whoosh. The room began to spin slowly. "No…"

"It's too young to have heritage status and too old to be economically maintained…."

His lips were moving but his voice warped in and out of focus in ears that thundered with sudden panic. *Demolition…* Her home. Her sanctuary.

"You can't…"

"It's all arranged." He frowned as he noticed her white-knuckled grip on the quilt. "Tori, are you okay?"

"You can't, Nathan. You can't." Her voice echoed in her head like a bad amusement ride. High-pitched. Discordant. But there was nothing she could do to stop it. "I can't."

"I found you a beautiful place, surrounded by trees. Right on the park. Only a few blocks from me. It's yours for a year. Longer if you want it. And if you want to come back here when the new building's up I can sort that, too."

His words washed in and out of her ears making little impact on her brain. *Coming back would require leaving.* The world dropped out from beneath her like the worst of free-falls. Except, abseiling down a rock face had never made her feel like this. She struggled valiantly to disguise how difficult it was to breathe. "I can't leave here, Nathan."

"Just come and check it out with me. I know you'll make it as nice as you've made this apartment. It has everything you spoke of that night."

She fisted his shirt and pulled herself closer to him, the fear clawing. "You're not hearing me. *I cannot leave here.*"

He stared at her, then looked around and then back at her with a deep, pained frown. "Tori, what's going on? It's just an apartment. It's not like you'll be homeless."

What *was* going on? Her whole body was reacting. Trembling. But she fought to hide it from him. He wouldn't understand how important this apartment was to her, how much she relied on routine to get her through each day since she'd lost Rick.

She barely understood it. Although she feared she was beginning to.

Nathan took a deep breath and watched her through narrowed eyes. "When was the last time you went outside?"

The ridiculous question distracted her. "With you. On the roof."

"I mean out on the street. When did you last go through the front door?"

She blinked. It was easy to recall those first days when she'd moved in, when everything was furnished, unpacked and in its place. Then there'd been a bunch of trips into the surrounding neighborhood to get her bearings. Then ever-decreasing errands the more she set up trades within the building for things she needed. She really scraped her memory…

Her heart thumped.

…and came up blank.

Her brows drew together. Suddenly she saw the past five years played back in fast forward. Every time she'd hedged. Every time she'd stalled. Every time she'd ordered in instead of dining out. Every single trade she'd offered the people in this building to ensure that the world came to her….

So that she didn't have to go out to it.

And it frightened the hell out of her. When had her entire life become a series of carefully controlled, deeply comforting routines? Her pulse started to beat at the fine skin containing it.

"I…" But she had no idea what to say next.

His eyes flooded with pity. "Have you tried to get help?"

Help? "For what?"

"Tori. You haven't been outside in…what…years?" He shifted closer to her. "You're agoraphobic."

Her laugh sounded brittle, even to her and her breath grew painfully tight. "Don't be ridiculous. I'm a mountain climber. How can I possibly fear open spaces? You've seen me on the roof. On the ledge. All that wide-open sky…"

Deny that, genius.

But he couldn't. "It's still not normal."

She pushed away, her breath still straining. "Normal? Are you really sure you're fit to preach about what's normal?"

His eyes narrowed dangerously. "Tori…"

But she was in pure survival mode and, just like last time, her body was making the calls on how best to get through this. She felt her lips curl up. "You've driven yourself into the ground trying to prove something to a mother who probably never even noticed. Did she even know how rich you were at the end there? Where you ended up?"

"Don't make this about me, Tori."

Every time he said her name it was like a warning. His tight tone said they were at DEFCON three.

And she ignored it completely.

"Why not? Isn't this exactly about you? Your desire to make more money? Your desire to prove yourself and beat your sucky childhood? To build something shiny and expensive? Did you get your revenge that way, Nathan, living the high life while she lived in squalor?"

"This has nothing to do with her."

"Oh, really? Did you buy your mother her own apartment with park views, then? Or do you save that sort of thing for the women you're sleeping with?"

He glared at her. "She always had a safe roof over her head, until the day she died. I bought out her lease. And then I bought the whole building."

What? She took three steadying breaths. "How many buildings do you own?"

His eyes glittered like dead sapphires. "Just the one."

And with those three little words everything came together. Apartment 8B. The notorious Domino. The way he'd subtly avoided meeting any of the building's old-timers. The way he was neglecting the building to rubble.

"*This* is the place where you were so unhappy?"

His silence was assent enough.

A deep nausea washed over her. "You bought the building you grew up in. And now you want to tear it down. Have you even been back into your family apartment since she died?

More silence.

She stared at him. "And that strikes you as normal, does it? Have *you* tried to get help?"

Throwing his words so brutally back at him only served to crank him up to DEFCON two. But his anger was underpinned by visible pain. "This is business."

"Oh, please! Anyone else would just move away and move on."

The way you did? her inner voice accused.

"Columbia is looking for new student housing in the area, Tori. I'll make a killing."

"Then why didn't you just sell out to them years ago?"

"I wish I had," he ground out. "Then I never would have had to—"

He cut himself off way too quickly to ignore and pressed his lips against whatever he'd been about to blurt. Hurt twisted in her chest. "Meet me?"

"I was going to say 'have this ridiculous conversation.'"

The ice in her veins solidified that little bit more. "You don't think it's significant that you've only bought one piece of real estate in your life and it's your childhood home? That you're demolishing it when you don't have to?"

"It's business, Tori. Risk is what I do. Sometimes I win, sometimes I lose, but my instincts are seldom wrong." His nostrils flared wildly. "And at least I'm out there, living my life amongst real people."

"And I'm living mine here," she said, her voice painfully tight. "Just differently to you."

Both their chests heaved. "It's not living, Tori. It's just existing."

Her throat ached from wanting to shout at him. And from the strain of not crying. "Huh. Funny, these past few days have felt pretty alive to me," she said thickly. She'd been gradually thawing out since the moment he'd first caught her up in his smoky gaze. His smile. His kisses.

He swore under his breath and grudgingly met her eyes. "They were. I haven't felt so...connected... Ever."

She was only a deep breath away from hysteria. "Me, too. Let's celebrate by popping a cork or ripping down a building."

His lips thinned. "Your sarcasm's not shoring it up any. It's only reinforcing that nothing good comes out of this building."

Tori stared at him. "So this *is* personal?"

His face took on a wild hue. "No. It's not. But I won't be sorry that the building and its misery are gone. A nice side benefit."

"Is that what I was this week?"

His face turned ashen. "No. You were not." He swallowed hard. "But even you have to admit your life here hasn't been a riot."

"Sorry to bust your theory but my life was perfectly crap before I moved in here, thank you very much."

His face shuttered over. "Your brother."

She pushed to her feet, past him out into the living room. "Einstein."

He pursued her out the door. "You're here because of him."

"I'm here because New York offered me a new life. A fresh start."

"No." The intent look in his eye was too all-seeing. "You're living in the most crowded and anonymous city in the country on the money Rick left you, sequestered in this tower like some kind of twisted fairy-tale princess, banished from the people and mountains you love, punishing yourself."

She spun on him, clutching the pillow close to her chest. "Punishing myself—for what?"

"For living. When he didn't."

Every molecule of oxygen sucked out of her body, rearranged itself in the atmosphere and then flooded back in on a rush of heat. She marched straight up to him and every step was on razor wire. Fear gripped her deep and low. "You have no idea what you're talking about."

He towered over her. "Really? Do you imagine I don't know a thing or two about guilt? I was the unplanned pregnancy that cramped my mother's style her whole life. I was the irritating expense as I outgrew uniform after uniform at school. I was the reason she had to drop a days worth of clients to clean the fetid apartment once in a while for Social Services to come around." He stabbed stiff fingers into his chest. "I grew up thinking my mother sold her body to anyone who had need of it so that *I* could eat a warm meal each day. And to top it all off I had to deal with the guilt of being so damned *relieved* when I finally realized she was doing it for money and not for me."

Tori flinched at the pain in his face and her whole body cried out in sympathy.

"So yes, Tori, I recognise survivor guilt when I see it because I survived my childhood and it took me a long time to let myself be proud of that." He stepped closer. "You lived when your brother died. And you think that deserves punishment. But you're wrong. Living is a gift, Tori, and finding the right person to live that life with is more extraordinary than anything."

Tears surged suddenly from nowhere and spilled uncontrolled onto her raging-hot cheeks. Nathan's lips squeezed tight against saying anything more and he stepped toward her.

She stumbled back—desperate not to hear the promise in his words, desperate not to tempt the hand of fate by embracing the tantalizing hint of happiness he offered—and consciously euthanized everything they had built between them.

"I killed my brother, Nathan." Her voice was hoarse and unnatural. "I killed Rick to save myself."

The only sound in the entire apartment was the tight wheeze of her own tortured throat. Nathan didn't even breathe. He just stared at her in horror.

Totally deserved.

Tori swiped at the tears spilling down her cheeks. "He was so much bigger than me, hanging over that abyss. His weight was dragging us both over. It took forever, slipping closer to the precipice. I scrabbled and clawed and tried to arrest my slide but I couldn't get purchase. Rick couldn't climb back up and I couldn't hold him forever." She heaved in a tight breath. "We both knew what had to happen, but his left hand was twisted up in the rigging—he couldn't reach his knife."

Her eyes dropped to shake the image burned into her retinas. "He was screaming at me to do it before he dragged me over, but I couldn't. I wanted to save him or die trying. Because I loved him more than the air we breathed." A shudder racked her body and the tears stopped flowing. They sucked back into her stinging orbits. A numb stillness settled over her instead. "But I got within a meter of the edge and, in that moment, right at the last moment I realized I was too afraid to fall. To die. So I did it. I held my breath, released my knife and cut the rope. And he fell."

Endless silence followed. And why not—there was nothing more to say. She'd said it all five years ago to the relentless line of strangers who investigated the accident. Nathan stepped towards her and she stepped back, crossing her arms in front of her.

His voice cracked when he finally spoke. "You had no choice. You would have both died."

She lifted anguished eyes to his. "I wish I had. Everything I've done since is just taking up air."

"No…"

"Maybe I am punishing myself. But Rick will never laugh or cry or be loved or watch sunsets or hold a sleeping child in his arms. Why should I get to?"

"So…what—you're just going to rot here in this apartment? Forsaking any goodness that might creep in under your defenses? Until you're old and senile and die alone in this apartment?"

Her chest squeezed hard and she thought immediately of Nancy. Was that why she felt so close to the older woman? Because she saw herself in Nancy? She straightened her back and the effort half killed her. Nathan was handing her the perfect excuse to end things between them. To do what she knew she had to. It would be better for him in the long term if she just unraveled the complicated tangle that had formed from her heart to his and tore it away.

She closed her eyes. In her mind she lifted a knife to the rigging of whatever it was that had brought she and Nathan together. Held them together now. "Yes." She took a long breath. "Starting with you."

He stared at her, his burning regard dark in bleached skin. But something about the raw pain she saw swilling in the twin depths made her pause her mind's knife. Offer him—

them both—one last chance. "Will you leave the building standing?"

His nostrils flared and his eyes blazed at her. "I can't, Tori. Not just because you can't go outside…"

Air sucked into her lungs of its own accord and it was strangely reinforcing. But it didn't do a thing to diminish the ache that filled her.

He wouldn't do it for her.

Because his own reasons were too strong.

Her heart cracked wider. "Then I don't want your new apartment. Or your charity."

She crossed to the refrigerator, snatched free the single sheet of paper stuck to its front and scribbled across it with her pen. His community order, fully signed off. She pushed it into his chest, and sliced the knife clean through the final golden filaments binding them together.

"And I don't want you to come near me ever again."

The ghosts of the building held their breaths.

Nathan stared at the order and then at her, deep and unreadable, although his chest pumped hard. "This is not really about the building, Tori." But then his lashes dropped and he twisted away and flicked a business card out onto the counter. "When you decide you need help—when you decide you need me—you know where I am."

She held herself perfectly rigid as he moved toward her front door. The door that had somehow come to symbolize her: as hollow and out of place as she always felt.

Except when she was with Nathan.

He stopped at the door and looked back at her, burning to say something. But he glanced down at the floor and then lifted carefully blank eyes back up to her and murmured a few words before disappearing out the door.

Tori waited until she heard the door latch quietly closed and then she took the pillow still smelling of him and hurled it, internalizing her scream so that it hurt more. So that the memory would be branded into her soul. So that she'd never again forget why she didn't let anyone in. Why she'd embraced this careful, controlled world where everything happened in the same way every time.

She and Nathan were not meant to be together. It was hard enough finding a perfect match for your outward qualities without also expecting your raging demons to get along. There was more than one way to be incompatible.

It had been a long time since her body had harbored intense pain—her routines and rules and cloistered ways had done their job in holding it at bay—but she felt it now, surging back in, raw and razored, at the thought of losing the man she'd only just found.

The man she hadn't even known she needed.

Her heart squeezed into a twisted pulp.

She stared around her now at the familiar sanctuary of her apartment. Her old furniture. Her familiar view. Her entire world. And she knew that, even if it *had* tiptoed up on her and taken over her life, this apartment was directly responsible for keeping her alive these past five years. For helping her breathe. For letting her heart beat. And it was going to be ripped into tiny pieces and hurled to the pavement at the hands of a man she'd given herself to, body and soul.

Nathan was going to rip her out of her safe life the way he'd come into it. In an explosion of timber shards.

Forgive yourself...he'd said right before he disappeared through her open doorway. But then he'd whispered the rest, and she'd almost not heard him over the roar of her frantic heartbeat past her eardrums. *Forgive yourself for choosing life that day*...

She folded her arms over her head and sank down onto the floor, releasing the pain on a stream of hot, blinding tears.

...but not for wasting it.

CHAPTER TWELVE

"YOU'D better get up here, Nathan. There's a woman hanging from your building and there are an awful lot of people starting to gather."

The moment Nate retrieved Dean's voice-mail message he knew exactly who the woman was and what she had done. He slid over to his desktop and fired up Sanmore's latest internet browser. He hadn't visited the webcam in a couple of weeks—every time he did it only reminded him of Tori's warm little apartment, of the wild, beautiful birds, and the wild, beautiful woman who cared for them. It reminded him of what he no longer had a right to dream of at night. But he still kept the link in his favorites folder. And he still hovered the mouse over it from time to time. The only thing that stopped him from clicking it was that he felt vaguely like a stalker.

She'd made it perfectly clear she wanted nothing more to do with him and he'd always been a man of sterling self-discipline. To the point of pain.

But better him in pain than her.

The website loaded and he paused for a nanosecond to look at some new imagery on the homepage—two robust, browning chicks that had been tiny balls of fluff the last time he'd checked.

His eyes flicked to the visitor-counter and widened, seeing a number in five figures. Low five figures, but still…That was a lot of people checking out Morningside's raptors in just a few weeks.

In the top corner, something about the thumbnail for the webcam didn't look right. As if it was blocked by something. He activated the cam and held his breath while it loaded.

"Oh, you are kidding me..."

There *was* something blocking the camera's view of Wilma and the chicks. A piece of card, propped up by a soda can, and kind of off center as though the wind—or an inquisitive falcon—had knocked it askew. It had a bold message in Tori's handwriting scrawled in thick, black ink.

Help save Morningside's falcons.
Help save their building.
Add your voice to the protest.
4:00 p.m., June 23

And that would be today. Nate's lashes drifted shut.

But then he couldn't help smiling. A normal person would have added a tastefully bordered HTML message to the home-page with five minutes' work. But Tori did nothing the normal way and her personalized message achieved two things. It added some raw urgency to her plea, which site fans would immediately respond to, and it blocked the birds from the view of those ten thousand plus visitors, effectively doing exactly what demolishing the building was going to do. Make them disappear. Which the site users wouldn't like. Maybe enough to get off their butts and travel up to Morningside for the protest that started—he looked at his watch—ten minutes ago.

Tori was an accidental genius.

And a total thorn in his side. She haunted him at night. She troubled him during the day. He caught himself making business decisions he thought she, rather than his shareholders, might approve of, and he spent way too long each day obsessing on which tenants had begun to move out and waiting to see her name show up on the report. So far most of the neighbors he knew had shifted to their new accommodations, even Mr. Broswolowski, whom he'd figured would have stuck in there with Tori. But he'd personally signed off on Mr B's relocation expense just two days ago so—other than Miss Smith who was scheduled for the end of next week—Tori was all out of friends in that big building.

Who was looking after her now?

The tenants' deadline was up in just a week. But if she was planning eleventh-hour protest rallies then she wasn't going anywhere soon. That meant she was holding out for the bailiffs. Or she was still in denial.

He groaned.

She didn't have a textbook phobia—that would be too simple and Tori was everything but simple. She had developed her own special blend of dysfunction; one that made her overly reliant on her ordered, predictable world, to counteract the damage she'd done by choosing life that day on the mountain. He'd looked into it to understand. To see if it truly was a big enough deal to throw away everything they'd shared. Apparently it was.

And accepting that was one of the hardest things he'd done. Forcing Tori back into the world would only hurt her more. Between them, they had two lifetimes of damage conspiring to keep them apart. And it wasn't often he met someone who trumped him in the screwy stakes.

He asked himself, again, what he'd been secretly asking himself for weeks—what she'd asked him.

Was she right? *Was* he demolishing Morningside for the wrong reasons? He had a written expression of interest from Columbia University's legal department telling him otherwise but he *could* have sold them the building right away. Let them do all the dirty-work with the tenants.

His heart heaved.

Let them throw Tori's world into disarray.

He missed her. Even the screwy parts. He missed the way she teased him mercilessly and laughed at him if he tried to talk up his achievements. He missed her warm body against his at night and the incredible rightness of being joined with her. He missed the wonders that he got to teach her and the amazing wilderness stories she got to teach him. He missed turning up on her doorstep at 4:00 p.m. sharp, knowing the day was just getting going.

But he didn't miss hurting her. Or forcing her to look at things she wasn't ready to face.

His gut lurched. He'd hated that.

He'd had a full private session with the psych that he'd lined up for Tori ready for the day she called him to ask for help— not that she ever would call, and the psych knew that even if it had taken Nate a while to catch on. He'd told Nate that forcing Tori back into the world was the fastest way to ensure she never healed. And given she'd thrown him out of her life for good, helping her more gently wasn't really an option. He could only hope that the looming eviction deadline would trigger some kind of change. But he'd expected it to be in the form of sticking an experimental toe out the front door.

Not arranging a rally for a thousand wildlife fanatics.

He could only imagine how intensely uncomfortable the very idea would have made her. Which said a lot about how desperate she must be feeling. And desperate people did desperate things. Like making a nestful of birds seem in more danger than they actually were.

Help save Morningside's Falcons.

Might as well have said *Please help me.*

He winced and snatched up his desk phone. "Karin, can you get the car out the front? I'm going uptown. And then get on to Tony d'Angelo at the NYFD…"

When he arrived, Simon had to let him out up the block because 126th Street was gridlocked thanks to the mix of people spilling out of the laneway behind his building. Young hippie types, older retired types, backpack-wearing corduroy types. Mothers with children. Hundreds of people. Traffic was still getting through, but it was car by car and walking pace to make sure no one got hurt. On foot was definitely faster.

Nate rounded the corner just as he had that first day and elbowed his way through the milling crowd, dodging the odd placard before it took his eye out. He glanced upward immediately.

And then his stomach flipped.

Dean wasn't kidding when he'd said *hanging from your building.* Tori dangled from the bedroom ledge one floor up from hers, fully rigged out in climbing gear, with a brightly decorated bedsheet saying Save Morningside's Falcons furled out below her. It took him only a blink to realize that she couldn't have opened 11B's bedroom window, so she must have climbed down the outside of the building to get to the ledge.

Crazy fool woman!

He looked around. The crowd was looking uncertain. Like a mob who'd forgotten why they were at a lynching. A bad feeling settled in his stomach.

"What's going on?" he asked a woman standing nearby. "Why isn't she doing anything?"

The woman shrugged. "Everyone was cheering as she shimmied down the building and unfurled the banner—" his stomach dropped clean away at that image "—but then she kind of just…stopped. We're waiting for something to happen."

"You care what happens to these birds?"

"Well, sure. There's not a lot of community spirit around these days. And *she* cares. Look at that. Who does that?"

His gaze followed the woman's finger upward again. There was definitely something spectacular and inspiring about a woman clinging like a backward starfish to the outside of a building. But then he narrowed his eyes and looked at Tori's posture.

Really looked.

She kind of just…stopped.

Nate sucked in a breath. Not stopped. *Froze.*

He sprinted for the building, fighting his way through more

and more people who were arriving and packing into the small space below until he got around to the fire exit at the base of the stairwell. He pulled his keys out and sorted through them until he found the one he needed and then flung the doors wide before running inside. The elevator would take a lifetime to get up there and Tori might not have that long. So he stuck to the stairs, not even counting the floors as his long legs ate them up.

By the fifth floor they protested and by six they shook with a hot burn. But the image of Tori hanging, terrified, from the building filled his mind and drove him onward. He visualized a scenario in which he got up there and she yelled at him for interfering. Called the cops on him. Slid her hands onto those beautiful hips and glared impatiently because she was actually *perfectly fine*, just…taking a breather.

He'd take that. He'd love that. Because it would mean she was okay. It would mean she was coping.

But deep down inside he knew she wasn't. She hadn't been coping for a really long time but she'd had everyone fooled. Her parents. Her neighbors. Him.

Herself.

Sometimes even the unrescuable needed rescuing.

As he passed the seventh-floor landing, his lungs pure agony, Nate realized that he wasn't going to be able to pull Tori up from the ledge outside 11B's sealed bedroom pane and there was no way he'd fit through her bathroom window. The only way he was getting her down *was* down and the only apartment that would put him close enough for that was his own.

His mother's.

His throat threatened to close right over and end it all here on the steps. He pushed through the landing doors and took a sharp left. The whole floor was ominously quiet, with most of the building now vacant. It practically echoed with the sound of his racing feet.

He didn't waste time searching for that little bronze key, hurling himself instead at the locked door. His whole left side

screamed on impact but the door creaked and shuddered. He
backed up and slammed again and the lock burst from its frame,
throwing him hard into the middle of what his mother used to
call the "receiving" room.

There was only one thing he'd received there and that was
an awful, early education.

The apartment was musty with age and dank with mildew
but otherwise empty of anything that would have identified
it as his. He'd donated the entire contents to Goodwill when
his mother had died and had called professional cleaners in
to scrub any echoes of their life from the nicotine-stained
walls. But memories still reached out and snatched at him as
he pushed himself to his feet and ran through to the bathroom.
The window resisted at first but he forced it open and stretched
through it.

"Tori!"

He couldn't see her but he heard her tentative response, tight
and small. "Nathan?"

Everything in him threatened to go wobbly at the sound of
her fear. But he forced himself to stay strong until she was safe
again.

"Tori, can you get back up?"

"I…I can't. I can't move…."

She sounded so much more than scared. Angry. Incredulous.
Distressed. Heartbroken.

He craned his neck around to the left and saw an old lump
of concrete sitting on the ledge. Dangerous, but maybe the only
way. He took a deep breath. "Tori, I need you to turn completely
away from the building. Can you do that? Face the Hudson."

He listened for her response but only heard a mewling sound
that could have been "yes" or could have been the falcon chicks
two storys up expressing their displeasure at the disturbances
going on all around them. He slid back through the window,
then wiggled an arm through ahead of him, just long enough
to reach the concrete lump. He grabbed it and brought it back
through into the bathroom. Then he sprinted through the old

kitchen, stripping off his tie and shirt as he went, and wrapping them thickly around his right hand and forearm before fitting the stone back into his swaddled fist.

His hands shook so badly he nearly couldn't tie off the swaddling. *Tori...*

In the master bedroom he yanked back the old curtains and a decade of mildew and dust exploded into the air. Nate fixed his eyes on the view outside, determined not to visualize what this room had once looked like or what had gone on here. He saw Tori's shoulder down at ledge level and the head she'd screened with her arms to shield it.

He lifted the rock and slammed it against the edge of the glass farthest from her.

The window cracked on first impact and smashed outward on the second. Glass fragments went everywhere and he hoped he'd managed to control the spray so it fell on the ledge and not on the protesters below. Tori turned toward him, wide-eyed and pale.

And wildly, patently, relieved.

His determination doubled. He used his wrapped fist to punch out the entire left hand pane of the bedroom window and then sweep the worst of the glass into the corner of the ledge. Then he unraveled it and threw the shirt aside and boosted himself out the window before he thought too much about the danger of what he was about to do.

Or how high he was.

Eight storeys seemed to swim in and out of focus below him. One minute the people below were just a bright sea of color and the next he was making out the tiniest and most inconsequential details. An overly large nose. A Lakers cap. And all of them with one expression in common—wide-eyed, excited disbelief that *someone else* was now climbing out onto the building's exterior. A half-naked man.

So much better than video games!

Nate dragged his focus back to the woman he loved and tried not to think about how far away the hard ground was and what it might do if he was to suddenly rush toward it. Or if she was...

Because he did love her. And it took a ridiculous incident to make him acknowledge it. He'd been half in love with her when he'd first kissed her in that elevator. And then their week together as lovers had sealed the deal. He'd loved her then but not been able to admit it.

Any more than he was prepared to admit she was right about this building.

Because he feared he'd be as bad at love as his mother and as just blind to his own failings.

"Tori..."

"Nathan, be careful!" Her eyes were as wide as those of the people in the crowd below.

He slid down into sitting position and hung his legs over the edge, close to where she hung suspended and the world lurched sickeningly. "I could say the same thing. What are you doing?"

"I'm trying to save the building!"

Even speaking made his chest ache. Five kinds of fear congealed in his lungs. "By fixing yourself to the outside of it? You think you wouldn't just be a convenient target for the wrecking ball?"

Slipping straight back into their usual, bantering dynamic helped take his mind off the fact that his entire future hung suspended in space and so, practically, did he. Joking seemed to help Tori, too. She loosened up just a bit.

"I used 11B's bedroom ledge to come down from so I didn't disturb the birds. I just wanted to hang the banner but then I looked around. At all the people. And I just... Everything just..." Her face folded.

He reached forward with his legs and hooked them around the taut rigging that held her weight, and she lifted her arms and grabbed his ankles immediately.

His smile was half grimace. "You've done this before."

Her voice tightened through clenched teeth. "This isn't the first time I've gotten into a tricky spot while climbing."

He swore and didn't bother to disguise it. "I kid you not—when I get you in you are never leaving the house again."

The irony of that made them both laugh, tight and strained. Nate locked his abs, tilted back onto his coccyx and contracted his legs back toward his body. The first little bit wasn't a problem because the rigging offered no resistance, but as he pulled, even Tori's slight weight dragged him forward a bit and he had to grip the concrete with what little nails he had. She turned in his grasp until she was facing him. The deathly pale bleach of her skin sunk home.

He had a sudden and crystal-clear vision of her, tear-streaked, exhausted and scrabbling inexorably down a mountain face, trying desperately to hold onto her brother while her heart ripped apart. He knew how he would feel if he dropped her now.

His life would be over.

A deep and a biding purpose flooded through him. He was going to build her a new life. "Hold on, baby. I've got you."

She locked her eyes on his, pale and frantic. "If you slide, you let me go."

He pulled harder and grimaced past the pain. "Not going to happen."

Her breathing was fast and urgent. "I'm rigged, Nathan. You're not. If you start to go you just let me go. I cannot lose you."

Lose you.

Not "lose you *like this*".

Absurdly, given the peril that they both faced and despite the deathly drop below him, his heart lifted. "You belong in my arms, Tori. We're not stopping until you're back there." He wriggled into a surer position. Every part of him protested. "The longer you talk the weaker I'm getting. Now shut up and start climbing."

She was still too low for the ledge, but she wasn't too low to climb his legs. She gasped a few instructions on how he could best brace himself and then she twisted the rigging in her fist and used it to take the bulk of her weight while her other hand clasped hard around his thigh for purchase.

She pulled. He braced. Then he tightened his legs under her armpits so she could release the rigging and reach for a higher point. She did, hooking her free hand onto his belt. It was worth every one of the designer zeroes it had cost as it helped pull Tori up and half across his lap.

So close.

He let go of one of his brace points and wrapped his arm around her torso and then used every fiber in every thread of every muscle in his body to pull them both back into a prone position on the filthy, pigeon-poop-covered ledge.

It might as well have been a down comforter.

He circled his screaming arms around her and pulled her hard up against him, the rigging protesting at the stretch, shards of broken glass slicing into his unprotected back.

Tori scrabbled to release the clips that kept her from Nathan and when the tethers swung free there was a joyful cheer from the crowd below. She flung her arms around him, reveling in the feel of his hard, shirtless body against hers, and she twisted her legs sideways so that one hundred percent of both of them was supported by flat concrete ledge. No chance of him sliding off.

No chance that she'd kill another man that she loved.

She buried her face into the sweat-covered curve of Nathan's neck and inhaled the heated scent raging off him. Every part of her started to shake and he absorbed her tremors straight into his skin. It didn't matter that the last time she'd seen him she'd thrown him out of her apartment. Her life. That she'd confessed her greatest shame to him and he'd accused her of wasting the life she'd chosen that day on the mountain face. That he'd lied to her about where he'd grown up. And that he was going to destroy her home.

All that mattered was that Nathan was here. In her arms.

And his heart was beating sure and hard and eternal against hers. For whatever minutes they had together.

She'd take it.

Eventually he spoke, his voice cracked and gravelly against her ear. "Are you hurt?"

Only inside. From so much. She shook her head.

"I need you safely inside, Tori. Can you stand?"

Her eyes dropped to his biceps. "My muscles aren't the ones twitching with exhaustion. Can *you* stand?" His color hadn't come back yet.

"Don't worry about me," he said. "You first."

She scrabbled over him, knowing he wasn't moving until she did. And more than anything in this world she wanted carpet under his feet. And, for the first time ever, under her own. She practically tumbled into the empty apartment and then rolled away from the window to make room for Nathan.

Through the window that was so much like her own, she watched him pull himself into sitting position on the ledge and sucked in a pained breath as she saw the shards of bloody glass sticking out of his back like some kind of masochistic body art. She glanced around and saw his torn-off shirt on the floor. She had it ready when he finally slid through the shattered window and landed with a thump next to her on the floor.

He looked baffled by his own weakness.

"Fatigue," she croaked. "And shock. Give yourself a minute for the adrenaline hit to pass." But then she lunged toward him and snagged his shoulder just as he might have leaned back against the musty apartment wall. Against the forest of broken glass peppering his skin. "You're going to hurt any moment, too."

She saw the moment he did. As the pain of thirty slices registered on his handsome face. The face she'd believed she'd never see again.

Compassion washed through her. She crawled around behind him and sat, spread-eagled, with her thighs either side of his hips to keep him from slumping backward. Worrying about him kept her from thinking about herself. About what had just happened. Just like getting Rick help gave her something to focus on when he died.

To hold herself together.

"Hold still." She picked at the larger pieces of glass, wincing as Nathan flinched. The easing of the blood confirmed they weren't as deep as she'd feared.

His voice was strained and low as he said, "Don't ever do that to me again."

"I have to get the worst pieces out—"

"I'm talking about the stunt you just pulled. I'm talking about looking up from a crowd full of strangers and seeing you hanging there, petrified, and at risk of falling."

Petrified. She had been, too. Completely overcome with an emotion that just froze every living part of her. Until she'd heard his voice… Her body shuddered with remembered relief. She picked more glass out and softly stroked every spot where she hurt him before moving on to the next. Then she paused.

"I don't know why…" She frowned at the unmistakable breathlessness of anxiety rising in her chest. Climbing was all she'd had left of her old life. "Do I not even have that now? I can't even climb a building without freaking out?"

He reached his right arm around behind him and curled his hand around her hip, holding her tightly against him. "I don't care. I'm just glad you're okay."

The awkward, tender touch broke her in a hundred places and gave her the strength to whisper something she'd realized as soon as she turned out there on the building face and saw all those people below her. All that vast, unfamiliar city stretching out beyond her. What he'd been trying to say the last time they spoke.

When she'd said such awful things to him to distract her from the truth of his words.

"I'm not okay, Nathan." Her eyes stung from so much more than the summer glare coming in the window. Her body heaved with a sob bursting to express itself. "I haven't been okay for five years."

He twisted around to see her but the pain of his shrapnel back stopped him with a jerk. Instead, he brought his left arm up over those powerful shoulders and snaked it around her neck and pulled her hard against his damaged flesh as though he just didn't care. Tori pressed her face against the hard angle of his jaw and did her best not to injure him further.

They both needed the contact before all else.

"I was terrified I was going to fall," she whispered against his ear.

He pressed his face back into hers. "There are much worse things than falling."

God, how true that was.

He turned toward her, bringing his lips mere millimeters from hers. But it wasn't their lips that met, it was their gaze. His breath was warm and comforting so close to her as he spoke. "Fear is good, Tori. It's normal. It means you have something to lose. Not fearing means not caring."

She frowned. How long had it been since she stopped caring about life?

"I tried to come to you."

His eyes darted towards her. "When?"

"About two days after you left. I wanted to show you I could. Show myself. But I didn't get past the sidewalk." She pressed her lips together to stop them trembling. "That was when I knew it had gone far enough. Knowing how I felt about you and still I couldn't…."

Her eyes misted over and tears choked her. She rested her chin on his shoulder, glad she couldn't see his reaction to her inadvertent declaration. "What's happening to me, Nathan? I'm normally the master of my fear."

"You haven't been mastering fear, you've been minimizing it. Avoiding it, by controlling your environment so tightly."

Her heart protested with a violent lurch. She traced her fingers carefully across his back and resumed picking at the glass, the hypnotic actions clearing her clouded, cluttered mind and forcing her chest to ease. Nathan settled back against her fingers and let her do it, giving her the breathing space she needed.

Was that what she'd been doing—avoiding her fears rather than facing them? She'd told herself she wanted to be safe… But maybe it was more that she wanted to be *Safe*—uppercase. She'd built herself a complicated world that meant she never had to jeopardize her boundaries, meet strangers, risk loss. A world that had seemed complete and varied and even rich until she shoved it up against the world of someone like Nathan and realized how homogenized and…beige…hers had become.

Worse, browned with stale air.

"I don't want to be Nancy. I don't want to live a life without risk. Why would I do that to myself?"

He spoke again, soft and close. "Two people died on that mountain, Tori. Except one of you kept breathing."

Everything in the room stopped. Pulse. Noise. The tiny particles of dust that danced like fairies in the shafts of light streaming in the window. Was that what she'd done five years ago? Stopped living? Was she truly the walking dead? In a rush of awareness she realized that was exactly how she'd been feeling for…a long time. Despite the neighbor friends. Despite the keeping busy. Despite the secret dreams of "one day."

Until a knight in such thick shining armor had barged his way into her familiar apartment and her safe, ordered life all those weeks ago.

Her breath resumed and the dust-fairies fluttered downwards. She pulled the final glass shard from his shoulder blade, kissed the vacant spot it left and then left her lips pressed to his flesh and murmured, "I feel alive right now."

Anyone else would have heard it as a come-on. But not Nathan. Because they were too similar. He knew her heart was suddenly beating as hard and as enthusiastically and as *vitally* as his. He knew her fear was still pulsing through her system, waking every long-dormant cell in her body with the clanging of bells. He knew how her flesh sang when it came anywhere near his.

Because he was part of her, too.

"It's what we do to each other," he said. "We bring life."

She wiped away the final trickle of blood and tossed the last glass shard to the tiny pile a few feet away from them. Then she pressed herself fully against his back as if to stem the claret floodtide. She slid her hands around under his arms and flattened them against his hot steel chest and let his strength soak into her.

"How do you know me so well?" she whispered.

He took an age to answer. "Because I am you."

She sat up straighter and he twisted around, bringing her half around onto his lap. "What do you mean?"

"Look around us, Tori. Where are we?"

It was only then she stopped to wonder about the empty apartment they were in. There was no way that the fastidious Barney would have let his apartment get like this, even before moving out last week. Which meant they were two floors down and not one. Which meant this was—

She sucked in a breath. "Your mother's apartment."

"I haven't set foot in here in sixteen years."

She glanced around. "Looks like no one has."

Sealed up as tight as his wounded heart. Tori sucked back an ache. It would have been bad enough hearing the raw pain in his voice without also seeing it tarnish those compassionate, brilliant eyes. "And you never came back here? Except to buy the building?"

His lips pressed extra-thin. "Even then I did it through a proxy. I had no interest in setting foot in this place. Ever."

Tori's stomach squeezed for him. "You planned to demolish it even then?"

"No. At first just owning it was enough. It was a statement I thought I was making for other people. For her, maybe. But I think I was really convincing myself of something."

Tori slid her hand up to cup his cheek. "Of what?"

Two pained creases appeared between his brow. "That I'd made it. I'd survived."

She stroked him carefully. "Those memories are part of who you are."

"Not the best part."

She winced at the self-loathing in his expression. "No. But they forged the best part. You can't deny them any more than I can pretend Rick's death never happened."

Much as she'd been trying. No photos. No family. Avoiding. *Oh.*

And just like that, the light streaming in the window might as well have shifted and fallen directly on them because the truth blazed golden and obvious down on the two of them, curled around each other on the filthy apartment floor.

They'd both enshrined their memories to protect themselves. She'd chosen to sequester herself away from hers. Nathan had entombed his whole childhood in this room.

"Were there no good times at all, Nathan?" Had he slid the stone shut on everything that happened?

Pain sliced across his face, more serious than the superficial wounds on his back. Those would heal. He looked around and shook his head. "It's hard to remember a single one. Not in here."

"Would you have felt differently about what she did for a living if she'd not been such a miserable parent?"

His eyes grew round with pain and then incredulity. "I just can't even conceive of her as a better mother."

She turned her hand and ran the backs of her fingers over his jaw. "What if she was disappointed in herself? That she wasn't a stronger person?"

"Then her whole life must have been a disappointment."

Tori frowned. "Imagine living with that. Knowing it was true." Nathan stared at her. She held his gaze. "I know something about self-loathing, Nathan. After a while it's hard to imagine you have any worth at all. It becomes possible to justify anything."

Look what she herself had justified.

His pain—old and entrenched—swamped her. "Hating her hurts you."

"I hate what she did."

Tori took a breath. "I think you hate what she didn't do."

"What's that?"

Gently, gently. "Put you first."

His eyes spat pain. "Isn't that what mothers are supposed to do?"

She thought of her own. The grieving woman she'd carefully partitioned out of her life rather than let comfort her. The woman who'd lost two children that day.

"Yes, it is. But when you're fighting for your psychological life there's not a lot of room for anyone else." Unless they force their way in. She curled her free hand around his as a silent thank you. "A lot of years can go by in the void, Nathan. It's a miserable, lonely place."

He stared at her, a deep frown cutting between blue, blue eyes. "Is that how you've felt? Are you lonely, Tori?"

No, I'm fine. The words instantly sprang to her lips. Because she was so used to saying them. Telling others. Telling herself. Ad nauseam.

Until she believed it.

But she looked back at the past few weeks and how she'd obsessed about saving this building. For Nancy, for the birds. How she'd stumbled back inside from that curb and let the fear cripple her into inactivity until the very last minute when desperation drove her to stage today's protest. How she'd forced Nathan from her mind but couldn't evict him from her heart. How she'd convinced herself he'd betrayed her and that it was no more than she deserved.

Was she lonely? She lifted her gaze. "Not right now."

"I missed you," he said, simply.

"I felt close to you, knowing you'd grown up in this building.

You were everywhere I looked. Forcing yourself into my consciousness. No matter how hard I tried to shove you down."

His lips twisted for the first time since he'd come smashing back into her life. The way he'd entered it originally. "That's me. Pushy. I'm sure you'll grow to hate it."

"I'm sure I'll grow to love it." Then, as his pupils flared, she raced on before the heat stained her cheeks. "It's not like you're exactly getting a prize in exchange."

"In exchange? I thought you didn't want me anywhere near you in the future."

"I was angry. And frightened. I overreacted."

"I'm demolishing your building."

"I know. And the thought makes me sick. Literally." As it had done many times over the past few weeks when the anxiety had just got too overwhelming. She pressed her lips to his knuckles. "But that in itself tells me something. A building should not have that kind of power over me." She held his focus. "Or over you."

His chest heaved.

"It's an inanimate object, Nathan. As much a victim of your childhood as you are. It's not responsible for what happened to you, though you've been punishing it all this time. Maybe forgiving the building is one step closer to forgiving the woman who lived here?"

Blue eyes glittered dangerously. Then they jerked around the room and came back to hers, conflicted. "You want to stay that much?"

With everything in me. But that in itself was not reason enough. Not anymore. She shuddered and sat up straighter. "I want this for you. I want to see you exorcise the bad memories and replace them with good ones, rather than just create a shrine to your unhappiness. No matter what glittering building you erect in its place."

His nostrils flared. But then the icy confusion bled out of his gaze and left a wounded blue in their place. "The building's

rapidly running out of people to make memories with. Wha
are you suggesting?"

She tossed her head back. "Renovate it. Reinvent it if you
want. Then invite everyone back and give it back its soul."

"What about you?" *Oh, so careful.* "How would you fee
about all the disruption?"

She took a massively deep breath. "I won't be here."

His voice tightened. "You're going to take the new
apartment?"

She shook her head. The very thought made her stomach roil.
"No. I'm not that brave. Not yet at least." He looked as confused
as she was uncomfortable. It had been a long time since she'c
taken any kind of risk at all. Talk about starting with a doozy!
She filled her lungs with the warm New York air streaming in
the window. "I'm coming with you. To your place. Until mine
is fit for habitation again. I think I'll be able to manage that as
long as you're there. If that's okay with you."

She fortified her heart and waited for the awkward silence.
The stuttered denial. The astonished laugh. But all she got
was...

"Are you serious?"

A barb of pure pain sliced low across her soul. Humiliation
hovered just at the periphery of her mind, gleefully rubbing
its hands together. Tori from yesterday would have cringed
and accepted whatever knock was her due. Tori today shook
her hair back out of her face and held his eyes. "Deadly. But if
you're not interested—"

His hand shot out and stopped her from scrabbling to her
feet. He stared at her, incredulous. "I meant, do you seriously
think I'm letting you out of my sight once I've had you for my
own? There's no way you're moving back in here."

For my own. Her heart set up a relentless thrumming.

"I like Morningside. And old habits die slowly." Surely he'd
understand how difficult this was going to be at first. There
was a time that a move would have excited her, not filled her
with dread.

He read very clearly between the lines. "Then I'll come back with you."

Hope welled unfamiliar and rusty in her chest. "You hate this building."

"I'd have a different...lens now."

What was he saying? The hammering intensified. "You'd go insane in my tiny apartment."

Inspiration blazed bright in his eyes. "I'm not thinking about your apartment. I'm thinking about a super-apartment up on twelve. We can merge the west end of the building. Give you those park views you wanted."

"Not Nancy's place?"

Nathan frowned. "Nancy Smith was the closest thing to parenting I got, growing up. Maybe it's time I tried to be a better son to her." He smiled. "That's if you don't mind us looking out for her."

Tori kneeled up and clasped his hands. "She can stay?"

"Until she wants otherwise. She might have to move into your place while the renovations on her floor are happening. Do you think she'll manage?"

"The question is, will you manage? Can you do this?"

"*We* can do this. Together. It's not going to be easy for either of us but a demon shared is a demon halved, right?"

Old anxieties surged forth. "What if we get it wrong?"

"Would you rather not try?"

She stared deep into those eyes and borrowed his courage. "No. I'm through hiding."

He pulled her forward into his arms and she braced her hands against his scorching chest as his lips branded hers. Her already swimming head spun at the first touch of lips she'd thought never to taste again.

"But for the record..." he said, as they surfaced for air. "We're not getting it wrong. This is about as right as I can imagine. I love you, Tori. In my own messed-up, dysfunctional way. I love your honesty and your vibrancy and, beneath it all, your courage."

The slope of a vast uncharted rock face loomed before her. One part of her shied away from the unfamiliarity of it all. But an older part—a braver part—remembered how it used to feel to discover new mountains. Her pulse pounded and her blood filled with bubbles of joy. "It takes one to love one. And I do love you. So much."

"Enough to commit to a future together?"

"What exactly are we committing to?"

"Each other."

The hands that squeezed hard around her heart protecting it, unfolded like a lotus, letting the muscle leap and surge back to full blood flow. "Forever?"

"Hey, if I'm ripping down walls for you, I need a long-term commitment."

"Is this a proposal?"

"This is a job offer. I'm going to need someone to manage the building and tenants for me. Someone I can trust not to let the place rot."

She pretended to think about it longer than the nanosecond it really took. The opportunity to have purpose again... "That sounds like a reasonable trade." Her eyebrows shot up. "Oh, my God...I just realised. The boy who started the whole trading thing—was that you?"

His smile broke her heart. "When you have nothing you tend to get creative."

"You're preaching to the choir."

"Viktoria Morfitt, your days of having nothing are gone. If nothing else, you will always have me."

She took a deep breath. "Again...is this a proposal".

Please. Say yes.

"This is a promise. When I propose I'm going to do it properly with a ring and champagne. Not on a manky carpet surrounded by broken glass with an angry mob waiting down below—"

"Oh!" Tori pushed out of his hold and surged to her feet. Her surprisingly steady, optimistic feet. "The protest!"

She raced to the window and used the curtain to shield herself from injury as she boosted back out onto the ledge. She pulled herself carefully to her feet but smiled back at Nathan as she felt his strong hands curl around the waistband of her climbing pants tethering her to him more surely than any metal fixing.

They'd lost some of the crowd but the majority was still there. They all snapped their faces skyward as she reappeared on the ledge her hands raised and their chants of "Save the falcons, save the building," petered out expectantly.

Tori took a deep breath and yelled down to them. "The building stays. The falcons stay."

A surge of energy burst up from below as the crowd roared with elation. Tori almost stumbled at the wave of positivity that buffeted her like a rising thermal current, but Nathan's hands kept her secure. As she knew they always would.

She turned back to look at him, at that gorgeous, twisted smile he got when he was feeling particularly pleased with himself. But this time she understood. She felt it, too.

As the sounds of wild cheering rippled through the streets, two brown shapes exploded from above into the sky, disturbed from their happy nest. Wilma and Fred soared upward, then turned and dive-bombed down a few floors before wheeling right and coming back up past Tori.

As though they were waiting for something.

And then it happened. Two more shapes, smaller, slower, infinitely less proficient, joined their parents on the warm, summer air and the four of them twisted and soared and wheeled toward the Hudson and the rich pickings of the pigeon-rich bridges.

Tori leaned back into the strength of Nathan's grasp and let her imagination take her. It was as though the falcons departed with the demons that had haunted his building—their lives— leaving it clean and pure and ready for a new beginning.

SIZZLE IN
THE CITY

WENDY ETHERINGTON

Wendy Etherington was born and raised in the deep South—and she has the fried chicken recipes and NASCAR ticket stubs to prove it. The author of nearly thirty books, she writes full-time from her home in South Carolina, where she lives with her husband, two daughters and an energetic shih tzu named Cody. She can be reached via her website, www.wendyetherington.com. Or follow her on Twitter @wendyeth.

1

"There is no such thing as justice—in or out of court."
—Clarence Darrow, 1936

The New York Tattletale
April 12

Financial Finagling?
by Peeps Galloway, Gossipmonger
(And proud of it!)

Hello, fellow Manhattanites! As tax day approaches, all the corporate yuk-yuks are frantically lining up numbers in neat little columns. *Yawn.* You and I know what *really* matters in this town—power and popularity. And it seems tycoon wannabe Maxwell Banfield finally has it clutched tightly in his overly tanned hands.

He's now the proud owner of The Crown Jewel, a popular luxury hotel on West 42nd Street in Midtown. Presumably, he'll offer the usual glamorous offerings in the hotel's restaurant, Golden.

But the real jewel in the Crown isn't the four-star eatery, it's the thirtieth-floor lounge, where it's rumored '50s movie star Teresa Lawrence once tossed her drink (a very stiff martini) into legendary singer Paul Casto-no's face, bringing an end to their tumultuous two-year marriage. In a fit of nostalgia (or perhaps the convenience of the notorious private elevator), the high-flyers of stage and screen still occasionally flock to the joint.

Let's hope Mr. Big Talker Banfield can keep his lucrative clientele happy *this time.*

After all, there were some rumors a few years back about a bit of book-diddling that the IRS wouldn't necessarily approve of. Even if that story was proved unsubstantiated, there's nothing wrong with repeating it *here,* is there, kids! Besides, Max has a social cushion and cache many of us would sell our designer bags and shoes for in a heartbeat.

He's heir apparent to his powerful father, the Earl of Westmore (that's the title of nobility held by the Banfield family of England and Wales). According to my compats in London, however, the future earl hasn't exactly lived up to his respected family name, given all his appearances in the tabloids. (And, *oh, dear,* there's yet another one!) It's rumored dear ole Daddy has cut his son off financially. But here he is, doling out cash for a luxury hotel.

Makes one go *hmm...*huh?

Certainly members of the peerage slithering away from a sticky situation has never happened before in *our* just and pristine land. So I'm sure those rumors about Max were, well...fraudulent. *Wink, wink.*

I, your humble squire, just write and wonder. Maybe Max has suddenly got savvy? Maybe he miraculously found thirty million dollars under his sofa cushions? You be the judge, Urbanites. I know I'll be hitting the streets to find out more.

Keep your ears tuned and your gums flapping!
—*Peeps*

"WE HAVE TO DO SOMETHING."

As Shelby Dixon shoved aside the newspaper, she sighed in disgust. "Where'd that crook Banfield get the money to buy a hotel?"

Her best friend Calla Tucker patted her hand in sympathy. "Apparently there are a lot more swindling victims besides your parents."

Victoria Holmes—her other best friend—narrowed her ice-blue eyes. "For thirty mil, there's a hell of a lot more."

Shelby sipped from her coffee mug and knew the bitter taste wasn't the drink she'd been served at Javalicious, where she and her friends gathered most Sunday afternoons in mid-town Manhattan.

Though she was originally from Savannah, Shelby had moved to the city to attend culinary school five years ago, started her own catering business after graduation and had no intention of ever leaving. She loved the vibrancy, the chaos and the struggle of the people and its urban maelstrom of clashing cultures and agendas. She'd adjusted to the size of her meager apartment that contrasted sharply with the extreme wealth of some of the homes she'd visited on the job. She'd learned to groan at the tourists gawking, wandering and clogging the subways, streets and cabs. She'd gotten used to the symphony of horns honking and angry shouts in a variety of languages.

She was home.

Moss dripping from lazy swaying palms was more her parents' style.

Thanks to Max Banfield and his fraudulent investment scheme, however, their seaside retirement had become a nightmare instead of a dream. Their savings account was shot, their spirits broken, their new condo on the verge of foreclosure and they were looking to their only daughter for salvation.

"He's got a rich father." Shelby's gaze flicked to the gossip article. "Maybe I could appeal to him."

Victoria shook her head. "You're chasing a dream. Guys like Max never pay. He's practically British royalty. He probably has an army of peons running behind him to clean up his messes."

"Don't be so negative," Calla said, exchanging a sharp look with Victoria. "Just because that lawyer you went out with tried to use you for your marketing contacts and clearly wanted to get his hands on your trust fund, that's no reason to be pissy."

"Sure it is," Victoria asserted.

Calla's eyes turned dreamy as she propped her chin in her palm. "I had a drink in that top-floor lounge last weekend. Very chic. Great lighting, cozy booths and a curving mahogany bar that probably seats fifty."

"Did Frank Sinatra—the ultracool 1950s version—jump out from behind the potted palm and sing you a tune?" Victoria asked.

Calla blinked. "Well, no."

Victoria swirled her finger in the air. "Then, whooppee."

Calla sighed—though not as deeply or hopelessly as Shelby had. "Come to think of it, the bartender was hotter than my date."

"Could we get back to my crisis here?" Shelby interjected. Normally her friends' opposing attitudes—positive for the ethereal blonde Calla and darkly realistic for the ebony-haired Victoria—were helpful. Today, they tried her patience. "We all have enough lousy date stories to fill the Hudson. Table the romance chat. I can't get the cops to do anything about my parents' case. And if I don't find a way to get their money back, they're going to wind up moving in with me."

"Talk about no romance," Victoria said sagely.

Calla bit into her scone—one Shelby had made and sold

to Javalicious on a weekly basis. She'd spent so much time cultivating relationships with local businesses that they cross-promoted and shared temporary employees and suppliers.

Was all that hard work in jeopardy?

Her parents couldn't live with her in her one-bedroom apartment, and she couldn't afford a bigger place, or continue sending them enough money to pay their condo mortgage. She'd already begged the bank for more time, putting up her catering company as collateral. What if she had to liquidate her business and move back home to support her parents?

That was her duty, she supposed, but it would break her heart. There had to be another way.

"How can there be despair and strife when there are delights like this to enjoy?" Calla said, licking blueberry scone crumbs off her lip. "This is your best creation yet, Shel."

Unfortunately, Shelby couldn't appreciate the compliment. "I don't sleep. I bake."

"Strife?" Victoria narrowed her eyes. "What is this? *The Canterbury Tales?*"

"If only," Calla returned. "Then we could call a knight to raise his sword and strike down the tyranny of injustice, rescue the princess from the castle and bring peace and hope to all the land."

"Darling," Victoria began, clearly making strides for patience, "you're a talented travel writer, but surely you're not thinking about moving into fiction."

"I could, you know." Calla nodded for emphasis. "How hard could it be?"

"I'd imagine quite—"

Shelby poked Victoria. "Hang on. Who's the princess in this story?" she asked Calla.

Calla cocked her head. "Your mother, of course."

"Why not me?" At the moment, Shelby figured she could use a knight or two to save the day.

"Because you're the knight," Calla said as if this were obvious.

Shelby and Victoria exchanged frustrated looks.

"Knives I can handle," Shelby said finally. "Swords aren't really my forte."

"And that chain mail would ruin the body-buffing treatment I got last week," Victoria added.

"Yeah." Calla bit her lip. "Maybe you're right. There has to be a better…" Calla's eyes sparked with inspiration. "We'll go Robin Hood."

Victoria peered into Calla's mug. "Did you add whiskey?"

Calla wrapped her hands protectively around the ceramic. "I added coffee, creme and caramel. I'm perfectly sober."

"Yet you suggested we involve Robin Hood in solving Shelby's parents' financial crisis," Victoria reminded her.

Calla scowled. "*You* brought up *The Canterbury Tales*."

Victoria nodded. "Because *you* started down Fairy Tale Lane."

"I was helping," Calla said, an atypical fierceness infusing her voice. "You, however—"

Shelby, holding up her hand, was beginning to feel like a referee. "Back to Robin Hood. Are we talking the costumes or the concept?"

"The concept, of course," Calla said. "I'm going nowhere in green tights and a short skirt after eating two of these scones."

"But you're suggesting we steal my parents' savings from Max Banfield," Shelby said slowly.

"Robin Hood didn't steal," Calla asserted. "He brought peace and justice to the land."

"By modern standards he was a vigilante," Victoria argued.

"Well, yes." Calla wiped her hands on a napkin. "But he was right, wasn't he? Fighting against the corrupt establishment? Helping people who'd been wronged and had no means or power of retribution? And I'm not suggesting we steal anything. I simply think we should take the law into our own hands. This investment scheme of Max's had to have affected a lot of people. We should find them and talk to them. We should band together."

"Shelby the Caterer and her Unhappy Retirees," Victoria said sardonically.

"We get proof of his swindling," Calla insisted.

"We get proof," Shelby repeated, both skeptical and curious of this obviously crazy idea.

"Sure." Clearly glad to have an eager audience, she leaned forward. "I'm great at research. How different could this be? We talk to his customers and his former clients. This new hotel gives us the perfect excuse. We could observe him, even interview him. I could pretend I'm doing a story on local entrepreneurs. We gather information and get proof that he's a lying, swindling creep."

Victoria's expression remained passionless. "Something nobody in the entire NYPD has been able to do."

"Only because they haven't really tried," Calla said, tossing a glare in her direction.

Shelby had to admit the idea of seeing that creep Max Banfield led off in handcuffs was appealing. But they all had jobs and businesses to run. Not to mention they had absolutely no authority to go poking around a criminal situation. What if Banfield had diplomatic immunity or something in America? Then the cops couldn't touch him, and she and her friends would get thrown in the dungeon for pestering him. "I appreciate you trying to help, Calla. But I have to agree with Victoria. I don't see how a caterer, a travel writer and a PR executive can solve a case the cops can't."

Calla stubbornly lifted her chin. "We can. We just have to—"

Victoria held up her hand. "Ladies, there's an obvious solution to this problem. I'll loan Shelby's parents the money to get by."

Shelby shook her head. "No. No way." When Victoria looked on the verge of insisting, she added, "They can't pay back a loan. The money they got from selling their dry cleaning business went to the down payment on the condo."

"A beachside condo won't be easy to sell these days," Calla said in an I-told-you-so kind of voice.

Shelby scowled. "No kidding."

"Our social lives are in a serious rut," Calla continued. "We need an adventure to break the monotony." She paused and grinned. "Plus, when is revenge against a creepy guy not fun?"

At this, even Victoria seemed intrigued.

Apparently, Shelby was staring desperation right in the eye, since the Robin Hood plan suddenly sounded like a viable option.

Victoria drummed her manicured fingernails on the table. "We've got one other problem."

"What's that?" Shelby asked, tensing.

"Robin Hood was a myth," Victoria said.

Calla cleared her throat. "Well, yes. That's a small wrinkle."

Shelby resisted the urge to drown herself in her latte.

2

"MR. BANFIELD, YOUR brother is on line one."

Trevor glanced up from the financial report he'd been reading to see his assistant filling his office doorway.

Hands planted on her ample hips, Florence Windemere scowled. "He's very insistent."

"I'll bet."

Max was, no doubt, caught in yet another mess of his own making. Who else could he call?

"Did he flirt with you again?" he asked Florence.

"Cheeky, that's what he is. Unprofessional, too."

Trevor smiled slightly at the flushed indignation of the woman who'd been his childhood governess after Max had gone off to boarding school at age eight—the year of their parents' divorce. "So was I at one time."

She drew herself to her full five-foot, one-inch height. "You were simply energetic, maybe a bit precocious and certainly a child. He's a grown man."

"He appears to be anyway."

Florence gave him a sage smile. "There comes a time, my boy, when you have to push the baby bird from the nest."

"Would you have given up on me?"

"He's not you."

"Which I, for one, am thankful. He *is* my brother, however."

"Older brother," Florence reminded him significantly as she retreated from the room.

Trevor understood her implication—the older sibling should be wiser, looking out for the younger. Somehow, almost right from the beginning, his family had been turned backward. And they'd all been paying for that quirk of fate ever since.

Bracing himself, Trevor lifted the phone receiver.

"Know anything about the hotel business?" Max asked him casually.

Way too casually.

Recalling the time Max had asked him about the hot-air-balloon business, only to have his ever-ambitious brother ignore his advice and buy four used ones with the ridiculous dream of them bobbing over and around the skyscrapers of Manhattan and/or Paris, Trevor knew he had to nip this blossoming idea in the bud. "It's volatile, labor intensive, multifaceted and in no way, shape or form an industry you should be involved in."

"Ah." Long pause. "Uh…okay. What'd ya think of that Jets game on Sunday?"

Trevor got a bad feeling in the pit of his stomach.

And not just because the Jets played football and it was the middle of April.

"What've you done?" he asked Max.

"Me?" he asked with affronted innocence that was well practiced and generally effective. "Not a thing. Though I did have a spicy dinner with a hottie from Venezuela last night. Maybe she's got a sister, you could come with us next time."

Max the Pimping Earl. Lovely. "I can get my own dates, thank you. Did you take Ms. Venezuela to a hotel?"

"No. My apartment."

"Did you eat in a hotel restaurant last night?"

"Uh, well— Hmm… Let me think."

He shared genes with this man. It was terrifying.

And since Trevor didn't have time to wait for the how-can-I-save-my-ass Max thought process to play out, he prompted, "Where did you have dinner?"

"I can't quite remember the name," Max said faintly. "It might have been a color."

"What color?"

"Hmm…red, maybe yellow."

"Where were you?"

"The Theatre District?"

"You're not sure?"

"I was half-pissed. We had drinks before at the top-floor lounge."

The Theatre District was clogged full of hotels. But a hotel with a restaurant whose name was a color—red, maybe yellow—and had a bar on its roof?

"Golden."

Max coughed.

It was mostly a tourist place, but the hotel had endured for more than fifty years and the lounge had its moments being hip and interesting, depending on the nostalgic whims of the NYC elite.

"Oh, damn. That's my other line. Gotta go." Max hung up abruptly but not unexpectedly.

Having flown into New York that afternoon from San Francisco, Trevor had grabbed newspapers at the airport, but other than glancing at the headlines in the cab, and answering a few pending emails on his phone, he hadn't delved further.

Max, at least in this country, was not front-page news.

An internet search on Max yielded thousands of hits on an article titled "Financial Finagling" in the *New York Tattletale*. The author's name was Peeps Galloway.

Talk about cheeky.

"Financial guru?" he muttered aloud as he read. "Since when?"

He had to shut his eyes when he reached the part about The Crown Jewel. *Bloody hell,* Max owned a hotel.

Clearly, their mother's most recent husband was gullible as well as rich, as their father had indeed cut off his oldest son financially.

At least publicly.

Trevor forced himself to read the rest, wincing when he read his father's title. He'd probably be getting a call from his secretary by tomorrow. Maybe even the old man himself. The heir apparent had indeed slithered away from several sticky situations, and yet again, it would no doubt be Trevor's responsibility to shove the mess under the rug.

He'd officially become his family's janitor.

Being the second son of the Earl of Westmore—who was related, by some convoluted and ancient way, to George III of England—Trevor had always known he'd have to make his way in the world. Nothing was going to be handed to him.

His brother would one day be the earl, and Trevor was largely superfluous. Like an insurance policy.

Frankly, Trevor had been relieved by his sibling's departure for boarding school and had blossomed under Florence's watchful, caring eye, even as Max fell in with a group of arrogant, troublesome boys who thought their future titles made them invulnerable.

The divorce hit him harder than you was a good excuse he got for his brother's behavior. *He worshipped your mother and doesn't know how to cope without her.* Or, *Max has the pressure of the title on his shoulders.*

During those days Trevor had resented being metaphorically shoved in a drawer and forgotten about, so he'd dreamed of becoming a teacher, then a poet, then a rock star. Thanks to Florence, he eventually learned to play to his advantages—athletic skill, a fair amount of charm, a strong dose of good sense and a trust fund to get virtually any venture started.

So, as his father mourned the loss of his marriage and Max had taken advantage of his distraction, Trevor had decided he'd run his own business. He'd be in control. He'd escape family obligations.

Not so fast, my boy.

Even after he'd left for America in his early twenties, he'd been dragged into Max's troubles. He made excuses. He'd reasoned with his brother. Apparently, no one else could. When his business became financially successful, he'd bailed out Max of several money crises.

Trevor had always understood his actions reflected on the rest of his family, on the ancestry to which he was forever linked by blood. Max loved parties, women and being important.

There were whispers that Trevor was the better successor to the title. That Max would never grow up. Yet, unless the line of succession was somehow eradicated, they were stuck.

Max was more like their mother—flighty and unpredictable. But while she was kind and generous, Max was inherently selfish. He expected others to pick him up when he fell down. Even at an early age, he managed to blame the crayons on the wall or the snags in the tapestries on his "energetic" little brother.

Yet Trevor and Max were bonded by a single truth—neither of them wanted to become their father. The stoic earl. Distant, but devastated by his divorce.

So Trevor had learned discretion and discipline at the stable hand of Florence. Nobody had to explain his partying the night away with hot women, too many cocktails and getting his picture printed in some trashy rag as a result.

Thirty odd years after their home life had imploded, Max had never learned that lesson.

Maybe they all should have realized that the crayons on the wall would lead to lousy financial and business management, gambling debts and embarrassing questions by peers and friends.

Trevor used to be proud that his father looked to him to help his brother, to coach him out of whatever ridiculous mess he'd landed in. There was no real harm in him—other than to his own family. But wasn't there a time to push the baby bird from the nest?

The intercom buzzed, and Florence's voice floated out. "Your father's on the phone."

"Brilliant," Trevor said sarcastically.

Project Robin Hood, Day Four
The Crown Jewel Hotel

A HOTEL SUITE'S BEDROOM wasn't the strangest place Shelby had used as a temporary kitchen and prep area, but it was damn close.

With a metaphorical shrug for the oddities of her job and praying the health inspector didn't make a surprise visit, she removed another tray of mini crab cakes from her warming ovens as the door swung open.

"I'm in with Banfield," Calla said, poking her head around the door.

Shelby set the hot tray on a trivet. "That was fast. You've barely been here fifteen minutes."

Calla grinned. "I'm pretty impressed myself." She pursed her lips. "'Course it helps that he's a dense and raving egomaniac."

"It sure can't hurt. Is Victoria here yet?"

"Just walked in."

"Make sure she stows her sharklike tendencies. She might scare him off."

"He seems pretty much dazzled by boobs, a heartbeat and a smile. V could manage him in her sleep."

Transferring crab cakes to a serving platter, Shelby felt a rush of excitement. This crazy Robin Hood plan might actually work.

Asking questions of the well-connected crowd, Shelby and her friends had learned Max was throwing a cocktail party in his suite to celebrate the "Under New Management" kickoff of the hotel. Victoria managed to get invited under the guise of offering PR services and promising to bring the press—aka Calla. She'd also suggested Shelby as the caterer, which Max had jumped on, presumably because his kitchen was currently understaffed, though Shelby suspected her undercut rates had pushed her to the top of the list.

She and her friends were going to mingle and listen, hopefully instigating themselves in Max's life and business, which would, presumably, lead to proof of his financial schemes. Or at least give them a new angle to take to the police.

Know thy enemy as thyself, right?

Calla was going to offer to interview him for a piece in *City Magazine,* one of her regular clients. The fact that she'd already secured their quarry's cooperation made Shelby all the more grateful for her friends' support.

"You're the best," she said to Calla as she added sprigs of lettuce and lemon wedges to decorate the platter.

"Remember this was all my idea," her friend said saucily as she flipped her wheat-colored ponytail over her shoulder and turned to leave.

Moving to follow, Shelby caught a glimpse of herself in the mirror on the wall. She'd made an effort to tame her wavy, shoulder-length auburn hair into artful curls. Only to have the thick mess turn frizzy beneath the heat of the ovens and the sweaty job of hauling all her equipment from her delivery van to the penthouse suite.

Oh, well. She had Calla and Victoria to dazzle Banfield. As long as she kept him and his guests fed, she'd done her job for the night.

Balancing the serving tray in one hand, she managed to open the door and ease her way into the main room without dropping anything.

At least until she hit what felt like a solid wall. With a grunt of frustration, she watched two precious crab cakes tumble toward the floor.

She was going to go broke saving her parents from financial ruin.

"Pardon me," said a silky, English-accented voice.

"No, problem," Shelby said, quickly glancing up, "I'll—"

She nearly dropped the entire tray as she got a look at the man attached to the exquisite voice.

Wavy black hair, blue eyes like the depths of the deepest sea and a trim physique encased in a meticulously tailored charcoal-colored suit.

Damn. Why doesn't my hair look better? was the only thought she could manage.

"I'll keep this one if you don't mind," he said.

Which one? *Me?* She was nodding before she'd even completed the thought.

As he straightened, she noticed the crab cake he was raising toward his mouth.

Wow, he has a great mouth, too.

Raising her gaze to his eyes, a jolt of sheer pleasure shot through her. She got the sense that he understood the effect he had on her. Or else he really liked crab cakes.

After chewing and swallowing, he sipped his cocktail—a martini with two olives—then smiled.

Though his eyes were steady as a rock, there was something fun and alluring about his smile. As if the rest of his perfection was hard-won. As if rebellion was natural and refinement a birthright he'd reluctantly accepted.

"You're the chef?" he asked.

"Yes," she managed to answer without stuttering.

"More crab than fluff," he commented. "Rare at these gatherings."

"I grew up in Savannah. It's a Southern-pride thing."

"Well deserved." He angled his head. "And the accent fits. I got the sense you weren't from here."

"You, either."

He nodded. "I was raised in London."

"That fits." Given the nature of her undercover plan, she wondered at the quirk of fate that had presented her with a flesh and blood James Bond in the middle of her investigative adventure. "Shelby Dixon," she said, holding out her hand.

"Trevor," the man said as he enveloped her small hand in his elegant, long-fingered one.

Their gazes held as they shook.

Shelby would have been happy to let their closeness linger for the next decade or two, but she was supposed to be working, both as a caterer and a spy.

A quick scan of the room noted several new guests. Max had assured her there would be no more than fifteen, but they were pushing twenty-five. Good thing she'd made extra hors d'oeuvres.

Drooling over the luscious Trevor No-Last-Name-Given would have to wait.

And why hadn't he given a last name anyway? Wasn't that odd? He was probably Max's bookie or possibly something even more nefarious. But by the time she'd considered this and turned to question him, he was walking away...directly toward Max.

The hotel owner-swindler welcomed Trevor with a hug and a broad grin.

"Well, damn," Shelby grumbled.

She should have expected this turn, as no man could be that perfect and have moral standards, too. If he was Max's investment recruiter, it was easy to see how the lousy crook had gotten his hands on thirty-million bucks. There was probably a line outside his office door to get in on the next deal.

Guests were starting to come to her to get a crab cake, so she reluctantly tore her gaze from Max and Trevor and roamed the room with her tray. After a while, she retreated to the bedroom to load up again, adding prosciutto-wrapped grilled-chicken bites, as well.

She passed Calla chatting up the hotel manager and hoped her friend was getting insightful info to use in their quest to bring Max and his schemes down. Full bellies and a cocktail or two were secret weapons in getting people to talk incessantly. Maybe she should share that tidbit with law enforcement.

She found Victoria next to the windows of the twenty-ninth-floor suite and offered her appetizer selections to her fellow conspirator, whose eyes were uncharacteristically dazed.

"I love New York," Victoria said, staring in Trevor's direction.

"He has an English accent, too."

Victoria's eyelashes fluttered as her face glowed with pleasure. "Oh, my."

"However..." Shelby said sharply, striving to bring Victoria back to her senses, "he seems pretty friendly with Max, so no matter how beautiful he is, he's now moved to second on the list of suspicious characters in this room."

"He's number one in my book," Victoria said, licking her lips.

"Helloo?" Shelby waved her hand in front of her friend's face. "Revenge? Vigilante justice? Any of these concepts sound familiar? *Max* is Project Robin Hood's Enemy Number One. He's our Sheriff Nottingham, our Al Capone. And anybody who cozies up to him is an accessory simply on principle."

"You're right," Victoria said slowly. She took a step in Trevor's direction. "I'll do some up-close and personal investigation."

Shelby caught her friend's arm. "Not so fast, Eliot Ness. I think observation is the best plan for now. Besides, I've already made contact."

"So?"

"I saw him first."

Victoria crossed her arms over her chest. "Really?"

"His name is Trevor."

"Trevor what?"

Blushing, Shelby shrugged.

"You can't be that committed to him. A conversation that didn't last long enough to get his full name? Get a hold of yourself. I thought he was Enemy Number Two."

Even more embarrassed, Shelby recalled her conversation that morning with her mom, who'd sounded so tired and defeated. The doctors had increased her anti-anxiety meds, and she was having a hard time adjusting. Not daring to glance at the object of her and Victoria's conversation, she rolled her shoulders. "He is," she said firmly.

And he was.

Except he was also the most beautiful man she'd ever laid eyes on.

No one could tell her fate wasn't enjoying a hilarious and cruel joke at her expense.

"Go chat him up," Shelby said to Victoria. "Maybe you can get his last name."

"Oh, no. This one's all yours." With a knowing smile, Victoria took Shelby's tray and glided away.

Well, she'd asked for it. She ought to be woman enough to take it.

After sending a glare toward Victoria's retreating back, Shelby started across the room toward Max and Trevor. Along the way, several guests stopped her to compliment the culinary offerings and ask if there were more. She assured everyone there was and indicated Victoria, who, despite her smart-ass tendencies, was one of her best and most loyal friends.

A definite BFF, since she'd gracefully conceded the path to Trevor and was currently doing Shelby's job, as well.

Trevor is a bad, bad man, her conscience reminded her.

Actually, she didn't know that for sure. Probable, but not certain.

She could only help her parents through this hardship if she knew the facts. This investigation was her duty as a daughter. This was business, not romance.

On the way toward her prey, she noted an unbalanced collection of the female population surrounding Trevor and Max. This phenomenon could be easily explained. Because, while Max had Trevor's dark coloring, his eyes were a muddy brown, he was shorter and more rotund than the sophisticated Englishman she'd met earlier, and there was a distinct shiftiness in his eyes.

Wow. She really needed to focus on what she was supposed to be doing here.

Yet another guest stopped her. "I'm dying for one of those delicious crab cakes," the clearly desperate woman pleaded.

Shelby cast a glance at her gorgeous goal. Like she'd get his attention in her wilted white chef's apron and limp hair anyway. However, he'd seemed to enjoy the crab cakes... "Okay, sure," she said to the desperate guest.

Retreating to the prep room, she assembled another tray of crab, but halfway through her task, she was startled by hot and mysterious Trevor walking in, then closing the door behind him.

"How do you know Max?" he asked without delay.

"I'm his caterer." His curiosity only furthered her suspicions of him. He was protective of Max. Meeting that alluring, blue-eyed gaze boldly, she added, "How do *you* know Max? You two seem like old friends."

"We know each other well," he returned vaguely as he moved toward her. "What about the writer and the icy brunette? You're friends with them."

"How do you know that?" she accused, wincing, as she realized she'd inadvertently confirmed his assumptions.

Some secret agent she was.

He smiled, confident and tempting. "I saw you talking to them earlier, just as you obviously saw me with Max. The brunette even refilled your food tray."

"You're observant."

"I like watching you." He brushed a strand of hair off her forehead in a surprising, quick and intimate gesture that made her mouth go dry. "You stand out in a crowd."

"You, too," she managed to whisper.

His penetrating stare unnerved her nearly as much as his proximity.

He was a friend of her enemy. He shouldn't fascinate her. She wasn't one of those women who went after bad boys, hoping to change them. She wasn't intrigued by danger or darkness.

And more turmoil she certainly didn't need.

But she didn't step back. If anything, this endeavor of justice was about standing her ground, standing up for her parents, who couldn't endure alone.

She wasn't about to retreat now.

3

TREVOR FOUGHT AGAINST THE impulse to slide his arms around the beautiful redheaded caterer. To find out the source of the worry behind her intriguing hazel eyes. To forget that he was only present to save Max from yet another of his follies.

But he was certainly losing the battle.

He wanted a taste of her as surely as he'd savored her food. Not so many years ago, he'd have indulged in the impulse to sweep her from the party, no matter about either of their obligations.

But he'd grown up, grown smarter and more successful along the way. Yet, as hard-won as his control had been, Shelby Dixon, with her fiery locks and petite frame, somehow tested it.

Reminding himself there were things in life more important than his own pleasure, he stepped back.

"You weren't suspicious when the owner of a hotel asked an outside service to cater his party?" he asked, hoping to get the conversation back to business.

She shrugged. "He's shorthanded in the kitchen." She paused a long moment before adding, "And my friend Victoria—the brunette who helped me earlier—is looking to get his PR business. I offered to help out."

That explanation made sense. He might be reading too much into this party and everyone attending…but then he had plenty of reasons for being suspicious of Max and anyone in his circle. "You'll certainly get future bookings after tonight, including ones from me."

"Good to know. What business are you in?"

This lot was a curious one. "Transportation, but I was thinking of personal needs."

Her eyes widened.

He smiled. "Mmm. Those, too. Though at the moment I was referring to social events. How do you feel about dinner parties?"

"As long as the check clears, I feel pretty great about them."

Beautiful and practical. He was smitten already. "A wise decision."

She walked over to a canvas bag sitting on the desk and pulled out a cell phone. "What day were you thinking about?" she asked, tapping the screen.

"Well, I—"

The blonde who appeared in the doorway was the writer Trevor had met earlier. "Shelby, where's—" She glanced at him before directing her attention to Shelby. "The guests are asking about crab cakes and lettuce wraps. You'd think these people hadn't eaten in a week."

"Free food brings out the animal in everybody," Trevor commented.

"Nice," the blonde said, pulling a tiny spiral notebook and pen from her blazer pocket. "Mind if I use that line?"

Trevor made an old-fashioned bow. "Be my guest."

She blinked. "Hmm. Hot *and* polite." She tucked the notebook away with the same efficiency in which she'd retrieved it. "More crab and wraps soon," she said, pointing to Shelby.

"I'm bringing out the last tray now," she said as the blonde backed from the room.

Shelby cleared her throat. "That's my other friend, Calla— she's a travel and lifestyle magazine writer."

"So I heard. She attempted to interrogate me earlier."

An uncomfortable expression crossed Shelby's lovely face "Interrogate? That's an odd description."

"But apt."

There was certainly something unusual about this trio of beautiful women appearing in Max's life, but he'd be damned if he could figure out what.

The title? Not likely. His father was hale and hearty and likely to hang around several more decades. And the status of dating the future Earl of Westmore didn't hold quite the same cache in New York as it did in London. Film or sports stars got much more notice.

The ladies also didn't seem after money. Good thing, since Max didn't have any, and would likely have less after a few months in the hotel business.

Plenty of people were eager for any work they could get these days. Maybe these women were simply hungry. In NYC ambition was practically a sport, after all.

Yet he didn't trust them—he didn't trust anyone easily. Never had, even without The Max Episodes to reflect on. People had used him many times over in an effort to get access to his powerful family, so he wasn't anxious to reveal too much to Shelby, no matter his attraction to her.

"You and your friends are quite a team," he said as she tucked her phone away and went back to loading her tray of appetizers.

"We stick together." She straightened with her tray resting expertly on her shoulder. "Much like you do with your friends, I bet."

Trevor nodded. "Naturally," he said, though he was embar- rassed to acknowledge, even privately, that he didn't have a

huge group of friends. He had acquaintances, business partners and lovers, but not a whole lot in-between.

Well, other than family.

He had an avalanche of family.

"The crab-cake devotees await," she said, heading toward
the door, which he opened. She cast a glance at him. "This is
the last of them, so I may need a discreet exit in a few minutes. Are you available?"

"Absolutely."

She handed him a business card as she strode from the
room. "Call me when you decide about that dinner party."

He glanced at the card and sighed. A strawberry dripping
in decadent chocolate sauce dominated the background. Shelby's name and contact information were printed in black ink
in the corner.

The idea of keeping his distance was a lost cause.

AT NEARLY MIDNIGHT, HER delivery van pulled into the hotel's
loading dock. Shelby and her friends moved her equipment
and reflected on a successful, if somewhat frustrating, catering event.

The food—and service, thanks to Calla and Victoria—had
been first-rate. The investigation had only led to more questions than answers.

Predictably, she'd run out of crab cakes and had to fill in
with more chicken wraps and cheese-stuffed tomato skewers.
She'd finished the party with luscious dark-chocolate truffles
filled with raspberry creme. Max and his guests had loved
every bite. She'd handed out cards by the dozens. Then, at
some point, despite his promise to protect her from the crab-
crazed crowd, Trevor had disappeared.

Poof, like a magician.

Or the longtime friend of a crook.

He was sneaky, no doubt about it. Somehow, while complimenting, flirting and getting all kinds of details about her her friends and their motives, he'd avoided revealing his last name, his true relationship with Max or much of anything about his own business. "Transportation? Bah."

For all she knew, he could be up to his gorgeous neck in trafficking—and she didn't mean black-market seafood.

"Sister, we have bigger problems than the Beautiful Brit," Calla pointed out. She handed over an armload of dirty serving platters. "I didn't get a whole lot out of Max."

"Of course you didn't," Victoria said drily, storing the last of the warming trays on the rack installed in the back of the van. "He's a *swindler*. He's an expert at deceit and misdirection."

"But I'm a professional information gatherer." Calla frowned. "He bragged a lot, which I expected, but refused to set up a time for my *City Magazine* interview, even though he'd agreed to do it."

"Empty promises," Victoria said.

"And," Calla continued, "he never gave many details about his plans or his partners of this new venture, if there are any."

"We did overhear the information about the investors' meeting scheduled for next week," Victoria reminded them.

"Investors for what, though?" Calla asked.

"Whatever his backup plan might be after he screws up this hotel thing." Victoria dusted off her immaculate black pantsuit as she climbed out of the van. "It's obvious he doesn't have a clue about the business. I talked to him for three minutes and knew that much. And he had cold eyes, dismissive, arrogant."

"I didn't see that," Shelby said, surprised by her friend's assessment.

Victoria waved off her concern. "Not important. I'm just put off by the subterfuge of this whole thing. I prefer the direct route, as you know."

Calla fisted her hand at her side. "We need to get invited

to that investors meeting." With a sigh, she sat on the tailgate of the van. "Somehow."

Shelby heard her own frustrated reflection echoed by her buddies, but her regrets were more personal. She knew she should be focused on Max, but Trevor dominated her thoughts. She'd all but thrown herself into the man's arms at one point. "Why did I blab to him like a starry-eyed gossip?"

Calla stared at her. "Max?"

"Trevor," Victoria answered before Shelby could. "And you didn't. You gave him your cover story."

Shelby resisted the urge to sink onto the floor of the van. "And my business card, my last name and, oh, yeah, yours and Calla's names and what you were doing at the party."

"What we were *allegedly* doing," Victoria insisted.

Shelby recalled the gleam in Trevor's eyes—and not just the carnal one. "He knew we were up to something."

"So?" Calla countered. "*He's* probably up to something, and Max definitely is. We're going to find out what. Remember, to think like a shark, you have to swim with the fishes."

Victoria planted her hands on her hips. "That metaphor is all wrong."

"Do sharks even think?" was Shelby's instinctive question.

"Don't sharks *eat* fish?" Victoria added.

Calla waved her hand. "Doesn't matter."

"It does if you're the fish," Shelby said.

"Which we are not." Calla helped Shelby out of the van, then they closed the doors. "We are women, hear us *holla*."

"That's roar," Victoria countered.

Calla shook her head. "Trust me, it's *holla*. I recently did a piece on urban slang."

"It doesn't matter if we bellow, shriek or wail," Shelby said, leaning against the van. "We'll still be two steps behind, and I still won't know anything about that Trevor character."

Calla patted her shoulder. "Don't worry about him. I'm all

over that." She cocked her head. "I've seen him somewhere
before. I just can't place the circumstance."

"And I'll start asking around about the investors' meeting
and what it's for." Victoria slid her arm around Shelby's waist
in a rare show of physical affection. "Max will need money for
this new project, so my family will be high on the list. Don't
stress out. We're going to get this guy."

Shelby leaned against Victoria and at the same time
grasped Calla's hand. Her friends' support meant everything.
They'd been through bad breakups, job losses and family
drama. They'd get through this crisis with the same bond of
solidarity they'd shared for years.

Footsteps echoing on the ramp leading from the hotel
brought Shelby out of her reverie.

She exchanged brief, wary glances with her friends before
peeking her head around the corner of her van to see the
source of the interruption.

Trevor.

"Good evening, ladies," he said as he approached the van.

Shelby, along with her coconspirators, were struck dumb
by the breathtaking sight of him.

His glossy hair gleamed blue-black beneath the streetlight.
His suit—which had to be handmade—fit his trim body and
broad shoulders to perfection. His dark blue eyes glowed with
power.

"Nice party," he said, and stopped directly in front of
Shelby.

"Ah...thanks."

After quick elbow jabs into her sides, Shelby's best buds
fled like vegans confronted with rare steak. They mumbled
excuses about checking the suite for leftover supplies, then
disappeared.

Ironically similar to Transportation Trevor's exit from the
party earlier.

"Where did you go?" Shelby asked—okay, maybe she accused. "You said you'd defend me if the crab-cake masses attacked, and you were nowhere to be found when the goods ran out."

"Sorry. I had to take an important call."

"From whom?"

He moved in, his tempting body nearly brushing hers and laid his palm against her cheek. "My father."

"Oh." Given the state of her family, Shelby wasn't oblivious to the idea that others faced the possibility of caring for their parents. "Is he okay?"

"Irate, but that's normal. So, yes."

The look in his eyes, plus his warm hand against her skin scattered her thoughts. "I'm glad, but what—"

Before she could draw another breath, his lips were against hers.

He touched nothing but her lips with his mouth and her cheek with his hand. The moment drew out, romantic, alluring and teasing, as if he was waiting for her approval, as if he knew he'd crossed a line, but was confident he wouldn't be shoved back.

Shelby had no intention of pushing him away.

She didn't know him; she suspected him. Of all manner of things.

But she moved closer. There was something about him she couldn't dismiss or forget. She wrapped her arms around his neck. Leaning into him, she initiated another kiss.

He responded with hunger and experience, angling his head and seducing her mouth with deep strokes of his tongue. Her spine seemed to melt, like chocolate in a double boiler.

She inhaled his warm, sandalwood scent, felt the heat and hardness of his body. He enveloped her like a blanket, though she knew there were layers of unknown to explore, feelings beyond pleasure and comfort.

When they separated, their gazes locked, their breathing labored, she could only manage one comment.

"All in all, it was a pretty damn great party."

The New York Tattletale
April 17

4

Party Like a Hotel Magnate
by Peeps Galloway, Gossipmonger
(And proud of it!)

A quick drop-in before your weekend in the Hamptons...

Oh, not spending your days at the luxurious retreat of the well-to-do?

Maybe you're drowning your sorrows over your tax bill at the local pub. Or possibly spending your generous refund at Bloomys or Barney's? (I hear there's a fabulous shoe sale at the later—just ask for Damon.)

Whatever your weekend plans...never fear, dear readers, I'll make either your shopping or your weekend shift at the tourist trap turn-and-burn palatable.

Speaking of tasty, I hear Max Banfield had an *ooh, la, la* soireé at his new hotel, The Crown Jewel, last night. Crab, so fresh from the sea the claws were still twitching, and chicken lettuce wraps were among

the food offerings, with the night ending in raspberry
creme-filled chocolate truffles.

Need I say yum?

No, I'm sure you have your own version of luscious-
ness to reflect upon.

Didn't I tell you about Damon?

—*Peeps*

Hotel magnate?

Was that a promotion over financial guru?

Trevor tossed aside the newspaper Florence had set on his
desk.

Instead of worrying about his brother, he stared out his
window, where the streets below teemed with the usual afternoon Manhattan chaos. He'd planned to spend the weekend
at his house in the Hamptons, but instead of anticipating the
escape and relaxation, his thoughts turned to the sensational
kiss he and Shelby had enjoyed the night before.

He'd crossed a line with her and didn't regret it in the least.

He should have been concentrating on Max and tempering
his latest mistake—or at least diminishing its press-worthy
moments—but instead Trevor'd found his attention straying
to the stunning caterer all night. The usual responsibility to
his family paled in comparison to her vibrancy and glowing
smile. As practicality seemed to be her mantra, he sensed even
she wouldn't approve of him being so distracted.

He was reminded of the genetic, and sometimes irrational,
impulses he'd inherited. Impulses that ruled his mother's life
and ones even his stodgy father had indulged in long enough
to produce him and Max.

Perhaps Trevor's rebel past wasn't so easily left behind.

And yet he'd been self-possessed enough to recognize the
determination in Shelby's eyes. Just as his mother had re-

solved to possess jewels, clothes and husbands, Shelby had her own goal in mind.

What, he wasn't entirely sure. But it somehow involved Max.

He'd confirmed only two things the night before—Max's financial windfall had indeed come in the form of their latest, wealthy, clearly gullible stepfather. And their father was monumentally annoyed about his name appearing in the American gossip rags.

Surely you can control this situation, Trevor, his father had said on a cell-phone call from his office in London. *I have important issues before Parliament to address in the coming weeks. I don't have time to explain this nonsense.*

I'll handle it, sir.

He's a grown man, his father had continued. *Reason with him. You're the only one he listens to.*

But Max didn't listen to him. He didn't take his advice or take responsibility. He wasn't even a grown man. Not really.

He went to Vegas and blew money. He ran up debts at the London card clubs and pubs.

In some respects, Trevor knew he'd failed his family. At the same time, he had the sense to not remind his father that *he* was the one who'd married and divorced the flighty, but beautiful woman who'd created Max, who was, in turn, creating the present problems.

You could be the first son, his conscience reminded him firmly. *Then you'd be required to follow in the earl's footsteps as well as adhere to every edict that fell from his lips.*

Not that Max was following this ancient rule.

Still, there were significant blessings in Trevor's life. Starting and ending without the burden of an earldom. He had his future well in hand, and it didn't include addressing Parliament, clamoring around a moldy country castle or lording over a London flat, no matter how tony the address.

He had a business to run.

With that bracing reminder reverberating in his mind, he turned back to his desk and the pile of contracts awaiting his signature.

Before he'd read more than a few paragraphs, the intercom on his desk beeped. "Shelby Dixon is here, sir," Florence said. "She doesn't have an appointment but assures me you'll see her."

Not only would he see her, he craved her presence.

He took a second to lift his eyes heavenward and repent any resentful thoughts of the last week. Since they were certainly numerous, Florence buzzed through again before he'd managed to respond.

"I'll see Ms. Dixon," he said into the intercom with what he hoped was a calm, professional tone.

In the intervening moments, his heart kicked against his ribs; his body hummed. He remained standing out of pride. She'd somehow found him, and he wasn't sure if he was impressed or concerned.

Attitude first, Shelby stalked into the room. She performed a mock curtsy in front of his desk. "Your Lordship."

"Ah...no." Suppressing a wince, he paused to drink in the amazing, furious sight of her before extending his hand toward the chair in front of his desk. He waited until she sat before he lowered himself into his own seat. "I don't have a title, though the doorman at my apartment building does persist in calling me Mr. Banfield. I prefer Trevor."

"Your father is the Earl of Westmore," she accused, her eyes more vividly green than the night before.

Perhaps rage brought out the distinctive color?

"He is," Trevor said calmly. "I'm the second son, however, so I'm only significant if my older brother dies." As his blunt words registered, shock flittered across her face. "No worries, he's in excellent health."

"Your older brother is Maxwell Banfield."

Since the connection had been made, he saw no reason to deny it. Though, like many times in the past, he wanted to. "He is."

"And you were at the party last night because…?"

"I was toasting my brother's success."

"You didn't tell me he was your brother."

He smiled. "Didn't I?"

"No."

"It hardly matters."

She crossed her arms over her chest. "I think it does."

Trevor shrugged. He loved her suspicious nature. He liked that she wasn't buying his story completely, and she certainly didn't appear impressed by his lineage. She should be sucking up to him, hoping for an introduction to his influential family or at least pushing for a booking.

Instead, she seemed genuinely, personally annoyed.

Wasn't that great?

"Did Max pay his catering bill?" he asked, wondering who exactly she was mad at and why.

"Yes."

"Did he come on to you?"

"No."

"I'm sorry. He's always had questionable taste in women."

"I didn't want him—" She narrowed her eyes. "You're pretending not to understand why I'm here and pissed off."

He reached deep for an innocent expression. "Why would I do that?"

"I have no idea."

As much as he was attracted to her, and had planned to call her with both a dinner invitation and a quote on catering a business event, he didn't know her well enough to throw open the family-closet door and let her see inside. He didn't want her to suspect how big an embarrassment Max was to

the family, or how Trevor was convinced this latest ventur
would be yet another failure.

Of course if Max's check didn't clear, or Shelby was a bi
fan of gossip mags, then his efforts at subterfuge would fail n
matter what Trevor did or didn't do. "Well, I'm pleased you'r
here, but I'm truly in the dark about why you're aggravated."

"You kissed me."

He didn't have to pretend to be surprised by that accusa
tion. "I've been complimented heavily in the past on my tech
nique. Can you be specific about why you're disappointed?"

Leaning across his desk, she propped her chin on her fis
"Can you explain why even absurd questions sound intelligen
when spoken with an English accent?"

Her sass and directness were enthralling—as well as he
proximity.

He tilted toward her. Their faces were bare inches apart
"That's a fascinating debate. Why don't we discuss it ove
dinner tonight?"

She simply shook her head. "Not so fast, Your Lordship
You kissed me while deliberately keeping your identity
secret. In fact, the only reason I found you was because Call
never throws anything away, and she uncovered a magazin
article about you landing a high-dollar contract last year." Sh
raised her eyebrows. "At least I know you transport legitimat
goods now."

"What did you think I transported?"

"Could've been anything."

"Like knockoff designers bags, I suppose."

"Yeah, maybe, but I don't like those. It's real or nothin
for me. I buy vanilla from Madagascar, for heaven's sake.
was thinking more pharmaceutical for your possibly illega
transportation business."

Terrific. The woman he had a massive crush on thought h

was a drug dealer. "All the more reason for dinner. There's a lovely Italian restaurant down the street."

She angled her head, considering him. The anger had been doused, replaced by interest. "Why didn't you want me to know who you were?"

"I don't like to advertise my family background. It tends to make people act…unusually."

"Suck-ups."

With a satisfied grin, he nodded. "Precisely."

"Why doesn't your brother talk like you?"

"Max puts on an American accent. He likes to blend."

By the way she cocked her head, Trevor assumed she found that as odd as he did, but he didn't really want to discuss Max's idiosyncrasies.

"I like your accent better." Her eyes smoldered into golden. "Is this Italian place down the street Giovanni's?"

Fascinated by the way her eyes changed in rhythm with her mood, he slid his finger down her arm. "It is."

A smile teased her lips. "I could eat."

"Excellent. Perhaps we could also work on my kissing technique. I'd hate to be a disappointment the second time around."

"Were you planning this practice during dinner?"

"I could wait till after. Or be persuaded to before."

Her gaze dropped to his mouth. "Let's see if the pesto sauce is as good as I remember."

Pleasure and anticipation raced down his spine. Their chemistry had been pretty electric the night before—maybe even more so because of the suspicion between them. "I'll speak to the chef personally."

"His name is Mario."

He walked around the desk and assisted her to her feet. "He's not your knife-wielding cousin or boyfriend, is he?"

"My cousin lives in Fort Lauderdale and runs a car wash and I don't have a boyfriend."

"I always thought the men of New York had good taste. Clearly, I've been misinformed." He opened his office door and allowed Shelby to proceed him. "I'm leaving, Florence."

"For the day?" His secretary's pink painted mouth rounded in shock. "It's barely after five."

"It's Friday. Go home. Enjoy yourself."

"Yes, I remember how. Do *you*?"

Trevor narrowed his eyes briefly as he passed Florence's desk. "Of course I do." The last thing he needed was Florence blabbing about his obsessive tendencies. Success didn't come without sacrifice, after all.

The irony that his secretary wanted him to slow down and have babies she could spoil, while his mother's worst nightmare was becoming a grandmother wasn't lost on him.

"But you'll miss out on your workaholic merit badge for the week," she called after him.

"Good night, Florence," he said, refusing to rise to her critique.

To his relief, Shelby laughed. "And here I thought we had nothing in common. My friends and assistants are always trying to get me to work less and play more."

"Easy to do when it's not your company on the line."

"Exactly."

Trevor pressed the button for the elevator, which arrived immediately.

"Is your brother a crook?" Shelby asked abruptly.

He nearly stumbled. It was rare for him to be knocked of stride, and this woman had done it twice in ten minutes. "No. Why do you ask?"

She shrugged as the elevator doors slid closed. "Just curious."

CALLA WALKED AWAY FROM a lovely spring evening, through the police-station door and into chaos.

The large, pitiful waiting room, painted a dingy gray and containing no more than ten folding chairs, strained at all the emotions and activity.

In one corner, a group of people stood in a circle, holding hands and praying. A trio of women cried in the other. A pair of children bounced and giggled on their chairs as a harried-looking woman stood nearby and yakked into her cell phone.

Lording over the masses, a bored-looking clerk sat behind a high, imposing faded wood counter and flipped through a magazine.

Lady Justice could hardly be proud.

But then Calla figured the police had a mostly thankless, as well as dangerous, job. They'd no doubt be grateful for her help.

Shifting her briefcase strap on her shoulder, she approached the counter. "I need to speak to someone in the fraud department."

The clerk never looked up. "Appointment?"

You needed to make an appointment to report a crime? "No, it's rather urgent. If you could just—"

"Is anybody in immediate danger?"

"Yes, I guess so. My friend Shelby's parents trusted this guy with their life savings, then he took off for parts unknown, but then we—Shelby, me and our other friend Victoria—read an article last week about how he'd bought a hotel right here in Manhattan. So, you can imagine how surprised we were. Where did he get the money to buy something like that?" She jabbed her finger on the counter to emphasize her indignation. "On the backs of gullible seniors, that's where. So, as you can see, it's imperative that I talk to somebody right away."

The clerk looked up, her expression weary. "Is somebody about to die?"

Calla blinked. "Uh...no, but—"

"Everybody's busy." The clerk's attention went back to her magazine.

It was no wonder Max Banfield was running around free as a bird.

But Calla had been a newspaper reporter in her hometown of Austin before she'd moved to New York and become a features writer. She'd navigated the turbulent waters of Texas politics, she'd interviewed presidents and kings, she'd even gone on safari in Africa last year. And she knew charm would get her further than bullying.

"I know you're extremely busy," she said sweetly to the clerk. "But I'm in a bind. I have important information on a fraud case that could really—"

"Are you high?" the clerk asked, nonplussed.

"No, of cour—"

"Do you know it's Friday night?"

"Yes, of cour—"

"Then go away."

Okay, maybe charm was overrated.

Before Calla could figure out her next move, a heavyset uniformed officer appeared at the end of the hall.

Calla rushed toward him before anybody in the waiting room could move. "I need to see somebody in the fraud department!"

His gaze flicked over her with a hint of male interest before he rolled his eyes. "Lady, I got—"

"Please. It's an emergency."

"It always is." He sighed and pointed down the hall he'd just emerged from. "Sixth door on the left. See Detective Antonio."

"Thank you," Calla breathed, barely resisting the urge to kiss his pudgy cheek.

"Don!" the clerk shouted, leaping to her feet.

"What the hell you want me to do, Mary?" he hollered back. "I got an attempted murder to deal with here."

Calla barely heard the renewed wailing from the waiting room, she was too busy scooting down the hall.

The sixth door on the left had the pealing, fading letters of Detective Division printed on the smoked glass. Drawing a deep breath and hoping not everybody inside was as cranky as the front-desk clerk, Calla turned the handle.

The room she entered was scattered with several metal desks, each containing a computer monitor and various personal items. A water cooler and coffee station took up most of the space in the back, and directly across from her was a closed office door that read Lieutenant Meyer.

Except for the distant ringing of a phone, it was blessedly quiet.

Better yet, only two people were inside—a woman in a well-worn brown suit, who answered the phone, and a dark-haired man, typing rapidly on a keyboard.

She approached him, confident when she revealed her information, he'd be interested. Detectives moved up the ranks by solving cases, right? Certainly this one would be no exception.

Up close, she realized his hair wasn't brown but black—thick, wavy and slightly mussed, as if he'd raked his fingers through the locks repeatedly. His hands were large, and his broad shoulders strained against the confines of his wrinkled black shirt, the sleeves of which were rolled up to reveal darkly tanned and muscular forearms.

This was not a man to be messed with.

"Detective Antonio?" she asked, hating the tentative note in her voice.

After a few more strokes of the keyboard, he lifted his head. His face was handsome and sculpted but hard. His lips might have been full but were flattened at the moment with a scowl. Eyes, green as a shamrock, but imparting none of the cheeriness of Ireland's symbol, stared back at her with vivid reluctance.

"Yeah?" he returned, giving her a quick look from head to toe.

His expression didn't soften with the perusal, and she found herself struggling not to be insulted. Granted, it had been a long time since she'd been the Cotton Bowl Queen, but she generally got a spark of interest from most men.

She'd even had her hair highlighted and gotten a glowing spray tan the day before.

Like that matters. Get on with it, girl.

She held out her hand. "I'm Calla Tucker."

He rose, but not before expelling a tired sigh. "Devin Antonio," he said, wrapping his hand around hers.

Fire darted through Calla's body at the touch of his calloused palm. She flinched at the sensation and yanked her hand back, but it continued to tingle in the aftermath. He must have felt something similar since he glanced from her to his own hand and back again.

Now there was heat and anger in his remarkable eyes.

Though the tingling lingered, making her light-headed, she ignored it. She was supposed to be helping Shelby, not flirting.

"Devin," she said after clearing her throat. "That's an unusual name for an Italian."

His scowl deepened. "It's Irish. My mom was."

"Oh, I'm sorry. She passed away?"

"Hell if I know." He extended his hand to the chair opposite his desk. "Have a seat."

"Thank you," she said automatically, though her thoughts

were whirling. She'd traveled enough to know war and despair existed everywhere and on many different fronts. But even in abject poverty she'd seen families stick together and work hard to make the most of their circumstances.

She found it incredibly sad that Detective Antonio didn't know that kind of comfort.

"Reporters are supposed to stay in the press room," he said shortly.

"I'm not a reporter." She waved her hand. "Okay, I was at one time. I'm a features writer now. Mostly for travel and life-style magazines."

"And you're here to do a story on me." He glanced at his watch. "At seven o'clock on a Friday night?"

"No story, and why does everybody keep reminding me about the day and time? Writers work at all hours. Silly me, I thought the police station was pretty much a 24/7 seven operation."

"It is, but not for me. I was on my way out."

"You were typing."

"Finishing up a report. Are you in some kind of trouble, miss?"

"It's Calla, and, no, not me. It's my friend Shelby, specifically her parents."

Before he could interrupt or, worse, throw her back to the front-desk diva, Calla told him about how the Dixons had given their life savings to Max Banfield, only to see it go into his pocket.

"I've got statements from six other couples right here," she concluded, fishing in her briefcase for the folder containing the transcriptions she'd painstakingly documented from her recorded phone interviews. "They all implicate Maxwell Banfield as the head of the investment company."

The detective didn't even glance at the folder she laid on

his desk. "Investments come with a risk. I'm sure Mr. Banfield explained that to his clients."

"But he didn't even invest the money. Weeks after cashing the check, the phone number he gave was disconnected and the office abandoned."

"Fraud is a difficult case to prove."

"Then your job must be pretty damn miserable."

He stared directly at her. "It has its moments."

Was that his attempt to compliment her or was she one of the miserable moments? The guy was impossible to read.

"Look, miss, I—"

"Calla."

"Fine. Calla." He shoved her folder across the desk. "I've got ten open cases to work. And it looks like one of them is going to be transferred to Homicide, since the harbor patrol found my suspect floating in the East River about two hours ago."

She pushed the folder toward him. "Then you'll only have nine cases. You've got room for one more."

"No. I'll have to work with Homicide exclusively for the next few days, catching them up on all the background, which means I'll be even more backlogged once they take over."

Frustrated, Calla rose and turned away from him. Shelby and Victoria were right. The only way they were getting results was to get them on their own. She was wasting her time with the hot, angry detective.

"These statements aren't admissible in court," he said.

Calla turned. He'd opened her file. Suspicious of his curiosity, she nodded. "I know. I have the digital recordings to back up everything."

He shook his head. "Doesn't matter. All these people would have to be interviewed by a cop."

"So interview them." She glared down at him, feeling better that she had the height advantage. "You guys know something squirrelly's going on. Mrs. Rosenberg lives right here in the city, and she told me she filed a report with you guys months ago. Why won't you help?"

"The case crosses state lines. That makes it federal."

She leaned over, bracing her hand in the center of his desk. "Oh, that's just crap. Unless Banfield walks into a bank with a loaded pistol, it'll be years before the Feds get around to this case. And why should he resort to violence anyway? He's doing just fine, smiling and lying and taking every meager penny these hardworking people have spent their lives earning. It's unconscionable."

He stood, taking her advantage with a single movement. "Where the hell are you from?"

"Texas."

"That explains it." He raked his hand through his inky hair, just as she'd imagined earlier.

The state of attraction along with dissent was foreign to her. When she liked a guy, she liked him. She had no idea what to make of this encounter. Or of him and where he stood.

"I'm not supposed to tell you what I'm about to," he said, sounding as aggravated as he looked. "But I don't want you going all Wyatt Earp on me and shooting down the guy at the local watering hole."

"Wyatt Earp's showdown took place in Arizona, not Texas."

"You're sure?"

She crossed her arms over her chest. "Pretty positive. Not to mention that happened about 130 years ago. Texans are independent and self-sufficient, not idiotic."

"Stubborn comes to mind," he muttered. "But whatever. I actually know about Banfield. One of our guys interviewed Mrs. Rosenberg, but we couldn't find anybody else to corroborate her claim."

"That's because Banfield moves all over."

"He's technically a Brit. And now he's bought a hotel in midtown."

For the first time, Calla realized there was more going on behind the detective's emerald eyes than resentment. "He certainly has."

He tapped her folder with the tip of his finger. "I'll look into the statements of the other victims, though you should know that people are reluctant to go on record about being duped."

"I have complete faith in your powers of persuasion, Detective."

"I'll contact you if I have any questions. You got a card?"

She pulled one from the front pocket of her briefcase and handed it to him. "I appreciate you taking the time to see me."

His mouth twitched on one side, as if he might actually be tempted to smile. "All part of the community-service motto."

"Good to know."

She turned to leave without shaking his hand again. She finally felt as if they'd reached an even keel. The last thing she needed was to incite her lust again.

"And, Calla…"

When she turned, she found his perpetual scowl in place—which somehow didn't lessen his attractiveness. His toughness made him all the more appealing. "Hmm?" she asked, perfectly aware she was staring.

"We'd really rather keep our information to ourselves for now. Let me look into this. No more victim interviews. Don't go to the press. Don't approach Banfield, don't talk about him, don't contact him in any way. Clear?"

A picture of the party the night before flashed in Calla's memory. "Oh, sure." She swallowed. "I imagine the NYPD looks down on vigilantes."

"You bet your cute Texas ass we do."

5

"IT WAS WONDERFUL, Mario—truly." Shelby smiled warmly at the handsome Italian chef. "I'd love to know what you put in the marinara sauce."

Mario waggled his finger. "Not even for you, *bella*. My great-great grandmother would never let me past the gates of heaven."

"We can't let that happen. How about a trade? I'll bring you four dozen of my chocolate-chunk caramel cookies, and you give me four jars of that sauce?"

With a smile, Mario nodded. "This is an excellent idea."

They agreed to trade on Tuesday, and Shelby picked up her wineglass with a satisfied sigh. She might be in a financial and emotional pinch, but the best things in life were sometimes easy to come by.

She directed her attention to Trevor, wondering if, with his privileged upbringing, he'd taken that kind of thing for granted.

"How nice of you to notice I'm still here," he said, drumming his long, elegant fingers against the table.

Impulsively, she covered his hand with hers. "Sorry. I get carried away by great food. Occupational hazard."

He lifted her hand to his mouth, brushing his lips over her

fingers in an old-fashioned gesture that left her breathless. "I agree the food has always been delicious here, but I've never gotten such exceptional service." He paused, his expression wry. "But then Mario never seemed enamored with my cleavage."

"Oh, good grief. He's married and has four kids."

"Yes, well, I'm not so sure his wife would be impressed by his close customer service."

Trevor's possessiveness should have bothered her. It didn't. "You're jealous?"

"I like cookies, too."

Delighted and charmed, she squeezed his hand and scooted closer to him in the intimate corner booth they shared. "How many do you want?"

"If Mario gets four dozen, I want five."

"I could also add dark chocolate and cranberries to yours. It gives the sweet cookies a hint of tartness."

"I like tart and sweet."

"Then that's what you'll have."

She'd gone out with him to spy and help her parents' cause—or so she'd told herself at the start of the evening.

She should be probing Trevor for information about Max and wondering if he'd told her the truth about his brother. Or if he actually knew Max was an amoral creep. Or if he knew anything about this investor's meeting. But she'd barely given the Robin Hood matter a minute's thought. In fact, she'd purposely avoided the subject of Max, as the more she enjoyed time with Trevor, the more guilty she felt for misleading him about her true motives.

Dinner had been delightful. Trevor was intelligent and attentive. He was determined and self-made, despite counting royalty among his friends. His wit had its British moments, but since he'd left his family's long shadow and come to New York at the young age of twenty-two, his ideas had a distinctly

American slant. And maybe, most importantly, the idea of him sharing DNA with a scheming, self-absorbed creep like Max Banfield seemed ludicrous.

She wished she could convince herself she was impressed by him because her last decent date had been months ago, but she knew deep down that Trevor would be impressive to anyone and in any situation.

"Should I bring the cookies Tuesday?" she asked.

"How about right after you deliver Mario's? Then they'll be dessert after I take you to a great steak house. Have you ever eaten at Palo's?"

She had—once. Victoria had treated her and Calla after Victoria had landed an important client but lost her latest lover because she'd spent so much time wooing the big client.

Shelby, however, couldn't afford to order so much as a salad there at the moment. Her stomach clenched. Was she using him again? Had her dip into spying, eavesdropping and vindictiveness already shifted her morals?

No, she decided quickly. Not yet anyway. She'd go to dinner with Trevor if they ate at a hot-dog stand on the street corner. And surely she could keep her personal relationship with him separate from her revenge quest. The subject of Max would be off-limits. Easy as pie.

"I'd love to have dinner Tuesday," she said. "Especially at Palo's."

He brushed his lips over hers, like a whisper…or a promise. "So date number two is secured even before the end of date number one? And here I thought my previous kissing technique would hamper me."

"Your technique is fine."

"Just fine?"

"You kissing me didn't aggravate me at the time—only later, after I found out who you were."

"But the Banfield men have established a reputation for

charm. My great-grandfather had a constant stream of mistresses, supposedly reaching double digits, and my grandfather had four wives. My father's broken the mold by staying single since he and my mother divorced, but it's early days yet. He's not yet sixty."

She raised her eyebrows. "How many do you intend to have?"

"One. But then I'm exceedingly picky. Much like you with whom you allow to kiss you."

"Sorry to be difficult. There are a lot of players in this city—and not only the kind in sports."

His gaze searched her face. "You think I'm playing you?"

No. Um, probably not. Besides, in light of her current agenda, she could hardly demand full disclosure from him. "Maybe we should try it again. The kissing, I mean, just to see if last night was a fluke."

"I look forward to the challenge."

The desire and promise in his beautiful blue eyes made her dizzy with heat. *Why me?* she nearly asked. He could have anyone—and probably had. Given his secrecy the night before, she wondered if she was trusting too easily and falling too quickly.

Yet logic dictated an unarguable fact—if Max had sent his brother out to romance women for his latest scheme, most notably the mysterious investors' meeting, he would have certainly picked Victoria. The suit she'd been wearing during the party had been Chanel, and a man as sophisticated as Trevor could certainly spot that kind of quality next to Shelby's serviceable black pants she'd bought on sale at The Gap.

Maybe he simply had a thing for redheads.

Regardless, she needed to stop overthinking every move and enjoy herself. She couldn't possibly hold Nearly Royal Trevor's interest for long.

The waitress arrived and cleared their plates, suggesting

Mario's coveted tiramisu for dessert, which they agreed to share.

When they were alone again, Trevor slid his hand down Shelby's back in a casual gesture that suggested he'd done it a million times before. He was clearly a tactile kind of person, reminding her of men in her native Georgia. The idea comforted, as she'd gotten used to more reserved New Yorkers. She'd learned years ago not to hug people unexpectedly the way everyone did down South.

"I was serious last night at Max's party, by the way," he said.

Max's name had her fighting a jolt.

Okay, so maybe not easy as pie, separating revenge and romance. It might be more like soufflé—lots of broken eggs and fervent prayers that the finished product wouldn't collapse.

Stalling, she sipped her wine. "Really? About what?"

"The dinner party I'd like to plan."

Relief washed through her. "Oh, right."

He angled his head, studying her. "You don't mind discussing business over dessert, do you?"

"No." She smiled, hoping to cover her brief discomfort. "I do my best work surrounded by food."

Enjoying cappuccino with their tiramisu, they discussed the details of a party he wanted to host for a potential new client and his top executives. He emphasized elegance, but nothing stuffy. His would-be clients were running a company started by their proud-to-be-blue-collar grandfather and enjoyed muscle cars and rye whiskey more than limos and fine wine.

Shelby suggested a steak and potatoes meal, plus a light salad tossed tableside. The meat would be acquired from her prime supplier and butter and cheese always made a popular accompaniment to any kind of potato.

Trevor agreed simplicity was best and told her his apartment address. She couldn't swallow her gasp fast enough.

"I did mention my business was fairly lucrative, didn't I?" he asked smoothly.

Actually, he hadn't. And even though Calla's article had given her a fair idea of his success, the reminder of the difference in their lifestyles was shoved into the brightness of reality.

"I figured you worked hard," she managed to say.

"So do you."

"Caterers don't make what transportation moguls do."

Laughing, he slid his arm around her waist, holding her to his side. "And yet we're all outpaced by guys who can throw a football sixty yards. It's a strange world sometimes."

After the check was presented, paid and whisked away, Trevor led her outside to a waiting cab.

"I'm surprised you don't have a limo and driver."

"I like being a regular New Yorker." He linked his fingers with hers, letting their joined hands rest on the worn black vinyl seat. "I especially don't like people waiting on me every minute of the day."

"I would have imagined you'd be used to that."

"No. As I said earlier, I'm the second son. My safety, education and general health was taken care of. But as for anything else, I was pretty much on my own."

"On your…" The coldness of his words hit her, even though he communicated no resentment. "Your parents?"

"My parents divorced—rather bitterly—when I was five. My father was busy with parliament. My mother became obsessed with screwing every tennis instructor in England. My father booted her off the estate when he found out, though I expect the abruptness had more to do with the gossip than unfaithfulness. I've always wondered if he still pines for her, no matter how inappropriate she was for him and his proper life,

ut instead of women, Dad focused all his energy in molding
he perfect heir." With a crooked smile, he shrugged. "Everybody copes with setbacks in their own way."

So Trevor was ignored in favor of *Max?* Shelby could
barely contain her outrage. "But—"

"Being on my own taught me self-reliance. I've never had
Max's obligations to the future title, never wanted them. Never
had to live up to anything but my own expectations, as long
as I did everything my father asked, of course." Regret filled
his eyes. "The divorce hit Max harder than me. He was de-
voted to Mum, while I had Florence, who was my governess
back then."

In other words, she was the only one who cared, Shelby
thought.

He stroked her cheek. "Your face is turning as red as your
hair. Don't be outraged for me. Remember, I'm related to
George the Third—yes, the one who fought the American
colonists. I have an excellent pedigree."

She stared at him in disbelief. "Who cares about that?"

He pressed his lips against her skin. "A great many people."

His breath stirred her hair; his scent stirred her senses.
Maybe her allure wasn't the color of her hair after all. Maybe
he liked her simply because she was normal.

Since his upbringing certainly wasn't familiar. At least to
her.

And all she'd done lately was complain about the burden
of her parents. While not living up to Daddy's expectations
certainly didn't excuse Max's swindling schemes, Trevor's
devotion to his family, flaws and all, was humbling.

She laid her palm against his chest, feeling the strong, sure
beat of his heart. "Why aren't you angry?"

"Because they're family. No matter our differences, I can't
unchoose them the way I can select my friends. And besides
the posturing and rules and general silliness, the Banfields

have been part of English society for hundreds of years. I have
a responsibility to honor them as best I can. I imagine you'd
do anything for your family."

Dropping her gaze, Shelby nodded. She was doing some
thing for her family, all right.

The cab pulled to a halt in front of the cozy, Chelsea-area
redbrick apartment building where Shelby lived. The street
lights illuminated the generous sprinkling of shady trees as
well as the front-porch pots filled with bright spring flowers.
It was a dream to live there.

Shelby's landlady was rich as a queen and charged her rent
ers a modest monthly sum. Thankfully, she'd hired Shelby to
cater her birthday party three years ago and fell in love with
Shelby's chicken cacciatore. She'd quickly become one of Mrs
Hines's beneficiaries, which had allowed her to move out of
Brooklyn and into the city.

Trevor paid the cabdriver, then he walked Shelby to the
door. "Business must be pretty decent," he said, his gaze
roving the building.

"I do okay." She explained about Mrs. Hines. "As long as
my tomato supplier doesn't bug out on me, and I make her
a spectacular birthday cake every year, it's like having rent
control."

"It's a great area. We're nearly neighbors. I live on 26th,
remember?"

He probably *owned* 26th, but at least Shelby could be proud
to show him her place. Very few people in her income bracket
could afford to live so well. "You want to come up for coffee?"

"I very much want to come up. But not for coffee." He slid
his arm around her waist and cupped her jaw in his palm. "I
should probably go."

Belying his suggestion, his mouth covered hers with assur-
ance, his tongue sliding between her lips in a teasing invitation that she felt to her toes. She leaned against him, feeling

his muscle tone and the heat of his body through his pristine white shirt.

Desire, hot and sweet, invaded her as it hadn't in a long, long time.

Or at least since last night anyway.

Everything about him called to her. She wanted to know if he'd been as scared to leave all he'd known in England, just as she'd been both terrified and excited to move away from her childhood home. She wondered if his father's indifference had spurred him to the great success he'd clearly achieved. She longed to know everything from his views on politics to his favorite music and foods.

She wrapped her arms around his neck and held him against her. The kiss went on with their hearts racing in sync and long, drugging sensations that seduced her more thoroughly than she'd ever known.

"Well?" he asked, pulling back.

Hazy from the sweet sensation of his kiss, Shelby fought to remember where she was—other than in his arms—what year it was or what planet she inhabited. Her gaze focused on his mouth as she wondered when she could have it on hers again. "Hmm?"

"Technique, my lady."

"Oh." She blinked. "Right. Yes, well…" She cleared her throat and prayed her brain would communicate something intelligible to her mouth. "Excellent work, your Lordship."

"Glad to hear it. Men do have an ego where these things are concerned."

"Yeah?" She blinked dazedly, as the look in his eyes wasn't ego, but hunger. "Yours should be secure, then."

"It'll hold till Tuesday." He pressed his lips to hers one last time, then started down the steps. At the bottom, he turned. "Are you sure you don't have a thing for titles? I wasn't kidding when I said I don't have one."

"Me, either. You started it with the *my lady* business."
Noting he was frowning and realizing this was a hot-button
issue for him, she added, "Frankly, I don't have a clue how the
English aristocracy works, and the only title I have a thing for
is *chef.* Good enough?"

His smile sent a renewed buzz through her body. "It's certainly a promising start."

He walked down the street, and she watched him until his
tall silhouette faded into the night.

She was fairly certain she'd fallen into a fairy tale. Hadn't
Victoria said Robin Hood was a myth when they'd started on
this crazy project? By agreeing to the plan had she somehow
challenged the time-space continuum and blurred the lines
between fantasy and reality?

"No," she muttered to herself, unlocking the door. "But
you've certainly been watching too many late-night movies
on the SciFi channel."

Despite the fact that Trevor was related to the man she'd
targeted for revenge, the attraction was enticing and exciting.
Why shouldn't she pursue it?

*Because, other than hot kisses and family trials, he's as
out of your league as the aliens in the movie you watched last
Friday night.*

Her practical voice also reminded her she was inching
toward the unethical side of the line. Hell, if she turned around
she'd probably see the line behind her.

But all she could think about was how to get closer to
Trevor.

6

BOUNCED!" SHELBY SHOUTED, slapping the offending, worthless check on the prep counter. "The man is a menace."

"I can't imagine why you're surprised," Victoria commented, flipping through a fashion magazine. "The guy's an idiot."

"He has a certain amount of charm," Calla said.

Victoria shook her head. *"Please."*

"Surely you recall that he's lured a lot of people into giving him their life savings," Calla argued.

"Not any people I know."

"Oh, right. You're infallible. Maybe you should sell savvy lessons." Calla smiled with mock sweetness. "Then again… that last client of yours and his organic toothpaste were both horrible."

Victoria slapped her magazine closed. "It was not. And what does that have to do with Max Banfield?"

From years of practice, Shelby tuned out her friends' bickering. It was like being caught at a tennis match between Pollyanna and Darth Vader.

Her thoughts instead turned to Max's upcoming investor meeting. Neither Victoria nor Calla had been able to get a lead on when, where or specifically what the meeting was being organized for. Max was either very selective about his invitees, or he'd simply been bragging at the party, and the meeting was a myth.

Trevor would know.

They were due to have dinner that night. She'd asked her friends to meet her in her kitchen because she was frantically baking cookies for both him and Mario, the Italian chef Trevor had accused of flirting with her on their Friday-night date.

She and Trevor had talked and texted several times since then. While she'd worked three events over the weekend, he'd spent the time at his house in the Hamptons. For some reason the dichotomy didn't bother her. But then she was currently involved in a delusion involving a mythical vigilante, so her judgment was shaky at best.

She'd gotten a stunning bouquet of flowers that morning. Trevor had admitted in the note that his secretary—aka Florence, the former governess—had picked them out, as he'd been in Boston since Monday morning.

So honest.

She'd prided herself on the same. At least she had a couple of weeks ago.

Now she was caught between what she needed and what was right. And that revelation went straight back to her plan to ruin Max. Was she getting justice, or was she unjustifiably vengeful? In her investigation, would she hurt those who were innocent? Should she be patient and hope the authorities would make him pay?

Eventually, anyway.

No easy answers. Like the most challenging of life's fights, not everybody could win, not everybody would be satisfied with the battle plan. Not all the lieutenants…

She whirled to her friends. "His assistant would know about the meeting."

Her friends stopped long enough to drag themselves from their debate and gave her identically confused looks. "Who's assistant?" Calla asked.

"Max's." The oven timer beeped, so Shelby retrieved the last batch of cookies. "Somebody's fielding calls, sending out invites and booking a conference room."

"He could be doing all that himself," Victoria said, though she looked speculative. "He could be holding the meeting in his own hotel."

"You really think Max is doing his own paperwork?" Calla asked, clearly doubtful.

"Exactly." Shelby ripped off her oven mitt and approached the kitchen's center island where her friends had gathered. "So there's a secretary, assistant or clerk who knows what's going on. We just have to get to her."

"Or him," Calla said.

"Her," Victoria insisted. "You really think Max is evolved enough to have a male assistant?"

"He has an office somewhere," Shelby said, hoping to head off another skirmish. "Let's find out where. Did either of you get his card?"

Victoria nodded. "I did, but no address. Just a phone and email."

"We could ask sexy Detective Antonio," Calla said.

"I don't care how sexy he is," Victoria said, raising her eyebrows. "Which you've reminded us of at least four times in the last hour, by the way. The last thing we need is a New York City cop catching wind of what we're doing."

They hadn't really done anything. Not yet.

Except lie, her conscience reminded her brutally.

"Max's card is a place to start." Shelby paced beside the counter. "What're we going to do when we find the address, though? March in and demand the assistant hand over the investors' information?"

"Maybe your boyfriend can help us out," Victoria said drily.

Shelby shook her head. "Trevor is far from my boyfriend, and I'm not getting him involved in this, regardless."

"Why not?" Victoria asked.

Shelby knew her excuse would sound lame, but she was going for it anyway. "I'm keeping him and Max separate."

"Separate?" Calla echoed, sounding doubtful.

"Does the phrase *sleeping with the enemy* ring any bells?" Victoria asked, typically blunt.

Shelby shook her head. "I'm not sleeping with him."

"Not yet," Victoria said.

"Trevor doesn't have anything to do with Max's schemes," Shelby insisted, transferring the cookies to a cooling rack.

Victoria swiped a warm cookie from the pan. "And you know that due to his good looks and slick, flirty smile?"

"Stop already," Calla said. "I happen to agree with Shelby." Before Victoria could follow through with another reality check, she added, "Which I base on hard evidence. He's loaded because of legitimate means. Why would he need a shady scheme?"

Victoria shrugged. "Some people do it for the thrill."

Calla narrowed her eyes. "Now you're being deliberately difficult."

With obvious joy, Victoria contemplated another bite of her cookie. "When am I ever easy?"

Calla and Shelby exchanged commiserating looks. Despite Victoria's healthy bank account and in-crowd business connections, she had plenty of issues to deal with. Her drive to succeed was a living, breathing, often invincible force that ruled her life.

Calla slipped her arm around Victoria's shoulders. "Never. It's part of your charm."

Smiling, Shelby moved the cooled cookies to a pastry box. "You know we're grateful for your honesty."

"We could all use a bit of bluntness at the moment," Calla added.

"Fine," Victoria said. "Ask Trevor about the investors' meeting."

Shelby closed the box. "He doesn't know anything."

Victoria leaned toward her. "Bet he does."

On the other side of the counter, Shelby mirrored her pose. "Bet what?"

Victoria brandished the remains of her chocolate-infused cookie. "My own dozen of these."

"What do I get if I win?" Shelby asked, wondering if she should patent the recipe, since it was such an obvious hit.

"The information about the investors' meeting."

Not a bad trade, really. Shelby would show her cynical friend that Trevor was one of the rare good guys. "Deal."

Victoria's only response was a triumphant smile as she polished off the last of the cookie.

Shelby had loaded her pastry boxes into the catering company's logo tote bags—one for Mario, one for Trevor—when complete comprehension over her agreement hit home.

She'd been goaded into asking Trevor about his brother.

"What have I done?" she wondered aloud as she sank against the counter.

"Remembered that you're supposed to be helping us help you help your parents," Victoria said calmly.

Shelby glanced around her kitchen, her pride and joy, the heart and soul of her business. If she had to sell everything and go home to take care of her parents, this would be nothing but a memory. Sure, she could start over in Savannah, but how many years would it take to claw her way back to the moderate success she'd worked and sacrificed to gain in New York?

What would she tell her employees, many of whom had been with her since the beginning?

And even if that potential nightmare didn't worry her, the idea of partitioning Max and Trevor into separate areas of her life seemed lame and most likely futile. Making Max pay was only going to come about through clever plans, total dedication and a whole lot of luck.

If she wasn't very, very careful, though, she wasn't only going to break a few eggs, she was going to burn them to ash

Victoria gave Calla a sage look. "She's more worried about upsetting Trevor than getting revenge on Max."

Shelby straightened. "I am not."

Though, admittedly, she was looking forward to seeing Trevor so much, she'd been preoccupied enough to reach for cinnamon instead of cayenne pepper when making jambalaya that morning.

"So you'll ask him about the meeting," Victoria insisted.

Sighing, Shelby reluctantly nodded. "Fine."

She wondered if she should ruin her date before or after she got her sixty-dollar steak.

A FEW HOURS LATER, SHELBY set down her fork with a different kind of sigh. "That was the most amazing steak I've ever eaten."

Staring at her over the rim of his wineglass, Trevor's dreamy blue eyes glowed. "It was a pleasure to watch you eat it."

Shelby cocked her head. "You're not some kind of weirdo who gets off watching women chew, are you?"

"No." He laughed. "Is there an epidemic of that kind of guy?"

"In this city, you never know."

"Yes, I suppose that's true. I'm simply glad we're compat-

ole in our culinary interests. A lot of women these days eat
othing but salad."

"Not me. I'd rather run on the treadmill regularly and eat
vell."

"Me, too."

He was just so damn likable, agreeable, as well as gorgeous. Plus, for a caterer, if the guy wasn't into food, then
utomatically there was going to be a problem.

*You mean, other than the fact that you're about to tell a
big fat lie to further your own agenda at the expense of his
amily?*

"Speaking of eating well…" she began, dismissing her con-
cience like a switch of a light. "I've ordered everything for
our dinner party on Friday. I got a beautiful tenderloin. I
could cut it into filets, but I was thinking about doing something more old-school. How do you feel about Beef Welling-
on?"

"As in the Duke at Waterloo?"

"That's the one. At first I thought the paté and puff pastry
were too fussy, but you can cut the dish at the table, which
makes things more homey. Even a manly man kind of thing."

"A manly man kind of thing," he repeated, looking con-
used.

"Yeah, you know, like a *Release the hounds!* bonding experience. Didn't you tell me these clients of yours have a hunt-
ng lodge in Ohio?"

"They do." He smiled suddenly, brushing his lips across
her cheek and sending her pulse into overdrive. "Brilliant.
They'll love it. You've thought of everything."

"That's what I get paid for. You're my client, so my goal is
o make the clients happy. Speaking of clients… Do you have
any idea what's involved in this investors' meeting of Max's?"

Trevor blinked. Complete bafflement suffused his face for
several seconds. "Investors'… Max? My brother Max?"

"Right. Another great client." She decided against mentioning the bounced check. "He told Victoria about some kind
of meeting for an investment project, but they got separated
during the party, and she never heard all the details. She asked
me if I'd talk to you, see if you knew what was going on."

Not a lie. Well, not all of it anyway.

Trevor said nothing, merely linking his fingers, then lightly
resting his chin on them. It was a precisely choreographed
pose—Central Casting's version of Deep in Thought.

His reaction made Shelby's mouth go dry. *He knows something.*

"Hmm," he murmured. "That's odd. He never mentioned
this to me."

"Does he usually?"

"He invests in various projects." Trevor chuckled but
Shelby could hear the tension underlying the humor. "Much
more adventurous than I am, certainly."

"That's strange. Victoria's pretty conservative."

"But she's wealthy."

There seemed little point in denying the obvious. Trevor
had had ample time to discover who Victoria was, but had he
taken the time? Maybe this was some kind of test of Shelby's
honesty?

Which you'd fail, by the way.

Shelby nodded. "Her last name is Holmes, as in the Holmes
Cardiac Wing at Midtown Memorial. As in Wyforth, Holmes
and Stein, law firm to the stars."

Trevor's mouth tightened. "I see."

"Do you think your brother's next project is really risky?"

Trevor's expression instantly cleared. "I'm sure it's fine.
Would you like me to ask Max about it?"

"Thanks, that would be great."

He linked his hand with hers. "For you, anything."

The warmth of his touch chased away the sharp edge of her doubt. She was getting paranoid, imposing her own troubles and uncertainties on his reactions. She'd asked; he'd answered. Was she supposed to interrogate the man? They barely knew each other. Maybe he did share secrets with his brother. She couldn't possibly expect to be privy to them all.

As they shared coffee and dessert of a rich and dark chocolate mousse, Shelby told him about her first attempt to make mousse for a family gathering, which was a complete disaster, top to bottom.

"Making truly great mousse requires considerable skill, doesn't it? How old were you?"

"Eight."

He coughed. "That's awfully young. You didn't ask your mother for help?"

"No way. Mom can't cook anything that doesn't come from a microwaveable box. My grandmother taught me. She was a great cook."

"Was?"

"She died three years ago." And, boy, could Shelby have used her advice at the moment. Granny would have known what to do about this swindling business. Though, given her fiery nature, she likely would have approved of the *any means necessary* avenue for justice. "She had a stroke playing the back nine of her favorite golf course."

"I'm sorry," Trevor said gently.

Shelby smiled. "She's probably still ticked off. Her score card showed she was on track to hit par."

"My father and his friends are obsessed with golf, as well. But then he has no culinary taste, much less skill, so he hardly compares to your grandmother. His favorite meal is well-done roast beef and boiled potatoes."

"Roast is comfort food," Shelby said neutrally. "I imagine it's stressful to be an earl."

"I doubt it's all that taxing. And he dictated roast three to five days a week. Probably still does. He likes predictability."

"And you don't?"

Leaning close, Trevor laid his hand on her thigh. "I like surprises."

Oh, good. You'll be thrilled when you discover I'm a big fat liar.

Shelby ignored the warning. Instead, she angled her body toward Trevor. The heat of his hand was separated from her skin only by her dress's thin, clingy fabric.

The fact that they were introduced through subterfuge was a vague worry. Desire hung between them, an impulse unfulfilled.

As yet.

Though his gaze dropped briefly to her lips, he continued. "The crazy thing was at Westmore Manor we had—"

"Westmore Manor. Seriously, your childhood home has a name?"

"The entire property has its own postal code. Is that helpful?"

"Not in the least."

He wrapped his arm around her waist. "I'm trying to compliment you, would you like to hear how?"

"Oh, please continue."

"At Westmore Manor..." He cast a glance at her, and she mockingly rolled her eyes. "We had an actual chef in charge of the kitchen. A highly accomplished French chef. He wanted to make Coquilles Saint-Jacques, Brie tarts and escargot with mushrooms."

"And your father wanted beef and potatoes."

"Chef Frances, carrying his German-made knives, ran cursing from the house one night during dinner when I was fourteen." Trevor's eyes lit with the memory. "But before that, I used to sneak down to his kitchen and try the food he *wanted* to cook. He had such passion. Passion my father was apparently determined to stamp out."

Shelby watched the shadow fall over his face. "Like with you."

"Not exactly. He wanted to control, more than omit." His expression cleared, the charm she'd become accustomed to reasserting. "But I didn't suffer for the challenges I've faced. Neither, I expect, has Chef Frances, since he now owns one of the most accomplished and prestigious restaurants in London."

"One you financed."

His eyes registered shock.

She flushed, self-conscious by her blurted response. "Just a hunch."

"You're a continual surprise—another compliment. The original one was that you remind me of Chef Frances." He trailed his fingers across her cheek. "Full of energy and passion."

She leaned into his caress. "A rarity in Westmore Manor?"

His smile flashed. "Not for everyone."

The man was amazing. Clever. Desirable. Interesting. What more did she need?

From the depths of her purse, Shelby heard her phone buzz, indicating a text message had come through. Wincing, she leaned away from Trevor. "Sorry. Do you mind if I check that? I have a big luncheon to cater tomorrow, and the hostess keeps adding to the guest list."

Gracious as always, Trevor said, "Go ahead. I have some difficult clients myself."

When Shelby pulled out her phone, she noticed the text was from Calla. She started to ignore it, then saw the beginning, Never mind asking T...

She clicked on the message. In full it read, Never mind
asking Trevor. We're going to break into Max's office instead

Oh, goody. Shelby the Caterer and her gleeful, oh-so-
passionate band of vigilantes seemed destined for the slam-
mer.

"WHAT ARE YOU UP TO?" Trevor demanded as he strode into
Max's office the next morning.

Seemingly unfazed by Trevor's abrupt entrance, Max
leaned back in his black leather executive chair. "Good afternoon to you, too."

Trevor braced his hands on Max's desk. "Investors' meeting. Ring any bells?"

"I hold lots of meetings. I'm a busy man."

"And an evasive one."

"I don't answer to you."

"I'll remember that the next time you invest in hot-air-
balloon rides."

Something was definitely going on with Max. Trevor knew
by now that strong-arm tactics would get him nowhere with
his brother. However, the idea of Max using one of Shelby's
friends, and the consequences that might ensue, had affected
his judgment.

Reaching deeply for his usual control, he lowered himself
into a wide leather chair opposite Max. His brother's business address was fairly shabby, but he'd made himself and his
guests comfortable in furnishings. "If you needed investors,
you could have come to me."

"It's a small project. Nothing you'd be interested in."

"Try me."

Max expelled a long-suffering sigh. "Real estate. It's a real-
estate investment."

"Where?"

"Downtown. A loft in the East Village. An artist died, and

his grandmother, who owned the building, wants me to find a contractor to divide the property into condos, then sell them."

Great day. Max knew less about contractors and real estate than he did about hotel ownership. His tendency was for poker and roulette. How he'd have better luck at a game that involved actual skill and judgment, Trevor couldn't imagine. "So the investors are for condos?"

"Yes."

"It seems awfully early in the process to be looking for buyers."

"The building is in a very desirable location."

"So you're going to get them to invest in a condo that isn't even built yet."

"It's done all the time."

"With established developers perhaps." Frustrated, Trevor rose and wandered around the office, full of books, artful lighting, polished cherry furniture, the latest electronics. A facade of a workspace. Like Max himself. "Who's going to build the condos?"

"I haven't decided. I'm taking bids."

"Don't you think owning a hotel and developing East Village condos are a bit too much to take on at the same time?"

Max's expression became petulant. "You handle multiple projects. Why shouldn't I?"

"Because you tend to lose interest rather quickly. Both hotel ownership and contracting involve commitment for more than a couple of weeks. How's your new girlfriend by the way?"

The abrupt switch in topic caused Max's left hand to jerk. He tried to cover the move by linking his fingers, as if that had been his intention all along. "Great. We're spending the weekend in the Hamptons."

"What's her name?"

"Julie. She's delicate, and needs me. She had a recent tragedy."

A horrible, but near certain, idea occurred to Trevor. "She wouldn't happen to be the former lover of a downtown artist, whose grandmother has just inherited a building?"

Red spots suffused Max's cheeks. "Now that you mention it…"

Trevor's stomach turned. The artist's body probably wasn't yet cold. And what had Max, and the fickle girlfriend, said to his grandmother to get her to agree to the condo development?

This was a step down—way down—from ill-advised, bordering-on-ridiculous business deals, from running up tabs in pubs and losing cash he didn't have to Vegas casinos. This was sleazy. Maybe Trevor should have expected his brother's continual downfall. Maybe he should have sent him home when he'd shown up in New York two years ago, claiming he wanted a fresh start. Maybe he and his father should have actually cut him off, instead of continuing to quietly bail him out. Though he'd hoped Max would see the futility of the path he was traveling, another part worried he was too far down the road to find his way back.

Still, Trevor's responsibility to his family legacy loomed. Max was the future of the Banfields, however much they were all concerned about what would happen when he eventually got his hands on the jeweled coffers.

"Deals like this are made all the time from inside sources," Max said, his tone defensive.

"Yes, I'm sure they are. Why should grief and ethics get in the way of making a buck?"

"Easy for you to say—you have a lot of bucks."

"I earned them."

"I'm entitled to them."

Angry by the almost comical twist of fate that had given his father an irresponsible heir and a dependable—though superfluous—second son, Trevor clenched his fist. He truly didn't want the title. Not that he could have it, even if wishing would make it so. The guilt over the fact that he didn't want Max's burden was no doubt what made him desperate for his brother to make a success of his life.

He and his father were bailing water out of a leaking lifeboat, though no amount of speed seemed capable of keeping the dream vessel afloat.

"How are bookings at the hotel?" he asked his brother, facing him with a smile and hoping to diffuse the tense atmosphere.

"Okay, I guess. I haven't talked to my manager in the last few days."

Like a toddler with a shiny new toy, Max was already bored with his. The only question now seemed to be which financial misstep would be the first to cause him to fall.

"You might want to check in with him," Trevor said as he moved toward the door.

"Yeah, I was just about to do that."

Trevor had his hand on the knob when Max called after him, "Do you know any contractors you can introduce me to?"

Over the years, Trevor had placated, enabled, tried the buddy system and bailouts. Nothing seemed to get through Max's unrealistic expectations. Florence wanted Trevor to push the baby bird from the nest. Time for some tough love.

And yet he could hardly refuse such a simple request.

"I'll send you some names. When is the investors' meeting?"

"Next Thursday at seven. Suite 1634 at the Crown."

Trevor suppressed a jolt. "That's fast."

"I need to judge interest before I start construction."

He needs money before he starts construction. "Of course you do." Trevor met Max's gaze with a glare. "If you embarrass this family again, I'm finished defending you."

Max frowned. "Since when have I embarrassed anybody?"

Trevor dearly hoped delusional tendencies weren't contagious. Especially since he was pretty sure they were hereditary.

7

"I CAN'T BELIEVE WE'RE doing this," Shelby said, staring out her van's windshield at the dimly lit back door of the building where Max Banfield rented his business office.

The differences between him and his brother were apparent not only in appearance, intelligence and integrity, but also success. The brick on the small midtown building was a dingy gray and sandwiched between a sketchy looking Chinese restaurant and a twenty-four-hour gym.

Of course, if Max rented in a luxury high-rise, they wouldn't have a prayer of breaking in, either.

"It's not like we're going to steal anything," Victoria said matter-of-factly.

"Actually, we are," Calla reminded them from the backseat. "We're stealing information."

"Should be no problem for a gang of criminals like us," Shelby commented sarcastically.

"We're not criminals," Victoria said.

Calla leaned forward. "Nor a gang."

Shelby was pretty sure those excuses wouldn't go over well

with the arraignment judge. "Before your mood-killing text,
was having a really nice time the other night," she said, pull
ing on a pair of fleece gloves, which Victoria insisted they
needed so they wouldn't leave fingerprints.

Victoria glared at her. "So sorry we interrupted you get
ting laid."

Shelby stared right back. "I've got several pieces of my life
hanging by a thread, so a little compassion wouldn't be out of
place."

Calla exchanged a look with Victoria. "Clearly, she could
use the sex."

Victoria pulled her own set of gloves from her handbag.
"She and the hot Brit can pick up right where they left off...
after we find out the details of the investors'— Duck!"

Shelby's head and Calla's nearly collided as they dived
toward the center console. Just over the dashboard, Shelby
saw a broad-shouldered guy carrying a huge canvas bag as he
exited the gym beside the office building. "That was close,"
she whispered as the guy ambled down the street.

"Who works out at ten o'clock on a Thursday night?" Vic
toria opened the passenger's side door. "Come on. I'd rather
not explain to some muscled gym rat just how innocent we
are."

Using the security key card Calla had procured that morn
ing by flirting with a lawyer who also rented in the building,
the women slipped inside via the back door.

With no security cameras to worry about, Shelby tried to
convince her racing heart they weren't in danger. In response
it ignored her reassurance and kept right on pounding.

"According to Calla's lawyer friend, Max's office is on the
third floor," Victoria said as she moved down the hall. "Let's
find the stairs."

"Why?" Shelby asked.

Victoria pushed open the stairwell entrance, took a quick

peek inside, then held open the door for the others. "Less chance of somebody seeing us."

"That's good planning," Shelby said.

"I went out with an FBI agent once." Victoria started up the stairs. "You learn things."

Calla fell into step beside Shelby. "Speaking of guys and learning, do you really think Detective Antonio was coming on to me?"

Victoria nodded. "With that *you bet your cute Texas ass* line? Definitely."

Shelby glanced at Calla. "You want to talk about your crush on the cop now? While we're in the middle of a B&E?"

"We talked about your sex life in the van," Calla returned. "And I don't have a crush on him."

"You haven't stopped talking about him for the last week," Victoria said.

Calla smiled. "Did I mention how sexy he was?"

"Several times," Shelby and Victoria said together.

"Still, he's awfully angry…" Reaching the landing, Calla started to tug open the third-floor door.

Victoria laid her hand over Calla's. "And a cop."

With a wince, Shelby joined them. "Considering what we're doing here, don't you think you should keep your distance from him, Calla?"

"That's some kind of advice, coming from you," Calla retorted, planting her hands on her hips. "You're practically in bed with our target's brother."

"Yeah." Shelby considered the benefits of being in bed with Trevor and quickly decided the risk was worth the experience—should she ever be offered the opportunity. "A valid point there."

Victoria cracked open the door. "Later, girls. Save the relationship chat for after our successful mission."

"Mission?" Calla angled her head. "Just how long did you date the FBI guy?"

Victoria didn't answer. She craned her neck around the door, presumably to check to see if the coast was clear. Which it must have been, since she waved Shelby and Calla into the hall behind her. "When we get into the office, Shelby will search Max's desk, Calla will—"

"How are we getting into the office?" Calla asked.

"How else?" Victoria answered. "My credit card."

"That only works in the movies," Calla said.

Victoria pulled her black Am Ex from her jacket pocket. "Nobody turns this baby down."

Bringing up the rear of the group, Shelby glanced behind her, certain she'd heard footsteps. The hallway was empty. Clearly, she wasn't cut out for criminal life. She increased her pace to stride beside Victoria. "I don't care how we get in, let's just get in."

They reached the office with Max's name on the door, and Victoria, her hand steady as a surgeon's, slid her credit card between the frame and the locking bolt. Like magic, the door popped open.

While Calla appeared astounded, Shelby poked her friends in their lower backs to get them moving inside. Closing the door behind her, she leaned against it.

The office consisted of a small reception area, some fake potted ficus trees and a modest oak desk for an assistant. The open doorway across the room led to a spacious office holding a black marble desk, black leather chairs and bookcases. Shelby could also see the edge of a leopard-print couch.

Predictably tacky, but plush.

But was Max really a master criminal? Maybe he'd gotten in over his head with a business deal, panicked and used the retirement project money—belonging to her parents and others—to cover his losses. Was she overreacting? Had she drawn her friends, as well as her potential lover, into a desperate mix-up?

Of course, he'd also evaded the police, lied, skipped town and denied any wrongdoing. He hadn't stood up for his mistakes. He'd run from them.

She fisted her hands at her sides. "Victoria, you search Max's office. Calla, look around the secretary's desk. I'll stand guard."

"Why am I searching?" Victoria asked.

"I'm...nervous." Shelby's hand twitched as evidence. She clenched her fist tighter. "Can we please do this?" She swore she heard the elevator jolting into movement. "You know, quickly?"

Her friends, bless them, said nothing and headed off to their assigned duties. Shelby pressed her ear to the door. *Silence.*

Great. They were going to get through this.

Everything was going to be fine. She was going to get Max on some kind of illegal activity. She was going to get her parents' retirement money back. She was going to get her lover's—well, *potential* lover's—brother arrested.

How—

The doorknob beside her hip rattled, then the door flew open, propelling her forward. She caught herself on the corner of the secretary's desk.

Whirling, she came face-to-face with the reason.

A black-haired, green-eyed, broad-shouldered man filled the doorway. Armed man, she corrected silently when her gaze zoned in on the pistol strapped to his side.

Well, hell. Detective Antonio.

His gaze cut past Shelby to Calla. "What the hell are you doing, Ms. Tucker?"

Victoria slid into the door opening opposite the cop. "Well, Calla," she said in a breathy tone, "for once you weren't exaggerating."

The detective was sexy all right. But he was dangerous. And not just because he undoubtedly had handcuffs and a badge in the pocket of his leather jacket. Furious heat rolled off him in waves, yet when those vivid eyes focused on Calla's face, the anger turned to hunger.

And not the kind Shelby satisfied with seafood au gratin.

He took two forceful steps inside the office, flicking the door closed behind him with the toe of his shoe. "Have you lost your hearing *and* your mind?" he asked, clearly directing his attention to Calla.

Though he wasn't anything like the guys Calla usually went for, Shelby distinctly heard her friend let out a needy sigh. "I'm great," she said, her face flushed an aroused pink.

The detective's response was to cross his arms over his chest while he continued to stare at Calla with both fascination and expectation.

Shelby glanced at Victoria, who shrugged.

Then, like a switch had been flicked on, Calla blinked. She glowered at the detective. "What I'm doing here is none of your business. What are *you* doing here?"

"Keeping you—" his gaze swept over Victoria and Shelby "—and your gang from committing a felony."

"We're not a gang," Shelby said, echoing Calla's earlier assertion.

"And we're not committing a felony." Cool as ever, Victoria leaned against the doorframe. "We're not here to steal—"

"Detective," Shelby said, bravely inserting her body between Victoria and the cop, "we're here to pick up some papers for…a friend."

Even to her own ears, the excuse sounded lame, but Victoria's confidence—as well as her comfort in having her father's powerful law firm on speed dial—wasn't going to fly with this guy. He looked fully capable of breaking rules, bones and laws to get what he wanted.

Those piercing eyes shifted their attention to Shelby. "Uh-huh. When did you get to be such good buddies with Max Banfield?"

"Well…" Shelby swallowed. "I catered a party for him recently, and we started talking, and…"

Victoria, her stride lithe and self-assured, moved toward them. "Are you arresting us for something?"

"How 'bout I start with trespassing?" he returned. "Maybe add in a little burglary?"

Victoria smiled as she pulled out her cell phone, and Shelby's stomach bottomed out. Surely this was a bluff. She absolutely did not want to end this night with an encounter involving her friend's austere father.

"Do you always wear gloves to retrieve papers for a friend?" the detective asked.

"It's the latest high-fashion fad," Victoria said, flipping her covered hand so calmly Shelby nearly believed her.

Antonio bowed his head, then shook it, obviously frustrated with the alternating lobs of lame and aggressive answers.

Calla rounded the desk, stopping mere inches from the cop. He lifted his head, as if he sensed her closeness. "Have you been following me?"

"Yes," he admitted. "And with good reason. Do you realize how much trouble you'd be in if anybody else had found you here?"

Calla jerked up her chin. "We had to do something about this case. You're not."

"I am. Though I'm obviously not doing it fast enough to suit you. I knew you'd do something desperate."

"But you're not going to arrest us."

"I ought to," the detective said, though he was clearly torn. "A night in lockup would do you a world of good."

Calla brushed her lips across his cheek. "Thanks."

The detective's gaze met Calla's for one humming moment before she stepped back.

"So glad that's settled," Victoria said, her tone amused. She dropped her phone back into her jacket pocket. "How about we all go down to Cooper's Pub for drinks?"

Looking grateful for breaking the tension, Calla smiled. "Sounds fun. Detective, I don't think I've formally introduced you to my friends."

Antonio pointed at Victoria. "Victoria Holmes, vice president, Coleman PR. Daughter of Stuart and Joanne, NYC VIPs, attorney and surgeon respectively." Nodding at Shelby, he continued, "Shelby Dixon of Savannah, Georgia, transplant to the city. Owner Big Apple Catering, daughter of recently fleeced victims John and Nancy." He lifted his lips in what might have been a smile. "Leader of the gang."

"We're not a gang," Calla insisted.

Antonio looked skeptical. "Organized effort at B&E in the middle of the night, complete with lookout. Preplanned gear and manner to evade law enforcement—dark clothing, fleeting and guilty glances down the hall, subversive attitudes, you get the idea. Sounds like a gang to me."

Victoria scowled. "I'm not getting a tattoo."

"Of course you're not," Shelby said, squeezing her hand.

She'd started this. She'd led her friends down this road. She was the reason their backgrounds were being investigated.

The detective was right about everything. "We're trying to save my parents' future," she said to him. "I appreciate your concern and your thoroughness." She exchanged a glance with Calla, whose eyes were pleading. "As well as your understanding at finding us in this…unusual situation. But we're done waiting. Max is, even now, preparing to swindle again. We need to find out what, when and where."

"How do you know he's working on a new scheme?" the detective asked.

Since *we overheard him recruiting investors at a cocktail party* sounded ridiculous, even to her, Shelby settled on, "We just know."

Antonio stared at her in disbelief. "Yes, Judge Mackland," he said mockingly. "I'm asking for a warrant based on a local caterer's assertion that she *just knows* a fraud operation is being conducted in a midtown office building."

"We don't need a warrant," Shelby said.

Both realization and anger shot into his eyes. "Hell."

Calla laid her hand on his arm. "Have you talked to the witnesses whose statements I gave you last week?"

"Haven't had time," he said. "This East River homicide takes precedence."

"Not for us," Calla said, her tone gentle in spite of his obvious frustration. "You told me yourself that fraud is difficult to prove, that witnesses are reluctant to come forward. You haven't been able to stop him. We can."

"As long as you don't do it on my shift," he muttered.

He might not be prepared to arrest them, but he couldn't help them, either. Shelby knew this might be their only chance. She already felt lousy for involving Trevor in their investigation. She was pretty positive she'd feel worse if she didn't get this information herself instead of relying on him to get it from his brother—based on her lie, no less.

"Why don't you guys go on down to the pub?" Shelby suggested. "I'll be there in a minute." She looked at the detective, then away. "I want to straighten up, make sure we haven't disturbed anything." Her gaze—compulsively, it seemed—went back to Antonio. "You know, out of respect."

The detective didn't move, even when Calla and Victoria headed to the door. "How do you know?" he asked Shelby.

Shelby pressed her lips together. The less the detective knew, the better. For all of them. Yet she also knew he wouldn't relinquish control without a grain of confidence in her determination. Without some sense that they were, ultimately, moving toward the same goal.

She wondered if his conscience was as torn as hers. Did the end really justify the means? Retribution at any cost? Could justice truly be blind? Who, ultimately, drew the line between what was right and what was wrong?

"There's an investors' meeting," she said finally. "We need to know when and where."

He held her gaze, then jerked around and headed toward the door. "I'll be outside."

"I'M SURPRISED YOU HAVEN'T asked me about Max's investors' meeting," Trevor said to Shelby as he stood beside her in his kitchen.

"Oh." Shelby's gaze danced away from his and onto the beef filet she was rolling in pastry dough. "Did you find out something?"

Momentarily distracted by her hands molding the pastry and wanting her touch against his own skin, he endeavored to focus on the topic. "It's a long-term project. He's rehabbing an old artist space into condos and looking for tenants to buy."

Shelby nodded. "Sounds like a great idea."

"As long as everything comes together." The last thing Trevor wanted to do was encourage Shelby's friend into investing with Max. Maybe his brother would fit all the pieces together, but Trevor wasn't counting on it. "She might want to wait a few months before investing."

"She might, but Victoria doesn't tend to live in one place for long. And if it's a hot property, she could jump in." Washing her hands at the sink, Shelby glanced at him. "When's the presentation?"

"Next Thursday night at The Crown Jewel. Suite 1634."

"Okay. I'll tell her."

"You don't want to write it down?"

She used the towel tucked into her apron strings to dry her hands, then tapped the side of her forehead. "I've got it."

"You're in work mode and want me to leave you to do your job."

She leaned into him, laying her hand against his cheek. "I'm glad you're here...particularly since this is your apartment."

"But I could do something else."

"You could set up the bar."

He kissed her forehead, then moved into the living room to follow her suggestion. As he polished glasses and checked the stock of liquors, he felt a pang of regret for the upcoming party. Though the clients he was entertaining were important, he'd much rather spend the evening enjoying Shelby's exclusive company.

When everything was organized to his satisfaction, he reached into the back of the cabinet for a bottle of Johnnie Walker Blue. Ridiculously overpriced, of course, but then the best things usually were.

He poured a small measure into two glasses filled with ice, then strolled into the kitchen, where Shelby was chopping celery. "Do you drink Scotch whiskey?"

She wrinkled her nose. "Not really."

He handed her one of the cut-crystal tumblers. "See if this changes your mind."

"I don't usually drink with clients before an event."

"It's barely a sip. Besides, you could make an exception for me, couldn't you? I'm more than a client, after all."

Her gaze searched his. "I guess you are."

He tapped his glass against hers, and the crystal pinged. "To us."

She smiled. "And to perfectly done Beef Wellington."

"I have complete faith in your culinary talents."

As she sipped her Scotch whiskey, the warmth of pleasur
lit her face. His body responded by hardening instantly.

Yes, he very much wished they could be alone tonight.

"Wow," she whispered, her tongue peeking out to strok
her bottom lip.

"I couldn't agree more." Though he wasn't referring to th
drink.

His guests would be arriving in twenty minutes, and in
stead of letting his caterer do her job, he was plying her with
Scotch whiskey and wondering how quickly he could get he
out of her clothes. What was wrong with him? One minut
he'd been relaxed, and the next he was fighting a tide of desire

He took business seriously. He'd never have enjoyed s
much success otherwise.

Maybe he was spending too much time around Max.

"Your place is beautiful," she said, glancing around, s
hopefully she hadn't noticed the tension inside him.

He forced himself to follow her perusal.

Two walls of his corner apartment were windows, provid
ing a spectacular view of the Manhattan skyline. The wall
were gray. The floors wood. The furniture minimal, with
clean lines dominating the design. Recessed lighting illumi
nated on artwork and showed off the spacious floor plan to it
best advantage. The kitchen and living room were separated
only by a long, curved bar.

The modern space of steel, glass and marble was a stark
contrast to the ornate, antique-ladened decor that dominated
his childhood memories.

Though sometimes he thought he'd ventured too far from
home.

"Have you been here long?" she asked.

"About a year. It's a lot of apartment for one person, but
couldn't resist the view. There's a terrace on the roof. Would
you like to go up?"

She glanced at her watch. "I can finish the salad while you and your clients are having cocktails."

Setting aside their glasses, he led her up the steel-and-glass block stairs to the terrace, which, unlike the apartment, burst with color. He didn't come here often enough, he reflected as he took in the many varieties of trees, climbing vines and flowers. A landscaping service took care of the plants, a cleaning service the rest.

"Ah, now this is more like you," Shelby said, running the tip of her finger over a purple pansy.

"How's that?"

"Warm."

He raised his eyebrows. "The apartment has three fireplaces if you're cold."

"I don't mean temperature. I mean more homey. You're a Brit. I figured you for a moss-dripping country house, old wood and busts cast in memory of some long-gone relative."

"That's my father's style. I prefer modern New York."

"Maybe so, but you could use one or two of these plants downstairs."

Laughing, he slid his arm around her waist. "The next time you come over, you can redecorate to your heart's content."

She looked at him askance. "Next time, huh?"

He captured her hand, sliding it up his chest to hook around his neck. "No clients to entertain, and I'll make you dinner."

Her eyes brightened with anticipation. "Okay."

Before he could stop himself, he'd covered her mouth with his. He deepened the kiss without delay, and she clung to him, pressing her delicate curves against his body to the point he had to stifle a moan.

Then she suddenly jerked back.

Her eyes wide, she blurted, "I need to check on dinner." She hurried to the stairs.

Closing his eyes, so he wouldn't have to watch her go,

Trevor fisted his hands at his sides and ordered his body to calm.

Shelby wasn't some fun and games girl he'd picked up a a party. She was the kind of woman a man had a relationship with, the kind you fell for.

She wasn't going to tumble casually into bed with him, and he found that the seriousness of taking that step didn't scare his bachelor soul as much as it had in the past.

But he needed to let her set the pace, and he needed to ge his mind back on business.

At least for tonight.

8

LOADING THE LAST OF THE coffee cups into Trevor's dishwasher, Shelby pushed the door closed and leaned weakly against the marble counter.

She'd survived.

And she had no idea how.

She couldn't remember a more torturous night in her entire life. The food had been perfect, or so the guests had said. To her, everything was overwhelmed by the memory of the Scotch whiskey she'd tasted on Trevor's tongue. Every time she'd heard his laugh, or saw his smile, she'd had to grit her teeth to choke back a surge of desire.

She'd had to suffer through the sparkling female guests flirting shamelessly with him, while she rushed around the party in plain black and wearing an apron. The blonde wife of the company's CEO had been so obvious, Shelby had been surprised she hadn't offered herself up to Trevor as the main course.

He'd been charming and polite through it all, even sending Shelby a wink or two when the blonde said or did something particularly obvious.

He'd also helped her carry dishes to and from the table, brushing her arm, touching her hand. By the time they'd reached coffee and dessert, she was so jumpy, she'd nearly dropped an entire load of dinner plates on her way back to the kitchen.

From down the hall, she could hear his voice, speaking in that smooth accent as he said good-night to his guests. A shiver rocked her body. She had to get a hold of herself. She was here as the hired help, not a hostess. If she didn't locate her professionalism, and fast, she was never going to get another booking out of Trevor or anyone he might otherwise be tempted to recommend her to.

He appeared in the kitchen, tugging on his tie to loosen the knot and stealing every breath from her body. "That went well."

"Everyone seemed to enjoy themselves."

Stripping off his tie, he laid it on the counter as he unhooked the top button of his white dress shirt. "Do you ever have a drink with a client *after* an event?"

His proximity caused a trickle of sweat to roll down her back. "Ah…sometimes."

He trailed his finger down the bridge of her nose. "How about the rest of that Scotch whiskey?"

"Well, I…" If she didn't get out of there, she was going to offer herself as the appetizer, main course and dessert of every meal he might want for the next week.

"You have somewhere to go?" he asked, his intent gaze pining her in place.

Had his eyes always been that bottomless pool of blue? Was it a trick of the light, or was she losing all her senses?

She laughed, which, to even her ears, sounded desperate. Yet another sense going south. "No, of course not."

"You have an early booking tomorrow?"

She shook her head. "I have a wedding to cater tomorrow night, but most of the prep work is already done."

"Good."

Grasping her hands in his, he led them to the bar, where he pulled out a bottle from underneath the cabinet, then poured them each a measure into a crystal glass.

"You didn't offer this to your clients," she said.

"They get good. You get the best."

He tapped his glass against hers, and they each sipped, never breaking their stares at the other.

"Will you stay awhile?" he asked.

She nodded, not trusting herself to speak. The taste of the drink had her mind zipping back a few hours into the past, when he'd kissed her in his own private garden of Eden, when he'd held her against him as if he couldn't bear to let her go.

Again, he took her hand to guide her to the sofa, which sat directly in front of one of the huge living-room windows. Did he sense she was contemplating a way to bolt from the apartment, or did he simply like touching her?

Either way, she was grateful for something to hold on to.

After setting their tumblers on the glass coffee table, he reached around her waist, tugging the tie of her apron strings. "Do you mind?"

She swallowed hard. "No. I should have thought of it. I'll get hollandaise sauce on your furniture."

As she reached behind her neck to undo that knot, he stopped her. "Let me," he said gently.

When she was free, he folded the apron and laid it on the table. He handed her cocktail to her, and they sat side by side on the sofa, each sipping silently.

"I should have hired servers," he said finally.

As she'd been staring at his elegant hand, wrapped around the crystal tumbler, she had to jerk her attention to his face. He looked worried. "I appreciated your help, but I guess you could have spent more time with your clients if—"

"That's not what I mean." He covered his hand with hers,

sliding his thumb across the back. "I wish you hadn't had to work so hard."

Always the caretaker. But she'd been running her own business a long time. "I get paid to work hard."

"Aren't you exhausted?"

She was pretty sure she could sprint from here to Harlem and she wouldn't knock out her nervous energy. Of course if Trevor wanted to volunteer another way...

She generally didn't sleep with guys after only a couple of dates. But then she usually didn't lie, connive and conspire either.

"I'm fine," she said.

"If you're sure."

"I am."

Trevor drained the rest of his Scotch. Had they really run out of things to say? Maybe he was the one who was tired.

"Speaking of getting paid, I owe you a check."

He started to rise, but she selfishly didn't want to lose his touch. She held tight to his hand. "You're good for it."

"I'll get it to you before you leave."

Silence fell again.

"You're not often this quiet," she said, feeling stupid for needing to interrupt the silence.

"You, either." Sighing, he brought her hand to his lips. "I'm trying to resist the urge to seduce you."

Her throat closed so quickly, she found it hard to breathe. "Really? Why?"

"I have no—" He stopped, apparently realizing the question had nothing to do with curiosity. His gaze slid to hers. Whatever he saw alleviated his worry. "Thank God."

He yanked her onto his lap, and their lips met. He laid one hand on the back of her head, angling her face so he could deepen the kiss. She tasted Scotch whiskey and felt hunger. Her body pulsed with need.

It had been a long time since she'd given in to sexual impulse. And never had a man like Trevor answered the call.

She fumbled with the buttons on his shirt, and he solved the problem by ripping it open, then following up by doing the same to hers. She'd imagined he'd be more controlled at a time like this, but she found herself thrilled by his impatience.

The passion in his touch electrified her senses, the ones she'd thought faulty. They'd obviously been looking for the right stimulation to come alive.

She let her head fall back as he slid his mouth across her cheek and down her throat. With a flick of his fingers, he unhooked the front-clasp of her bra and filled his hands with her breasts.

She moaned and let the sensation overwhelm her. Briefly, he pressed her palms against the heated muscles covering his chest, then drifted downward, to the button on his pants.

Either determination or the promise of fulfillment made her fingers steady. She undid the button, then the zipper, her fingertips brushing the tip of his erection.

"Bedroom," he muttered, swinging her into his arms.

He set her down next to the bed, which had a steel frame and was covered in a charcoal-colored spread. "I need plants in here, too, I guess."

She gripped the edges of his shirt and pushed them down his arms. "Sure. Later."

They undressed each other with impatient tugs and a few rips. He swore he'd buy her a new shirt after tossing her tattered one onto the floor. Thankfully, he kept condoms in his bedside table, so the process of protection was a momentary interruption.

When he pressed her back to the mattress, his body braced over her, their gazes met and her heart stuttered to a halt.

She hadn't imagined the pool of emotion in his eyes. It was there so vividly, she felt the piercing need of it and the significance of the moment wrap themselves around her as surely a their bodies longed to join.

He kissed her as they became one, bringing unexpecte tears to her eyes.

Then all she knew was pleasure.

They moved together as if they'd been born for the purpos The frenzied hunger became long, deep strokes of discover and wonder. His body was a combination of lean muscle an raw power.

She found a million places to kiss him, to slide her tongu over his smooth, hot skin. Everywhere he touched her i return, she caught fire. Every movement intensified her ex citement.

As the scent of desire filled the air, the world around then fell away. All she knew was the rhythm of their bodies, th press and slide of his touch, their skin growing slick with sweat.

His muscles quivered from the effort of holding back. "Le go," she whispered, placing a kiss at the base of his throa "I'm with you."

That was all the encouragement he needed. His hips move faster, deeper, stronger. The coil of need inside Shelby tight ened further. The tension couldn't possibly hold for long.

Even as the thought passed through her, her body pulsed gripping him and bringing wave after wave of satisfaction crashing over her.

The sensations were so intense, she barely acknowledged him following her into paradise. She clutched him in ecstasy and gratitude.

He collapsed on his side next to her, his heavy breathing stirring the tangled hair against her neck.

Her head resting on his pillow, she turned her face toward him.

Damn, he was beautiful.

Even more so flushed and satisfied, his radiant blue eyes lazed.

She needed him more than was wise. Her life was a heavy, troubled mess, but she felt light in his arms. Maybe she was escaping, maybe she was running from her conscience, but he made her heart stop and everything else acutely breathtaking.

"You okay?" he asked, cupping her face, his thumb brushing her cheek.

She smiled. "Pretty great, actually."

He kissed her lingeringly. "Me, too." Turning onto his back, he held her next to him so that her head rested on his bare chest. "I was afraid I'd botch this."

She paused to stare at him. "Sex?"

He grinned. "No, I knew that would work out."

"Work out?" She thumped his chest. "Don't go all gooey and romantic on me."

He flung out his arm, then clasped his hand over his heart. *"For where thou art, there is the world itself. And where thou art not, desolation."*

"Okay, too gooey."

"It's Shakespeare."

She pressed her lips together. "Sorry. It's lovely."

"Dramatic, certainly." Clearly not offended, he tucked her head against his shoulder. "I was afraid to botch *us*."

As a picture of her and her friends breaking into Max's office flashed before her, she fought tensing up. "How would you do that?"

"We haven't known each other long. I didn't want you to feel pressured into sleeping with me."

"I haven't." How amazing was he, concerned about her emotional state? Especially since she was the one botching things. How was she ever going to explain this business with Max? "Though it's all happened a little fast."

He slid his hand down her back, both comforting and sending renewed tingles of desire through her body. "I know."

"Scary?"

"No." He kissed the top of her head. "Well, maybe."

"I think it's supposed to be uncomfortable...to a degree. There's something powerful between us, but it's fuzzy. Whether or not it'll come clear..." She shrugged. "Time will tell."

"Nicely put. Uncertainty is the reason I left home. I wanted some."

"You *wanted* uncertainty?"

"Yes, though I know it sounds strange. In London, my life was planned. It had been decided generations ago. I was supposed to follow the family legacy and go into politics, teaching or the clergy. I was supposed to marry a proper English girl of good breeding. And, of course, continue to breathe— just in case."

"Sounds cold."

He squeezed her. "I thought so, too."

"So you came to New York, started your own business and became a huge success."

"You make me sound bolder than I was. I did have a healthy trust fund to draw from."

"And a family who expects perfection."

"Yes." He turned on his side, so they faced each other. "What does your family expect of you?"

He was making himself vulnerable to her. He'd told her things, shared memories and worries she suspected he'd shared with few people. If she cared, which she did, she could hardly give him any less.

"They expect nothing," she said, meeting his gaze head-on. "They want my love, my respect. They want me to be happy. I want the same for them in return."

"Life isn't that simple."

"Isn't it?"

"No, but it should be."

He pressed his lips to hers, then gathered her closer. Their wrapped-around-each-other position had nothing to do with sex, but with understanding. Appreciation. Promise.

She immersed herself in his touch. Her revenge paled against her need to be with him, but her family responsibilities lingered, and she'd dragged her friends into this conspiracy, as well.

Closing her eyes, to both her obligations and her deception, she trailed her fingers across his chest. No matter how new their relationship, she couldn't continue to lie to him and sleep with him. She was going to have to tell him about the Robin Hood plot.

But when—and how?

Because she knew one thing for certain. Her parents did expect something from her.

They expected her to be honorable.

Project Robin Hood, Day 18
Continental Apartments, The Penthouse

I can't believe we're doing this.

Standing in front of his office windows, Trevor reflected on Shelby's statement earlier that day when they'd met at his apartment and nearly tore each other's clothes off in their haste to satisfy their need.

"I can't, either," he murmured to the empty room.

After spending most of the weekend in bed with her, he'd been unexpectedly called out of town on Monday and just returned to the city at lunchtime. In the cab from the airport, his fingers had tingled with the need to touch her, a weakness he couldn't seem to set aside. So he'd called her and asked her to meet him at his apartment.

Bold. Maybe even bordering on crazy.

But then his desire for Shelby was that powerful.

How had he survived four days without her touch? Without the sensation of her body becoming one with his?

She was right in thinking their relationship was moving fast. But he didn't want to slow the pace. He wanted more, more and more.

But was he being fair to either of them? His job was hectic, his family commitments complicated, bordering on impossible. Was he crazy to drag her into that chaos? Was this the right time to get involved with anyone, much less a woman he cared about as much as he did Shelby? Max was messing up his life for the eight hundredth time, and there seemed no end in sight.

In addition to the ridiculous and risky business decisions of the past—the hot-air balloons being followed by an Alaskan king-crab fishing business—Trevor now had to wonder where his brother had gotten the money to buy a luxury hotel.

Turned out their latest stepfather had not bankrolled him. When Trevor had called his mother and chided her for giving Max money, she'd claimed innocence. She'd actually laughed when Trevor had questioned her about the amount needed for the hotel purchase. Apparently the new husband was well-off, but not flush enough to hand over millions to a stepson he hadn't even met.

Max hadn't attended their New Year's Eve wedding, as he'd been mooching off a friend who owned a house on sunny Antigua.

So where had the cash come from? Building condos on spec was one thing, but a real-estate transaction would have required paperwork, legal signatures, a big, fat check.

Was it possible one of Max's long-shot investments had actually paid off?

Given his lousy luck at the card table and the debts he'd

...un up from Vegas to Monte Carlo, Trevor didn't see how his brother had earned thirty million dollars gambling. Whenever he earned the slightest bit of a profit at a venture—the estate sale and auction house he'd started with a couple of mates from school came to mind—he turned around and blew it on a boat or car or monthlong ski trip.

So how'd he get the funds to buy The Crown Jewel?

Considering Max's attitude when Trevor had last questioned him, the only way he was going to get answers was to conduct his own discreet inquiries. He needed to stay informed, since not only would his father continue to question him, Trevor would certainly be expected to clean up the fallout and head off the media when whatever Max was up to went sour.

His office doorknob rattled, and Trevor didn't have to turn to know Florence had entered.

Her sigh was heavy. "If you're going to brood, you might as well go home. Or go find that lovely ginger-haired girl and take her to dinner."

His pulse thrummed at the image of Shelby. "She had to work."

"So take your lovely and loyal assistant to dinner."

Trevor glanced over his shoulder, not surprised to see Florence's bright pink lips pursed as she fluffed her highlighted blond hair. "Much as I'd like to I already have plans."

"Go out with a friend. Go to your fitness club. Read a book. Relax."

He shook his head. "I mentioned I already have plans, didn't I?"

"Humph. I bet with that ungrateful brother of yours. He doesn't count."

"I'll be sure to give him your best wishes when I see him."

"See him?" She charged toward the desk with the same determination she'd once used to convince him that without the ability to add and subtract, his trust fund wouldn't do him any good. "Popin, you need to stay as far away from him as possible."

Thirty years later, the endearment still made his ears hot. "I can handle him. Why don't you head home?"

She didn't move. "I think I should come with you, make sure he doesn't take advantage."

"He won't. I'm checking up, not handing over a check."

"I should hope not."

Trevor rounded the desk and kissed her temple. Though she wasn't officially family, she was the best part of home. "Don't worry. I have your idea about pushing out the baby bird under advisement."

Florence looked skeptical. "I suppose his lordship is worried about what the scoundrel is getting into and dragging you into the muck along with it."

"He relies on me to keep him updated," Trevor said neutrally.

"Just remember he needs you more than you need him."

Though Trevor nodded, he knew nothing was further from the truth. He wanted his father's trust and admiration. Maybe it was the curse of the second son. Maybe it was because he saw his father's struggle to be confident with his heir. Maybe he was a sap.

At the door, Florence glared at him over her shoulder. "You're not messing around on that ginger girl, are you, love?"

Trevor grinned. "A beautiful woman who makes cookies and doesn't care a whit for my bloodline? Certainly not."

As soon as his assistant left the room, however, Trevor returned to staring at the horizon. Brooding was apt. Florence wasn't one to mince words or feelings when she cared so deeply. She'd gone from being a caretaker, to a mentor, to a friend.

Though he'd had his share of women he'd *messed around,* playing at romance and true relationships, he wasn't playing now.

Yet the closer he and Shelby grew, the greater the chance he'd learn what a wash-up his brother was. Plenty of respectable women in London had tangled with Max and heard of his reputation to the point they wouldn't associate with any Banfield.

Not that anyone would say so publicly. The whispers and pitying stares his father received were almost worse. Frankly, Trevor wasn't sure how much more the old man could take.

Why he was more annoyed than ever by his brother's lack of appreciation for all he'd been given, he didn't know. Why Shelby was different, he wasn't sure. He only knew he did and she was.

And, he admitted, how deeply that passion would go might change the course of his life forever.

9

Hotelier Misfortune?
by Peeps Galloway, Gossipmonger
(And proud of it!)

Did you survive Tax Day, Manhattan?

My buns and my pocketbook (And you *know* that's a Louis Vuitton classic tote, don't you?) are still chapped. Not sure we're getting our money's worth down there in D.C., but that's a whole different kettle of fish....

Speaking of fish...a friend recently had dinner at Golden, the premier restaurant inside The Crown Jewel—you know the hotel recently bought by financial guru *(cough, cough)* Max Banfield—and his thirty-six-dollar entrée wasn't gently sauteed in butter and herbs as advertised, but fried beyond recognition.

And, no, darlings, I'm not transferring to the culinary review page, I point this out to draw attention to the real flambé, namely the chef shouting in both English and Italian that he'd had enough of the deplorable situation at Golden and he was "so freakin' outta here." (Not sure of the Italian translation, but it involved quite a few hand gestures, you get the idea.)

My friend overheard all this with several other diners, by the way, because Golden's recent transfer of ownership has also included cramming so many tables onto the restaurant floor that the waitstaff has to turn sideways, which is practically illegal in nearly every southern state.

Questionable management *and* a renowned chef on the run? Sounds like Golden—and The Crown Jewel, in turn—could be in serious trouble.

Maybe you should have your fish fried over in Brooklyn for half the price, instead?

Keep your ears tuned and your gums flapping!

—*Peeps*

SWIPING HER FINGERS THROUGH the long, platinum blond wig, Shelby stared at her reflection in complete dissatisfaction.

The hairpiece had come from a nearby costume store on 21st, but since they leaned toward the elaborate, she looked like a cross between Marilyn Monroe and an aging Playboy bunny.

With way less than C boobs and lacking a professional hairdresser.

This is never going to work.

She wanted her parents' retirement money back. She wanted Max punished. She was crazy about Trevor.

No way all those things could come together successfully. A soufflé destined to fall, a steak predetermined to burn.

At least the suit looked nice on her. Since it was Victoria's, it probably cost more than Shelby made in a month. Which led her to consider yet another negative in her life—the potential loss of her business.

No matter that she was trying like hell to make everything work out, everything seemed destined to clash. Her irritation

was running over into her deception to her lover and her in
tense feelings for him.

She'd left him earlier as he'd tucked her into a cab in fron
of his apartment building. Supposedly, she was meant to be o
her way to her catering space. Which she had gone to. *Briefly*
Instead it was time for Robin Hood to kick into action.

She pointed at herself in the mirror. "*You* are a bad, bac
girl."

Grabbing her bag, she left her apartment and hailed a cab
Today, maybe today, this whole nightmare would be over. Ir
her disguise, she planned to lure Max into letting him swin
dle her. Then the police would stop following her around and
concentrate on the real problem.

Though Detective Antonio had been remarkably under
standing about ignoring their burglary attempt, he was stuck
"being Homicide's bitch," as he'd so succinctly described the
night they'd all gone to the pub, so Max was living high and
preparing to ruin more lives.

And that just burned her cornflakes.

Plus, if the cops ever did get close, the rat would no doub
sense the trap and simply move on to the next city or country

And just how did her sophisticated lover fit into all this?

She knew Trevor couldn't be part of Max's schemes, bu
there was no way a man with his intelligence was completely
ignorant of them. Maybe she was lying to him, but he wasn'
telling her everything, either.

"An excellent basis for a loving and lasting relationship."

"Talking aloud to yourself is a sign of delusion," the cabbie
informed her. "I'm right here, ya know. Like talking to a
shrink."

"Are you married?"

"Was. Three times in fact."

Yikes. "I'm going back to talking to myself now."

He shrugged. "Suit yourself."

Shrinks and delusion aside, he got her to The Crown Jewel in record time. Let the subterfuge begin...

After paying the cabbie, she walked into the hotel, trying to emulate Victoria's confident stride and I-could-own-the-world-if-I-wanted attitude. As she crossed to the elevator, she felt a moment of panic when she regretted not asking Victoria and Calla to come with her.

She'd insisted they stay away, afraid Max would recognize the three of them together, regardless of disguises. They'd supported her so much, but she had to take this step alone.

Approaching suite 1634, she rolled her shoulders. She was going to ruin this lying, smiling crook and get her life back.

"THAT'S *fascinating,*" Shelby said, laying her hand on Max's arm as she smiled at him.

Max shrugged without modesty. "Yes, I do have a knack..."

From his other side, a dark-haired woman linked her arm with Max's. "Certainly you do, darling. Over there are some investors you should talk to." She sent an icy glare toward Shelby. "You'll excuse us, won't you?"

Shelby clenched the stem of the wineglass she'd barely taken a sip from. "Sure."

Knowing her plan's foundation was shaking, she glanced around the room, wincing as her gaze passed over the scrimpy crowd and the hors d'oeuvres table. She'd have been more effective catering this disaster. This wasn't a gathering of people flush with cash who could afford refurbished condos in the East Village. She knew that because everybody here seemed like she usually did, and she had no money.

These people were here to be seen, schmooze the future Earl of Banfield, have a free glass of wine, a complimentary plate of crappy food, then hopefully meet people flush with cash.

Max soaked in the expectant atmosphere like a fish moving

water through his gills. He showed off schematics of condo
with spectacular views via a 3-D slideshow presentation dis
played on the wall behind the food table. He assured every
one the project was "well under way" and the address woul
be "the" place to call home in six months.

As a completely biased observer, Shelby noted he promise
neither too much nor too little. He was a pro.

At least her parents hadn't been swindled by an amateur.

Though, hang on—

The brunette who'd absconded with Max had guided him t
a woman of about fifty. She had professionally coiffed silve
hair—certainly not a costume wig—wore a gray suit an
matching shoes that Shelby had seen online going for a pric
with a comma in it.

She looked capable of investing in something besides time
in front of the mirror. So among the posers, Max had attracte
some actual possibilities.

Hang on to your pocketbook, lady.

Clearly Shelby's was safe. Max had paid scant attention t
her, much less asked her to stroke out a deposit check. Wha
was she doing? A caterer launching her own sting operation?
She felt like a fool.

Time to call for reinforcements.

She withdrew to a quiet corner of the room and dialed Vic
toria's number from her cell. "This isn't working," she whis
pered into the phone. "He's barely spoken to me."

"In that suit?" Victoria asked in disbelief. "The man's blind
as well as idiotic."

"The tacky wig is spoiling my look," Shelby said.

"I told you to dye your hair," Calla said calmly, obviously
listening in on Victoria's end.

"I'm not—" Shelby stopped. She was lying to her lover an
dragging her friends into criminal conspiracy, but she drew

he line at *dyeing her hair?* Something wasn't working, all ight. And it was her own sense of logic.

Her mania for justice.

Then, from the other side of the room, an unanticipated vent changed everything.

Trevor walked in.

Her stomach clenched, and she must have made some noise ut loud, since Victoria asked, "What's wrong?"

"Robin Hood's arrow just went way left of the target."

"What the—"

"Gotta go. I'll call you guys back."

Her heart pounding, she frantically judged the distance be-ween herself, Trevor and the door. Max hadn't recognized er, but he'd only seen her once, and then in the capacity of servant. He probably wouldn't have remembered her even vithout the disguise. But Trevor knew her well.

Every intimate inch of her.

Thankfully, the posers descended on Trevor quicker than hey had the bartender. Women flirted; men jockeyed for po-ition to shake his hand. He was definitely somebody with :achet. After so many years in the catering business, it was :heering to realize she could predict human behavior more .ccurately than some psychologists.

Her triumph was short-lived, however, as Trevor glanced lowly around.

Sipping her wine—for real, this time—she kept her face n profile and hoped the wig hid some portion of her face. \t least Max was in the back of the room. As soon as Trevor noved in that direction, she was going to skedaddle, as her ;randmother used to say.

When he took a few steps in his brother's direction, she nched the other way. A woman and two guys obviously veren't going to let Trevor escape them, so they matched him tep for step, the woman keeping up a rapid pace of conversa-

tion that would hopefully be either fascinating or distractin
enough to hold Trevor's attention.

Then suddenly, inexplicably, he stopped. His head snappe
in her direction. She sucked in a quick breath, and for a heart
beat, they stared at each other.

He blinked first, and she nearly broke into a run as he
spoke to the people around him just before he strode towar
her.

Her heart pounded as if she were an animal trapped in
cage.

Tough it out, girl. Maybe he didn't recognize her at all
Maybe he simply liked her suit. Maybe he wanted to know
where she'd bought her wig.

"Shelby, what are you doing here?" he asked when he
reached her side.

"Well, hell."

"That wig is awful," he said, his tone amused but his eye
conveying his confusion at seeing her. All the pieces hadn'
fallen into place yet—her asking about the meeting for Vic
toria's sake, who was nowhere in sight, her telling him they
couldn't go out tonight because she had a catering job.

She licked her bottom lip. "I can explain."

He slid his hands into the pockets of his suit pants and
waited.

"Meet me in the lobby in ten minutes," she blurted.

Then, she skedaddled.

SITTING NEXT TO SHELBY at the lobby bar, a glass of fine Scotch
in his hand, Trevor fought for calm. "You don't have a cater
ing job tonight, do you?"

She played with the stem of her wineglass and didn't look
at him. "No."

"You lied to me."

"Yes."

He clenched his hands around his glass and resisted the urge to hurl it into the mirror behind the bar. "Would you mind telling me why you said you do?"

"I'm sorry," she said, looking at him finally.

He noted the bleak expression in her eyes and fought to remain calm. "For what?"

"For lying. For what I have to tell you."

In the time she'd fled Max's investors' meeting, she'd taken off the ridiculous wig, false eyelashes and heavy makeup. She was Shelby again. Although she was Shelby before, too, even with the additions. She couldn't hide the way she stood and held her body, her lovely face, those inviting lips. Not from him.

"Okay." He couldn't think of anything else to say.

"Your brother swindled my parents out of their retirement savings."

"He—" Trevor shook his head, hoping to clear it. Whatever he'd been anticipating, that hadn't been it. "Max? The guy upstairs?"

"Yes."

He let out a laugh, then sipped his drink. "You're mistaken."

"I'm not."

She proceeded to tell him about the fraudulent investment schemes, Max cashing checks from seniors, then skipping town. Cops were investigating, though so far they didn't seem prepared to make an arrest. And Shelby and her friends had decided to take matters into their own hands when the wheels of justice weren't rolling along rapidly enough to suit them.

Project Robin Hood.

And what a fairy tale it was.

"Max is irresponsible, but he's harmless," he told her firmly.

Her eyes widened. "Do you consider swindling retirement money out of seniors harmless?"

"Absolutely n—" He stopped. This whole thing was a mistake. It had to be. "He wouldn't do that. I'll admit he frequently makes poor decisions, gambles too much and his grand ideas don't usually work out, but he wouldn't deliberately con anyone."

"But he has."

"He hasn't."

"I have proof."

"Where?"

"Not with me. It's at my apartment. The cops have a copy, too. Your brother won't get away with another scheme. I'm going to make sure of it."

"Well, I certainly hope your future efforts are better than this evening's debacle. Cheap disguises aren't your forte, my dear."

"It was going just fine until you showed up."

"So it's *my* fault you had to abandon your undercover operation? Didn't cast me in a role for your little drama? You slept with me to spy on me, I guess. To see if I was part of Max's latest scheme."

She looked away quickly, and his heart jumped.

He'd made the wild accusation because she'd hurt him by lying, and because he didn't want to face his own doubts about Max, didn't want to believe he'd sunk so low.

But it was true. He could see it in her eyes. He was a pawn in her plot for revenge.

He set aside the rest of his whiskey because he wanted its burn down his throat just a little too much. His body went numb all on its own.

She laid her hand over his, and the pain, somehow, expanded in a radiating wave. "I slept with you because I like you. I like you a great deal." Determined, she searched his gaze until he held hers. "But I did accept your first dinner invitation hoping to find out more about Max. I wanted to be sure you weren't part of his fraud."

"And since I passed, you decided to climb into my bed willingly." He snatched his hand away. "Thanks."

"Trevor, please. I know I made a mistake by lying to you. But the only thing I wasn't completely honest about was Max. Everything between us has been real and…wonderful."

"It *was*."

"You don't want to see me anymore?"

How could he? He'd turned to ice. "No, I don't."

"Okay." She reached into her bag and pulled out a ten-dollar bill, which she set on the bar as she rose. "Please don't invest with Max. I'm sorry, but he really is a swindler, and I'm going to see that he pays."

Trevor said nothing.

The fact that she'd accused his brother of unsubstantiated fraud was minor compared to his relationship with her crumbling like ancient stone.

He hadn't been made a fool of in romance since sometime in primary school. Yet his need for Shelby had blinded him to her true motives, to the harsh truth that she'd been using him to get to his brother. He was a dupe. Nothing more.

If he could only convince himself of that fact, he'd be free.

Project Robin Hood, Day 19, 4:00 p.m.
Javalicious Cafe, Midtown Manhattan

"HERE ARE THE PICTURES Shelby took at the investors' meeting." Calla slid a disk across the table to Detective Antonio. "They're not too great. She took them with her cell phone."

"While trying to be covert."

Calla nodded. The coffee she usually enjoyed had left a

bitter taste in her mouth. "Um, the covert part didn't go s‹ well."

"I really am working on the case," the detective assure‹ her. "She didn't have to screw up her love life."

Calla worked up a smile. "Sympathy, Detective? Hov unlike you. I should get you out of the office more often."

His gaze held hers for a fraction longer than was profes sional, the fathomless green seeming to draw her closer. " can be pleasant."

"So I see. We've been sitting here for nearly fifteen min utes and you have yet to warn me off your case."

He scowled. "That's about to change. You and your friend need to back off. Banfield obviously didn't buy her as a poten tial investor, and his jilted brother is bound to tell him abou the three of you trying to spoil his plans. Leave this to th‹ professionals."

Calla shook her head. "No can do. Shelby is more deter mined than ever. She seems to think if she exposes Max Trevor will forgive her."

Antonio shook his head. "Doesn't work that way in my neighborhood."

"I'm sure it doesn't, but people who cook well are ofter quite obsessive."

"So tell her to obsess over fruits from Bora Bora some thing."

"Her mind's not really on delicacies at the moment. From what I gather, she's butchered quite a lot of meat in the las twenty-four hours. Did you read my story on Bora Bora?"

"I did. It sounded like a nice place."

"A nice place?" Calla rolled her eyes. "It's one of the mos breathtaking, exotic, peaceful, romantic islands in the world From the peaks of the volcano piercing the sky, to the watei reflecting impossible shades of turquoise and emerald, it's almost impossible to capture its magic, even in pictures and videos."

"Right, nice."

She sighed. "How about you stick to your job, and I'll do mine?"

He tapped his finger on the disk. "Exactly my point. You and your friends pack up your disguises and save them till Halloween."

"Where's the adventure in that?"

"You appear to find plenty of adventure without sticking your nose into a cop shop."

Pleased, not discouraged, she smiled. "You read more than one article."

"I had to make sure you were who you said you were."

"You could have done that in a ten-second Google search."

Despite her pleasure, or maybe because of it, his stare was confrontational. "I like to be thorough."

"Me, too. Why were you suspended three years ago?"

Pain, then shock flittered across his handsome face for a split second before he blanked his expression. He leaned back in the booth and stared at his coffee mug. "I wasn't thorough."

Regret pulsed through Calla. She'd expected him to say in-house politics or the like. She certainly hadn't meant to cause him pain. She started to grasp his hand, but was afraid of making things worse. Instead, she linked her fingers in front of her on the table, keeping a safe distance from him. "Did you like my articles?"

"I read more than one, didn't I?"

Just when she thought they might become friends—or more—he withdrew again. *Calla, you really screwed that up, didn't you?*

As expected, he scooted out of the booth. "I gotta get back," he said, tossing a few bills on the table. "Coffee's on me."

"Detective," she called when he would have turned awa
She held up the disk. "Don't you want this?"

He plucked it from her fingers, taking care not to touch he
"I'll see if our techs can clean up some of the images."

"Take note of the attractive brunette at Max's side. Sh
could be an accomplice. She introduced herself to Shelb
simply as Alice."

"Not Marion?" When she cocked her head in confusio
he added, "You and your buddies seem to think of yourselve
as Robin Hood's gang. Wasn't there a maid Marion?"

"Marion was on our side." She pursed her lips as the cas
ing slid into place. "And, actually, Trevor would be Mario
for our purposes. Betraying the wealthy, unscrupulous sid
to fight with the rebels for truth, justice—"

He held up his hand. "Sorry I brought it up."

"You're right, of course. He hasn't exactly joined our sid
has he? Well, Shelby is holding out hope."

"Right, hope." He shook his head, as if the concept wa
foreign to him. "Peaceful relationships aren't exactly my spe
cialty, so tell your friend I'm sorry."

Watching him walk away, Calla sipped her coffee. Ther
was a heart beneath all that turmoil, but its beat was kind
erratic.

10

LONELY AND UNWILLING TO go with Victoria and Calla out to the clubs for Friday-night fun, Shelby got out of the cab so she could wander up the pedestrian-only portion of Broadway.

The bright-light craziness contrasted sharply with the intimacy of her neighborhood. The people she saw every day and knew by name diverged from the dazed and dazzled expression of the tourists clogging the streets. The sights she took for granted were glaringly present now—towers of steel, brick and glass, cracked sidewalks, attitudes worn like designer clothes. And noise, noise, noise.

Traffic was a bitch. Rent was beyond the reach of nearly all. Dreams were made and destroyed daily, probably even hourly.

Yet it was hers. Loved, feared and respected.

She'd come to the city to make it big, like millions of others. And she was doing pretty damn good. No matter how much Trevor meant to her and how much she regretted the way she'd handled things with him, she wasn't giving up on

her dream. To do that, she had to make sure her parents g
their own dream back.

He had to protect his family. She could hardly expect hir
to believe her, stand with her, when her goal was his brother'
punishment.

So, for now, they had to be on opposite sides.

The evidence she'd promised him was in her bag. Sh
wanted him to see it, but didn't want to bear the brunt of th
anger in his eyes. Eyes that had once looked into hers witl
desire and adoration.

Regardless of his family obligations, he had a right to knov
who he was defending.

She walked over to eighth, which was considerably quiete
and hailed a cab to his apartment building. Standing on th
sidewalk after being dropped off, she looked up at the risin;
column of glass and steel and was pretty sure its tip piercer
her heart.

The ache in the center of her chest spread, and for a momen
tears filled her eyes.

Blinking them away, she nodded to the doorman on duty
Thankfully, she didn't recognize him, nor he her. She wasn"
sure she was up to explaining she wasn't coming to see he
lover, but to further incite her enemy.

She walked to the security desk.

"Ms. Dixon, how are you this evening?" Fred asked.

She'd met him the night she'd come to cater Trevor's party
Had that been only a week ago? "Great," she lied. "I jus
stopped by to drop this off for Mr. Banfield." She handed hir
the packet of evidence she'd compiled against Max.

Probably confused, but too much of a pro to show it, he
took the envelope. "Yes, of course."

"Thanks. Have a good night."

"You, too."

She turned to leave, then stopped. He was so close, and

he'd apparently lost all common sense in the last twenty
econds.

"Is he in, by any chance?" she asked Fred.

The guard checked his computer screen. "He is. Would you
ke me to call up?"

"No." She shook her head for emphasis. "No, I really...
'ould you please?"

Fred smiled and picked up the phone on his desk. He was
robably familiar with babbling females asking about Trevor.

Shelby wandered a few feet away. If she overheard Trevor
houting to Fred *hell, no, that woman isn't ever allowed in my
'partment again as long as she lives,* she was certainly going
o lose it. As she paced, she crossed her arms over her stom-
ch as if she could hold herself together with so little effort.

"Mr. Banfield would be pleased to see you."

Shelby ground to a halt and blinked. "He would?"

"Yes, miss. Would you like to take this up as you go? Or
vould you prefer me to deliver it later?"

"Ah..." She was still stuck on *pleased* to see her. Cer-
ainly Fred had added that part to be polite. "I'll take it." She
'lutched the packet in her shaking hand. "What the heck."

"You're cleared for elevator two."

"Thanks."

"Ms. Dixon?"

When she glanced over her shoulder, Fred was smiling. "He
ooked a little pale and distracted earlier. He'll be glad to see
'ou."

Clearly Fred's detection skills weren't the sharpest.

"I'm sure he will," she said, proving her lying skills were
oned to a razor's edge.

During the elevator ride up, she called herself crazy over
ind over. She nearly picked up the emergency phone to call
'red and ask him to cancel the express ride.

Drawing all the courage she could muster, remembering

she was a rebel at heart, she shuffled out of the elevator an
down the hall. The apartment door was open. Her heart kicke
against her ribs as if it was frantic for escape.

No doubt her instinct for self-protection.

As she reached the doorway, she realized he was listenin
to Sinatra. The icon's voice filled the apartment as if he migl
be singing into a microphone while standing on the dining
room table. "My Way" had never sounded so good or so des
perate.

Holding the envelope against her chest, she ventured insid
tapping her knuckles on the door in a perfunctory announce
ment as she moved into the foyer and closed the door behin
her.

No response.

Well, Old Blue Eyes kept singing, but no reaction from
Trevor.

The effect was remarkably unnerving, probably his inten
tion. He had a right to be angry, to blame her for ruining ev
erything between them, to resent her for planning to get hi
brother arrested.

As she entered the living room, she searched the dimly li
area for him, finally spotting him standing in front of the win
dows, an amber-filled crystal glass in his hand, the city light
seeming to surround him.

"I was trying to get drunk," he said quietly, not turning
around.

He could have punched her and caused less misery.

"I see," she managed to say. The tears sprung to her eye
yet again as she let her gaze rove his solitary form. "I'll se
this down and go."

She was laying the folder on the coffee table when his voic
startled her, louder and firmer. "Why did you come here?"

She could have brought the packet of information withou

ver talking to him. She'd pushed herself to face him for one
eason. "To apologize."

"You did that already."

"Not well." Commanding her feet to move, she crossed to
.im. Before he could stop her or she could change her mind,
he laid her palm against his chest. She clutched his shirt. "I'm
o sorry I screwed this up. I'm crazy about you, and I'll never
ie to you again. I was desperate to save my parents, and I lost
•erspective. I have no idea how we'll reconcile this thing with
Vlax, but I want to try. Please don't let my mistake ruin us."

His face was in shadow but she could smell the whiskey,
omehow enticing and familiar even though she'd driven him
o this dark point and regretted doing so.

"I never get drunk," he said slowly, his beautiful voice a
•it slurred.

Carefully, she took the glass from his hand. "So don't now.
'orgive me, instead."

Reaching out, he cupped her cheek. "I made mistakes of
ny own."

The relief rose up, nearly choking her. "Oh, yeah? Tell me
.ll about them."

His arms surged around her, and she dropped the glass on
he wood floor, where it shattered. But though she jolted in
:hock, his grip never slackened.

He tightened it instead, picking her up and carrying her
oward his bedroom.

As he removed her clothes, he kissed every inch of exposed
:kin. The tenderness clogged her throat with gratitude. He for-
3ave her with every touch, stroke and sigh.

Sinatra's voice continued its melodious seduction, clear and
:ure, familiar and renewing. His words accompanied their
need, the movement and rhythm of their bodies merging as
)ne. With full knowledge of all that still stood between them,
:hey climbed walls and broke through barriers.

The hunger she had only for him filled her, drove her t happiness and fulfillment, reminding her that what was ir tense and sudden could also be warm, meaningful. Makin her admit her feelings for this man were both complicated an simple.

They lost themselves in the night, in a legendary voic and passion that flew to new heights. And yet promised eve higher soaring into the clouds.

When she faded back to reality, he was there, holding he head against his shoulder, his breathing sure and strong.

"You warned me not to give Max money," he said, absentl stroking the hair off her temple.

"You shouldn't."

"I *should* have known I wouldn't be rid of you right then.

Raising up on her elbow, she pinched him. "Rid of me huh?"

"I had a stupid moment where I thought it would be easier.

The desire was back in his crystal-blue eyes, and she foun herself wishing she could stare at it forever. "I've had a fev of those lately. They're hard to shake."

"Not this time." He traced her cheek with his finger. "You protected me. Even though I didn't believe you about Max."

"Did you tell him about my plans?"

"No. Did you think I would?"

She shook her head. "But Calla's detective friend warne us you might."

"Detective Antonio's a cynic."

"No kidding, but I still—" She stared at him in surprise "How do you know anything about him? All I told you wa his name."

"I have my ways." He kissed her gently. "Come on, let' eat."

Glad the volatile subject of Max was set aside—at least fo

e moment—she looked down at her bare body. "We're not
ally dressed for going out."

"We'll find something here. You didn't forget how to cook
your despair over losing me, did you?"

She snagged his shirt off the floor and shrugged into it.
Luckily for you, no. I butchered a lot of meat, though."

"Can I pause and say *yuck* without sounding too un-
anly?"

"Sure." She grinned. "I think you've firmly proven your
manhood tonight."

WITH SKILL AND INGENUITY she managed to put together an
mazing pancetta carbonara, which Trevor devoured.

He'd been running on caffeine, nerves and fear since the
ight before. The relief at being able to enjoy a meal while
ooking across the dining-room table at Shelby was powerful.

He held out his hand, which she took. "Let's talk."

As he led her to the sofa, he could feel tension spike inside
er. He wasn't crazy about jumping into the trouble with Max
o quickly after their reconciliation, but he had to let her know
where he stood, what he'd discovered. In return, he needed to
ee the evidence she'd gathered.

Maybe, just maybe, they'd find a way to resolve this im-
ossible situation.

"You're not the only reason I was upset tonight," he began,
olding both her hands in his. "I've been doing some research
f my own."

"About Max."

"Yes. I talked to Antonio and assured him I wouldn't warn
Max, as he thought I would. Then I called a friend who's a bit
igher up the chain than our pessimistic detective."

"How high?" she asked, her tone rising.

"A rung or two up the ladder of command. Max is in a great
eal of trouble."

Her shoulders slumped in relief. "You believe me."

"Yes." He leaned forward, pressing his lips to her forehea "I was wrong not to before."

He'd been duped all right, but not by Shelby, by his ow brother.

"We all want to see the best in those closest to us," she sai

"I was worried about Max embarrassing the family nam about worrying my father. I wasn't worried about him hur ing anyone else."

The brown in her hazel eyes darkened. "I'm sorry."

"You didn't do anything but try to protect your own famil Exactly what I've been aiming to do. Though without suc cess."

He thought of the earl, of the upcoming conversatio he'd have to hold with him. The disappointment and frus tration that would follow. Then he recalled the last time he' dragged an irritated Max away from Vegas—after paying of his debts—without so much as a thank-you for bailing hi out before he got in deeper. He remembered all the empt promises Max had made to everyone in the family, swearin he was going to settle down, or at least stop humiliating th Banfield name.

Trevor was sick of the excuses and promises, the misman agement and disrespect. Based on his friend's information a the NYPD, Max's future could be even more perilous than hi past.

Damn, how had everything gone downhill so quickly? Hov had Max moved from poor decisions to outright fraud? I would be unbelievable if Trevor wasn't there to see it himsel His brother frantically treading water, poised to slide farthe under the surface.

He would stop the slide, all right. Trevor was going to se to it personally.

"Do you mind if I stand?" he asked Shelby. "I'm not leaving you, I simply need to…move."

"You haven't failed, Trevor," she said gently, watching him walk away.

"I have."

"You have no control over Max's decisions."

"I should."

"How?"

The simple question fired his temper, something he rarely let loose. "Because it's my responsibility."

"Why?"

"Because that's what I do!" He slid his hand through his hair and tugged, hoping to get a hold on his frustration. "I thought I was doing it well. My family *expects* me to do it well."

"Max is clever. He works a room by being unthreatening, by not pushing too hard, by appearing to know less than he does."

"But he is all those things in reality."

"Which is why the ploy is effective."

"I should have known," he said, clenching his fist. "I've been bailing him out often enough, I should have seen what was really going on."

"You've been bailing him out?"

He heard the astonishment in her voice and held up his hand. "Not in the way you think. A lot of gambling debts and bar tabs, sure. I've paid off the paparazzi not to publish embarrassing pictures, but mostly it's been ridiculous stuff. He wanted to start a company that would give tourists hot-air balloon rides through Manhattan."

"There's very little open space. How would—"

"Exactly. It was preposterous. Then there was the time he bought a pair of fishing boats, intending to catch Alaskan king crabs."

"Isn't that really dangerous?"

"He was going to hire people to do the actual work. At lea until he saw the insurance he'd have to carry on the business

"Which I'm assuming he didn't investigate until *after* he bought the boats."

"You know him well."

"I'm beginning to. So how did you bail him out?"

"I found someone who could renovate the boats, add bett navigational equipment and the like, then resold them at profit."

"And who invested in the upgrades?"

"I did."

"Who got the profits?"

"I split them with Max. I'm not a complete fool." Thoug right now, he certainly felt like one. "I was trying to teac him something. To show him that mistakes can be recovere from, that a wrong step can sometimes lead to a right one."

"If you're you."

"Not only me. Anyone with a kernel of sense—"

She lifted her eyebrows.

"Ah, yes, well… You have a point there."

"And what Max is doing now isn't a mistake, it's on pur pose."

He sighed. "I know. Buying the hotel sent off glarin alarms for me, too. I had no idea where he got the money fc that."

Shelby looked astonished. "Retirement and condo scam would be a safe bet."

Trevor's stomach twisted. "You're undoubtedly right. But the time of his big grand opening party, I didn't know. That why I was there the night we met."

"You said you were there to toast his success, as I recal You hugged him."

"I was there to find out how he'd acquired the hotel and t

arn him to stay out of the gossip columns. I wanted him to
now I was watching him."

"That's why you were so suspicious of me and my friends,"
e said, her eyes alight with understanding. "Why you didn't
ll me your last name."

"I didn't give you my last name for the reason I told you
en—finding out about my family tends to make people
ange." Despite the seriousness of their conversation, he re-
alled her flushed face and direct gaze meeting his across a
ay of crab puffs. He'd fallen hard for her and her succulent
od immediately. "I liked you exactly as you were and didn't
ant to spoil it. But, yes, I was suspicious of you. I like to
eep tabs on Max's associates."

She glared at him. "So you can buy them off?"

With a wince, he nodded. "I'm sorry to say I have before.
's time to push the baby bird from the nest, Florence, my
ssistant, is fond of saying. My lack of willpower has led to
isaster."

"It's admirable you tried to save him, but you do realize
e's a lying, no-good, son-of-a—"

He snagged her hand and pulled her to her feet and into his
rms. "Such passion from the Yank. And my mother is quite
ice actually. She has extremely poor judgment in matters of
e heart, however."

"Nice to know Max comes by his lousy qualities naturally.
low much of your time, money and energy have been wasted
eeping him from drowning?"

He kissed her forehead and let her comfort wash over him,
ven though she was kind of annoyed with him. "Too much."

"It's pretty weird to be called a Yankee."

"Mmm." He kissed her the tip of her nose. "I'll keep that
n mind." He kissed her cheek, then kissed his way along her
hroat.

She planted her hand against his chest and pressed back.

"You go over there. I'm sitting down. I can't think with yo touching me."

Capturing her hand, he held on by his fingertips, which was a decent metaphor for their relationship. "But later…?"

A smile flirted at the edges of her mouth. "We'll see ho it goes, Your Lordship."

"I've always thought formal titles were products of gene ations passed, and certainly not anything due me." He pla fully tugged her against him. "But I'm beginning to see wh my father enjoys the perk."

He pressed his lips to hers, lingering longer than he shoul but not as long as he wanted. Then he led her to the sofa ar stepped back, as requested.

"I went to the hotel party to see how Max had gotten thir million dollars, which I suspected had come from our ne stepfather, but wasn't sure. I never dreamed he was actual conning anyone. I went to the investors' meeting because b that time I knew for sure Max was into something sleazy. H told me about the real-estate project, converting the decease artist's space to condos. I also learned he's romantically i volved with the artist's former lover."

"Yuck."

"Well said."

"He's getting desperate."

"I agree. The morality and legality of his projects and h judgment are falling at a rapid pace."

"Desperate. You're so cute when you're wordy."

The unexpected compliment stirred him. "Come over her and say that."

She shook her head. "You need to read that first." Sh nodded at the folder on the coffee table. "It ain't pretty."

Trevor would have rather prodded a live snake, but he kne Shelby was right. Could it be any worse than hearing her sa she was involved in her own undercover sting operation in a

ffort to expose Max's alleged crimes? Could it be any worse
han two respected NYPD officers telling him his brother
eally was under investigation?

He looked through the folder with a sickening heart. Sev-
ral statements by would-be retirees, including Shelby's par-
nts, documented giving Max their life savings to invest in
ertificates of deposit, only to have him skip town with their
noney and leave behind only broken dreams and fake certifi-
ates.

Yep, it was worse.

The woman he cared about, who'd shared his bed and
rightened his life, was a victim of his own brother's greed
nd unscrupulous behavior.

Still carrying the folder, he wandered around the living
oom. The scent of garlic, cream and bacon lingered in the
ir. The indulgent aroma reminded him of the people who
ouldn't indulge, who wondered how they'd make the next
ent payment, how they'd survive without their savings.

While his brother cashed checks and looked toward the
ay the family coffers would open to him completely. While
revor sat in his high-rise fortress of privilege.

He sat next to her on the sofa, close enough to touch, but
till apart. The whole bloody business was starting to sound
hakespearean.

"Do you want to hit me?" he asked her.

"No." She glanced at him askance. "Though I wouldn't
nind taking a swing at good ole Max."

"The line will no doubt be forming around the block any
ninute."

"It's already formed."

"I suppose it has."

But would he join?

He couldn't stand with Max against Shelby, but could he
eally battle his own family? Should he allow his brother to

take the full brunt of the consequences of his actions? Es
pecially considering Trevor had enabled him along the way

Certainly he had to do something.

"When I talked to the police, they told me that thoug
they don't have jurisdiction over the scheme he conned you
parents with in Savannah, there's a complaint from Mrs. Iri
Rosenburg, who lives right here in the city." He tossed th
folder onto the coffee table. "Quite a resume."

"He gets around." She laid her hand on his thigh, and h
linked their fingers. "And the past is quickly catching up wit
him—one way or another. When Calla talked to Detectiv
Antonio, he agreed to reinterview Mrs. Rosenburg for furthe
information."

"But he says there's a body in the East River—"

"Not anymore, I guess. Still, the detective has problems c
his own. Not to mention there's something about him."

When she didn't elaborate, Trevor prompted. "Somethin
about him…?"

"I'm not sure. Except that he's sort of supporting us an
sort of annoyed we're invading his space. Mostly annoyed,
think. Oh, and Calla is hot for him."

"How wonderful for them."

She didn't comment on his sarcasm. She knew as well a
he about all the barriers that remained between them.

"Detective Antonio also made an effort at convincing m
to talk you out of going any further with your personal ver
detta."

"Like I said, mostly annoyed."

"Did you really break into Max's office?"

She lifted her chin. "I'll refrain from answering that ques
tion without my attorney present."

"You didn't think I'd tell you the truth about the meeting
You had to get proof?"

"I'd already asked you to check with Max when my buddies came up with the alleged break-in at the office."

"And you didn't want to wait for my answer before committing the alleged break-in?"

"That, and I didn't want you in the middle. I didn't want you right where you are—forced to divide your loyalties."

"The evidence against Max is piling up."

"Knowing and acting against him are two different things."

The fact that she understood the position he was in didn't make the decision any easier. "Yes, it is."

"I guess you agree with the detective? You think my friends and I should step back and let Max go until the police can catch up."

He met her gaze directly. Brother or not, Max had crossed way over the line between right and wrong. As sick inside as he was about the whole business, he couldn't let Shelby and the others go on alone. And while he wasn't at the point where he could hand over his only brother to the police, he knew Max had to be stopped. "No, I think we need to handle this ourselves. I want in on the Robin Hood project."

11

"I HAVE A FAVOR TO ASK first, though."

Shelby's ears were still ringing from Trevor's announcement and not entirely prepared to hear his request.

"I've been—"

"Are you sure about this?" she interrupted.

"I am. Max can't continue on this path. He's hurting people. He stroked her cheek with the tip of his finger. "Namely, you."

"So you're doing this for me?"

"Mostly. Is that a problem?"

Her heart squeezed in her chest. "I guess not." At least not until she completely fell for him. Their relationship had started with lies and vigilante justice. They had nothing in common other than Max and their desire. How could anything lasting come of that?

"I've been concerned about Max's behavior for a while," Trevor continued. "Babysitting him used to be easy, even second nature." He shrugged. "I watch him to keep him from embarrassing the family and the title we've held for more than two hundred bloody years."

"Because your father asks you to."

"Now, yes. Publicly, he's cut Max off. He was practically humiliated into doing so by his peers, even though I think

e's convinced he'll turn around one day and find a clone of
imself staring at Max's image in the mirror."

"You never told me delusion ran in your family."

Trevor's smile was as weak as her attempt to joke. "They
must, since, in the beginning, I was truly trying to help. We're
brothers. I wanted to support him. But I've been resenting him
lately and feeling guilty about it. Now, given that his actions
have gone far beyond embarrassment, I feel foolish."

"And angry? It's okay to be angry."

"Believe me, I am." He squeezed her hand. "But I'd like
you to do something for me before going forward with your
plans."

"And that is…?"

"I want to give Max an opportunity to apologize and make
restitution."

She leaped to her feet. "No. Absolutely not. We're way past
apologies."

"And restitution," he reminded her calmly. "Obviously,
your parents are struggling. Their financial situation has
driven you outside the law. If I can get Max to pay…"

"It's not only about the money."

"What's it about, then? Revenge?"

"You're damn right it is!" She attempted to pace off her
fury, only to find her temper snarling even louder. Freakin'
rich people. If they didn't like how their life was going, they
bought a new outcome. How many demanding, irrational,
privileged jerks had she placated and served and…

Whose checks she'd cashed to live the life she wanted.

Stopping, she curled her hands into fists and tried to think
rationally. Trevor wasn't Max. And being a jerk wasn't limited to those with money.

Facing her lover, she crossed her arms over her chest.
"After all the suffering he's caused why does he get to write a
check and make it all go away? No. I want him prosecuted."

"You want him punished."

"And what's wrong with that? Too uncivilized for you, Your Lordship?"

Slowly, he rose to his feet. His blue eyes had hardened like ice. He clearly didn't like her mocking his family title, especially since she'd used it often as an endearment. "You want people to take the law into their own hands? To ignore rules and procedures? To decide who's guilty among themselves and pass judgment and sentencing?"

"There are times when desperate measures are needed."

"And who decides that? *You?*"

She certainly didn't want the days of the Wild West again, but when the law turned its back on hardworking, if somewhat gullible people, somebody had to step up and make things right.

The law isn't turning its back. Lady Justice is simply moving too slowly.

What would it hurt to give Trevor this opportunity so they could fight for the same side? Max wouldn't dish out a dime to her parents or anybody else. She'd bet her new deluxe convection oven he'd laugh in Trevor's face when he made his reimbursement request.

"Fine," she announced. "But I have no control over any charges the police eventually manage to scrape together."

"Agreed."

"And Max will pay. Not you."

"I'd be glad to—"

She glared at him. "*Max* will pay."

"Your parents shouldn't continue to worry. Let me help."

"I'm helping them."

"A loan?"

"No." Drawing a deep breath, she fought against the humiliation of her lover knowing she'd failed to protect her family

rticularly when he was so adept at sheltering his. "Thank
u, but no. This is my fight."

"Mine now, too. My family has lived by a code of honor,
yalty and civility for generations. I can't let this go."

"Neither can I."

"So we agree."

Close enough to touch, yet she felt as though they'd trav-
ed miles in opposite directions.

She didn't like the distance. There would be battles enough
contend with. It'd be nice to have him beside her.

She looped her arms around his waist, laying her head
ainst his chest. His heart beat soundly against her cheek.
Even if Max agrees to restitution, you'd better hire him a
arn good attorney."

Sighing, he held her against him. "I will. Still, he's hardly
criminal mastermind. Certainly not front-page news."

She pressed her lips to his jaw. "The gossip columns seem
love him."

"Don't they just?"

"Bet Daddy isn't happy about that."

"No, he definitely isn't." Trevor's mouth twitched with
musement. His eyes thawed. "Daddy?"

"It's a Southern thing. What do you call him?"

"Sir."

"Not *my lord* or *milord*? That kind of thing?"

"In public, I do. In private he relaxes the rules."

Shelby rolled her eyes. The guy sounded like a true stuffed
irt. How fortunate was she that his son—the insignificant
cond one—was so deliciously passionate.

She bumped her hips against his. "I think *milord* is sexy."

"Do you?" He slid his hands down her backside and held
r against his body. "Instead of getting revenge on Max, we
uld knock him and my cousin off, and I'd have quite a few
tles coming my way."

Sizzle in the City

"Oh, yeah?" She glided her tongue across his bottom l and reveled in the way he tensed. "Name them."

"There's the Earl of Westmore, of course."

She unfastened the buttons on his shirt. "That's your f ther's title, right? Even without Max in the picture, you'd on get that when he passes away."

"True, but—"

She slid her hands across his bare chest, clearly distracti him. His skin was warm, but she knew she could make it h "So now we're knocking off three people. Too complicate What else?"

"My second cousin's the Viscount Carlton."

"That's pretty hot."

"Is it?"

"If you're into that kind of thing." She shoved his shi down his arms, then dropped it on the floor. "What about yo Without us committing patricide or fratricide or...whatev killing a cousin might be."

"Very formally I'd be the Honorable Trevor Banfield, b I have no actual title."

She unbuttoned his pants. His erection pulsed against h hand. "What a shame. I'd like you so much more if you di

He closed his eyes as she stroked him. "You lie."

"See what a good vigilante I am?"

She backed him to the sofa and let go of him long enoug to strip off her clothes. Naked, she straddled him, rubbing he self against his hardness, enjoying the building of tension, th desire that slammed her body and soul.

He braced his hands on her hips, encouraging her to roc with him. "The best I've ever seen."

Protection was essential before their hunger climbe beyond the point they could think. Before they became one

Still...for the moment, she liked the teasing.

"Titles are kind of boring," she said.

He cupped the back of her head and angled her face for is kiss. "I so agree," he said hungrily before he captured her nouth.

He tangled his tongue with hers. The potency of his warm, amiliar sandalwood scent, and the obvious need to be with er, have her, left her trying desperately to catch her breath.

"I was thinking we'd play master and maid," she said gainst his lips.

"You sure you don't want to be the duchess?"

"Hell, no. Besides, I already have a French maid's cos-ume."

"Do you?" He tongued his way down her throat. "Make it n English maid, and you've got a deal."

She halted her teased rubbing, planting her hands against is shoulders as she leaned back. "You want to be diplomatic ow?"

"I have to be loyal to the motherland."

"Uh-huh." She climbed off his lap and rose. "I'll get my tuff together, go home and sew a tiny little British flag to my ostume." Glancing over her shoulder, she wiggled her bare utt and pointed at him. "You wait right there till I get back."

She'd barely taken another step before she heard him charg-ag after her.

"Have pity, milady," he rasped in her ear as he lifted her ff her feet and carried her to his bed.

roject Robin Hood, Day 22
)ffice of Maxwell Banfield Inc.

TELL ME ABOUT FIRST RATE Investments," Trevor asked his rother on Monday morning.

"It was a business I owned for a while. Things didn't work ut."

Typical Max. Nothing concerned him except his own neck.

Was he oblivious even now to the grave jeopardy he was i
Did he have any instinct about how far apart they'd grown i
the last few days?

Trevor glanced around the office. It communicated conf
dence and prosperity but seemed overdone. Trevor had alway
noticed something was wrong. Because Max had poor tas
or because there was something truly wrong?

"Mind if I sit?" Trevor asked him casually.

Deliberately insulting, Max glanced at his watch. "I hav
a meeting in twenty minutes."

Trevor held on to his temper just barely. He thought of
Shelby, of how much she meant to him. Of how desperatel
he wanted this whole disaster over with, so he could concer
trate on her. On them.

In between her catering jobs, he and Shelby had spent th
weekend in bed. Again.

He was starting to see a pattern form, and he liked the pi
ture.

"This won't take long," Trevor said, lowering himself int
the chair in front of Max's desk. He and Shelby had come u
with a strategy, and he hoped to hell it worked. "One of you
former clients came to me and said you swindled her and he
husband out of their retirement savings."

Max's casual pose and expression disappeared. "Who
When?"

"It hardly matters. Did you?"

"Did I what?"

"Swindle them."

"Of course not." Max clenched his hands together. "How
could you ask me something like that? I connect people wit
good deals, but not every investment works out."

"Invest in what?"

"For retirees I generally recommend CDs."

"CDs are pretty secure." *Unless there are no CDs.*

"Who are these people?"

"The Rosenburgs. Nice couple. Even nicer apartment on ark."

"I remember them," Max said, nodding sagely, though revor caught the whiff of another false note. His brother ad no memory of taking their hard-earned money. "Shame he project didn't pan out."

"How did the…" Trevor bit back the word *scheme* "…projct fall apart?"

Lurching to his feet, Max shrugged. "I don't really rememer."

"Think."

Max's gaze darted to Trevor. His tone had burst his brothr's self-indulgent bubble.

"You have to reimburse your clients."

"No, I don't. I told them there are risks with any investment."

"But you didn't invest the money."

"I gave it to a friend to invest."

The accusation had been a guess. One he was disheartened o have confirmed. "What friend?"

"A—a stockbroker." Max's face flushed—either from anger r embarrassment. Or guilt. "He's the one who said he was uying CDs. Get the money from him."

Trevor didn't believe him. Seeing his brother through helby's eyes had changed him. There was no friend. He'd never intended to invest the money.

And yet, whether it was old habits or protective instincts, revor couldn't resist giving Max one last opportunity to save imself. A window to crack and reap the benefits of having owerful family backing. "Your friend skipped town with the money. It's your responsibility to compensate the clients who rusted you with their savings."

"All my funds are tied up in other projects."

"Sell the hotel and get the money."

Max laughed. "You're not serious."

Trevor stood. "I am."

"I've done nothing wrong. Is there anything else? I hav business to see to."

Trevor wished his conscience would clear. He'd given Ma every benefit he could think of, only to have his offers re jected. Yet his brother couldn't possibly know the extent o forces moving against him.

For that, Trevor was sorry.

"You're making a mistake," he said quietly as he turne and left the office.

"EAT THIS. YOU'LL FEEL better."

Trevor stared at the huge cupcake with pink icing Shelb offered and shook his head. "I don't see how." But the dam thing was so silly—and it was Shelby offering it, after all, s he bit into the treat anyway. "You knew it wouldn't go well.

"It didn't go well?" Calla asked gently.

He'd come to Shelby's catering space as promised afte the meeting with Max. He hadn't expected to find her friend Calla and Victoria there, too, but he should have. The whol gang was officially gathered together.

Even though he was wild for Shelby, he could see how an number of men would be distracted by her mates—serious but glamorous Victoria and ethereal blonde Calla, whos name, as well as the frothy cupcake, suited her kind tone o voice.

"He laughed at me," he admitted to the ladies.

"Damn." Victoria reached for her purse. "Shel, I owe yo twenty."

Seeing Trevor's confusion, Calla explained, "Victoria be Shelby that Max would beg you to save him."

"And Shelby bet on laughter?" he asked.

"Yep." Calla shook her head, either at the entire mess or possibly at Shelby's inexplicable prognosticating skills. "I ought he'd go crying to Mama."

"You know him well," Trevor said, his gaze locking on helby's.

She rubbed his shoulder. "I'm sorry."

As he sat on the stool next to the kitchen's center island, e pulled her between his legs and wrapped his arms around er waist. He hadn't realized how much he needed her understanding until now. "He was a complete ass."

"I was afraid of that."

He tried to smile. "Not *I told you so?*"

"Not this time." She stroked his cheek. "You had to try."

He captured her hand, kissing her palm. He wanted to hold er, taste her, lose himself in her touch, but knew indulgence as a luxury. His needs would have to wait.

"How sweet," Victoria commented, clearly impatient.

Calla sighed. "Isn't it just?"

"I have a one o'clock meeting," Victoria said. "Could you uys make out later?"

Trevor aimed a genuine smile at Shelby. "Absolutely. What's our next step, Ms. Hood?"

"Cute." Shelby squeezed his hand before she stepped back nd faced her friends. "We set a trap."

"That didn't work out so well at the investors' meeting," alla said, her gaze darting to Trevor.

"So we plan better this time," Shelby said.

"A better disguise might be a good first step," Victoria ointed out.

"And we do it together," Calla insisted. "Last time you went lone. This time, we're together, whatever the plan."

"Maybe," Shelby hedged. "We'll have to see how things ork out."

"We broke into—"

Shelby waved Victoria off before she could finish her sentence.

"I'm part of the gang now, right?" Trevor asked. "Don't get to learn the secret handshake?"

Victoria poured more coffee into her mug, then refreshed everyone else's cups. "I was going to say we broke into Max's office together."

"And got caught," Shelby reminded her.

"There's a trend of us getting caught," Calla said, looking worried. "Maybe we should leave this to the police."

Victoria pursed her lips. "What a shame, especially since we were going to appoint you detective liaison."

"What's that—" Calla stopped and narrowed her eyes. "You're teasing me cause I have the hots for Devin."

"Do you?" Victoria asked, clearly delighted. "I had no—" She stopped her taunting after a sharp look from Shelby. "We can't stop now. We're finally getting somewhere."

"They're right, Shelby," Trevor said. "You started this together. You have to let them—and me—help."

"I will. I am," she added with more force. "But you also need to understand what you're risking. What if the unpredictable Detective Antonio decides to arrest us all for interference or whatever?"

"That would be obstruction of justice," Calla said, scowling. "Very difficult to prove, especially since we're helping justice."

Victoria sipped her coffee. "Bottom line? We need new evidence to bring to the police, something that will force them to step up their investigation."

"Where are we gonna get that?" Calla asked. "We've talked to everybody we can find that Max swindled."

"What about this new condo thing? That can't be legit." Victoria looked to Trevor for confirmation.

"Based on Max's recent track record, I'd say he's not being

ompletely honest with his investors." He paused. He had to
hift his thinking. Instead of protecting him, he had to reflect
n ways to prosecute his brother. It was a disturbing, if nec-
ssary, change. "At best he's using the new investors' money
) fund the condos. There's no way he has the capital to start
onstruction on his own. At worst, he has no intention of
uilding anything."

Clearly frustrated, Shelby shook her head. "So we wait for
im to cash the checks of new victims, wait some more to see
vhether or not he builds the condos, then drag everybody to
ie cops' front door?"

Calla lifted her finger. "Ah, sorry, but that doesn't sound
ke a well thought-out plan."

"Are we capable of coming up with a better plan over
offee and cupcakes?" Victoria asked.

Shelby frowned. "What's wrong with my cupcakes?"

"They're delicious," Calla said. "I think Victoria was won-
ering if we should have a more serious venue. And more time
) consider all the options."

Shelby planted her hands on her hips. "You think we're
onna come up with a brilliant plan if we go to a boardroom?"

"Maybe it would help if we gathered in Sherwood Forest,"
Victoria returned.

"Ladies," Trevor began as he stood. Diving into the fray
etween three women was no doubt a homicidal endeavor, and
e dearly wished he had the NYPD and their sharpshooters
s backup, but with tempers and frustration running high, he
vas hoping to head off a major disagreement. "Between the
our of us, our brilliant minds, research expertise, plus a bit
f cunning and guile, I think we can find a way to fool Max."

"Oh, wow." Calla blinked. "He is good."

Victoria's icy eyes gleamed. "Are you sure you don't have
brother I can seduce?"

In addition to being into Shelby, he was utterly charmed

by her friends. Despite his family's track record with relationships, he felt oddly at home. "I do, in fact, have a brothe Unfortunately, he's the guy we're trying to send to prison."

Silence permeated the kitchen. Even the fan in the convec tion oven, cooking the next batch of cupcakes, seemed to sto rotating.

Then the ladies started laughing. Calla broke first, and th others followed. They hugged each other, and he stood apar yet he felt privileged to be present at all.

Smiling, he leaned against the counter. "If anybody interested…you might want to know Max is likely using swi dled funds to keep the hotel running. Maybe there's an angl we can use there.

"I promise I'll help you. We're going to find a way t punish Max and get back the money." He approached ther so he could link hands with Shelby. "You're not alone any more."

12

"MY FRIENDS LIKE YOU," Shelby said, pressing her lips to Trevor's bare shoulder.

He dragged his mouth across her jaw. "I like them."

They lay side by side, replete from sex and still tangled together as if touching each other might be banned in the next hour.

The warmth of his body, the scent of his skin, enveloped her in desire and comfort. The conflicts and problems they were facing seemed a distant concern, even inconsequential.

She glided her hand across his chest, and his muscles twitched in response.

"I like you better, though," he said, slipping his arm around her to pull her against him.

She linked her arms around his neck as his mouth found hers. His tongue moved past her lips, and arousal flowed down her back, tingling all the way to her toes.

When they parted, she trailed kisses down his throat. "You like touching me."

He moved his hands down to cup her backside. "Every chance I get."

"I don't mean only now. Whenever we're together."

"You're very touchable."

"It's more than that."

His eyes looked starkly blue against the white sheets an his glossy black hair. "My father is restrained. I promise myself a long time ago I'd be different."

"Your father stamps out passion."

"He's not vindictive, just extremely proper. Are you tryin to kill the mood?"

"I'm trying to find out things about you."

"Like what?"

"Anything. Everything. I can predict Max's moves easie than I can yours."

"I would hope I'm a bit more complex than him."

She smiled. "Good point. So your dad's restrained, whic I'd pretty well guessed. What's your mom like?"

"Not restrained." He trailed his finger along Shelby's thig "She's like you—she says what she thinks."

"Does she? How did she get the attention of a restraine English earl?"

"By being blond and buxom. This is a very odd conversa tion to have naked."

"You want to get dressed?"

"No."

"So I guess you have your dad's coloring."

"Most of the Banfield men have dark hair, if that's wha you mean. Max is the odd mix."

"In more ways than his appearance." She slid her finger through Trevor's hair. Its silky texture sent a flare of nee deep inside her belly. "Is your dad as good-looking as you?"

"He's an uppity Brit who bedded and married a wild, spon taneous, stunning buxom blonde. He's got some game."

"Do you guys get along?"

"As long as I do what he says."

Playfully, she poked his shoulder. "Come on. You can d better than that."

"We have a decent relationship, though we had some rough mes when I was a teenager and resentful of Max the Would-e Perfect Heir. Like every father and son, I expect. He'd ither I wasn't an expat, and we're not especially close, but I now he's proud of my success. And he's glad I don't gamble his private London club, then fail to pay off my debts."

The whole deal still sounded cold to her, but not every imily was as boisterous as the Southerners she grew up round. "What about you and Max? Do you get along?"

"Now I'm getting dressed."

Trevor rolled out of bed. Shelby only got a brief glimpse f his leanly muscled body before he stepped into his pants nd fastened them. Tucking the sheet around her, she bent her lbow and propped her head on her hand.

She couldn't restrain a grin. They shouldn't make sense ogether, but they did. At least in the moment. Damned if he idn't make her crazy happy.

"You have to get dressed, too."

She scowled.

He extended his hand. "Come make dessert."

Reluctantly, she did as he asked, though wearing his rum-led white shirt still carrying his scent, changed her attitude.

In the kitchen, she found peaches, eggs, marsala wine and ugar, which she made into a simple Italian dessert.

Trevor licked the first bite off his spoon and moaned. That's incredible."

She pressed her lips briefly to his before digging into her wn cup. "It's called a zabaglione. Be sure you don't say that nstead of my name the next time we're in the throes of pas-ion."

"It's not quite that good." He linked their hands. "Let's go p to the terrace."

Once they'd ascended the stairs, Shelby noticed an addition

among the abundance of bushes, trees and flowers. "Whe did that come from?"

"I bought it today," he said, leading her to the chai longue. "Homey, don't you think?"

She smiled wryly. "I do. Just one?"

"Ah, that's the best part." He reclined in the chair, the guided her down to lay back between his stretched-out leg

As they finished their desserts, his warmth surrounded h like the blossoms on the plants. The vibrant, chaotic city la below, but that was beyond the balcony walls. Inside tho walls, they were cocooned in their own private world.

"Which one should go downstairs?" he asked, setting the empty glasses aside and tucking his arms around her.

Remembering how she'd said he needed plants in the apar ment, a different kind of coziness enveloped her. "A couple the trees, plus some pansies. They'll get plenty of sun in fro of the windows around the dining room."

"You've given this some thought."

"My mom's into gardening. I think the instincts are geneti Do you not want to talk about Max?"

Against her stomach, his hands tensed. "We'll have to eve tually, I guess."

"Would you rather separate your lover from your brother adversary?"

"Yes, but I don't see how."

Since Shelby had tried, and failed, she could heartily agre

"Besides," Trevor continued. "I'm a coconspirator."

"Because of me."

"No." Kissing the top of her head, he squeezed her. "We partly. I do want to help your parents, but I want to get rest tution for everybody else Max swindled, as well. It's my dut to—"

"This isn't only about duty." She turned so she could se his face. Barely lit by the city's glow, he still took her breat

vay. Maybe all the more because this mess mattered so much
him. "You want to help because you're worried about ev-
ybody involved, not just my parents."

"Sure I am. What he's done to them is wrong."

"But here's where we're different. I'm doing this for my
mily. If it wasn't for them, I'd be off making pasta and
uces and letting the cops do their job. You're here because
u see a wrong that should be righted."

"I'm here because my brother is causing all the problems."

She turned on her side, laying her head against his bare
est. "But not only problems for me."

"Not only," he agreed.

"You're very noble."

He chuckled.

"You think the earl would approve?"

"In theory. He'd be happy if my nobility kept his name out
f the gossip columns, but since it's his heir who's due to be
cked by the cops, he's going to fight us with his last breath."

The full extent of what Trevor was risking suddenly
ecame clear. Would he lose his father's respect as well as
is brother? "He'd side with an unscrupulous swindler over
u?"

"Max is the heir."

Such resignation. Yet Shelby couldn't imagine the man who
red Trevor would set aside the law and all his principles to
rotect a son who cheated people to cover his own mistakes.
he wasn't exactly up on British law, but surely he could dis-
herit Max if he went to jail.

"I choose to hold out hope for the best." She traced her
nger across his skin, though she had the feeling she and the
arl wouldn't get along, should they ever meet. "You're hurt
y Max's betrayal."

"Yes."

His pain, encapsulated in one word echoed through h
"You tried to help him."

"I thought I did. Now, I'm questioning everything. Mayb
should have let him fail years ago. Maybe I'm the reason he
come to this."

"You're not."

"If I'd stopped him sooner, he wouldn't have had the mea
to swindle your parents."

She'd sensed Trevor's guilt long before now, and she wante
that particular obstacle gone. She shifted to stare at him. "M
made his own choices."

"So you've said. But he's going to cheat at least one of tho
people we saw at the condo investors' meeting."

"We'll contact them. Get them to help us. Or we'll talk
employees at the hotel and see what they know."

"That's too many people who could tell Max we're askir
questions. If we're going to contact potential investor
shouldn't we be warning them?"

With regret, Shelby shook her head. "This is where yo
and I are gonna part ways on justice. What we need is fres
evidence. Like Victoria said. Something to take to Detectiv
Antonio and say *here's what happened last week*."

"And sacrifice other families?"

"What else can we do?"

He stroked her cheek, then kissed her tenderly. "We ca
enjoy the terrace."

Max was set aside—a neat, but necessary solution.

For now.

Eventually, they'd have to resolve the matter before movin
forward.

Trevor tightened his hold around her waist and pulled he
on top of him. "You can also tell me how good-looking I am

"Can I?"

He chuckled, then pressed his lips to the pulse point beneath her ear. "Please."

She understood he was asking for more than compliments. He needed a distraction. "I was sandbagging." She let her legs fall on either side of his thighs. "You're breathtakingly gorgeous."

"No kidding?"

"Uh-huh. And when you smile, I get all tingly."

"Remind me to smile a lot."

Since she wore only his shirt, and he wore only his pants, it took minimal effort to lift, unbutton, roll on protection and have them both sighing in pleasure.

As Shelby rocked against him, she closed her eyes, wanting to vividly experience every stroke, every gasp.

His breath was hot on her skin; the night air was cool on her back.

When his tongue flicked against her hardened nipple, she fought to find her breath.

But she didn't succeed.

He overwhelmed her—in a good way. He challenged and intrigued her. And she wanted him like no other.

At times, when their eyes met, she could hardly believe his was the face she saw.

She stewed, baked and grilled. She whipped and stirred. She served.

She didn't lose herself.

Except now. Except with him.

Bracing the heels of her hands against his shoulders, she rolled forward, then back with her hips. He surged deeper inside her and shoved down the shirt she was wearing.

As his lips caressed her breast, she let her head fall back. She wrapped her arms around his head and held him closer still.

Tucked against each other, nothing could come between them.

He moved but still held her, never separating, as he hook-
her legs around his hips, then hovered over her for a mome
before sinking his body between her thighs.

She gasped as she encountered the bracing impact of th
chair beneath her, the intense pleasure of him filling her. Sh
saw the green of the plants, the midnight sparkling sky ar
the intense blue of his eyes.

His hands cupped her breasts; his mouth devoured her ski
She felt his tongue against her throat. His teeth nipped h-
earlobe.

The fire and beauty of what they were doing washed ov-
her as she hit her peak. She jolted. Her body pulsed in tin
with his. She felt his breath against her cheek.

She was falling in love with him.

His touch, his words and his heart.

Lying with him, she couldn't imagine anything separatir
them. But Max was there, in a way. And if she ruined Ma
would that destroy everything else? No matter what Trevo
felt now, how he wanted to make everything right, how mud
he desired her, she knew the possibility lurked.

Was she willing to risk Trevor for revenge?

"GOOD MORNING, CHAMBERS," Trevor said into the phone. "
my father available?"

"No, sir."

Though it was 6:00 a.m. New York time, it was eleven i
London. Time enough for the earl to have had his breakfas
make calls, address correspondence, but not late enough f-
lunch.

I left a beautiful woman sleeping in my bed for this?

Trevor made an effort to keep the impatience out of hi
voice. "Thanks, Chambers. I'll call his cell."

"I'm sorry, sir. It's unlikely you'll be able to reach him. He
in flight."

"To where?"

"To New York," the house manager said calmly, not realizing the bombshell he'd dropped.

"He's coming here?" Trevor said woodenly.

"Yes, sir. I thought you were aware. He went to New York his morning. He should be there sometime this evening."

"How...interesting." Trevor's grip tightened on the receiver. Thank you, Chambers."

"Good day, sir."

As Trevor disconnected, he heard shuffling behind him. He turned to see Shelby heading toward him. As seemed to be her wardrobe preference of late, she wore only his shirt, her fiery hair was mussed and she'd never looked more beautiful.

Lazily, she wrapped her arms around his waist and tucked her head beneath his chin. "If you ever have the urge to call me before the sun comes up, resist."

The tightness in his stomach over his father's impending visit eased. "The last thing this city needs is a cranky, sleep-deprived caterer."

"A little coffee will help—especially since sleeping with you doesn't lead to much rest—but I think I can manage breakfast."

"Don't you want to know who I was talking to?"

"Do you want me to know?"

He wanted to share everything with her. Though they'd only known each other a few weeks, she'd become an essential part of his life. If they could get through this ordeal with Max, maybe they'd have a chance. "How do you feel about having dinner with an earl?"

She jerked her head up. "You know another earl besides your father?"

"I do, actually. But my father's the one who will be coming to dinner. Expecting to surprise me."

In a purely feminine gesture, she tucked her tangled hair behind her ears. "When did you find that out?"

"Two minutes ago."

"Okay. Is he going to yell at you?"

He nearly laughed at the mental picture of His Lordship, Earl of Westmore, in a screaming match. "No."

"But he's pissed about something."

"Undoubtedly."

"Max?"

"That's a safe bet."

"So we probably shouldn't tell him about Project Robin Hood."

Her calm acceptance dispelled his nerves. If anyone was used to his father's cold temper, it was him. He'd protected and defended Max at the earl's direction, he could hardly be blamed for this awful business now. His conscience reminded him often enough of the missteps over the last few years.

"Probably not," Trevor agreed.

She let go of him and shuffled to the kitchen, where she stuck her head into the fridge. "How do you feel about eggs?"

"I know I can make them." He took the carton from her hand. "You don't have to wait on me."

She took the carton back. "I like feeding people. You, in particular. It's a compulsion."

Before he could so much as blink, she was cracking eggs and whipping them together in a bowl. "I thought your father was all about manners and social etiquette."

"He is. When it suits him."

"So showing up uninvited doesn't violate some highbrow rule?"

"Probably."

"When will he be here?"

"A few hours."

She poured the eggs into a pan on the stove. "Where do

ou want to go? I may need to meet you there, depending on ow my prep work goes today."

"I expect our conversation will be personal. How about if pick something up, and we eat here?"

"Take-out food?" she asked in horror. "Are you trying to nsult me?"

"My father pops into town without notice. I don't expect ou to cook for him."

"But you want me to meet him?"

It was a bit early for a meet-the-parents date, he guessed. But everything about this relationship was different from all he others. Plus, he had to admit a certain curiosity for how is father and lover would take to each other. "I'm going to ave to tell him about Max—all of the evidence against him. 'd like you to be with me when I do."

"I'll be there, and I'd like to cook. He'll be less cranky if e's full."

"What a dreamer you are." He scooped the eggs onto two lates, then handed her one, while he leaned next to the coun- er beside her. "Okay, then. But I'm buying all the ingredients, nd you're not serving us."

"Deal." She devoured her eggs. "I could use a kitchen as- istant."

"There are quite a few things I can accomplish in the kitchen." He polished off his breakfast. Taking her empty late, he set it aside and moved between her legs, which she vrapped around him. "Should I demonstrate?"

She smiled. "Mmm. That would be nice." But when he noved in to kiss her, she planted her finger on his chest and eld him back. "However, since now I have a dinner to prep s well as my regular work, romance is going to have to wait."

He trailed his fingertip across her cheek. "Anticipation can e good."

"After we get rid of Pops, I'm all yours."

He winced. "You're not really going to call him Pops, a you?"

"Nervous, maybe?" She scooted off the counter. "Can borrow your shower?"

"Depends. Can I join you?"

"Multitasking. I like it." She snagged his hand as the strolled toward the bedroom. "What would Max do if h thought his shaky operation was collapsing?"

"What do you think he'd do?"

"He'd run."

"Yes, I think he would. We need to be careful about how we approach him and the people around him. I believe I mad that point last night."

"We're watching him, but keeping a low profile. Which dirty, low-down operation is the most vulnerable?"

"You're so adorable." He pressed his lips to hers. "I thin the hotel's in trouble, and the condo investment is obviousl his next target, but—" He stopped, as something she'd sai sank in. "You're watching him? How?"

"We trade off. Victoria and Calla have been bearing th load over the last few days while I've been…busy with you. She let go of him and moved quickly toward the bathroom door. "I really should get in the shower."

When he caught up to her, he wrapped his fingers aroun her wrist. "How are you watching him?"

"The usual way—by following him everywhere he goes.'

13

"IT'S ABOUT TIME YOU GOT here," Victoria said as Shelby
climbed into her friend's Mercedes. "Max is coming out any
minute."

"Sorry. My prep work took longer than I thought. How do
you know Max is coming out?"

"I gave one of the valets twenty bucks to text me when he
was on his way."

"With the budget of this operation rising like a geyser,
we're gonna have to squeeze that putz's wallet until he bleeds
to recoup our losses."

"Here, here."

"As if things weren't complicated enough, Trevor's father
is coming to New York."

Victoria stared at her in disbelief. "When?"

Shelby glanced at her watch. "Anytime now."

"He just decided to fly over an ocean to chat?"

"Apparently."

"The timing can't be a coincidence."

"No, I'm sure it isn't. I expect he's come to complain to
Trevor about how he's handling Max. Or maybe his viscount
cousin has landed himself in a scandal they expect Trevor to

clean up. Or maybe he's decided to actually appreciate t non-criminal son he has."

"Wow. Who curdled your cream this morning?"

Shelby grinned. "Actually I had sex and eggs for brea fast."

"At the same time?"

"Consecutively." She poked her friend's leg. "You shou try it, then you wouldn't be getting those scowl lines arour your mouth."

Victoria flipped down the visor and stared into the mirro "What—" She shifted her glare to Shelby. "That wasn't nice

"Sorry, I'm a little punchy. I didn't get much sleep." Sh smiled broadly. "You know, more se—"

"Oh, look, there's Max."

Instinctively, Shelby slid down in her seat as she watche the hotel mogul-condo developer climb into a cab in front The Crown Jewel.

Victoria slid out into traffic a couple of cars behind hin and Shelby made a note of the cab's tag number, so they cou be sure they were following the right one.

The cab headed south, so he could be going to his offic the condo site or anywhere between 42nd Street and Lad Liberty.

At a stoplight, Victoria flipped down the mirror again.

"Cut it out," Shelby said. "You're freakin' perfect, a always."

She raised the mirror as the light turned green. "My sp consultant should send you half the tip I'll be giving her whe I go in for a full treatment tomorrow."

"Yeah, sure." How somebody as stunning as Victoria coul have doubts about her appearance, Shelby would never unde stand. "What should I wear tonight?"

"Something besides Trevor's sheets."

"That's really funny."

Victoria shrugged and turned left as Max did the same. It's a reasonable warning, Miss Nympho."

"Jealous?"

"Insanely."

"Seriously. Do I wear jeans? My chef's jacket? Your black Chanel suit?"

"Yes, no, and dream on." Victoria glanced at her. "Relax. He may be an important man, but he's still just a man. Puts his pants on one leg at a time, et cetera."

"I'm not worried about the title thing. But he's Trevor's father. If he hates me, Trevor's going to dump me."

"No, he won't. Trevor's his own man. Cook the father something. You'll feel better."

"I am."

"Pasta?"

"I wish. The earl is apparently a fussy eater. Basic meat and potatoes kind of stuff." Shelby wrinkled her nose. Culinarily repressed people weren't her forte. "I considered making escargot or *cervelles au beurre* just to be bold, but in the end decided on roasted chicken and vegetables."

"*Cervelles au beurre?* Isn't that—"

"Cow brains in butter."

"I don't even want to know where you get those."

Amused, Shelby angled her head. "I've seen you tuck into a prime filet a time or two. What's the difference?"

"Brains are icky."

To hear her posh, sophisticated friend say *icky* was truly funny. Which was probably why her mood didn't take a nose-dive as she realized Max was on his way to his downtown office.

Same old, same old. No clandestine meeting with a loan shark or shady accountant they could document and add to their file of bad deeds.

Victoria pulled to the curb, and they watched Max alight

from the cab in front of the tacky Campbell Building they'
broken into less than two weeks ago.

They were approaching the one-month anniversary of Pro
ect Robin Hood, and they were no closer to getting reveng
on Max than when they started. She experienced a whole ne
respect for the difficulties of Detective Antonio's job.

How much longer could she expect her friends to give u
their time, emotional support and money for the cause? An
was her heart even in it anymore?

Given the space Trevor occupied in her emotions, sh
couldn't cause him pain. And while this whole mess was ce
tainly Max's fault, the doubts about whether or not she coul
go through with her vindictive plot were growing.

"If you need to get back to your chicken, I'll wait," Victo
ria offered, leaning her seat back and pulling her cell phon
from her purse.

Shelby laid her hand over her friend's. "No. Let's go."

Victoria's gaze probed hers. "He could leave here and mee
with one of his potential investors. Didn't you say contactin
one of them was our best option? Don't we need new evidenc
to take to the police?"

"Yes and yes. But right now we need to go get a drin
somewhere."

"It's not five o'clock."

"It will be by the time we get to Marque's. Let's set thi
aside for tonight. Tell me what's going on with you."

Victoria shifted the purring luxury car into gear.

SHELBY RAN PAST TREVOR as he opened his apartment door fo
her. "Sorry I'm late. I tried to do way too much, then I go
caught up with Victoria's concern for her promotion, whic
she completely deserves, but—"

"Hey." He snagged her by the shoulders and pulled he

against him. His blue eyes radiated desire. "I missed you today."

Her heart fluttered.

He was freshly showered, dressed in jeans and a black sweater and smelled like manly heaven.

Victoria had been right to keep her outfit casual. She wore roughly the same thing, though she'd tossed on her chef's jacket to keep from spilling anything on her clothes while she cooked.

He captured her mouth, angling his head to give her a thorough welcome that drove away all thoughts of family, food and frankly anything but the flow of need through her veins.

Unfortunately, when they separated, reality returned.

She cast a glance down the hall. "Is your father here?"

"No." He wrapped his arm around her waist and led her into the living room. "He checked into his hotel a few hours ago, called me to say he was in the city, then informed me he was having tea, contacting a few people, and he'd be arriving at seven."

"Did he say why he was here?"

"No, but we know my brother is on his agenda."

"Yeah." She flopped her head against his shoulder. "I've had a martini. I think I'm loopy."

"Remind me to take advantage of you later."

"That sounds—" She halted as they reached the end of the hall. "Oh, my." Trees, bushes and flowers suffused the living and dining rooms. Not the jungle of the terrace, but an artful setting that fit Trevor exactly. "You've been working hard today."

Embracing her from behind, he placed a lingering kiss on the pulse point beneath her ear. "They add a certain something, don't they?"

Her heart, already committed to him beyond everything sensible, contracted. "It's something, all right."

"How about some coffee?" he asked, letting go as he move into the kitchen.

She was going to need a lot more than coffee, but tha would do for a start. "Sure. Did my supplier send over ever thing for dinner?"

"He did." As she pulled the chicken out of the fridge, Trev ran his hand over her hip. "According to Fred he seemed pret possessive of you."

She swung around to the stove. "Fred in security dow stairs?" When he nodded, she added, "The relationship b tween a caterer and her supplier is sacred."

"As long as all he gives you is carrots and potatoes…"

When she trailed her finger down the center of his chest, h tugged her to him. "You keep me pretty satisfied otherwise

"Do I?"

"Definitely." She kissed his jaw. "But there are miles t go…"

"I know."

Trevor, too, was frustrated with the obstacles that conti ued to bombard them. Along with trying to get past the secre they'd kept from each other and the unexpected speed bum of his father's visit, Max was standing in the damn road.

But no matter Max's mistakes, Trevor couldn't help b struggle with the idea of moving against him and siding wit a woman he'd known only a few weeks.

He was crazy about Shelby. He craved her presence, he touch, her laugh. She was his lover and friend.

Yet how could he reconcile his actions? How could he tur his back on his family loyalty?

As the chicken cooked, he and Shelby shared coffee at th counter. He told her about his day, and the normalcy of hi work helped his mind shift from the turmoil they were goin through. By comparison, the complications of logistics, trans

rring goods from one county, state or country to another,
emed simple.

She shared the silliness of the luncheon she'd catered that
'ternoon, where the client had asked for a vegetarian menu,
nly to have several guests complaining about the lack of
eat.

"Did you tell them their host had requested the menu?" he
sked as the sun descended and the lights of the city flicked
n.

"No way. The client is always right, especially this one,
ho lied through her teeth and said she hadn't requested veg-
arian but instead told everyone that I'd bragged about my
eat produce supplier. I do have one, by the way. But she left
ut the part where she told me several of her guests couldn't
ossibly eat flesh." She rolled her eyes. "Though nobody
emed to have a problem with leather bags or shoes."

The thought of Shelby having to apologize for a mistake
e hadn't made was maddening. "So you took the blame?"

She shrugged. "She's a good client, and I've gotten plenty
f bookings from her friends, too. Rich people are an odd
rowd sometimes, but I need them." Her gaze flicked to his.
No offense."

"None taken."

"I also produced a container of chicken salad that I'd made
or a just-in-case scenario, and three of the women liked it so
uch, they ordered several large servings each. In the end, I
ot future business and was able to add to the client's bill by
harging her for something she hadn't ordered but neverthe-
ess saved her party."

"How practical."

"A necessary trait in the food-service business. Especially
hen the household coffers are as modest as mine."

As soon as the words were out of her mouth, she shook her
ead. "Sorry." She set down her coffee mug and crossed to the

oven, presumably to check on dinner. "I seem determined point out our differences tonight."

"I understand practicality. I employ it myself every day.

She opened the oven, releasing the mouthwatering scer of roasting chicken into the air. "Every business owner doe I guess…if they want to be successful."

Her spirit was so strong. Her generosity and jaunty attitue a balm to the problem they found themselves mired in.

He hoped his father didn't ruin the mood with what wa guaranteed to be harsh judgment on how Trevor was mana; ing Max. He'd stopped asking long ago why the younger ha to watch out for the elder. Max was special, after all. The Hei Not to mention Max wasn't capable of managing to plan h daily meals, much less his entire life.

For a few minutes, they'd been talking about their day li a real couple. Could that become the norm? Could they hav a future together?

No easy answers. No simple path.

Weren't the best things in life worth a fight?

"Even my father is practical," he said, rinsing their mu; and placing them in the dishwasher. "Every year aroun Christmas he'd threaten to turn off the heat if my brother an I didn't stop opening the door every five minutes."

"I imagine Westmore Manor isn't known for its insulation

"It was built in 1674. Additions and modernizations ca only do so much."

"I bet." She cocked her head. "Now that I know you so. intimately, I can't imagine you toiling around a bleak ol manor house."

"It's pretty luxurious actually." He gave her a teasing smil "And not even the servants toiled. And Father put a padloc on the door to the dungeon after he heard me threatening t capture the girl next door."

"To play doctor, I'll bet."

"Certainly not." He put on a face of mock insult. "At the me I wanted to be a solicitor. I couldn't wait to practice my oss-examination techniques."

"Uh-huh. How cute was this girl?"

"Quite." He crossed to her, lifting her onto the counter and oving between her legs. "A redhead as I recall."

"Such good taste at so young an age. I don't have to curtsy hen I meet him, do I?"

"My Father? Hell, no." Clearly, he wasn't the only one with ore on his mind than dinner and *how-was-your-day-honey?* onversation. He grasped her wrists, gliding her arms around s neck. So normal. So easy. So right. "Frankly, I can't wait see what the orthodox earl makes of my rebel Yank."

"I hope, for your sake at least, we don't come to blows. He's ing to blame you for the mess with Max, isn't he?"

He decided not to answer her question about blame and rile er too soon. "I hope the same—for his sake."

"Fine, so I'll help you pat his hand, assure him everything's eachy with his Number One Son, then ship him back across e ocean so we can get on with our dastardly plan to ruin lax."

Trevor pulled her closer to hide his wince. *Ruin.* He was lanning to ruin his own brother.

"You smell really good." She nuzzled his neck, scattering is guilt over Max. "Last week, after you told me to get lost, bought your cologne to remind me of you."

His heart skipped a beat. "Did you?"

"It made me feel closer to you. Especially since I thought ou'd never speak to me again, much less touch me."

He tightened his grip around her waist. Her hips bumped s. Physical need rode high, even as everything between them se even higher, preventing them from being truly connected. 'd never have been able to stay away, even if you hadn't ome to me."

"Do you feel like we're standing on the edge of som
thing?" she whispered. "It might be great. It might be a c
saster."

He hadn't been scared of anything or anyone in a lon
long time. But he well remembered the helpless sensation. I
couldn't go back.

She braced her hands on either side of his face. "We'll—

The intercom buzzed. "Mr. Banfield?"

Reluctantly, Trevor let go of Shelby and crossed to tl
speaker. "Yes?"

"Your guest has arrived," Fred said. "He's coming up
elevator two."

"Thank you."

Trevor took a deep breath, then released it. Was he reac
to placate and ultimately lie to the man who'd raised him?
man he loved and respected? All for the greater good?

With a sigh, he headed down the hall. Robin Hood wou
be so proud.

SHELBY BUSIED HERSELF in the kitchen while Trevor answere
the door.

The chicken looked perfect, roasted to a light golde
brown, the vegetables scattered around as if a stylist had a
ranged them for a cookbook photograph. The table was s
with white china, silver and sparkling crystal.

Provided she didn't blab out her plans to ruin the futu
earl, who was, in truth, a creep instead of the respected ge
tleman he should be, she might survive the night.

As she stripped off her chef's jacket, she heard both men
voices in the hall. They sounded so similar, she couldn't te
whose was whose. She supposed she should have expecte
the likeness, and the idea made her feel somehow closer to tl
man who'd sired the man she loved.

But sad at the same time. She and Trevor had a bond, but
ot a likely future.

As father and son rounded the corner into the kitchen, she
inked. The resemblance didn't stop at the way they sounded.
This is how Trevor will look in twenty-five years.

Well, except for the tweed suit.

"Sir, this is Shelby Dixon," Trevor said.

"Good evening, Lord Westmore. How was your flight?"

"Fine. Thank you." He glanced at his son. "I didn't know
ou had company. Perhaps we should schedule our meeting
or the morning."

Trevor slid his arm around Shelby's waist. "I wanted you
 meet Shelby."

The earl's gaze shifted between the two of them. "I see."

Up close, Shelby could see the differences in the two
en beyond age. The earl's mouth was smaller, tighter. His
yes weren't as vibrant as Trevor's, and an air of disapproval
eemed to emanate from him.

"She's an important part of our discussion." He smiled at
er. "And she's a trained chef who offered to make dinner."

"A cook?"

Shelby accepted the earl's appraisal and judgment silently.
he'd been too hasty with the thought that they were going to
e compatible.

"A chef," Trevor corrected, and Shelby heard the sup-
ressed anger in his tone.

It was gonna be a long, damn night. "Why don't you make
ou and your father a drink? He looks like a martini kind of
uy."

The earl's eyes registered surprise.

"I'll throw together a salad," Shelby finished.

Trevor slid his hand up her back, a silent gesture of sup-
ort, then escorted his father into the living room.

"Trevor, it looks like the botanical gardens in here. Do you have a cleaning service?"

Shelby rolled her eyes and headed for the fridge. She hop her supplier had sent the wine she'd ordered. She opened th bottle of premium chardonnay and poured a healthy glas With Trevor's budget, she'd splurged, and the reward in tas and quality was well worth it.

If she and Trevor had been dating six months, if she wasr half out of her mind with worry for her parents, if she wasr hell-bent on vengeance against the great and wonderful he if, in other words, they were a regular couple, maybe they have a chance at a real relationship. Maybe his dad's appea ance wouldn't be so difficult. She wouldn't feel so vulnerab and defensive at the same time.

She chopped salad ingredients and tossed them with fres varieties of lettuce. She set both the salad bowl and her ha full wineglass in the fridge.

She was going to need all her wits about her to get throug dinner.

When she walked into the living room, tension lay as thic as the low-lying clouds outside the windows. A storm wa brewing—both indoors and out.

Both men stood as she entered. Their manners were as er grained as their DNA, after all.

"Would you like a drink?" Trevor asked as he approache her.

"No, thanks." She looked into the clear blue of his eyes ar leaned into his caress across her cheek. "I'm good."

They sat on the sofa with Trevor between his father and he and the earl caught up his son on the news in London and the manor. It was generally a list of names and accomplish ments, hirings and firings, births and deaths, but there wa a moment or two when a twinkle appeared in the earl's eye and the charm that had developed fully in his son was eviden

During dinner, the polite conversation continued. No mention of Max the Swindler or the fact that Trevor was sleeping with a woman considered a mere domestic. The earl was politely complimentary of the food, but since bland roast beef and potatoes were the benchmark, Shelby didn't take offense.

After polishing off a dessert of peach cobbler, which Pops ate every crumb of, the earl pushed back his chair and rose.

"I suppose you're wondering what brought me here so unexpectedly."

Seeming calm, Trevor sipped coffee. But Shelby knew his expressions well. He was bracing himself.

"I assume you're here because of the publicity Max has been getting lately," he said.

"I thought you had the situation here under control, Trevor." The earl's hands, resting at his sides, curled into fists, and the temperature in the room dropped at least twenty degrees. "But obviously I was mistaken about the seriousness with which you regard your family. I'm here because a New York police detective called me to ask if I was aware a woman had filed a complaint against my son for fraud and did I have a comment on those potential charges."

The earl's eyes turned to ice. "Would *you* care to comment, Trevor?"

14

SHELBY SUCKED IN A shocked gulp of air.

She wanted to reach across the table and grab Trevor
hand, but his stoney expression stopped her.

Antonio? What the hell was he doing? Why was he inte
fering again? Supposedly oh-so-busy following her and h
friends in addition to his East River homicide, he must ha
found a vacant spot on his crowded calendar.

The earl opened and closed his hands in silent condemn
tion, as he apparently struggled to gather his temper. "Wh
are these lies about fraud and nonsense? You told me you ha
Max under control, Trevor." He braced his hand on the tab
as he leaned toward his son. "What if this gets out? The ta
loids are ruthless."

Guess he hadn't struggled too hard.

"We have a lot more to worry about than the press, sir
Trevor said stoically. "The suspicion of fraud isn't a lie."

Shelby goggled at Trevor. Why wasn't he defending him
self? He was supposed to keep Max under control? What
joke.

"Max isn't merely overextending himself or investing i
businesses without preparation," Trevor continued. "He's a
tively swindling people."

The earl's face turned stark white. "He's not. He can't be."

Resignation in every line of his body, Trevor rose. "He is."

Shelby remained rooted to her chair. Even with the earl's ¦sty attitude, she knew it couldn't be easy to hear his child ¦as a crook.

"The woman Detective Antonio referred to is one victim," ¦evor explained. "Shelby's parents are another. And there are ¦ore."

The earl glanced at Shelby, then dismissed her just as ¦ickly, and she felt less sorry for him. "How could he have ¦tten himself into anything illegal? I thought you were ¦atching him."

"I can't follow him around every minute," Trevor returned. ¦nd he got himself into this mess. I've tried to help him, tried ¦ counsel him. On your orders, I've bailed him out of debt ¦d scandal. No matter what, he keeps falling."

"Ridiculous." The earl lifted his chin. "He's a Banfield. His ¦oodline is impeccable, his future secure. Obviously you're ¦t doing enough, or things would not have progressed to this ¦vel. Can you talk to the detective? Keep this development ¦iet?"

"This development is an illegal investment scam." Trevor's ¦ne rose in disbelief. "He stole money from decent, hard-¦orking people."

The earl shifted his gaze to Shelby. "According to *your* ¦rents, I suppose. And yet you seem quite close to my other ¦n. How…convenient."

"Convenient?" Rage coursed through Shelby as she surged ¦ her feet. "Look here, buddy, I'm—"

Trevor grabbed her hand, giving it a long squeeze. "Shelby, ¦ease."

Tears clogged the back of her throat as she watched the ¦ruggle in every line of Trevor's body. Love welled up in her, ¦king her breath.

Her revenge wasn't for her alone anymore. It wasn't a fu‐
ous impulse, or an act of desperation. She needed to end Ma‐
schemes for her parents, for the other victims and definite
for Trevor. The blame he bore was misplaced.

She nodded and let go of his hand, though she remaine
standing, anticipating the next blow.

"I have talked to the detective, sir," Trevor said in an ama‐
ingly composed tone. "He's busy doing his job, not givir
press interviews. But that's hardly—"

"While you're distracted with your bedmate, our fami‐
name is fodder for the gossipmongers. Do you know how th
makes me look? Do you understand the ramifications for yo
brother's reputation? Do you care at all for the ancient and r
vered name you were blessed to be born with?" He jabbed h
finger against the dining table. "Fix it."

The muscle along Trevor's jaw pulsed.

Shelby dearly hoped he didn't grind his beautiful teeth
dust.

"I'm doing my best," Trevor managed to say. "You didr
need to come all the way here and reprimand me like a fiv
year-old."

Disbelief radiated from the earl. "Is that what you'v
learned in America, disrespect for your father?"

Okay, that's it.

She didn't want to embarrass Trevor, but she was do‐
being bullied by this pompous, overbearing *gentleman*. Sh
marched around the table and stood nearly toe-to-toe with th
earl. "Why is it Trevor's responsibility to handle Max? He
a grown man. It seems to me that if everybody *stopped* ha‐
dling him, he'd be where he belongs—jail."

The earl's face turned an alarming shade of red. "Th
future Earl of Banfield incarcerated? Young woman, yo
cannot possibly understand the ramifications of that outcome

"Sure I do." Shelby crossed her arms over her chest. "Ever

nily has some relative who stole a car, or went streaking
rough the quad during college or drinks too much and hol-
s at the TV newscasters. For the Dixons it's my crazy uncle
rry, who spends half the day sitting in a lawn chair under
s carport sniffing paint thinner."

Trevor smiled. His father looked horrified.

And Shelby felt much better. "A couple of years in prison
ght do Max a world of good. It would surely be cheaper for
u two. Plus, when he gets out—all freshly rehabilitated—
u can plan a great public relations campaign. Second
ance for Wayward Heir. A friend of mine works for the
st PR firm in the city. She'll fix you up."

Trevor, used to her outspokenness, looked interested by
r spin on the the situation, which made her feel less guilty,
well. Max deserved to pay for his crimes, but he wasn't an
il psychopath. A little time behind bars might be the tough
ve he needed.

By contrast, the earl appeared incapable of speech. Which
as surprising. With a kid like Max, Shelby had figured him
r an expert in hostile communications.

"The press is hardly our biggest concern, sir," Trevor said.
Ie's going to need a good lawyer."

"It won't come to that," the earl insisted.

Good grief. Did delusion run in the family? The man in-
sted Trevor manage Max's life and mistakes, but didn't trust
s judgment?

"Regardless," the earl continued haughtily, "I'm sure Trevor
is the funds to recover the Dixon family's losses."

Trevor's body jerked as if he'd been struck. "You don't
iow Shelby, sir," he said slowly. "Because I'm certain if you
d, you'd greatly regret insulting her integrity."

Shelby didn't flinch from the earl's jibe. He was, after all,
ing exactly what she was—protecting his family. He also
dn't realize just how personally she was taking that quest.

Just as she was determined to bring Max to justice, he'd
doubt do everything in his power to keep her and Trevor ap
once Project Robin Hood's secrets came out.

Still, she wasn't deterred. "And if you knew me really w
you'd know it isn't wise to come between me and somethi
I want."

TREVOR FOUND HER SITTING on the chaise longue, scowling
the trees.

"I'm sorry I spoke to him like that," she said, not soundi
sorry at all.

After her warning to his father, she'd stormed up the sta
to the terrace. He'd let her go, knowing she needed to cool c

Surprisingly, his father hadn't commented on her abru
exit or the confrontation over Max. He'd simply thanked h
for dinner and left for his hotel.

Not sure how much time to give her, and definitely n
wanting to be added to the growing list of Banfields she'd li
to slug, Trevor had cleaned up the dessert plates and cups.

The caffeine and tense conversation had him wired, so
wandered around the living room for a few minutes befc
spotting a particularly pretty pansy. Snapping off the blosso
he'd twirled it between his fingers as he mounted the stai
Just when he thought they'd found some common ground, t
world tilted sideways.

"How many years in prison would I get if I punched ou
cop?" she asked.

"Quite a few, I'd imagine."

"How about English nobility?"

"Would you rather if I'd done more to defend you?"

Her eyes fired as she stared hard at him. "I can fight n
own battles."

"But you don't have to fight them alone, and I'm not tl
enemy." He handed her the pansy blossom. "I come in peace

She brought it to her lips. "Thanks. They're edible, you
know."

He hadn't brought it for her to eat. Maybe he should have
given her more time and space. Or more flowers. Still, beneath
her anger and defensiveness, she was hurting, and he wanted
to be there to comfort her as long as she was down.

He sat on the end of the chaise. "If you glare at the trees
like that the leaves are going to fall off."

"What the devil do you know about horticulture?"

"Obviously less than I do about comforting my girlfriend."

Surprise forced the irritated lines from her forehead. She
raised her eyebrows. "Girlfriend?"

He'd let the word slip, though it was true. But now didn't
seem like the opportune time for that discussion. "Problem?"

"No." With a sigh, she scooted next to him and laid her
head against his shoulder. "I really am sorry I argued with
your father."

"You shouldn't be. You were right. And, he started it."

"Maybe he's still bitter about us kicking his butt at York-
town."

Laughing, he pulled her onto his lap. "I wouldn't entirely
rule that out." He kissed her softly, feeling the tension drain
from her body. Finally, he was getting the hang of comfort.
"We made a good team tonight."

"You controlled your temper better than I did."

"I have more experience."

"Does he think I'm an ill-mannered lout?"

He kissed the underside of her jaw. "If he does, he didn't
say so."

"Did he tell you to dump me?"

"No, and I wouldn't even if he did. I don't take orders from
him."

"Except when it comes to Max."

Irritation rolled over him. He might have been furious—she wasn't right. "Not anymore. I'm on your side, remember▮

She stroked his face with the pansy. "I don't want an▮ body taking sides. Max shouldn't come between you and yo▮ father. And neither should I."

"Don't worry about it."

"But—"

"Max started this, not you."

She searched his gaze, her eyes filled with anxiety and d▮ termination, the same emotions that churned in his stomac▮ "And we're going to finish it?"

"We are." He skimmed his mouth across her cheek. "In t▮ meantime, I know how you can support me."

"Remember you're not alone, either."

"As it happens the kind of comforting I have in mind ▮ best done in pairs."

Project Robin Hood, Day 24
Paddy's Bar

"HAVE YOU LOST YOUR mind?" Calla demanded as she s▮ onto the barstool next to Detective Antonio. "Why'd you c▮ Trevor's father?"

Pausing with a beer bottle halfway to his mouth, the dete▮ tive scowled. "Why are you always bothering me?"

"I live to be annoying. A trait you ought to be famili▮ with."

"What'll ya have?" the burly bartender asked.

Calla noticed most the patrons around her were enjoyi▮ beer or amber-colored liquids. Asking for a diet soda wou▮ probably get her tossed out on her butt, but dear heaven it w▮ barely noon. "I'll have what he's having," she said, flicki▮ her thumb toward Antonio.

"How did you find me?"

She glanced around the rustic, Irish-themed tavern. There ere more cops than shamrocks in the joint. "This place is ross the street from your precinct house. I took a wild guess. hat are you doing in here in the middle of the day?"

"I pulled an all-nighter and just got off shift. Are you my other now?"

"You could use some guidance and discipline," she mut-red, then took a sip of her beer. Grimacing, she set it down. Why did you call Lord Westmore?"

"Hello? You people are the ones butting into my case, doing y surveillance. I figured you'd appreciate me trying to shake ings up. Somebody or something's got to break."

"But we have a plan, and you're going to screw it up. We're ying to be low-key here. If the earl tells Max you called, he's ing to hop out of here like a rabbit with his cottontail on re."

Antonio blinked. "A rabbit with his—" He stopped and ook his head, as if the reference were too ridiculous to an-yze. "Is the earl going to tell Max?"

"No. Trevor met with him this morning and asked him not . Shelby says the earl doesn't believe Max has done anything egal."

"Then what's the big deal?" He took a long swallow of beer. And what plan do you have? You chicks need to stay out of is case and let me do my job."

"Chicks? This isn't a farm. We're women—and best friends esides—and we're gonna do what we have to in order to put at slimeball out of commission."

Antonio leaned toward her. Their faces were bare inches art. She could see golden flecks in his deep green eyes. What plan?"

The man was the most contentious, aggravating, bossy… xier-than-sin— She stopped her internal tirade and cleared r throat. "We're still considering our options."

"Hell." He polished off his beer and laid some money ⊙ the bar. "See ya, Jimmie," he called to the bartender.

"Where're you going?" she asked. She'd come to scold hi A lot of nerve he had not to even stick around for her censu

"Home. To bed."

A vision of his rumpled dark hair and naked, leanly mu cled body tangled in soft cotton sheets wavered before h⊙ She grabbed the bar to steady herself before calling after hi⊙ "You could help, you know."

He barked out a laugh. "Under your direction."

"Naturally."

"No, thanks."

"Shel, there's a guy named Henry Banfield out here to s⊙ you."

Elbow deep in floured dough, Shelby glanced toward Pe⊙ hovering in the doorway between the front office and t⊙ workroom. "There is?"

"Yep." Pete angled his head. "Trevor's father?"

"Uh-huh."

"Uh-oh."

Shelby put on a brave smile, though her stomach was ra⊙ idly tying itself in knots.

Pete kept the bills paid and answered phones a few da⊙ a week in between classes at NYU. Someday, he'd be a br⊙ liant accountant. She felt fortunate to have his good sense ⊙ the payroll.

"Send him on back."

"I could tell him you're busy."

"No." She headed to the sink to wash her hands. S⊙ couldn't imagine whatever the earl had to say would be e⊙ couraging, but she didn't see how delaying the confrontati⊙ would help. "I'll see him."

"Okay. I'm gonna transfer the phones back here and take f. I've got a world-history midterm tomorrow."

"Yeah, sure. Thanks, Pete."

She heard voices in the front room, then Lord Westmore tered the room.

Dressed in a tailor-made charcoal-gray suit—not tweed— looked more like his son than ever.

Shelby swallowed the lump in her throat as she dried her nds. "Good afternoon, your lordship. What can I do for u?"

His hands clasped behind his back, he wandered around e room, pausing at the stove top. "Chicken soup?" he asked.

"Just chicken," she said, wondering where this was going. as he casing the joint or assessing its value? Either way, she ubted the earl had troubled himself to come to her kitchen chat about culinary endeavors. "I'm making chicken pot- es for a charity luncheon tomorrow."

"Really?" He actually smiled. "I enjoy a good chicken tpie."

"Do you?"

"Though I'm especially partial to roasted beef."

"Trevor mentioned that."

"He thought the meal was dull. But I like tradition."

"My mom made grilled-cheese sandwiches every Tuesday ght when I was growing up. 'Course, that was probably be- use it was the only thing she knew how to make without rning the house down." She halted the urge to continue mbling. "Were you expecting to find Trevor here?"

"No, I came at this time because I know he's at his office." e stopped on the opposite side of the center island. "You and y son have become quite close recently."

Then again, maybe she'd rather talk about food. "We have."

"You met when you catered a party for Max."

"That's right."

"A party you and your friends used to garner informati⟨
about Max and his allegedly illicit business ventures."

She braced her hands against the counter. *Yes, it starte⟨
with a lie. Thanks for the reminder.* "Do you have a poi⟨
your lordship?"

His gaze met hers. "You're very direct. You remind me ⟨
my former wife. Different coloring, of course, but full of fi⟨
and independence. You know what you want."

"Yes."

"But you're not capricious and unreliable."

"No."

"And right now you want my son?"

Shelby pursed her lips. "It took you quite a while to g⟨
around to that."

His face flushed. "I have difficulties communicating wi⟨
women at times."

"We're all just a little bit different," Shelby said sardon⟨
cally. "It must be frustrating."

"Simply maddening."

"So you came here to find out if I'm using him? For h⟨
rich friends as potential clients or the luxury of sleeping ⟨
his high-rise apartment?"

"Maybe both."

"With his looks and success I imagine he's caught the a⟨
tention of a number of women who're interested in the… Let⟨
call them *benefits* that come with being involved with him⟨

"Yes, he has."

"Did you warn them off, too?"

"Sometimes."

"Sorry, my lord, but, as they say in my neck of the wood⟨
that dog won't hunt here."

Looking resigned, he nodded. "I was afraid of that."

Though she didn't have to like it, she understood his su⟨
picion. A father should safeguard his son—even if he's t⟨

econd, just-in-case one—like a daughter should honor her
arents. They were alike in more ways than either of them
ranted to admit. "As much as I long to tell you that my rela-
onship with Trevor is none of your damn business, I'm aware
our intent is to protect him."

"He cares for you very much."

"I feel the same. He's already offered me money for my
arents. I won't take it."

"Not yet."

She shook her head. "Not ever."

After holding her gaze a long moment, he again nodded.
I believe you." He paced the length of the island, then back.
And I misjudged you." He shrugged. "It happens, though I
ke to think not often. There was my wife…" He trailed off.
But then I have Max and Trevor, so I can hardly call the re-
ationship a mistake.

"I was young and impulsive—hard as that may be to be-
eve now."

"It is."

"Perhaps I learned from my mistakes. Or lost my nerve.
But family obligations, and the title, require a decorum Trevor
sn't burdened with. He has more freedoms. I imagine that's
vhy he chose to live in America. As a result he's done more
vith less."

"You might try telling him this. He needs to hear it."

"Yes, well, we need to get through this Max business. Do
ou really think he deserves to go to jail?"

"At the very least."

The earl sighed. "Bloody Americans, bent on retribution."

"You *are* still pissed about us kicking your butt at York-
own."

He chuckled, and the humor made her ache for Trevor all
he more. She was crazy about that smile, and the events of the
ext few days were likely to determine how often she might

get to see it in the future. "Are you aware my ancestor led th attack?" he asked.

"And got his butt kicked."

He inclined his head, the elegance of the gesture certainl genetic as she'd seen her lover do the same thing many time "I hope you make him happy."

"Me, too."

"Do you love him?"

"Yes."

She'd answered instinctively, probably rashly, but sh couldn't regret the truth. There were too many deception slights and injustices already.

"Have you told him?"

"No."

"Don't wait. Trevor deserves to be happy, and I think yo do that very well."

She thought so—for now anyway. The lies and the plot were incredible obstacles to overcome however. When th business with Max was over, would she always be a reminde of his brother's downfall? And what if they didn't get enoug evidence to have him arrested? Would she grow to resen Trevor?

"As long as we're sharing confidences," the earl added, should admit there are times I wish Trevor could have bee my firstborn and heir. If the birth order had simply been re versed."

Wishing for something impossible to change seemed like giant waste of time to Shelby. "Why does birth order matter?

"It does" was all he said.

But if Max went to jail, couldn't he be disinherited? Sh didn't know how that kind of thing worked in the U.K., bu with enough political and legal wrangling, she imagined any thing was possible.

"Trevor would make an excellent earl," Shelby agreed.

As the words escaped her lips, fear surged through her.

What if that happened?

He would have a seat in the House of Important Noble ople, or whatever they called it. He'd have to go back to gland. His wife would be a *countess*.

She wasn't countess material.

And even without the title, he was still British nobility, and e was a caterer. He moved goods back and forth around the rld; she boxed cupcakes and sold them to the neighborhood ffee shops.

She was a fool to think she could hold on to the man she ved so deeply.

The earl crossed to the stove, lifted the stock pot lid and in- led. "You're an excellent cook." He glanced at her over his oulder, and she fought to focus on him instead of the dread thering through her veins like poison. "Sorry. It's *chef,* isn't I expect you can make lemonade quite easily."

"Lemons and sugar."

"I'll leave that to you."

The metaphor between her and Trevor's relationship, king something good and sweet out of something that rted bitter wasn't lost on her.

But it didn't give her the hope the earl undoubtedly in- ded.

"So, during my meeting this morning with Trevor," the rl continued, "after viewing the evidence compiled against ax, it occurred to me that my burden on Trevor has been great. I realized I could assist instead of order or criticize. what exactly goes into making a chicken potpie?"

15

TREVOR WALKED INTO a scene in Shelby's catering kitchen t
caused him to come to a halt in the doorway.

His father was wearing an apron and stirring something
the stove. Calla and Victoria were sitting side by side on
counter. Each had a plastic bowl in their lap and flour on th
hands. Shelby was dipping a ladle into a pitcher that look
remarkably like lemonade.

He blinked at the homey atmosphere. Something was rea
wrong and really right.

Father is wearing an apron.

That was probably the wrong thing.

"You're having a party and didn't invite me?" he ask
entering the room.

"We made lemonade," his father said with a joy on his fa
Trevor had only seen a few times in his life.

Calla toasted him with a V-shaped crystal glass. "A
lemon-drop martinis."

"Chicken-pot pies have been promised," Victoria said
her usual dry tone. "If Henry will get a move on over there.

"Henry?" Trevor managed to echo.

Shelby put down the ladle she was holding and closed
distance between them. "Hey."

Just that quickly, the world narrowed to two. He braced his hands on either side of her waist. "Everything okay?"

"We've had our strange moments."

"Was one of those tying an apron around the lofty Earl of Westmore's waist?"

"Oh, yeah. He got through it."

"And you?"

"I'm great." Though there was a hint of tension in her smile, she moved closer, brushing her lips across his cheek. "Even better now."

"*Aw,* look how cute they are," Calla said.

Shelby grinned. "Calla's had two lemon drops already."

Trevor pulled Shelby tight into his embrace. It was like coming home, only better. His kissed the top of her head. "I can tell."

Desire crawled through his veins as she loosened his tie, sliding it from around his neck and looping it around hers like a scarf. She linked their hands. "Come join us."

He'd thrown himself in with Robin Hood and her compatriots. He supposed it was time for some merriment.

Though there was also hard work—stirring, chopping, kneading, rolling, scooping. With the potpies for Shelby's luncheon stored in the walk-in fridge, the gang was left to make their dinner.

Unable to face a potpie after all the ones they'd slaved over, they formed dumplings from leftover dough and added chicken and vegetables. They poured fresh stock, thickened with flour for the broth. Shelby directed his father on how to bake a loaf of herbed bread, and Trevor opened the wine.

Gathered in folding chairs in the back corner of the kitchen, they feasted. Not even a party in Sherwood Forest could have competed.

"I don't want to ruin the mood," Trevor said, "but we need to talk about Max."

Victoria groaned. "How 'bout I just run over the creep t[
next time I'm following him?"

When the earl's face registered shock, Shelby patted h[
hand. "Sorry, Henry. Victoria's even more direct than I am[

"Quite all right, my dear." The earl offered her a slig[
smile. "Max can't continue hurting people. He has to chang[
his life. The Banfield name is at stake."

Ever since their talk that morning, Trevor was finding h[
father's change of heart a little unnerving. He appreciated t[
earl not warning Max of the forces moving against him, b[
he wasn't sure how to take his father's active involvement [
the Robin Hood project.

The fact that, apparently, it came down to the family rep[
tation shouldn't have been so surprising. It was also entire[
possible the old man was as pissed off at Max as Trevor wa[

Calla frowned into her water glass. "Detective Antonio [
out of patience with us. If we're not careful, we'll be the on[
behind bars."

"I think we're all tired and frustrated," Trevor said. "W[
need to expose Max's crimes and end this."

"We need a better plan than the last time we confront[
Max," Shelby pointed out.

"I've been giving that some thought," Trevor said. "Ho[
about if we're honest?"

Victoria gestured with her fork. "I'd bet my Mercedes Ma[
knows zero about honesty. It's worked pretty well for him [
far."

Trevor sipped his wine. "Well, we won't be telling him e[
erything. Just enough to lure him into our trap."

"Which is?" Shelby asked.

"We're not having any luck contacting anybody from t[
investors' meeting or finding proof of defrauded victim[
Shelby hasn't already documented, so what if we're the fre[

vidence? What if we go with Shelby's original idea and
ecome Max's next mark?"

"We, as in all of us?" Calla asked, glancing around the table
nd looking doubtful.

"We'll plan everything together, but I think we need one
nvestor, and I have the perfect woman in mind."

Everyone fell silent as they all looked to Shelby for her re-
ction.

"I'm fine with being the would-be victim," she said. "I
nink I'd enjoy the end result all the more. But how? Do I pull
ut the blond wig and false eyelashes again?"

Victoria frowned. "I vote no on that part."

"I wasn't thinking of Shelby actually," Trevor explained
uickly before they ran full tilt with costume ideas. "How
bout my administrative assistant?"

"Florence?" the earl and Shelby asked at the same time and
the same disbelieving tone.

Trevor tried not to take their reaction as criticism. "Yes,
lorence. Max was at school when she was my governess, and
nly met her a few times. She recently came out of retirement
work for me, and Max hasn't ever bothered to come to my
ffice here in New York. He won't recognize her, and more
nportantly we can trust her.

"I'll bring her to the next investors' meeting, and we'll say
e has family money she wants to invest in one of the new
ondos. Simple. He'll trust us, because he'd never dream I'd
etray him. I've invested too much effort into bailing him out
f trouble."

Shelby cocked her head in confusion. "Does Florence have
mily money?"

"Does she need the actual cash?" Calla asked. "Why not
st say she does? He gave you a bad check. Let's return the
vor."

"I think the money should be real for this to work," Shelby

said. "If he cashes the check and it clears, won't that be stro[n]ger evidence for the police? A paper trail?"

"Hold on." Trevor scowled at Shelby. "What bad check?"

"Sorry," Calla said, shoving a bite of bread in her mou[th] and looking guilty.

"The check from Max for my catering services at th[e] hotel," Shelby admitted. "It bounced."

Trevor ground his teeth together. "You have to let me—"

"No, I don't." Shelby shook her head. "I knew the ris[k] of him stiffing me going in. It was my decision to go ahe[ad] anyway."

"There's an easy solution to the problem of the money[."] Victoria said, "I've got plenty—"

Shelby waved her off. "No. It's too big of a risk."

"*I'm* giving Florence the money," Trevor said firmly.

Shelby narrowed her eyes. "Oh, no you're not. We're n[ot] using your money, either."

Trevor laid his hand on her thigh, squeezing it lightly [to] calm and reassure her. "She'll be borrowing it to get to Max[."]

"Unless he takes off before we can get him arrested." H[er] expression was mutinous. "And I don't like dragging Floren[ce] into this. I'll be the mark."

"Florence doesn't mind," Trevor insisted. "Trust me, she'[ll] enjoy the adventure."

Shelby seemed on the verge of offering another excus[e] when Calla said, "If you're the mark, Trevor will have to d[e]posit the investment into your bank account."

Shelby's face turned white. "No. He can't."

The earl abruptly covered Shelby's hand with his. "Th[at] isn't what I meant earlier."

She focused on him. "I know."

While Trevor, and presumably the other women, re[]mained confused, his father added, "How about if you u[se] my money?"

"No way." Shelby jerked to her feet, tossing her napkin on : table. "I appreciate everybody's help, I really do, but all you are spending way too much time and energy on this. keep researching and looking for people willing to give tements to the police. There'll be no more surveillance or :ak-ins or any of it. I can do this."

"On your own?" Victoria finished for her.

"That's not fair," Calla said. "We want revenge as much as u do. It's not right what Max is doing."

"You need us," Trevor said, his voice tight with disappoint-nt. Why wouldn't she trust them? Him especially? The ache his heart spread. He loved her, and she was rejecting him.

"Let your friends help, Shelby," the earl said quietly. "They nt to share in the responsibility."

"Shelby, why don't you come to the meeting, too?" Trevor ggested. "You can pose as Florence's daughter or niece, iybe her secretary. You'll be right there to make sure noth-g goes wrong."

Shelby stood rigid, and Trevor fought for the words that uld convince her. *All for one, and one for all?*

Oh, wait. That was *The Three Musketeers.*

Tentatively, Calla raised her hand. "I could use some extra sh. Any of you guys want to deposit a big, heaping pile of n my bank account, I'm cool with that."

Her silly offer broke the tension.

"Okay. Hell." Shelby looked skyward, then dropped into r seat. "We'll do it. It's a good plan." Under the table, she :ed her fingers through Trevor's. "But Max is already sus-:ious of you. You questioned him about his CD investment, d he knows you're watching him. What if he senses the p?"

"He'll take off like a jackrabbit," Calla said.

Victoria drummed her fingers against the table. "We've me too far to risk spooking him now."

"What if I escort Shelby and Florence to the investme
meeting?" the earl offered.

Before Trevor could be little more than shocked by his
ther's offer, he continued. "Naturally, he won't suspect me
trapping him."

"Are you sure you want to be that involved?" Trevor ask
his father.

"Love isn't always easy, son," the earl said, resignation
his eyes. "I want to be there."

"Provided your sudden appearance doesn't scare him
death," Victoria said drily.

"He won't be scared," Trevor said, certain it was true.

Having his powerful father there would make Max bol
than ever. After seeing his brother through Shelby's eyes, he
gained a bit of insight into his character just as she had. M
would puff up like one of the hot-air balloons he was now r
torious for wanting to buy.

Trevor exchanged a meaningful glance with Shelby, w
nodded. "I think it could work."

All for one.

Condos for Sale!
by Peeps Galloway, Gossipmonger
(And proud of it!)

On guard, fellow Manhattanites!

Did you hear one of our beloved avant-garde ar-
tistes in the East Village has gone on to that great Pi-
casso painting in the sky? Yes, I know, let us all shed
a tear into our whiskey sour. (Which is *the* hot drink
of spring, by the by.) He will never be forgotten by all
who cherished his groundbreaking work.

But we all must go on…on to the real-estate section
of this quality publication, as an oh-so-discreet ad for a
new condominium development has been placed. (See

pgs. 9 and 10 for the full-color spread.) Through a delightful real-estate agent named Alice, you, too, can get all the deets on the budding project. And even get in on the ground floor of what's sure to be Manhattan's new IT address!

One scoop you won't get from the lovely Alice, though, is the brainchild behind this development. (You know I know, and you know I'm going to let you know. 'Cause, you know, we're buds.) It's Max Banfield! Imagine our very own, newly crowned hotel mogul and future earl already branching out to other ventures! It makes a shoe diva proud, doesn't it?

Apparently those stories of trouble over at the Crown were greatly exaggerated. Who would start such an unsubstantiated rumor? The nerve of some people.

(For a list of my own sources, please present yourself to 700 Pennsylvania Ave, Wash, D.C., and check out that charming old document under glass called The Constitution. Amendment number one is a doozy.)

Be sure and invite me over for a cocktail when you move into your new lush pad!

—*Peeps*

oject Robin Hood, Day 26
e Crown Jewel, Suite 1634

ᴇʟʙʏ ᴘᴏsɪᴛɪᴏɴᴇᴅ ʜᴇʀsᴇʟꜰ behind Henry and Florence as they de up in the elevator.

"Relax," he said, glancing at her over his shoulder. "It'll be er soon."

She nodded, but her thoughts drifted back to the last time e'd been in this building, when the betrayed look on Trevor's face as he'd confronted her in her ridiculous disguise for⊃ her to admit her plot against Max.

Much had changed; some couldn't be altered.

Deception had dominated her relationship with Trev⊃ How could anything honest and true bloom from that s⊃ beginning? How could chemistry and a bond over a self⊃ crook form the basis of love? How would their differences⊃ upbringing, income and status ever merge?

"Let him come to you," Victoria said, her voice comi⊃ through courtesy of the tiny earpiece Shelby and the oth⊃ wore.

Jerking back to reality, Shelby drew deep breaths as s⊃ watched the elevator's lit numbers advance higher and high⊃

"Don't fidget," Florence whispered, turning to stare at h⊃

She'd probably said the same thing a thousand times⊃ Trevor in church while he was growing up.

Appreciating the confidence in Florence's sturdy fra⊃ and kind brown eyes, Shelby nevertheless shook her hea⊃ "I'm supposed to be the mousy niece who keeps track of ⊃ checkbook. I'll be more convincing if I twitch."

"We need to make a copy of our small film for an awa⊃ committee as well as the police," the secretary said matt⊃ of-factly.

When Shelby frowned, she added, "You're quaking lik⊃ sparrow caught in a hurricane."

Annoyed at herself, Shelby rolled her shoulders, pleas⊃ to discover her spine was still in place. She wasn't afraid⊃ Max nearly as much as what would happen once he was ⊃ of the way, and she and Trevor had to face the unlikely ev⊃ of their relationship continuing.

"The earpiece works quite well," Henry commente⊃ "Maybe I should get one of these systems for Hastings."

"Hastings?" Shelby asked.

"My house manager," the earl said.

Shelby pictured a stern-faced, gray-haired butler in a three ece black suit. She was so out of her league with these ople.

She also had no idea where her friends had gotten the sur illance equipment, complete with an audio bug in Shelby's ng and a mini camera hidden in the arrow-shaped charm ound her neck. Or why they felt such extreme measures re necessary. But she expected they'd enjoyed the intrigue.

At least somebody was having fun.

The triumph and anticipation she should feel wasn't there. nxiety and dread were, however, present in great supply.

"Remember I'm with you," Trevor said, via the same ear one. "You can do this."

Shelby closed her eyes briefly and took a deep breath. hough not near her physically, her lover was manning the cording equipment in a rented hotel suite. Victoria was al ady at the investors' meeting posing as a potential victim. alla was in a rented van outside, prepared to follow Max hen he left.

What could go wrong?

As Henry and Florence strolled into the suite with her shuf ing along behind, she noted everything was set up like the evious gathering, though with a few prosperous additions. ne slide show was now accented by a physical model of the ilding once it was developed into condos. The food table as more opulent and included an ice sculpture in the shape a swan. The room was more crowded, and the attendees ore affluent.

Max had been working hard.

They'd barely crossed the threshold when a waiter offered orence and Henry glasses of champagne. She was ignored.

Perfect. Not only did she have no intention of toasting any ing, Shelby would be most effective if she wasn't memo ble.

Henry urged their trio toward the model encased in a gla display. The prospective condo building was a ten-story tov of glass and stone. Tiny trees and people dotted the sidewall A park, complete with potted flowers, iron benches and pla ground equipment, set off the east end of the property.

"It's perfectly peaceful," she said quietly.

"Appearances can be deceptive, my dear," Henry sai smiling at her.

"It's a facade," Florence added.

"It certainly is," Shelby agreed.

"Your lordship."

Careful to keep her face angled downward, Shelby turn as Henry did toward the man with the worshipful voice. Ma naturally.

Through her large, dark-rimmed glasses, she looked pa her lanky brown bangs and noticed the scumbag's widen eyes as if he'd been presented with a plate of diamonc "Father, you're here."

"I am," Henry said, shaking his son's hand, his tone war but not overdoing it. "I popped into town to see you at Trevor, and he told me about your project. I wanted to s you, naturally, and I thought my friend Florence might be i terested."

Florence shook Max's hand as Henry introduced ther Shelby was pointed out as Florence's *quite efficient* niec Rosemary.

Shelby waited for recognition. She held tight to the leath portfolio she'd brought both as a prop and a place to sto Florence's all-important checkbook. Surely they'd all be d nounced as frauds.

But Max barely glanced at her—all his attention was f his father and his friend.

"She's going to love this development," Max said, all smi and welcome. "Let me show you around."

He dragged them from one end of the room to the other, inducing them—well, mainly the earl—to everyone in sight. elby finally understood the fawning, false as it might be, t Trevor had endured through his life. Grown people, supsedly independent-thinking Americans who elected their ders instead of birthing them, fell over Henry like a prince. vas ridiculous and embarrassing.

She'd been somewhat anxious about meeting the earl. hile her concern had mostly been over meeting the father the man she loved, intimidation over the title had come into y. The fact that he lived in a social and economic structure yond her realm couldn't be ignored. Celebrities were worpped; teachers were underpaid.

Wasn't that what the Robin Hood legend had been all out? The balance of nobility and greed. The divide between ve and have-not. The compulsion to give and take.

And, for her, the desire to resolve injustice.

Through the whole ordeal, Trevor sent encouraging advice ough her earpiece and Victoria kept a distant eye on their gress around the room.

Shelby was wrapped in the embrace of her friends, and e'd never felt so comforted—and so afraid of what would ppen when they let go.

"It's so beautiful," Florence said, gazing with fake rapture the slide show Max provided. "I'd love to live there."

"But you can," Max said, his voice low and coaxing. "A mmitted deposit, and all this can be yours."

Shelby felt Henry's hand press into her back. "A commitd deposit of what?" she asked Max.

"Twenty grand," he said, not looking at her at all but Florce. "That's all I need."

It was considerably less than they thought he'd want and uch more than she wanted to give. But then she wouldn't llingly give the man cab fare.

Which is probably why, after she wrote a check to Maxw
Banfield Incorporated, her hand jerked as if in protest wh
she extended it toward her "aunt" to sign.

"Do it," Calla said in her ear.

"End it," Trevor added.

Shelby handed over the check.

Was she ending one crisis only to have her heart broke
How could she and Trevor take what was begun with lies a
make magic?

She was fresh out of lemonade.

"Do you think he'll cash the check?"

With Shelby's head resting on his chest, her bare thi
slung over his as they snuggled in his bed, the last thing
earth Trevor wanted to do was talk about Max.

"He'd be silly to cash a check that large. The bank has
file a report of any single withdrawal of more than ten tho
sand dollars." He stroked her bare back with the tips of I
fingers. "Still, he'll probably run to the bank in the mornin
even though it's Saturday. The key is where he deposits it. T
money should be held in an escrow account reserved for t
condo construction."

She pressed her lips against his skin. "And you don't thi
he'll do that?"

He closed his eyes and fought to concentrate on the que
tion. "I don't think he can spell escrow."

"You're sure your friend at the bank will call when M
comes in?"

"Yes."

"And if he withdraws the money?"

"Then, too. Stop worrying."

"You're the one who should be worrying. It's your mone

"I'll get it back."

She sighed. "My stomach's in knots. How does Detective tonio do this everyday? I'd go crazy."

"He doesn't have a personal stake in his cases."

"True."

Another kiss to Trevor's chest, and he grinned. He knew needed to talk through her concerns, but damn it was hard.

"He didn't recognize me," she said softly.

His heart jumped. "Antonio? When did you—"

"No, no." She patted his shoulder. "See, I'm not the only who's worried."

He tightened his hold on her. He wasn't troubled, per se. st anxious to end all this intrigue. He had quite a lot to say Shelby, and he wanted her untroubled and happy when he l.

"Max," she continued. "He didn't recognize me as the ca- er from the party. He didn't recognize Florence or suspect own father had turned on him."

"Did you expect him to?"

"I guess not. But we're taking a lot of risks now. If any one int of the plan goes wrong, we'll lose him."

"Then we'll just have to find him again. He'd contact me entually."

She lifted her head, her eyes dark with apprehension. "I n't wait that long. I want this over. I'm tired of it hanging er our heads."

He hugged her and kissed her gently. "Me, too."

When he would have deepened the kiss, she propped her- lf up on her elbow. "Still, this ordeal has had its moments. ou should have seen the expression on Max's face when spotted the earl at that meeting. He looked like he'd been nded the keys to Fort Knox."

"I'm sure."

She gave a faint smile. "How 'bout ole Pops? He handled e scene like a pro."

Trevor couldn't suppress a wince. "You didn't call him th
did you?"

"You're not worried about twenty grand, but you're co
cerned how I address your father?"

He thought about it for ten seconds. "Yes."

"I called him what he asked me to—Henry."

And that was a marvel in itself. "I've never seen him be
charmed by anybody in my life. But then you're pretty cut

"Cute?"

He traced her jawline with his finger. "Stunning. Brav
Wrapping his hand around the back of her neck, he pulled l
close. "Irresistible."

She laid her mouth on his, exploring at first, then increa
ing the intensity. Her lips were sweeter than any dessert ev
conceived, even in her clever mind. He'd never tire of t
scent, feel and taste of her.

She pressed her feminine heat against his erection. I
groaned and fumbled for the condoms in the bedside tabl
drawer, but she snagged his wrist, pining his hands above I
head.

"Let me," she whispered before she proceeded to destr
his self-control with her mouth and body.

Passion flowed from every part of her. Her breath was I
and ragged as she kissed her way down his throat. She glid
her tongue teasingly over his nipples, and he hardened to t
point of near explosion.

When she rolled on the condom, she took her time doi
so.

Meanwhile, he was using every ounce of willpower he ha
But when she lifted her hips and welcomed him inside I
body, the glorious pleasure of it overtook everything.

How was it possible to want somebody so much? To ne
to the point that nothing else existed but her?

They moved together as if born to be joined, and when

maxed, her moans of satisfaction sparked explosions like
e aftershocks of a violent earthquake.

Love deluged him with its wondrous power when she col-
sed on top of him, her heart galloping in time with his own.

So beautiful and perfect.

Nothing could part them.

16

"THE MONEY'S IN HIS personal account."

Trevor made the announcement to the gathered gang
Shelby's kitchen on Saturday morning.

Panic not relief jolted through Shelby. They were one s
closer to meting out justice, and when the ax fell, Trevo
brother would be broken, defeated, forced to repay the sw
dled funds and jailed.

Wasn't that the vision she'd dreamed of for months? Ev
years?

So why was she sick inside? Why wasn't she thrilled?

"Hot damn," Victoria said from her perch on the counte

"What's next?" Calla asked, her tone excited.

No one seemed to notice Shelby was on the verge of te:
or that she'd clutched her hands together to keep them fr
shaking.

"We go to Detective Antonio and tell him everything
Trevor said. "The personal deposit is enough to bring Max
for questioning. Added to everything else, probably an arres

"Probably?" Shelby jumped on the word.

He frowned, whether because he sensed her tension or fr
her abrupt tone, she wasn't sure. "It's obviously not up to u

d at this point, we need help from the police. They need to
t court orders to freeze Max's accounts."

"I agree with Trevor," Victoria said with a decisive nod.
What if Max decides to take off with the money?"

"Do you agree, sir?" Trevor asked his father.

Looking tired, Henry nodded. "I'm resigned to the idea
at Max has to be stopped from ruining any more lives. I'll
re an attorney for him. Right after I give him the dressing-
wn of his life."

Calla gave Shelby a brief hug. "We set him up. It's time for
etective Antonio to take him down."

Yes, she wanted this over, but she was terrified that when
was, she would lose Trevor. They'd begun with lies. They'd
nded over revenge. Who'd want to build on that? "I think
e should watch him another day or two."

Trevor approached her and took her hands in his. "Let's be
ne with all this. I know you're ready."

"What if we haven't done enough?" *What if I've gone too
r?*

"Your family would be proud," Henry said. He winked at
r. "Though I'm a bit sad to see my days as a gullible mark
me to an end. I believe I could have had a nice career in the
eater."

"Lord Aberforth is always looking for patrons for his son's
ays," Trevor said drily. "Perhaps you could invest."

Henry's eyes widened. "Aberforth? That barking duffer? I
ouldn't give him—" He stopped, obviously noticing Trevor's
nile. "Very amusing, son."

Trevor and his father had become much closer over the last
w days. Could she take some credit for that? Did it balance
e bomb she'd dropped on the family?

Trevor turned back to Shelby. "The ending of the earl's
:ting career notwithstanding, wouldn't you be overjoyed to

let this burden go? You've proved to the police that it's ti▸
to take this case seriously. Let them do their job."

She noted the antsy looks on her friends' faces. They▸
given so much of themselves to her cause. She met Trevo▸
gaze and saw no hint of the foreboding brewing inside h▸
His eyes were clear, blue and perfect.

But for how much longer would he look at her that way▸

She tried to smile. "You're right, of course. After all th▸
time, it just feels strange to be near the end."

"Hot damn," Victoria said again, scooting off the count▸
and dropping to the floor. "I'm headed to the beach. Call ▸
when they've got the jerk in custody." She sailed out the do▸

"I'll call Detective Antonio," Calla said, hitching her pur▸
on her shoulder.

"I'll do it," Trevor said. "He's going to be pretty annoye▸
You shouldn't have to take the brunt of his anger again."

Calla glanced at the door Victoria had gone throug▸
"You're sure?"

Trevor nodded. "Absolutely. Go to the beach."

"Bye." Calla ran after Victoria.

Fearing she might collapse under the weight of her drea▸
Shelby pulled away from Trevor. "I should get to work on t▸
Perry wedding."

"Are you okay?"

"Fine." She nearly ran to the walk-in fridge. "I'm real▸
behind with the prep."

He followed her. "Let me help."

"No." She frantically gathered produce at random. "Enj▸
your Saturday. You and your father go to the park or som▸
thing."

He slid his arms around her from behind and nuzzled h▸
neck, exposed by the ponytail she'd gathered her hair int▸
"I'd rather stay here with you."

She nearly jumped out of her skin. "No! Thanks," she ded in a softer voice.

None of these feelings for each other were real. He'd see t once Max was arrested, once there was nothing to secure em together. Once this mess hit the media, and his father ied on him to soothe the hole in his life and save the family me from total disgrace. He'd realize how different they re. He'd break her heart.

He drew her around to face him. "What's wrong?"

She couldn't meet his gaze. "Nothing." She skirted around n. "I just need to get to work."

"How about a celebration dinner tonight? Father, you ould join us."

The earl nodded. "That sounds lovely. My last night in the y. Where do you recommend, Shelby?"

"Sorry, I can't go," Shelby said, laying out her ingredients d having absolutely no clue what she was going to do with em. "The wedding, remember?"

"We can help," Trevor said. "The Banfield men look quite shing in a tuxedo."

"Don't be silly." Shelby drew a knife from the block and gan chopping celery. "You guys go and have fun. Take him Giovanni's."

Trevor exchanged a look with his father. "Maybe it's best Shelby doesn't come. You should see Mario, the chef, trip er himself to please her."

Shelby rolled her eyes as Trevor no doubt expected her to.)h, good grief. That's such an exaggeration."

Trevor leaned toward her, brushing his lips over her cheek. Jot by much. He needs to be reminded you belong to me."

The desire and possessiveness in his eyes made her heart ntract. Her throat threatened to close. She couldn't hold on uch longer. "I'm sure you'll be happy to tell him."

"Count on it. You sure you don't want help?"

She pointed the knife at him. "Out."

Laughing, he held up his hands. "I'm going, Chef. I going. Call me later." After one last kiss, he and his fath left the kitchen.

When she heard the door close behind them, the tears sh been fighting fell unheeded. Under the weight of her sorro she collapsed into a chair and cried.

Project Robin Hood, Day Twenty-nine
Offices of Banfield Transportation

"HE'S WITHDRAWING THE money."

"What?" Trevor was sure he'd misheard his friend fro the bank. "How? When?"

"Now."

"All of it?"

"He's closing the account. Wants five thousand in cas and the rest in a cashier's check. What do I do?"

"Stall."

Trevor slammed down the phone, raced past Florence, th hailed a cab outside his building. "First Union Bank, on 5t he said to the cabbie. "Quickly, please."

While he cursed himself for having not anticipated th turn of events, his heart pounded and reminded him Ma sudden flight wasn't the only problem he would have to fa that day.

Shelby was running from him, too.

She'd claimed exhaustion on Saturday night after the we ding she'd catered. Yesterday she'd gone to brunch with hi and his father, but she'd been distracted and jumpy, then to him he should spend time with his father, since his flight w departing that afternoon.

Last night, though she'd spent the night at his apartme

seemed to be going through the motions when they made
e, and she'd been up and gone at dawn this morning.

She should be happy, eager to celebrate their victory. What
s wrong? Had he done something to upset her? He'd gone
ough everything that had happened over the last few days,
1, while stressful, he couldn't see what could have caused
h a turnaround.

And now, if Max got away, would she blame him? Would
y spend all their time looking for him? Instead of after-sex
1dling would they worry and plan their next move for re-
1ge?

The possibility made him want to bang his head against
nething solid.

When he reached the bank, his friend was standing on the
ewalk out front.

"I'm sorry," he said when the cab pulled to the curb and
vor opened the door. "We tried to go slow, but he's insis-
1t and agitated. My clerk is putting the cash in stacks now.
'll be coming out any minute."

"It's okay. Go back inside. I'll follow him from here."

"Good luck."

Trevor nodded and ducked back in the cab. Reaching into
wallet, he pulled out a wad of twenties and handed them
the driver. "Could you wait at the end of the block?"

"You got it, pal."

He should call Shelby, but his mind was racing so quickly,
couldn't think what to say. Using the side mirror, he kept
1tch on the bank's front door, and nearly fell off the seat
1en Max exited, looking around furtively and toting a brown
1ther briefcase.

Trevor had the faint, irrational impulse to laugh. When had
s life become a spy movie?

"Get ready to go," he said to the cabbie, watching Max raise
s hand to hail a cab.

Trevor's driver did a professional job of getting in lin few cars behind Max's cab. As they inched through midd traffic, he called Shelby and explained what was happeni

"We should have been watching him," she said, her vo low and strained.

"Too late to regret it now. Call Victoria and tell her to co get you, then ring me back, and I'll update you on wher am."

"Okay. What are we going to do if we catch up to him?

Frustrated and edgy, Trevor speared his hand through hair. "I have no idea."

"We'll think of something." She paused, then added i shaky voice, "I'm so sorry, Trevor. This is all my fault."

"It's *not*," he said firmly. "Call Victoria."

He disconnected and let his head fall back against the se

"You need the cops, buddy?" the cabbie asked.

"Among other things," Trevor said bleakly. "Don't lose t cab, and you can be part of the big bust."

"Cool."

In true NYC style, he was thrilled to be part of the acti instead of intimidated by the possibility of danger.

"Where are you?" Shelby asked when she called a few m utes later.

"That was fast."

"Victoria and Calla were already on their way here."

"I'm going through the Midtown Tunnel."

"He's headed to Queens? What—" She stopped. "H going to LaGuardia."

"It would make sense."

"It doesn't actually, but we're right behind you. Call wh you know for sure."

"That the cops?" the cabbie asked, weaving around a b to keep Max's cab in sight.

"My girlfriend."

"And she's a cop?"

"She's a caterer."

"Uh-huh."

"I promise I'll buy you a beer later and tell you the whole ory."

"Ought to be a doozy." The cabbie met his gaze in the rear- ew mirror. "Mind if I ask who we're followin'?"

"My brother."

"Better make it two beers."

Max was indeed headed to the airport. The ladies caught to Trevor's cab, so he was able to wave to them through e back window. Victoria looked determined, Shelby wor- :d and Calla was on the phone—no doubt with Detective ntonio.

Trevor had called the detective himself but had only gotten s voice mail. Maybe Calla was having better luck.

What was Max thinking? What was he *doing?*

With the bank account on watch, they'd called off the sur- illance on Max. None of them had had any contact with m all weekend. What could have spooked him to send him nning to the airport with a briefcase full of cash?

At the airport curb, Trevor gave the cabbie his card. Thanks. Call me and I'll tell you how it turns out."

"Appreciate it, but I think I can guess." He turned and inted to a car a little ways ahead—one Detective Devin ntonio was alighting from accompanied by two other men. Those your cops?"

"Yeah. Thanks again."

They'd been waiting on Max's arrival. How had they own he was coming?

"That's Antonio," Shelby said, jogging up beside him.

He linked their hands. "Come on."

They rushed through the sliding doors with Victoria and

Calla right behind them. Victoria's car was sure to get tow‹
but none of them cared.

Max was hustling toward the security line as if the de‹
himself were on his heels, which—though his brother mig
not yet realize it—he was.

How he thought he'd get through with a suitcase full
cash, Trevor had no idea. Panic and bad judgment were Ma
forte.

Badges flipped out, Antonio and his compatriots a‹
proached Max. He stumbled and tried to look shocked a‹
innocent, though he was clearly sweating and guilty. Smoo
as silk, the cops took him by his arms and relieved him of t
briefcase, escorting him to the far end of the facility with on
a few passengers and airline employees even noticing the d‹
turbance.

As DETECTIVE ANTONIO and his group approached a do‹
tucked behind one of the airline check-ins, Trevor walk‹
up to them. "Good afternoon, Detective. You've been busy

"Well, well, if it isn't the Nosy Caterer and her band
happy chicks." He smiled sardonically at Trevor. "Plus o‹
rooster."

Trevor knew their chances of getting information out of t
police were brief, so he held his reaction to Antonio's inst
in check. "Do you mind if we tag along? We've been tryi‹
to get in touch with you."

"Yeah, I got your messages." His gaze swept the grou‹
pausing ever-so-briefly on Calla. "Come on."

One of the guys with Antonio opened the door with a k‹
card, then led them all inside the airport security offices. Wi
little fanfare, they moved past the main desk and down a ha‹

That's when Max's head whipped around. He glared
Trevor as he struggled like a scalded cat. The cops on eith‹
side, being bigger, stronger and obviously experienced wi

rious criminals, subdued and cuffed him with almost no fort.

"You!" Max screamed at Trevor. "You did this."

"Swindled millions through nonexistent investment hemes?" Trevor lifted his eyebrows. "I don't think so, dear other."

"You're such an idiot." Max's mouth twisted, his eyes glit-red with rage. "You don't know half of what I've done. I can t away with anything I want. I'm the future earl."

In shock, Trevor found no clever words came to his lips. le brother he knew, the charming, not-so-clever boy had llen away, leaving a desperate, hate-filled crook.

"And *her*." Max jerked his head toward Shelby. "I knew actly who she was at the condo meeting. That's why I de-ded to cash out and go back to London. These cops can't uch me there."

In his rage, Max had somehow failed to grasp that he as very much in American custody and getting to London ouldn't be as easy as strolling onto a jet.

"I helped you because you're family," Trevor said, keeping s tone even, though he felt as if he'd been punched in the omach. "How could you do this to Father?"

His face mottled, Max lunged toward Trevor, only to have e cops subdue him once again. "Traitor! That's what you are. lon't know what you said to Father to get him to go along ith your stupid little domestic there, but you can bet I'll tell m all about your ridiculous traps. He'll have me out of here less than an hour."

Trevor pitied him, since he knew that wasn't going to ippen. But he also longed to strike back. Nobody insulted helby.

And they still had the winning hand. While Max might ive recognized Shelby, their plan had accomplished its al—Max was right where he belonged.

Leaning toward his brother, Trevor let his own fury sho
"You can bet I've learned my lesson about helping you. You
on your own from now on."

"*Wrong.* I can't wait to watch Father force you to clean
behind me. Again." Max laughed as the cops forced him do
the hall. "See you soon, little brother."

In the midst of his disappointment and anger, Trevor h
the odd sensation of being tossed back in time.

He recalled a birthday he was supposed to spend with l
mother, but instead had been jarringly sent back to Westm
Manor because his mother had decided to spend the time
Puerto Rico with her latest lover.

The earl had welcomed Trevor back home with his usu
dignity and restrained pleasure. Max, however, hadn't be
the least thrilled.

Resentment had flashed in Max's eyes. He'd clearly want
Father, and the attention, all to himself.

Should they have figured out then how far down he wou
go, how greedy and lacking in conscience he'd eventual
become? Maybe Trevor would ask himself that question l
the rest of his life.

Shelby squeezed his hand, bringing him back to reality.

He wrapped his arm around her shoulders and held on. M
had made his own bed. *She* was his future.

"Always liked a good family reunion," Antonio cor
mented.

The detective took Trevor, Shelby and her friends into o
room, while the other two cops ushered Max into another or

"How did you find him?" the detective asked, standi
while everyone else found a seat in the small conference roo

"How did you know he was coming here?" Trevor returne

Antonio shook his head. "You first."

Even with chicks and a rooster present, Trevor wasn't in t

od for a game of chicken. He only wanted to know what
s going to happen now.

So he recounted the condo-development project and the
p they'd subsequently laid for Max.

"Inside connections at the bank, huh?" Antonio nodded.
ot bad—for civis."

"And we'll be perfectly happy to go back to being civil-
s," Shelby said, "if you'll tell us why you're finally arrest-
g Max."

The detective propped his hip on the table. "Oh, I have a
g list of charges I'll be filing. While you people were at-
ding fancy parties at the hotel and doing some really obvi-
s and lousy surveillance, I was doing my job."

Calla gave him a shaky smile. "We never doubted you—"

"What do you mean lousy surveillance?" Victoria broke

"Nice car," he answered. "The salary difference between
execs and cops is a crying shame."

"Detective, please." Shelby's hands were clenched so
htly, her knuckles had turned white. "What's going on?"

Trevor laid his hand on Shelby's thigh as Antonio explained
at he'd been doing while the Robin Hood gang was orga-
zing their sting operation.

Based on Mrs. Rosenburg's complaint, plus the evidence
elby had gathered, he'd gotten a court order to search and
g Max's office, which allowed them to learn about Max's
mbling problem.

In addition to swindles and schemes, which the police had
tten his bank records to prove, he'd borrowed against the
lue of the hotel to pay off heavy gambling debts. The de-
ctive was certain he could bring Max in for questioning and
t a confession, since, with the questionable people he owed
oney to, jail was the safest place for him.

"But Max got a call from his bookie this morning, warning

him that he'd run out of patience. Max, who'd spent the la
few days preparing for a trip, buying a one-way plane ticket
London, cashing checks at various banks all over town, hu
up and called the airline to move up his flight to today." T
detective shrugged. "I decided it was time to show my han

Trevor looked at the women around him, all stunned a
just a bit disappointed. While they'd thought they were
clever with their disguises and vigilante plans, the police h
been quietly building their case all along. Their surveillan
had been organized, sophisticated and yielded actual resul

Antonio sensed their letdown. "The fact that he's got
this stolen cash on him will add to my case, though, so ni
job there. And now I know why he was planning to he
to London in the first place—more bad disguises on Mi
Dixon."

"So we helped," Calla said slowly.

"Sure. I'll let Miss Dixon's parents know when Banfield
assets have been sold off. They should get their original i
vestment back." The detective scowled. "But do me a fav
and go back to your catering, writing, advertising, transpo
ing and whatever. This kind of thing is best left to the profe
sionals."

A GLASS OF SCOTCH IN his hands, Trevor watched Shelby pa
his living room.

"Do you think we helped at all?" she asked. "Or was A
tonio just blowing smoke up our skirts?"

"I'm not wearing a skirt." And the shock of seeing h
brother's complete lack of conscience had him way more a
itated than the detective's thorough and professional inves
gation. "Sit down and have a drink with me."

She looked at his extended hand, then away. "Don't yo
want to go see him?"

"I called a lawyer, just as my father asked me to. Max w

ly spend the night in jail and be arraigned in the morning.
 may have to stay there until the trial, considering he's a
ght risk."

"And you're not upset?"

"Hell, yes, I'm upset. Come here and comfort me."

He'd said it to make her smile. She didn't.

She crossed her arms over her middle, as if she were ill. "I
't be a countess."

He set aside his glass. "A countess? What are you talking
out?"

"Max is going to jail. Won't he get disinherited or some-
ng? You'll be the earl. You have to go out with ladies,
ybe even princesses. I'm not either."

Her voice had risen to a high-strung pitch. He leaned for-
rd, resting his arms on his thighs. At least he knew what
d been bothering her the last few days. "Max won't be disin-
ited. The title will come to him on my father's death, even
e's in prison. That's the law. My father's hale and hearty,
you've seen, by the way. What's this really about?"

"We're too different. We're never going to work out. You're
bility. I'm a caterer."

He fought to hold on to his patience. Whatever reaction he'd
pected from her, this certainly wasn't it. He'd put a bottle
champagne in the icebox, for pity's sake. "I'm not nobility,
I've explained several times. I'm a man. One who—"

"A mogul, then. Wouldn't your father be happier if you
ted a polished English lady?"

The grim finality in her tone pushed him to his feet. "My
her genuinely likes you, as if that even matters." He tried
draw her into his arms, but she jerked back, and a fissure
panic darted through him.

His touch rejected, he slid his hands in the pockets of his
cks. "You're very much a lady, and I'll buy you a damn
wn if you want to be a princess."

Her gaze flew to his. "No. I don't." She whirled away. " don't belong together."

His heart stopped for several beats.

"You can see that, can't you?" she asked, rushing on, aware that her doubt was crushing him. She flung her arm the air as she faced him again. "We have nothing in comn I don't belong in this place. You volunteered yourself and *Earl of Westmore* as tuxedoed waiters for one of my cater events. I can't do that to you. It isn't right."

"Neither I, nor the bloody Earl of Westmore, are afrai hard work."

"That's not what I mean." Tears flooded her eyes. "I your brother arrested. Have you already forgotten that?"

"You're not putting Max between us anymore. I helped him there, and I don't regret it." On some level he underst her guilt. He should have done something about Max soo He should have understood how far his brother had fallen. they shouldn't be blaming each other, they should be turn to each other, not away. "Can we not talk about him for on For one night?"

"I don't see how."

"Sure you do. We change the subject." He walked to l laying his hands on her shoulders. "I love you."

Fear, not happiness, leaped into her eyes. "You don't m that. You're upset."

His heart breaking into pieces, he shot back, "I do me it."

Had he honestly expected her to fall into his arms, conf her undying love and they'd live happily ever after?

Yes, he had.

"We started this relationship on a lie," she reminded h

"I don't care."

"I do." She grabbed her bag off the coffee table and hea

vn the hall. "We need some time apart. Time to figure out
his is real or not."

"I don't."

She turned, and a tear slid down her cheek. "I do."

He pressed his lips together to keep from begging her to
y. "I'll be here."

She said nothing, the door clicking shut her only response.

ᴇᴀᴛʜɪɴɢ ᴀs ɪғ sʜᴇ'ᴅ ʀᴜɴ a mile, Shelby stumbled out of the
vator and into the lobby of Trevor's building. "What am I
ng?" she muttered. "Where am I going?"

He loved her. Seriously? *No freakin' kidding?*

Hope and happiness she hadn't let herself feel earlier
shed over her. Trevor didn't say things he didn't mean. He
n't do things he didn't want to.

"Can I help you, Ms. Dixon?" Fred asked.

"I— No. I just— I need a minute."

She wandered to the front windows and pressed her fore-
ad against the glass.

Her dreams had literally come true. Max in jail; Trevor re-
ning her love.

Why was she panicking?

She was being flighty and unpredictable—exactly what
'd assured Henry she wasn't. And she definitely knew what
 wanted. She wanted Trevor. Differences and all.

True, the journey to this point had been complicated. But
hey could get through the ordeal with Max, starting on op-
site sides with deceit and family loyalties between them,
ning forces, compromising, surviving and still loving
:h other at the end... Well, it seemed they could likely get
ough anything.

True justice was illusive, but true love was easy. If she
nted to find it badly enough.

She was running, plain and simple. She wasn't weak like

Max. And if she had to wear a crown and learn to curtsy be with Trevor, then that's what she'd do.

It's not wise to come between me and something I wo she'd once said to Henry.

It was time she proved her challenge.

Looking around, her gaze fell on the elevators.

She couldn't run back to him without overcoming one obstacle. A sense of déjà vu washed over her.

Hadn't she once paced this same lobby, taking a chan on seeing Trevor again? On them finding a way to turn v geance and mistrust into hope?

Humiliated, though that was the least of her worries, walked toward the security desk. "Uh, Fred," she said, cle ing her throat when her voice croaked out like a rusty whe "Can I go back up?"

Fred, naturally, looked utterly confused. "Well… I'm s posed to clear everybody, every time."

"But I'm a knight who's raised her sword to strike down tyranny of injustice. I've rescued the princess from the ca and brought peace and hope to all the land." She leaned ward and whispered, "So I'd really like my reward now."

Fred was half smiling, half alarmed. "What reward?"

"The Honorable Trevor Banfield."

Whether he thought she was sincere or crazy, Fred neve theless nodded. "Elevator three."

Impulsively—proving she might be unpredictable times—she kissed his cheek. As she rushed to the elevator, called over her shoulder, "Don't tell him I'm coming, pleas

On the ride up, she remembered Trevor's face when sh told him they didn't belong together. When he'd told her loved her, and she hadn't believed him.

She'd hurt him.

Maybe he should have spent some of that tough love on brother years ago.

But then they never would have met.

And that scenario absolutely didn't fit with her fairy tale.

When the elevator doors opened, Trevor, anxious, beauti-
and determined, was standing there.

She blinked. "My lord."

He yanked her into his arms. "My love."

Then he was kissing her as if she was his whole world, as
e'd never let her go, no matter how far and fast she wanted
run.

He didn't know, at least not yet, that she wasn't going any-
ere without him ever again.

Arms wrapped around each other, they shuffled into his
rtment.

"Why'd you come back?" he asked, his mouth hot and
ngry against her cheek.

"We spent enough time apart." She placed her hands on
her side of his face. "And I think I might be a bit impul-
e. Oh, and I love you, too. I think I forgot to mention that
lier."

The smile she adored blossomed on his face, and she
nted his lips on hers as soon as possible. And forever. "You
finitely left that part out." He slid his arms around her waist.
gain, please."

She slid her arms around his neck. "I love you."

He kissed her, his devotion to her never more precious.
Vhen I'm with you, I'm complete. I think I knew that from
first moment I touched you."

"And tasted my crab cakes."

His eyes gleamed. "That, too."

"No matter how fast this has happened, how unlikely a
uple we might be, I believe in us." She slid her hand through
s hair, relishing the silken texture, scarcely able to believe
was all hers. "This is real. The future could bring anything,
t we'll face it together."

He hugged her tight against him. "That's what I call a g⟨
plan."

"My best."

"I wasn't kidding about my talent with tuxedos. I ⟨
always fill in as a waiter at one of your events."

"After I see you in this tuxedo, your lordship, I'll consi⟨
it."

"Consider, will you?"

"Well, the view without a tuxedo is pretty impressive.
I'm sure you'll do fine. In the meantime, we're overdue f⟨
celebration. How are you at opening champagne?"

He grinned and guided her to the kitchen. "Why don⟨
demonstrate?"

* * * * *

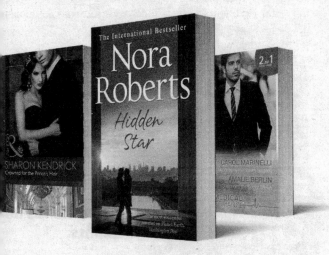